TURNING POINT

ELITE RESPONSE FORCE BOOK ONE

P R ADAMS

PROMETHEAN TALES

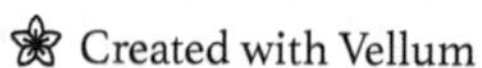 Created with Vellum

ALSO BY P R ADAMS

For updates on new releases and news on other series, visit my website and sign up for my mailing list at:

http://www.p-r-adams.com

Books in the On The Brink Universe

The Stefan Mendoza Trilogy

Into Twilight

Gone Dark

End State

The Rimes Trilogy

Momentary Stasis

Transition of Order

Awakening to Judgment

The ERF Series

Turning Point

Valley of Death

Jungle Dark

Chariot Bright

Dawn Fire (2018)

<u>**The Burning Sands Trilogy**</u>

Beneath Burning Sands

Across Burning Sands

Beyond Burning Sands

<u>**Books in The Chain Series**</u>

The Chain: Shattered

The Journey Home

Rock of Salvation

From the Depths

Ever Shining

DEDICATION

For the service members who served in Mogadishu, Somalia, in 1993.

1

---

12 December 2174. Approaching Bellar Frontier Colony.

No matter the improvements new spacecraft offered, Meyers always found them disappointing. In the case of the Javelin, he couldn't put a finger on what was missing or amiss, but he was sure it was something. The vessel was larger, faster, and had better systems and weapons than anything the ERF had in its fleet. It was also more comfortable than any military vessel Meyers had ever been inside. Even filled with personnel, it felt roomy.

He ran an almost delicate hand through his blond hair, then he stretched his legs and rolled his shoulders, but he couldn't get the tension out of his lean body. That tension reached his eyes as well, bright blue against the bloodshot sclera. His hooked nose wrinkled at the creaks and pops of his joints rolling up through his armor's audio sensors. The noise momentarily drowned out the soft hiss of the gunship's air recycler and the murmur of conversations going on somewhere in the near-dark. His movement drew an arched eyebrow from the man seated directly opposite, Master Sergeant Carl Paxton, the platoon sergeant Meyers hand-selected for the mission. Paxton was short, dark-eyed, and wrinkled. He had a nose that looked like it'd been broken and never properly set. They were both secured to their seats by padded harnesses, black in the Javelin's dim light, but Paxton seemed relaxed, possibly even comfortable. Meyers felt that if he wanted to successfully execute his first mission as the Elite Response Force's battalion commander, he would need someone like Paxton.

Temporary battalion commander, Meyers reminded himself. That qualifier brought a sigh of relief, at least until he remembered who and what he was responsible for, temporary or not.

Seated to his right were members of Squad One. Most of Squad Two sat to Paxton's left. Most of their gear was secured to the floor between the rows of seats. The rest of the two squads were spread between the other Javelin and the older Arrow shuttle that was hauling support personnel and the rest of the gear. Even in the newly acquired Javelins, the air had already taken on a lived-in smell.

A gentle tone echoed in Meyers's earpiece: they were approaching the final communication point with the *Valdez*. Paxton tapped his helmet, signaling his intent to seal up for the call.

Meyers sighed, then he sealed his helmet as well and connected to the channel invite. He hated the secrecy. His men deserved better than all the secrecy.

He glanced at the bulk of Corporal McNutt, Squad One's leader. His square jaw seemed clenched in perpetual anger, and his dark blue eyes were almost black in the dim light. To McNutt's right, Private Rebecca Starling's dark eyes darted left and right, and she bit her full, bottom lip and absently brushed a stray, black curl from her forehead. She was absorbed in what was probably a tech manual based off the static glow of her earpiece's projected display. Meyers considered her a welcome reminder of how much things were changing.

Not just men, he reminded himself. *Soldiers.* And they all deserved better.

It was just another part of the job that he would have to deal with until the Special Security Council got off its collective ass and found a real replacement for Rimes.

As if there ever could be a replacement for Rimes.

"Captain Brigston, this is Colonel Meyers on Javelin Zero-Zero-One." The rank, the position…it all sounded so strange to his ears.

"Go ahead, Colonel." Brigston's voice was clear and calm, no doubt the luxury of long odds that the *Valdez* task force would face any sort of threat.

"We're approaching rally point. Comms check, please."

"Lieutenant Oppert, Arrow One-Six-Three."

"This is Ensign Nunoz, Javelin Zero-Zero-Two."

"Ensign Hassan, Javelin Zero-Zero-One."

"Agent Barlowe. Intelligence Bureau."

"Captain Brigston, *Valdez*."

"Paxton, Master Sergeant, sir."

Meyers rolled his eyes. "Thanks. Camille, check your signal—"

Paxton's raspy cough broke over the channel.

"Shit." Meyers closed his eyes and lowered his chin as close to his chest as the harness allowed. "Lieutenant Oppert, please check your signal. There's some static on your…there, that fixed it."

"It's this goddamn system software." Oppert's voice had an edge to it that could have been from the stress of flying the old Arrow shuttle on such a critical mission or could have been caused by the software she was complaining about.

Or it could have been a more personal problem. Meyers could picture her face—round, a light spray of freckles, green eyes—scrunched up angrily.

It would take weeks to repair things with her.

"They'll get you squared away just right when we get back to Plymouth, ma'am," Paxton said, his voice honey sweet. "Fit you up in one of these."

"Should've had Zero-Zero-One." She sounded sullen, bitter.

"Let's—let's stay focused on the mission brief." Meyers focused by rubbing his thumbs against his forefingers, then he brought his hands up and shared out a workspace with the others. "Four hours to touchdown. Jerem—Captain Brigston, any intelligence updates?"

"Nothing. We've been monitoring the communications buoy and riding its signals down to the planet. Weather is still a mess in the southern hemisphere, but it doesn't have a huge impact beyond a couple hundred kilometers over the equator, and you'll be on the tail end of what's there when you go in. No indication they're aware of our approach, no indication the target's even on Bellar."

"He's down there. They wouldn't have sent us all the way out here if they weren't absolutely sure." Meyers certainly hoped the Intelligence Bureau and the United Nations were right. Sending the ERF to one of the frontier colonies was a bold move that could easily backfire, and by every indication, the Special Security Council desperately wanted to improve its relations with the colonial governor, who had only ever offered a cold shoulder.

"Well, he's staying off the Grid," Brigston said.

"Do they even have a Grid?" Ensign Nunoz didn't sound like he was joking.

"There's a robust one in Ardennen." Brigston cleared his throat. Meyers imagined Brigston's pale-brown eyes squinting patiently, his bronze-colored cheeks being sucked in. He was probably fiddling with his uniform buttons and trying to force a smile onto his plain face. It was how Brigston coped with his discomfort at being in command. "Unfortunately, we see very little from Turning Point, so we have to assume it's not quite so capable."

"Or they don't care about the outside world." Ensign Hassan's normally quiet voice was hard to hear over the noise that had crept back on the connection.

Meyers scanned the display; the noise was coming from Oppert again. "Lieutenant Oppert, your comm—"

Oppert cursed and disconnected, and an awkward silence settled over the connection.

"So, Turning Point," Meyers said to break the silence. He brought up the latest data Barlowe had sent out. It was the sort of thing Rimes would have been on top of, something Meyers knew he needed to get better about studying. "Any updates from imagery analysis, Agent Barlowe?"

Barlowe cleared his throat, a soft sound. Everything about Barlowe was soft. He was small, slight, and quiet. His hands were delicate, his eyes and lips almost feminine. How he'd made it through the Commando Q course without serious injury had always mystified Meyers. "A couple things. I've sent an update to the designations—power and telecommunications facilities, some of the other infrastructure management facilities. Don't be fooled by the description. This settlement may have been put together by displaced and criminal elements, but they seem to have done well enough getting things together. There's plenty of prefab and quick-fab construction, more than enough to house the entire planet's population."

Ensign Nunoz snorted. "Like anyone else is going to settle in a city full of criminals."

"What constitutes criminal can be pretty arbitrary, Ensign. Most of these people were political prisoners, victims of tyrants, for-profit prisons, and the criminal justice systems that were modified to support those."

Meyers could hear the resentment in Barlowe's voice. His history with the criminal justice system wasn't common knowledge. "Thank you, Agent Barlowe. Anything more on Mr. Waverley?"

"No." Barlowe's voice caught as he blew out a loud breath. "But he has to be somewhere around Turning Point. Anywhere else, he would have shown up."

Meyers quickly looked over Waverley's portfolio: Chad Milton Waverley, top-flight management and finance education, entered the metacorporate world at thirty-six after the company he was running was acquired by one of SunCorps's corporations. Fourteen years to rise through the SunCorps ranks, eight years as CEO of SunCorps. One minute, earning eight figures and cited as the key to SunCorps's growth and success, the next, given up by SunCorps as an effort at appeasement to the United Nations.

Waverley wasn't the problem; he was the sacrifice.

Or, Meyers thought, maybe we are.

Oppert reconnected, her signal barely in the green. "Sorry, Colonel. This fucking system is a joke. I'll do a full-blown reset after the call."

"It's just for this mission." Meyers wondered if that was true. The Arrows were relatively new vessels, and they could probably be salvaged with a few upgrades and some long overdue maintenance. It wasn't like military budget cuts were going away anytime soon, especially with everyone trying to appease the metacorporations.

"You're just under ten minutes out from radio silence, Colonel," Captain Brigston said. "Any final information you need from the *Valdez*?"

"Thanks, I think we're good for now. Good hunting."

"Colonel Meyers, could I get a moment?" Oppert sounded like she wouldn't take no for an answer.

"Sure." Meyers waited for the others to disconnect. "Camille, you can't—"

"This goddamn piece of shit crate isn't space worthy, Lonny. And I'm the senior pilot—I should be flying Zero-Zero-One. Or we could've waited another day for Zero-Zero-Three's repairs."

"Is that what this is really about, flying a Javelin?"

"It's disrespectful to put your best pilot in this can—"

"You're the only one who can handle One-Six-Three."

"And you stuffed your support team in here with the gear, castoffs, like—"

"That support team is as valuable as any other group we have."

"And you have no right, no right to ignore me like you did yesterday. You can't just—"

"You were drunk, Camille."

"Lonny, dammit, listen to me. Kara's dead. It's been a year. You have to move on."

Meyers looked around the cabin, as if he expected someone to be watching or listening. Most of the soldiers were caught up in their own worlds or were sleeping. Even if his helmet were open, they wouldn't care what he was talking about. "Let's talk about this when we get back to the *Valdez*, okay?"

"No, it's not okay. You keep pushing me away. You probably gave me One-Six-Three to keep me away from you."

"I gave you One-Six-Three because you're the best pilot we have. It's that simple."

"Yeah, well, everything isn't simple. It's complicated. You can't just compartmentalize your life like some problem you want to solve a piece at a time. We had something before Kara came along. You can't just ignore that because it's inconvenient."

"Inconven—" Meyers pressed his fists against his helmet's faceplate. "Camille, I'm your commanding officer for now. I can't have a relationship with you."

"Another thing to hide behind. Nice."

Meyers had to choke back a frustrated laugh. "You think I want this mess? Rimes put me in for this brevet position before he went on his suicide run against Theroux and those SunCorps proxies. After he made a sacrifice like that, I couldn't turn the SSC down, especially when they promised to find a replacement. That would've been disrespectful to them. And Rimes. He gave his life to stop that alien mind control device they were using. I think I owe him something after that, don't you?"

"The ERF's tainted after what Rimes did. No one's going to want the command. You know that, but you don't want to talk about us."

"Will you please just...just for..." Meyers groaned. "There is no us. While I'm your commanding officer, there can't be."

"When we get back to the *Valdez*, we're—"

Oppert's signal dropped to half-strength, and then to nothing. A second later, it came back.

"Camille, you're breaking up."

"This fucking piece of—"

"Just reset your systems. We'll...I'll talk to you once we get the camp established on-planet, okay?"

"Fine. Don't you dare think you can lock me out of your tent." Oppert disconnected.

Meyers shook his head. He wanted to shout, but he wasn't sure even his helmet could contain his frustration.

A soft chime indicated someone wanted a private connection. Paxton.

"What's up, Master Sergeant?"

"I think I might ask you the same, sir. I've seen enough fights from one side to know woman trouble when I see it." Paxton tapped his helmet's faceplate. "Man twists and jerks around like that, he's either taken a couple AP rounds in the gut, or some gal's got him by the nuts."

"Thanks, Master Ser—"

"Lieutenant Oppert, she's very popular with the men. You ever see what she barely wears to play volleyball, sir?"

Meyers blushed. "Lieutenant Oppert doesn't engage in fraternization."

"Not saying she does, sir. Just saying she has a little emergency box on her rather ample right cheek, if you follow. You know, break glass in case you want a good time?"

"I get the picture."

"She's like one of those old combustion engines. Get that hood up, there's all kinds of moving parts in there. Volatile and tricky, sir. Gotta know what you're doing."

"Thank you. I don't think it's appropriate to discuss the lieutenant's moving parts or volatility, do you?"

"Oh, I don't mean anything by it. It's always good to have someone who will spread..." Paxton coughed. "You know, sir. Good cheer. The boys don't have a lot of women to choose from. Doctors, nurses, pilots." His helmet turned toward Starling. "And now, well, things're complicated."

Meyers glanced sideways through his faceplate, darkened so that Starling couldn't see him. She was an attractive enough young woman, with milk chocolate skin, full lips, and a cute, button nose. She was a little smaller than most of the men, but she'd made it through the Commando Q course, the first woman to do so. She was tough. It suddenly dawned on Meyers that Paxton's point all along might not have been Oppert but Starling.

"If you're concerned that a female on the operation is going to be a problem, Master Sergeant Paxton, let me make it clear right now that I won't allow it to be."

Paxton chuckled. "Might want to check that with Corporal Gerhardt, Colonel. Heard him drop a few words that might be considered insensitive."

Meyers shut his eyes and counted to ten. Rimes said long ago it was an effective way to fight off panic and anger. Gerhardt and Zacharowski—"Titan" and "Ski," their preferred Delta Force nicknames—had been nothing but problems since their transfer from the last operational Delta unit. As a squad leader, Zacharowski was a mess, a loose cannon more concerned with one-upmanship than teamwork and discipline, and he was an enabler for Gerhardt's bad behavior.

"I'll make clear to the corporal that women are to be treated with the same respect shown to men."

"He wasn't just insensitive about Starling being a woman, Colonel."

"You're kidding me."

"Corporal Gerhardt's got the sort of mouth on him used to get folks taken out behind the barracks and—"

"I'll take care of it, Master Sergeant."

Meyers closed the channel and glanced at the team seated around him. Squad One was composed of survivors who had been away from the main camp on Plymouth when the metacorporate forces attacked. They were a mix from all over the world. If Gerhardt had some sort of racial hang-up, it would need to be snuffed out quickly. The last thing Meyers wanted was to screw up the ERF. A lot was at stake with the mission, and it already felt like things were coming apart.

A countdown filled the upper right corner of his helmet display, and a chime immediately sounded.

They were heading into the atmosphere.

2

12 December 2174. Stratosphere above Bellar Frontier Colony.

RATTLING FILLED the Javelin as the straps securing the gear to the middle floor strained under the G-forces. The full-bright interior lights revealed soldiers holding tight to harnesses. They were descending hard, taking advantage of the narrow window they knew for certain wasn't covered by even the most primitive sensors planet-side. What they were doing carried some risk, but Meyers had brought along the three best pilots the ERF had. They could handle it.

Imagery from the belly cameras ran beneath icons of the ships. Oppert's Arrow showed a pale amber on its operational readout.

Meyers opened a channel to the pilots. "One-Six-Three, I'm showing you amber on your ops-readout. Are you okay?"

"I'm green across the board, Colonel. Maybe you should trust your best pilot."

"Lieutenant, if you would—there, you've just gone full amber." Meyers straightened in his seat. "Please check your systems."

"I'm looking at my readouts right now. Everything's green."

Meyers wrestled with the idea of closing out the call, but it didn't seem right. With all the Gs they were pulling, the smart systems were piloting the ships, but if Oppert showed green on her console, it was likely that's what the smart systems would see as well.

"Lieutenant," Ensign Hassan said, "I can see you now. Your pitch looks off, and you're drifting from the formation. Your right wing has—"

"Dammit, I'm telling you I'm green across the board."

Hassan swallowed. "You don't feel any—"

"Of course I feel it, Genevieve. I felt it the second we entered atmosphere. That's the way this bitch handles."

Ensign Nunoz's comms activated. "Lieutenant, maybe this is just another glitch?"

"Fine. Goddamn piece of..." Distortion rumbled through Oppert's signal. "Shit."

"What?" Meyers pushed forward against the harness.

"I reset the indication and console display system. Now I've got red..." There was an unfamiliar edge to Oppert's voice. "Shit. Yeah. The smart system's still not seeing those readings, apparently, and I can't just reset the whole system. We'd tear apart at this speed without controls."

"Can you do anything, maybe just hold it steady while the system resets?" Meyers's stomach turned as the amber of One-Six-Three's display dipped into red.

Oppert snorted. "Right. Just blinking and talking to run the systems like this leaves me weak. Why not try to fight a control stick, right?"

The red darkened.

"Tell the systems to level off, then. Force it not to put so much strain on the airframe. Hassan, Nunoz, ideas?"

"If she gets the system to level off, Colonel, she's going to be at risk of detection," Nunoz said.

"We'll deal with that if it happens, Ensign. Can she do it?"

"I can do it. Just—" Oppert's signal became a series of squeals and screeches.

"Camille? Camille?" Meyers realized he wasn't sounding like a commanding officer. "Lieutenant Oppert?"

"—and now—"

More squeals and screeches. One-Six-Three's color lightened ever so slightly, until it was almost amber again.

Meyers's guts twisted. He'd been the one to sign off on One-Six-Three even being brought along. Zero-Zero-Three should have been ready by the time they arrived, and even another day of delay would have been okay. Camille should have been piloting a Javelin—his Javelin. He'd been selfish.

"She is leveling off and slowing, Colonel," Hassan said. "That right wing doesn't look good, but it is not doing what it was before."

"Thank you, Ensign." Meyers shut his eyes for a moment. The odds of detection were extremely small, but it was a new risk they had to account for. "Please adjust to match One-Six-Three."

The rattling intensified as the Javelin shifted, then things seemed to calm significantly. Meyers caught a shift in Paxton's helmet, as if he was looking for an explanation. Meyers sent a quick audio-to-text update over a private channel.

"I-I think it's okay now," Oppert said. "I don't know if this piece of shit is getting off-planet again, but it seems to be stabilizing."

One-Six-Three was solidly in amber now.

"Colonel, we are north of the equator, ten minutes out from entry to the desert south of Turning Point," Hassan said. "We will need to descend more soon."

Meyers checked the belly camera displays. The planet was a dark emerald sea beneath them, one of the broad expanses of dense vine and scrub jungle. "I don't know if I like the idea of an aircraft that can't tell when it's tearing itself apart flying nap-of-earth. We've already risked detection once. I think—"

"I can reset the systems in a minute," Oppert said, calmer now. "We're past the worst of it. I can handle it."

"You're sure?"

"I'm good."

Meyers glanced at One-Six-Three's amber indicator. The Arrows often flew dangerously close to their limits. "You tell me the second anything changes."

"Don't I always?"

Meyers tried to relax, but it felt like the G-forces were still pressing against his heart. Reviewing mission objectives and intelligence analysis did nothing to help. Rimes had always seemed capable of maintaining calm and distance. It was critical to ERF operations, but it was something Meyers couldn't imagine himself ever mastering.

Night quickly settled over rolling hills, and long shadows turned into near complete darkness. The Javelin descended steeply.

"Approaching desert edge," Nunoz said. "One-Six-Three, you've got a bit of—"

"Yeah, yeah. My right aileron is not happy at all." Oppert's voice carried a playful tone. "Shit, guys, you don't have to treat me like a baby. I've got it."

The Javelin began rising and descending as moonlit dunes flew by close beneath the belly cameras. Meyers tapped a beat against the harness as the ETA display counted down. They were close now, the mission imminent. In just over a minute, they would be rolling out, and his orders would be the difference between life and death, success and failure.

"One-Six-Three, you've got that roll back."

Nunoz's voice brought Meyers's attention back to the aircraft status indicators. One-Six-Three had dipped closer to red while he was looking at other things. He squinted at the terrain flying beneath them—dunes, flat stretches, the occasional outcropping.

"I know, Nunoz." Oppert sounded frustrated.

"Lieutenant Oppert." Meyers barely managed to stop himself from calling her Camille. The idea of her visiting his tent had been distracting. "You're dipping into the red again."

"It's that damned ailer—"

One-Six-Three completely disappeared from the display.

"Lieutenant Oppert? Camille?" Meyers reset his display. "Ensign Nunoz, what happened?"

Nunoz swallowed hard. "One-Six-Three's gone, sir."

Gone. Meyers tried to wrap his head around that. Camille. His support staff. Most of their gear. "Where's the...where's the emergency beacon?"

"It could be destroyed."

"Get us down."

The deceleration and course adjustment pressed Meyers hard against his harness. In his mind, the image of Oppert's shuttle disintegrating in a fireball kept playing in a loop. Had she hit a dune? Had the systems spontaneously failed and somehow caused the shuttle to tear apart? Or had something shot the Arrow down.

He had to know.

3

————

12 December 2174. Karpov Desert, South of Turning Point, Bellar Frontier
Colony.

MEYERS CLUTCHED the harness that held him in place as Paxton herded the
others out of the Javelin. It would have been easier for Meyers to lose
himself in the order and predictability of commanding the troops, but the
moment called for more. He glanced out the airlock, open all the way
through to the desert outside. On the ground, the dunes were an almost
blue-gray in the moonlight. The air was cool and clean on his face. Sand
rattled off the hull in a steady breeze.

Breathable, he reminded himself. Bellar's gravity wasn't much greater
than that back on Earth, and they'd spent the entire trip out under something heavier to prep for it. It really was a very promising colony, despite
being so far out from everywhere.

He slipped the harness off and stepped outside, stopping at the base of
the ramp. The soldiers were huddling, muttering. They already knew, or at
least suspected, what had happened.

"Master Sergeant Paxton." Meyers turned toward the Arrow's last good signal. There was still no emergency beacon. He wasn't getting any readings from the personnel, either.

"Colonel?" Paxton was looking in the same direction, although he was doing a better job of hiding it.

"No transponder, and I'm not picking up any life signs from crew or passengers."

Paxton squinted and screwed up his face. That was about all the emotion he seemed capable of showing.

Meyers powered down his scans for the missing soldiers' signals. There were a few possible explanations for not picking them up so far out, not all of them involving death. "Let's get the Rovers assembled, get the netting up, and build out the operations center. One klick perimeter, wide sensor array. I'll want Squad One with us."

Paxton turned toward the huddled soldiers.

"Wait." Meyers held up a finger. "What's the local time? Something like two in the morning? We're fifteen klicks out. Let's get Barlowe and Starling inserted into Turning Point. Civilian garb, lightweight BAS gear. Use the second Rover."

Paxton turned back just enough to lock eyes. "Alone, Colonel?"

"Have Zacharowski support them."

"Zacharowski, sir?"

Meyers wondered if he might be pushing the idea of team building too early. It seemed the sort of thing Rimes would do. "Better to find out now what we've got, don't you think?"

Paxton's grunt was almost lost in the wind.

"All right. Send Perkins along," Meyers said. "You can never have too many snipers."

"You remember Corporal Viet was in One-Six-Three, sir? Sergeant Banh's sniper?"

"Shit."

"Yeah." Paxton turned back to the soldiers, now clustered by squads, and waved them over. "Listen up! Corporal McNutt, your team's on Rover assembly. Both units assembled in ten minutes. Go! Sergeant Banh, your team's got camouflage netting and ops assembly. Move it!"

Banh's dark eyebrows arched, and he raised a wiry arm, waving for his team to follow as he ran to gather gear.

Paxton turned to Zacharowski. "Sergeant Zacharowski, your team's got perimeter sensors. One klick, wide array, then double time back here. You're going on a field trip. Private Starling and Perkins, you're with Zacharowski. Let's get it done!"

Other than McNutt, the squads were in motion before Paxton finished with his orders. Zacharowski not questioning why they were going with wide dispersal of the sensors was the same as acknowledging that everyone knew One-Six-Three was out there somewhere.

"Master Sergeant Paxton?" McNutt glanced over his shoulder as his squad began unloading gear from the Javelins. "Perkins and Starling, what gives?"

Paxton crossed his arms over his chest. "Not your concern, Corporal."

"My squad, my concern, least that's how I reckon it."

"Fair enough. They're going into Turning Point."

McNutt looked over at Meyers but said nothing else. He ran over to help his squad with the unloading and Rover build-out.

Meyers strolled around to the front of the Javelins and scanned the horizon with his Battlefield Awareness System's settings at maximum. He glanced at Paxton. "Anything on your BAS?"

Paxton nodded. "Coming up now. Seems a little sluggish."

"Yeah."

Wireframe overlays laid out what Meyers already knew: his soldiers were hauling kit into the center of camp and breaking out the tools and components they needed to fulfill their assignments, and the Javelin pilots were checking their vessels, probably focusing on the chameleon skin effect on the hull.

But there was nothing out there in the desert, nothing but quiet.

Sand crunched as someone came up behind him. He turned to see Burrows, eyes wide as he scanned the same black horizon.

"It went down? The Arrow?"

"Looks like it." Meyers looked back to where the soldiers were assembling the Rovers. Pumps inflated the frames from a set of flat panels, then fuel cells hardened the panel skins into shapes that snapped together. The simple drivetrains were already being slotted to the undersides while the balloon wheels were inflated.

"Any idea where?"

"We know where it disappeared from the sensor readout."

"No transponder?" Barlowe looked down at the sand. "That's odd."

"What's the range on those? We're probably twelve, fifteen klicks out, depending on how it..." Meyers thought of Oppert—Camille—and what it must have been like in the last crazy moments. Maybe everything happened too fast for her to feel anything.

"The—" Barlowe pointed toward the Rover assembly area. "You, um, doing a recon?"

"I want to see if we can recover anything. Maybe survivors."

"I was thinking, maybe I could give the gear that we have here a look, see if there was something we could put together to deal with that Grid they've got in Turning Point. I was really counting on the gear in the Arrow."

Meyers clasped his hands together in front of his face, realizing too late it was the sort of thing people did when in prayer. "About that. I'm going to need you and Starling to go into the city."

"Into the city?"

"Not alone. Ski's taking a couple people from his squad. They'll protect you."

Barlowe exhaled and licked his lips. They quivered in the moonlight. "The Intelligence Bureau's role here is just...I'm supposed to be an advisor. Your team."

"My systems and intelligence analysts are out there somewhere." Meyers pointed toward where he guessed One-Six-Three was. "I'm not putting you into combat, Ladell."

"You saw my analysis. That place is a war zone. They kill each other over border disputes, insults, supplies. I'm still dealing with things from the war."

"I thought we weren't going to judge these people off their history."

"Six-month-old data isn't quite history, Lonny."

"You're going to be okay."

"Shit. Look at my hands." They were shaking. "Jack told me what we did during the war…"

"I understand. You're not a Commando anymore. I get it. I'm not asking you to do anything other than to look at their Grid, okay? See things with your own eyes. We need to know what's going on, see if Waverley's showing up on any of the Grid traffic. No gunfights, no infiltration. I promise."

Barlowe nodded. "Okay. You…you think it's safe to send Starling in?"

"She was a Commando. She can take care of herself. Unless you're saying otherwise?"

"No. She's really good. She picks things up really fast. But…she's smaller than me." Barlowe brought a hand up to the top of his helmet, almost a salute.

Meyers chuckled. "She could probably kick your ass."

"Mine, sure. You want her out there with…" Barlowe shrugged. "You did understand that most of the people in Turning Point were incarcerated, right?"

"So were you."

Barlowe winced. "I'm not saying they're all bad people, but prison changes—"

"No one gets special treatment. She signed up for the ERF. She feels she's ready for this. Do her a favor and give her the chance to prove otherwise."

They both turned at the whispery crunch of sand beneath boots. Corporal McNutt was approaching, head down so that his thick, black hair covered his face. He was only 180 centimeters tall, but he was broad-shouldered, long- and thick-limbed. And fast.

Barlowe looked back at Meyers. "I'll do what you ask. Just, you know, keep in mind what I said, okay?"

"Sure." Meyers turned back to McNutt. "Everything all right, Corporal?"

"Yeah, think so, Colonel." McNutt's Kiwi accent was barely noticeable, but it was there. "Got the Rovers ready, if you want to check them out?"

"Good. Have your squad mount up. Oh." Meyers nodded toward Barlowe. "Private Starling's going with Agent Barlowe."

McNutt squinted and tilted his head. "Into the city?"

"Into the city. We need to see if we can get onto their Grid."

"Just the two of them? Seems risky, don't you think?"

Meyers heard a bit of his own resentment of authority in McNutt's tone. It was both annoying and reassuring. "There's not an ERF operation that doesn't involve risk, Corporal. Zacharowski's squad will be providing cover. Are we going to talk about this or get moving?"

McNutt bowed slightly and pointed toward the waiting Rovers. Meyers strolled to the passenger side of the nearest vehicle—Rover One—and slipped into what passed for a seat. Behind him, a two-and-a-half-meter flatbed stretched over six wheels. The flatbed was raised maybe one and a half meters off the ground, and the lids of flip-seats ran all along the edge. When the lids were lifted, footrests would telescope down and out, protecting riders' legs from the wheels. McNutt slid into the driver's seat and twisted to look back at his squad.

"Mount up."

One of McNutt's men—Calderon, Meyers thought—leaned in close to McNutt. "Everything okay, Boss?"

McNutt looked straight ahead. "Becky's going on a sightseeing tour—Steven's providing overwatch. Everything'll be hunky-dory."

Calderon shot a quick glance toward Meyers, then settled into the seat immediately behind McNutt. Despite being shorter and leaner than McNutt, Calderon still cut an impressive figure. In the dark, his eyes were as black as the low patch of hair on top of his head.

McNutt pulled something out of his right breast pouch and lowered his head. Whatever the thing from the pouch was, he squeezed his fist around it while the squad mounted up. When the last of the squad was belted into the flip seats, McNutt returned the item to his pouch and pushed down on the accelerator pressure plate. The Rover kicked out sand and lurched forward.

When they were clear of the camp, and the drone of the Rover's drivetrain had combined with the rising wind to provide some background noise, Meyers leaned in to McNutt. "You don't appreciate Private Starling being separated from your squad?"

"We're a tight unit, Colonel. What we went through, there'd be something wrong if we weren't."

"Everyone who fought in the war saw hard action."

"Yeah, no one's saying otherwise. We just got to know our enemy up close and personal, that's all. Widowmaker, y'know?"

Dunes rolled by at a leisurely rate, and Meyers thought back to the deserts of Sahara, where the war had started. There was a dead zone there, a place where systems became unreliable. Widowmaker was worse. A lot worse. A place like Plymouth, with its smothering soup of an atmosphere and primordially brutal animal life that could have chewed up and spat out Sahara. And the Widowmaker region of the planet was the worst.

Meyers leaned closer. "They're not going in alone, just remember that. And they're not there to engage."

"You think that's enough?"

"Sergeant Zacharowski's been tasked to send three—"

"Ski's a fucking hotdog, right. Fucking beats off to his little Delta patches."

"They're just going to provide overwatch in case there's trouble. We don't need trouble." Meyers straightened back in his seat. "Understand me, Corporal?"

"Yeah, seems like I do. Colonel."

Meyers turned back to the dunes. He ran his hands along his legs and tried not to think about Oppert and the people who'd been on One-Six-Three. He tried not to second-guess his own decision to put Barlowe and Starling under Zacharowski's care. It made sense. Banh's sniper had been in One-Six-Three. McNutt's squad was still coming together, and they needed to improve their relations with Zacharowski's squad.

A faint beep sounded in Meyers's helmet, and he leaned forward.

"Transponder signal." He pointed to their left.

"Yeah, getting it now," McNutt said. The Rover turned. "Smoke. Straight ahead."

Meyers stiffened, and his heart raced. The transponder signal was still a few klicks out, but the glow of fires was visible at the base of a dune a hundred meters away. He closed his helmet and opened a private channel to Ensign Hassan. With the thermographic enhancement, the horizon glowed with bits and pieces of heated metal.

"Genevieve, you have a minute?"

"I do, Colonel. What is it?"

"We're about fifty meters out from the wreckage. The transponder signal's about three klicks northeast. How likely—" One-Six-Three flashed through his thoughts, as if he'd been in the cockpit. The blue-gray dunes were so vivid he could make out individual grains of sand and pebbles, then it all blurred and became a sheet of solid gray.

"Colonel?"

The Rover came to a stop next to the piece of smoking debris. It looked like it might be the tip of one of the wings. A string of shallow trenches ran back from the wing to darkness at the edge of his helmet's sensor range, as if the wingtip had flipped end over end for a good distance.

"I was just curious how large a debris field might be. For a ship the size of the Arrow."

"Oh, yes, I understand. Well, it would probably depend on what they hit. We were flying at over 300 kilometers per hour. If she were to have hit a boulder, or even a sizable dune, it could have torn the wing off, or it could have pulled the Arrow straight down into the ground."

Meyers climbed out of the Rover and stumbled toward the next closest piece of debris. The sand dragged him down as if it were lava.

"Does three kilometers..." Meyers swallowed and wondered if the pain he was feeling was the sort of thing that had aged Rimes so quickly.

"Could the ship have been torn apart over a three-kilometer area? Yes. Absolutely. Colonel?"

"Yes?"

"I am sorry for your loss. Lieutenant Oppert was a good pilot, and I very much enjoyed her company."

Meyers opened his faceplate and doubled over, trying to take a quiet, deep breath. "Thanks, Genevieve." He disconnected as the crunch of boots in sand announced someone's approach.

"More a bit beyond the dune," McNutt said from a respectable distance. "Body parts, too. Don't see much hope of survivors."

Meyers stood and brushed sand from his knees as he thought through the chalks for One-Six-Three. Camille, Corporal Viet, Lieutenant Genêt, Corporals Torres and Rohmer, Private Lumley, Lieutenant Espinoza,

Corporals Shane and Leialoha, and Sergeant Sheff. Pilot, sniper, platoon commander, medics, intelligence analysts, systems specialist; no signals showed from their suits. A good chunk of their ammo, most of the operations center equipment and medical supplies, part of their water extraction gear, half their food.

The mission wasn't a bust. Not yet.

Meyers straightened. "Who's your runner?"

McNutt looked back toward the soldiers spread out between the Rover and the wreckage. "After Perkins? Calderon, I reckon."

"Send him north, helmet closed, channel open. Watch on thermo and UV for any parts—machine and human. Have him tag them, then have the rest of your squad collect and bury the human parts in a single grave."

McNutt didn't say anything, but he tensed up enough that it was clear he didn't care for the assignment.

"I'm taking the Rover up to collect the transponder."

Meyers trudged past McNutt and slid into the driver's seat, then checked the system readout. The Rover was at ninety percent power, more than enough. Meyers pressed softly against the accelerator and swerved through McNutt's squad. Once in the open, Meyers closed his faceplate and accelerated.

Once again, heat blobs tagged where One-Six-Three had broken up in the desert. He set the BAS to automatically tag anything that stood out. He'd tagged 278 items by the time he came to a stop next to the transponder signal. He walked over to a black piece of curled fuselage maybe three meters long and half as high. Ribs poked from the top of the fuselage, silvery white in the moonlight. The black box was secured in the crook where a horizontal support rib joined the two vertical ones.

Meyers squatted next to the fuselage and immediately jumped back, gasping. Instead of sinking into the sand, his knee had bumped into something solid just below the surface. He leaned forward and brushed away the sand until he could see what he'd knelt against.

Wind whipped away the last grains of sand, revealing a section of armor.

"Shit."

He brushed away more sand and ran his hand along the length of the armor, finally exposing enough to get a grip on whatever it was. He tugged, and a leg came free. The BAS registered it as Sheff, the systems specialist. Meyers set the leg behind him and returned his focus to the transponder. Although it was secured to the airframe, it was supposed to be easily removed from its mount. He turned on his helmet lamp and searched around the mount, finally spotting the clips on the third pass. He released them and pulled the black box free, then he set it in the foot rest area on the passenger side. He took a deep breath and headed back for the leg, carrying it to the Rover and setting it on the flatbed.

Suddenly, his BAS display shifted. It was minor but enough that he noticed. He scanned for whatever it was that had changed, then he realized it was the display of the One-Six-Three personnel chalk. Three vitals were glowing on the display, rising and falling.

There were survivors.

"Corporal McNutt, we've got survivors!" Meyers slid into the Rover and headed toward the signals.

"You sure?"

"Three signals, 207 meters east of the transponder. One of them's very weak, the other two...weak. Lieutenant Genêt, Corporal Torres, and Private Lumley." Meyers cursed below his breath. The BAS should have been transmitting those signals, just like the transponder should have been transmitting the second the Arrow crashed.

"Why didn't they show up before now, Colonel?"

"I don't know. Maybe their systems are damaged. Maybe they're so wounded the suits have been drained just keeping them alive."

"Or maybe it's a bad signal."

"They're just ahead. It looks like a whole piece of the fuselage tore away."

Meyers jumped out of the Rover and ran toward the section of fuselage. Against the midnight blue sky, the frame was black, lying on its side, four seats still secured to it. One of the seats was twisted and caked with black blood and sand, but the other three held soldiers. His soldiers. They were twisted, their limbs limp and misshapen, but they were alive.

"Corporal, they're alive!" Meyers glanced through the clear faceplates of each soldier. Their faces were bloody and bruised, and their eyes were closed, but the signals said they were alive. "Anyone on your team have even rudimentary medical training?"

"Corporal Cho."

Meyers wondered what Rimes would do in a situation like this. It felt wrong abandoning wounded, possibly dying people, but there was no other choice but to go back for Cho.

"I'm heading back. Have Cho start running toward me."

"Yeah, he's like a rabbit already."

Meyers had the Rover at top speed in seconds, and the vitals readout of the survivors filling the center display at ten percent opaqueness. He slammed on the brakes once he realized he was driving straight at Cho. Once Cho was in the Rover, Meyers lifted his faceplate. He would have to rely on the earpiece's projected display for the drive back.

"Survivors, sir?" Cho's faceplate was up, and he was breathing hard. He looked sleepy, the result of heavy epicanthic folds. Muscles worked beneath the pale skin of his broad face.

"Three. Lieutenant Genêt's not looking so good, but she's stable. They're all a mess. Broken bones, probably internal bleeding. Can you handle something like that?"

Cho blinked rapidly, then he nodded. He looked back at the flatbed. "Is that from one of them, sir?"

"Sergeant Sheff."

Cho blew out a breath and stared ahead, still blinking rapidly.

Meyers brought the Rover to a stop next to the section of fuselage and let Cho out, then spun the vehicle around and backed it up so that it was parallel to the fuselage and close enough that any movement could be minimized. Cho was already looking at Genêt.

"Multiple fractures, sir. I'm pretty sure they've suffered spinal damage. The harnesses can only do so much."

Meyers was well aware of the limits of the body, the armor, and the safety systems. "Do what you can."

"I want to go ahead and rigid up their armor, y'know, lock everything up as is. Hopefully minimize any damage from moving them."

"Can we move them? Just the two of us?"

Cho tapped something into Genêt's torso control panel, then stepped back. "I think so, sir. It'll be hard, but, yeah. The lieutenant's ready now. You—"

"Sure." Meyers took up a position on Genêt's right side.

"I'm going to disengage the harness, and then we'll both grab this hook on either side of her torso armor, okay, sir?"

"Got it." Meyers licked his lips and placed a hand just wide of the harness, ready to grab at the hook on his side that Cho had pointed out.

The harness clicked, and Cho lifted it clear with one hand while grabbing the hook on Genêt's left side.

"Okay, sir, now we lift her straight up and out of the seat. The armor's going to go rigid, and she'll be at full length until I turn that off. Ready?"

"Ready."

Genêt's weight was more than Meyers had expected. It wasn't just the armor and kit, but the way they had to lift her straight up, relying almost exclusively on upper body strength and doing their best to minimize jostling. They set her on the flatbed, both of them grunting and gasping from the exertion.

Cho ran an armored forearm through his open faceplate, dabbing at sweat beaded on his forehead. "Two more to go, sir. You up for this?"

"Yeah." Meyers was ready to take a break, but there were people—his people—counting on him.

By the time they got Corporal Torres on the flatbed, even Cho looked ready for a break. Cho was a slight man, but he had as far as Meyers could recall above average physical evaluations. Meyers had seen enough of Cho's personnel files to know there was some sort of gang history, things that had cost Cho a shot at following his father into the metacorporate world. It was something Meyers could empathize with.

"Lumley's a big guy, sir," Cho said between gulps of air. "Why don't we take a second before we move him? Won't make a difference to his condition."

"All right, sure." Meyers turned and shook out his arms as he walked away from the Rover. His heart was hammering so loud in his chest that he almost missed the chime coming from his earpiece. It was Barlowe. "Go ahead, Ladell."

"Lonny, we've got trouble. Big trouble." Barlowe was whispering, but his words were clipped and seemed to pop over the channel, despite a hum that indicated he was at the edge of quality comm range. "We're being followed."

"We. You and Private Starling?"

"Yeah. We traced the Grid signals to two potential hubs. I went for one; she went for the other. It's predawn here. The streets are mostly empty. It should've been safe." The line went quiet for a moment. "Anyway, we can't shake these guys."

Meyers froze. The probe was supposed to have been safe, easy. "Can you...I don't know, get them into an alley, knock them out?"

"These are big guys. Big." A motor hummed somewhere in the distance. "I don't know."

Meyers thought back to McNutt's description of the fighting they'd done in Widowmaker. "I think Starling will be okay, if that's what you're worried about."

"I'm worried about me, Lonny." Barlowe's voice rose as he spoke.

"Okay. Who's covering you?"

"Ski's sniper? Titan, I think. He can't get a clean shot, if that's what you mean. We had to go in deeper than we wanted. They have roadblocks. It's crazy."

"Stay calm, all right? Tell Ski to get someone to a position ahead of you, someplace you and Starling can meet at. Understand? There were a bunch of buildings in the imagery that looked empty or half-finished. Any of those nearby?"

The channel was silent except for the hum.

"I see one. I'm signaling Becky now. This is messed up, Lonny. It's like a war zone down here. They've got vehicles patrolling with armed men. Automatic weapons. It's like—"

Barlowe closed the channel.

Meyers spun. "Okay, Corporal Cho, let's get this wrapped up and get back to base. We've got problems."

Cho massaged his neck through his armor. "Sure, sir."

Meyers took up his position at Lumley's side and waited for the click that would signal the harness was unlocked. Aching arms were a minor thing to deal with compared to what was going on in Turning Point. Meyers's guts twisted at Barlowe's description of the city. They needed to eliminate Waverley and get off Bellar before the colonists were even aware the ERF were on-planet. A war zone was exactly the sort of complication they needed to avoid.

4

———

12 December 2174. Karpov Desert, South of Turning Point, Bellar Frontier Colony.

THE OPERATIONS CENTER amounted to a man-made cave, four meters on a side, two and a half high. The floor and walls—mostly bare—were the same sort of inflatable materials as the Rovers, kept rigid by charges from embedded batteries. Sand crunched beneath Meyers's boots as he crossed to a cargo case and set his helmet down. The structure was empty except for him and Banh's squad. His nose burned from the plastic smell of the walls, like someone had just squeezed the structure out of a giant tube of polystyrene.

Meyers turned his attention to the wall of displays Banh's team was still fiddling with: perimeter sensor data, video feeds from McNutt's crew working the wreck, and grainy video feeds that could have been anything.

It was the team in Turning Point.

Meyers wiped sweat from his brow and tried to calm down enough to let his armor and the night air cool him down.

Paxton descended the gentle entry ramp and came to a stop in front of the static-filled monitors, fists planted on his hips. "Sergeant Banh, where the hell's our video?"

"The signal is quite weak, Master Sergeant." Banh stared at the monitors intently. In their glow, it was hard not to notice that his right eye was larger than his left. It was the sort of thing usually corrected during childhood. The asymmetry was also visible in his hairline, which came closer to his barely visible eyebrows. He waved at one of his soldiers, who sprinted out of the center. "We are trying to run a concentrator using the Javelins' systems, but only so much can be done. It is the signal."

"Sergeant Zacharowski, this is Colonel Meyers. Can you hear me?"

"Got a lot of noise on the line, but I hear you." Zacharowski's voice was mostly distortion and stutter, but the BAS cleaned the signal more with each word.

Meyers shared his comms with Paxton. "We hear you. Go ahead."

"I got Titan and…uh, Perkins feeding me video. Our little birdies are holed up about 200 meters from our position."

"That's good. I'm going to need you to use your BAS as a collector. Consolidate your team's signals into one feed, join the bandwidth from your team's suits, and transmit the final signal through the Rover."

"I have my team running their systems hot, keeping them ready to act. Situation's under control."

"If you had the situation under control, Sergeant, I wouldn't be talking to you right now."

"Your intel team screwed up, but we'll get them out. Don't you worry. Probably need to get McNutt's squad trained up. Perkins got dinged up putting up a sensor. Sloppy."

Zacharowski's cockiness felt too familiar to Meyers, who heard his own younger voice. That cockiness ate at him now, just as McNutt's resentment of authority had earlier. "Over a bad communication channel, I understand that might have sounded like a request, Sergeant Zacharowski. It wasn't. Send me the consolidated signal."

Meyers muted the connection and turned to Paxton. "What's this about Perkins getting dinged up?"

Paxton shrugged. "Went quiet when he was supposed to be putting up his sensor. They found him woozy, some scrapes on his armor. Probably the wind knocked the sensor into him."

The explanation didn't sound very likely, but Meyers couldn't imagine someone assaulting Perkins, either. Meyers moved closer to the grainy video, giving Banh and his team a chance to step back and away from the potentially uncomfortable engagement. Seconds passed with Paxton clearing his throat as the only sound, then a soft squeaking sound caught Meyers's ears. He was grinding his teeth. He muted his earpiece again; Master Sergeant Paxton did the same.

"Sergeant Banh, why don't you and your team check on that concentrator." Paxton sounded calm, his words barely more than a suggestion; Banh and his team exited the operations center at a jog.

"Zacharowski thinks he's still Delta," Meyers said. The display bowed beneath the soft tap of his finger. It was just a specialized section of the wall, a few micrometers deep, but when the video feed was good enough, it was like looking through a window.

"We have latrine pits to dig—" Paxton's voice was lost in the jumbled audio that accompanied a sharpening video feed.

"You getting this?" Zacharowski's voice had just a hint of annoyance.

Meyers scanned the imagery as it built out into a three-dimensional display. Zacharowski's BAS was creating a fairly low-resolution image to best use the available bandwidth. The imagery was good enough to give Meyers what he needed to not feel blind: vehicles moving in the distance, choppy, grainy, but good enough; buildings that were a composite of live video and wireframe overlays; green dots and names indicating ERF positions. In the areas outside the concentration of ERF personnel, the images were static, drawn from the existing intelligence data. The place looked practically medieval, with several packed-dirt roads to go along with the blacktop of the main streets. There were prefab and quick-fab buildings, some of them rising three stories, all of them simple and weathered. Potholes, garbage, and rocks cluttered roads and alleyways.

"Coming through now," Meyers said. "Can you put your snipers on the channel without losing too much bandwidth?"

"Adding them on. Titan, Perkins, you're on an open channel with the colonel and me."

"Picked a good night for hunting, Colonel. Awful dark out there. Makes it hard to pick out the targets. They're all dark, I mean." Titan's voice was loud and casual.

Paxton's mouth twisted as if he'd just bitten into a chunk of rancid meat.

"Thank you, Corporal Gerhardt. I get that the situation isn't ideal." Meyers tried to insert a little sting into his choice of using Titan's real name over his treasured Delta nickname, but he wasn't sure how effective that would be over such a distorted connection. "Sergeant Zacharowski, tell me what I'm seeing."

"We inserted here." Zacharowski drew a line that traced through the static imagery to the south and stopped just shy of the green dots. "These are mostly quick-erect buildings, typical early-stage colonial stuff. I deployed Titan and Perkins to the highest rooftops, then I sent Barlowe and Starling in. No real activity to speak of at this hour, but when they crossed this road, they picked up tails." He traced a path that seemed to match the jumpy images of the vehicles.

"And when they tried to extract—"

"No luck. So they've moved through some of the buildings in that area. Some are apartments; some are abandoned. Can't just sit still, though. Not much longer, anyhow."

"Should've made a run for it." Titan snorted. "Can't see them, night like this."

"Best cut that shit right now," Perkins said. Even over the bad connection, his hostility came through loud and clear.

"Aw, Perkins, I didn't know you liked a little dark meat on the side. Why don't you just pay attention to getting a clean target for once, huh?"

Meyers felt his cheeks burn at the racial undertones in Titan's comments. "Corporal Gerhardt, I think it's best if you limit your commentary to relevant input going forward. Sergeant Zacharowski, we'll discuss this later."

Paxton tapped his crooked nose in approval.

Meyers took in a breath and bit back saying anything further. There were rumors Titan was a problem, but there had never been any evidence or details provided. Hearing it out in the open...

It wasn't time to dwell on personnel problems, Meyers decided. "In your estimation, Sergeant, have they been made, or is it just curiosity?"

"Curiosity, I'd guess."

Meyers drilled down so that he could see where Barlowe and Starling were. Two buildings, one of them small, were all that separated them. He connected to Barlowe.

"Ladell, I've got visual from Zacharowski. Can you talk?"

"Yeah." Barlowe's voice was a whisper. "My tail's somewhere outside—" A faint squeaking sound sneaked into Barlowe's audio. "Shit. Okay, he's inside. I can see him silhouetted in the doorway."

"We need to keep our footprint here to a minimum. I need an honest assessment from you. Can you fall back to Zacharowski's position without engaging?"

"No. He has a gun. Assault rifle, I think. Okay, he's moving in. Bugging out."

Meyers winced, then he switched to Starling's channel. "Private Starling?"

"Colonel? I-I got a problem."

"I know. I'm getting a video feed now. It's not very good, though."

"I'm sorry, sir. I got some clothes. From the locals. Hanging out to dry, I mean. We were tapping into the Grid when—"

"That's fine. Can you update me on your situation? Can you lose your tail?"

"I think so. I can try."

"Good. Agent Barlowe's trying to shake his tail now. He's forty meters west-southwest of your position. Looks like there aren't any working streetlights in that area; is that correct?"

"It's like moving through the woods without a moon."

"All right. I'm going to have Zacharowski deploy some support. I want you to move to the closest of their signals. Can you do that?"

"My BAS is a little choppy, sir."

"We're all having problems. When you get close enough, it should work out."

"Moving now."

"Excellent."

Meyers switched back to Zacharowski's channel. "Barlowe's not going to be able to lose his tail, but Starling's giving it a try. Who are your best with hand-to-hand?"

"Hand-to-hand? Shit, draw their tails into the open, and we'll pop their tops."

"I don't want any killing if we don't have to, Sergeant. Two men, have them deploy and push their signals to max strength so they show up on Barlowe and Starling's BASes. If we can get out of there with—"

Distant popping sounds mixed with shouted curses.

"Ain't happening, Colonel. We've got automatic fire and muzzle flash."

"Deploy those men, now!"

Meyers reopened his channels with Barlowe and Starling. Gunfire flooded Barlowe's channel. "Ladell? Ladell? Private Starling?"

"He's just firing wild!" Barlowe was gulping air. A ricochet careened close enough for his earpiece to pick it up. "They're crazy."

"Someone's after me, Colonel!" Starling sounded a little more under control, but panic could be just around the corner. "Can I shoot?"

"Run. Use cover. Move toward the signals you see on your BAS." Meyers muted the connections and activated the channel to Zacharowski. "I see Cisneros and Allen moving in. They need to get it into another gear."

More gunfire came through; this time it was Starling's channel. Her breathing intensified, and she let out a deep sound, the sort of sound you make when you have the wind knocked out of you. Meyers dropped his eyes to where Starling's vitals should have been, but her signal was too weak to do anything more than handle audio.

"Private Starling, are you—"

"Running like hell, sir." Her voice was louder. "Banged into a wall."

On the display, Barlowe was moving toward Cisneros, but there was a sizable gap; Starling was doing better closing with Allen.

Paxton leaned in closer to the display and shook his head. "Hell, my momma could move faster than that, Colonel. I thought Agent Barlowe was a Commando?"

"More than a decade ago."

Paxton snorted. "Might want to work on his cardio some."

Meyers drilled down on the display. Starling was clearly moving faster, but Cisneros seemed to be moving faster toward Barlowe than Allen was to Starling. Gunfire chattered over the channel again.

"Allen has visual on Starling," Zacharowski said.

"The bogey?" Meyers imagined himself in the situation, jogging down roads in the dark, watching for shadows slightly darker than other shadows, leaping over those, hoping he didn't turn an ankle on a rock or pothole.

"Visual now. Allen is moving into an alley."

Meyers unmuted his line to Starling. "You should see an alley ahead of you."

"Left. He in there?"

"Yes. Drop once you're past him."

Starling's green blip hit the alleyway, and gunfire combined with what must have been raining debris. She spat and cursed, and then it sounded like she hit the ground hard, her blip parallel to Cisneros's. A voice shouted, loud, along with what might have been a magazine being slapped home, and then there were more indistinct, muted sounds, like a scuffle, interrupted by gunfire, and then a cry cut short.

Meyers turned to Paxton, who shook his head. "Starling?"

"It's all right, Colonel. Allen was fighting over the gun, so I hit the guy with a rock. He's down."

"Get back to Zacharowski."

Their blips headed south, and Meyers turned his attention back to Barlowe's green blip. Cisneros was close, separated by a large building.

Meyers opened the channel to Zacharowski. "Send Cisneros into that building." Then Meyers flipped the channel to Barlowe. "Building ahead of you. Cisneros is entering on the opposite side. Head for his position."

Barlowe grunted what might have been a breathless acknowledgment. His blip moved toward the building and then moved into it. Rattling, banging, a gasp, then the same sounds close enough for the earpiece to pick up but far enough away it was hard to be sure what, exactly, was coming through. Barlowe's gasps and grunts quickly drowned out everything else, then it sounded like he hit the ground, and a loud voice started shouting.

"Don't you move, mother fucker! Don't. Move." The voice was deep, the accent strange, tinged mostly with a Latino twist.

"Okay." Barlowe's surrender sounded complete and authentic.

"Who the hell are—" The deep voice let out a shout, and then things became quiet.

Meyers cocked his head, as if that might help him understand the situation. "Barlowe, what's going on?"

"Cisneros...fighting him. They've got knives."

Knives, Meyers thought. It wasn't going to end well. "Get out of there. Head for Zacharowski's position."

Meyers switched back to Zacharowski's channel. "When you get Barlowe and Starling back, send them straight back to the Rover. Have Allen escort them."

"Cisneros just reported in."

"And?" Meyers already knew what had happened.

"He had to kill the guy."

Meyers turned away from the displays and locked his hands together.

"What do we do, Colonel?"

"Wait until he gets back to you, then pull out."

"Allen said these guys are big, like they're on something."

Meyers thought back to Rimes's experiment with Munoz before the ERF was formed and how tough it was sparring with the guy. It always seemed like any fight was one mistake away from a serious injury. "Let's hope we don't have to deal with them anymore, then. Get your people back here alive, Sergeant."

"Understood."

Meyers closed the channel and sighed, keenly aware of Paxton watching out of the corner of his eye. Outside, McNutt's team was pulling into camp, grim-faced from burying the dead. Meyers was down nearly a third of his force, and all they had to show for it was a dead local, possibly what passed for law enforcement in a city like Turning Point.

There was no backing out of the mission now. It was the sort of thing Rimes had managed to handle with ease, but Rimes wasn't there anymore. The ERF had survived him, and now it was Meyers's problem, and he was failing spectacularly.

5
—————

12 December 2174. Karpov Desert, South of Turning Point, Bellar Frontier
Colony.

MEYERS PACED the operations center floor, absently wiping at the fine sheen
of sweat on his forehead. The structure interior was warmer now that the
sun had risen outside, and ventilation and human occupation had provided
a lived-in smell that made the sharp, plastic smell more tolerable. He
absently noted the different sounds produced when he stepped onto a
shallow pool of sand rather than on a few grains or a scattering of pebbles
or the rare clear patch of the rigid surface. Any sound was better than the
hesitant muttering between Barlowe and Starling, each seated on a cargo
case maybe half a meter from the wall of displays. They'd been at it—hacking, analyzing, muttering—since their return from Turning Point, and there
wasn't the slightest hint of confidence in their voices.

"Okay you two," Meyers said as he came to a stop. "Give me something.
Anything."

Barlowe glanced over his shoulder at Meyers, then sighed and rubbed
his forehead. "We...there's nothing."

"What do you mean there's nothing?"

"Waverley's an extraordinarily wealthy man, used to living a life of luxury. You've seen the report provided by SunCorps—human staff of thirty, twice as many robotic and autonomous assistants, four residences. It's a footprint that should stand out, even on a planet of a billion people. On a planet with a population like Bellar?" Barlowe stood and tapped one of the displays, and a series of overlays settled over Turning Point. "Power consumption, food and water, bandwidth use—everything that would signal a potential disproportionate footprint—and we have nothing."

Meyers moved closer to the display. "What about here? This whole section around...what is that, a harbor?"

Starling squeezed between Meyers and the display. "Technically, it's Turning Point, sir. The automated barges from Ardennen come down to this point, drop off their cargo, pick up supplies, then return upriver or down into the bay and along the coast. I'm not sure where they go down there, but some of the imagery we have shows them. We pulled down a live feed for a few seconds this morning. The harbor has the only functional security cameras worth tapping into. At least that we can get into without hacking. It looks like there are three barges tied off right now. I think there's a security team there, too. Maybe six people. But it's not the best security. If you look here, there's a fence around the harbor compound, but to the south, where it opens up on the desert, there's a pretty good gap—"

Meyers shook his head. "I'm not interested in the logistics, Private."

Barlowe's head jerked up. "Logistics are all we have to work from, Lonny. We don't have any idea who's in power, how the population is distributed, what their economy is based on, nothing. What we both saw when we went in is consistent with extreme poverty, but we only had a chance to see the southern part of the city. Over on the west side, there were these huge displays on the rooftops. Maybe twelve or fifteen meters high. It looked like they were looping...I don't know. Propaganda?"

"Definitely propaganda. Violent stuff. And I don't mean the barges are tied off like they're anchored or something, Colonel." Even whispering, Starling's voice was husky, and her deep Alabama accent broke through. Pain was evident in her eyes.

"Then what do you mean?"

"Like they was—were—stolen. Robotic ships like that, they manage their own securing. It's just safer that way. No risk of accidental damage if someone ties something up to them and their sensors don't pick it up. But they got chains all along the hull now. It looks like someone tore up the engines, too."

Meyers looked at Barlowe. "So, what? These people stole the barges?"

"We think so. Or they're holding them for ransom, maybe. Like pirates." Barlowe seemed to consider joining them at the displays, but then he just stared into the distance and began manipulating the images through his earpiece and the components of the BAS he was still wearing beneath his clothes. "We don't know the implications of that, not without getting more data. But what we're guessing is the larger footprint you see in that area just represents..." He squinted. "The alphas?"

"That's the power center of the city?"

After glancing at Barlowe, probably for assurance that didn't come, Starling said, "It makes sense, sir. I mean, based off what Ladell explained."

Barlowe's eyes focused on them again. "Losing Espinoza and his team is going to make this really hard. You've got two people trying to run systems and make sense of the data instead of five." He nodded toward Starling. "Becky hasn't had any training in analysis, so she's doing a lot more than she should have to."

"We're all doing more than we should have to. This whole operation is exactly that. There should be a blockade up in orbit. We should have two ERF companies down here tracking Waverley. The UN should have sent an envoy to establish diplomatic relations with whoever's in power in Turning Point. But we don't have any of that, and I wasn't given a choice when the directive came down, so we have to accept the risks and work with our current resources."

Meyers realized he was close to shouting, so he shut up and returned to pacing. It wasn't fair to be mad at Barlowe and Starling. It was the lack of support, irrational expectations, and all the early setbacks that were eating at him, not the two of them.

When the heat was gone, he turned toward the displays again. Barlowe and Starling seemed determined not to look him in the eye.

"Okay. So we don't have Waverley, but we've got a disproportionate use of resources along the harbor area. Could he be hiding his footprint somewhere in there, spreading it out somehow?"

"Sure. And there are some really nice-looking buildings that would probably be ideal for someone like him." Barlowe drilled down on a pair of buildings, one of them more of a complex, walled in, with nearby smaller buildings. It wasn't too far from the harbor. "I'd guess right here. And there's a lot of traffic going in and out. But it's been that way for months."

"So, too long for it to be Waverley."

"I think so. Maybe we tear the data apart and find otherwise, but if you're asking me right now to make a guess based off what we got, I wouldn't consider that a very likely target."

It was too early to start chasing low-probability leads. They needed a breakthrough, but it didn't seem likely they would get one soon.

"All right. We have a couple other possibilities. One, he's not here, and SunCorps lied to the UN. A wild goose chase. We pack it up and head home. We'll need a lot more evidence before we can claim that. Two, he's not in this area. Maybe he's up in Ardennen. Again, SunCorps lied and we missed on our analysis. We don't have enough data to make that call, right?"

"No."

"So, ideas?"

"We need to get an understanding of the power structures. Those haulers that seemed to be on patrol. We saw what looked like checkpoints —sandbags, people hunched down. It was like a war zone."

Starling nodded. "They had assault rifles, sir. There wasn't anything about that in the data. Who supplied those? Do they have anything heavier than that?"

"Those haulers had guns mounted on them," Barlowe said. "I'm sure of it."

"Mounted guns?" The idea seemed absurd to Meyers.

"Armored bubbles." Barlowe stood and ran a finger up and down what looked like it might be the main north-south road through the center of town. "They were moving up and down here. Two things stood out to me. One, one of those looked like a heavy hauler. I don't know, like construction or mining stuff. A flatbed, armored cab. Two, I know I saw an armored bubble on the flatbed, and I think I saw at least one other one. Automatic, heavy caliber. That big hauler, the gun looked really big, like an anti-aircraft type weapon. Maybe a railgun."

"Armored haulers? Railguns?" Meyers looked Turning Point over, trying to imagine why and how anyone would have armored haulers with anti-aircraft guns. "Does that match anything in the data we have?"

Barlowe shook his head.

"Not that I saw, Colonel." Starling seemed embarrassed. "I'm sorry about missing the details about the haulers."

Meyers shook his head. "So, we need to send people in. Is that what you're saying?"

"There's not a better way to get a feel of what's going on than to ask around and listen." Barlowe looked down. "I could go in. I think we'd have a better chance in daylight of fitting in, or at least not drawing attention."

"You said these men pursuing you were big. Pumped up, shooting up?"

"Yeah. There must be a good flow of steroids and growth hormones."

"And you don't think you'll stand out?"

Barlowe didn't seem to take offense. "Oh, not everyone was big. Just over toward the west side. It was bad there."

"You have anyone else in mind to go along?" Meyers glanced toward Starling, whose eyes went wide.

"Not Becky. Cisneros, maybe. I heard Spanish coming from some of those haulers."

"How's your Spanish?"

"I grew up around Phoenix. It's passable."

"Get with Cisneros. See if those clothes you brought back fit him. I didn't see anything outrageous—jeans and a shirt, right?"

"No indications of cultural oddities. The big guys seemed to all be wearing...muscle shirts?" Barlowe glanced at Starling.

"Wife-beaters." Starling looked from Barlowe to Meyers, blinking, mouth open as if she'd said something embarrassing. "That's, uh, what my dad called 'em."

"Muscle shirts is fine," Meyers said.

Barlowe looked back at the displays and tapped the north-south road. "I think it was more that we were spotted in sensitive areas and ran when we were confronted, otherwise we might have fit in. Well, me, at least. The man chasing me, I'd guess he was Afro-Latin. Becky?"

"Hispanic, I guess?" She still seemed off-balance, embarrassed. "I don't know. Caramel skin? Is that right sounding?"

"Yes. Cisneros and me," Barlowe said.

"I'll talk to Pax—" Meyers caught a flurry of movement out of the corner of his eye and realized it was a display showing the feed from one of the cameras near the Javelins. He bumped up the volume. Soldiers were huddling, then running, and a few seemed to be scuffling or coming close to it. It was quickly broken up by Paxton's gravelly bellow.

And then Paxton was strolling through the men, like a king, fearless. He was shorter than most, barely more than 175 centimeters tall, but he was thick through the chest and just in his presence managed to radiate danger.

Meyers hustled to the exit and opened a channel to Paxton. "Master Sergeant Paxton, what's happening?"

"I was just wondering the same thing myself, Colonel."

Meyers jogged along the edge of the camouflage netting of the nearest Javelin, then curled through the open space between the two vehicles and the operations center until he could see the men gathered around. He was already certain in his gut that he knew what was going on. He pushed through the men, who were slower to open a path for him than they had been for Paxton.

Or Rimes.

Everything was different now, Meyers reminded himself.

He came to a stop behind Paxton, at the nose of the second Javelin, where three men held McNutt back and two more stood in front of Titan. He was wiping blood from a flattened nose.

Paxton spread his legs slightly and clasped his hands behind his back. "Gentlemen, if I were to go strictly by appearances, I would infer there was some sort of altercation between Corporal McNutt and Corporal Gerhardt. Does someone want to dissuade me of that?"

Sergeant Zacharowski—one of the men holding Titan back—brushed dirt from his uniform and smiled. There was a red welt forming on his jaw, as if he might have caught a punch himself. "No altercation, Master Sergeant. Just doing a little sparring."

"You son of a—" Titan launched himself at Zacharowski but was hauled back by Cisneros, who seemed to put a little something extra into the effort.

Paxton turned toward McNutt, who sported a scrape over his right eye. "Corporal, does Sergeant Zacharowski's account match your reckoning of the situation?"

McNutt stopped pulling against the soldiers holding him back and straightened. His eyes were squinted tight so that the dark blue of the iris seemed almost black. His face, normally verging on a warm gold, was darker, almost a red-gold. "Reckon so, Master Sergeant." Perkins, who'd been draped over McNutt's back, patted him on the chest.

Paxton cocked an eyebrow at Meyers. "Looks like a little training gone too far, sir."

Meyers wanted to call bullshit. He wanted to address what he guessed was behind the incident, clear and unequivocal. But a part of him said that approach felt all wrong. "Sergeant Zacharowski, Corporal McNutt, please follow me to the Operations Center. Sergeant Paxton, if you and Sergeant Banh could see to it everyone understands that there will be no more overzealous sparring incidents before joining us, I would appreciate it."

"We'll do that, sir." Paxton waved the soldiers in. "Gather 'round, people."

Meyers waved for McNutt and Zacharowski to follow, then set a quick pace. When he reached the entry to the building, he stopped. "Agent Barlowe, Private Starling, take a break. You two deserve it. Clean up, get something to eat, see if you can catch a nap."

Barlowe and Starling appeared in the entry. Starling's eyes widened at the sight of McNutt and Zacharowski, but all she said was thank you to Meyers, and then they were gone.

Meyers entered the structure and settled onto one of the cargo cases. He pointed the men to two of the other cases, then set his hands at his side and tapped out a quiet beat. "I wanted to have a talk with you earlier, Sergeant Zacharowski, and I think my failure to do so probably led to this situation." He raised a hand when both men looked like they might interrupt him. "Ten years ago, I probably would've kicked the shit out of Corporal Gerhardt myself." He glared at McNutt. "And I would've been wrong. We're a team. Undersized, under-prepared, and we've already lost people without even engaging the enemy. This sort of thing, it's unhealthy."

"Making jokes about shooting one of my squad, that's okay?" McNutt's color was hot again.

"Corporal Gerhardt was way out of line. And Sergeant Zacharowski's going to handle that, aren't you?"

"Titan just likes to get under people's skin."

"Especially if that skin's a little darker than his?" Meyers cocked his head. "I've seen his type. How the hell he made it into ERF is beyond me, but if he has a repeat of this behavior, he won't be in much longer. Am I clear?"

"I hear you."

"Another thing, Sergeant. This isn't Delta. You'll find I don't get hung up on formalities, but there will be some level of decorum. Try throwing a few 'sirs' or 'colonels' in when you address me." Meyers turned back to McNutt. "You two are in positions of leadership. Your behavior sets the expectations for your squad. If they see you acting professionally, they'll follow suit. Am I clear?"

"Yeah, you're clear, sir," McNutt said.

Zacharowski just stared for a moment, simmering. "I hear you, Colonel."

"Good." Meyers opened a channel to Paxton.

"Am I done briefing the troops, Colonel?" Paxton asked.

"I think we're ready to have a chat when you and Sergeant Banh are."

"We're on our way."

Meyers closed the channel and looked back at Zacharowski. "Corporal Gerhardt made a comment about Private Perkins not getting a clean target. Was that more of Gerhardt's act, or was it related to this injury Perkins suffered setting up the sensors?"

McNutt turned on Zacharowski. "Injury?"

Zacharowski shrugged. "No one saw it, and he doesn't know what happened."

"Do you think it was the injury, Sergeant?"

"No, sir. Perkins kept saying he didn't have a clean line-of-sight, even when his video feed showed otherwise."

"Corporal McNutt, is there something going on with Private Perkins? We only have two snipers now. I need them both focused on the mission."

McNutt looked down. "Perkins is fine, Colonel."

"Is something wrong with his kit, then?"

"He didn't miss a shot, did he?" McNutt's brows were bunched up, and his head was thrust forward. He closed his eyes and ran a hand over his face. "His wife's up the duff, and she's pressuring him to come back to Earth."

"Up the duff?"

Sergeant Banh took three steps into the room and stopped, eyes darting from one person to another. "Training completed, Colonel."

Paxton cleared his throat as he entered the room. "We talking about Private Perkins's wife, Colonel?"

"We are."

"Pregnant, Colonel." McNutt shifted slightly on the cargo case. "Her father runs a successful enough business; he can take on someone without any skills and train him."

Meyers wasn't sure how to react to that. "So it's not about the promotion to corporal?"

Paxton snorted. "Oh, it's definitely about the promotion. Dangling that out there as an incentive to re-up didn't sit well with him to start, and now he's lost his nerve."

"It's not nerves," McNutt said. "He's not sure it's right to be killing another man, what with being so close to separating, that's all."

Paxton squared his shoulders. "Right up to the second you turn civilian, you're obligated to follow orders, even if those orders are to kill someone, Corporal."

"Perkins knows his obligations, Master Sergeant. It's a...personal thing."

"Well I can check the agenda again, but I'm pretty sure no one scheduled a personal thing." Paxton took a step toward McNutt. "You need to get your squad together, Soldier."

McNutt's brow bunched up again, and Meyers sensed they were on the edge of another sparring incident, one that would be impossible to overlook. "Master Sergeant Paxton, maybe you and Corporal McNutt could have a talk with Perkins, just review his options, go over the incentives for continued service. No matter his decision, we need him to get his head into the situation. Agreed?"

McNutt seemed to relax. "I can do that, Colonel."

"Excellent. So, let's get on to the reason I called you all in here." Meyers sighed. "Here's the latest on the mission: We're no closer to Waverley, and we aren't likely to get closer anytime soon. What we're going to do next is see if we can infiltrate Turning Point, gather some HUMINT. Sergeant Zacharowski, Agent Barlowe asked for Private Cisneros. You think he's up for it?"

"He's up for it."

"I heard he got cut in that knife fight."

"Bruised and a little scrape. We're almost done fixing his armor. He'll be fine."

"Master Sergeant Paxton, your thoughts?"

"Someone gets knocked off the horse, you don't wait to put them back on it, Colonel."

Meyers wondered how quick Cisneros might be to go to a lethal option after getting stabbed while trying to take his target down alive. The risk was just another thing to be taken on.

"See if you can find something he can wear in those civilian clothes Private Starling brought back. We'll try inserting them at dusk." Meyers paused long enough for anyone to speak up if they disagreed with the plan; no one did. "Dismissed."

Another dangerous decision that quickly started to gnaw at Meyers's gut. With each new act, they became more committed.

6

12 December 2174. Karpov Desert, South of Turning Point, Bellar Frontier Colony.

MEYERS LOOKED AWAY from the display he'd been staring at, rubbed his jaw, and paused the app that was crunching the data. His legs were stiff, and his eyes ached. It felt like he was slowly cooking in the Operations Center.

He stood and stretched and realized that he needed a break.

Barlowe paused the video he was examining. "You should get some sleep."

"I will. When you're back safe." Meyers thumbed the canister on his hip that dispensed stims, then flipped the bitter little pill into his mouth. He pulled his water bottle from his other hip and washed the taste away, all the while squinting at Barlowe and Starling's screens. When he couldn't make sense of what they were looking at, he walked toward the exit. Sand spiraled in the late afternoon air, glittering a pale aqua.

"Anything new?" he called over his shoulder.

"No," Barlowe said.

"I'm still working on the Grid problem, Colonel." Starling sounded as tired as Meyers felt.

"We could sure use a breakthrough." Meyers looked at them, saw the fatigue in their eyes. "I know you're doing what you can, but we've got a lot of things piling up."

Barlowe glanced over at Starling. "There are only two of us, Lonny."

Meyers twisted and stretched, loosening his limbs until the tightness lessened. The stim would take a bit to break down completely, but there was already a faint tingling at the tips of his toes. "You've always come through. We've always found solutions. We can figure this out."

Starling hid her face in her hands, then she stood up and rushed past Meyers. "Excuse me, sir. I need to go rinse my face." Her voice quivered.

Meyers waited until she was gone, then said, "What was that about?"

Barlowe looked back at his display. "I think we need to talk."

"You need to leave soon. I'd rather you spend your time looking through the—"

Barlowe walked past and stopped a meter outside the building.

Meyers blinked. "Okay, I guess we need to talk right now."

When the wind hit him, it felt warm and invigorating. He'd lost awareness of his own smell, something he couldn't ignore when the wind sucked it out of his suit and slapped him with it. He needed a shower and a nap.

Barlowe headed away without a word, the wind at his back.

Meyers followed, almost at a jog. "What's up?"

"Becky has an idea, and I think it's a good one." Barlowe slowed and cast an eye at the camouflage netting that whipped over the tents set up opposite the Javelins, then he sped up again. "I think it might be good if you let her pitch it to you. You know, give her credit for it."

"Wait, what?"

"I said you should let her tell you about her idea and give her credit for it."

Meyers stopped and grabbed Barlowe's shoulder. "Wait a minute."

Barlowe shrugged Meyers's hand off with some effort and glared. "I don't think so. I don't think I'm going to wait any longer."

Meyers looked around. They were surrounded by blue-gray dunes and dancing sand spirals. He could see the tents, but with the wind, they were almost certainly out of range for their voices to reach anyone. "What's going on? What's all this about?"

"This? This what? Someone finally telling you you'd better back off? Hm?"

"I...I don't..." Meyers rubbed his forehead. "Did I miss something?"

Barlowe glanced back toward camp. "You're missing everything."

"Whoa! Slow down. My brain's stuck in neutral. Explain what's going on, okay?"

"Sure. Where d'you want me to start?"

"How about with this? This whole blow-up?"

"Okay." Barlowe crossed his arms over his chest. "When was the last time you took a nap?"

"On the Javelin. Um, I don't know. Forty hours ago?"

"You think that's a good idea? Making decisions running on stims and desperation?"

Meyers wanted to say that Rimes had managed to do just that for years, but there was no way that would fly. "Okay, that's not helping. Can you get to the root of this?"

"That is the root of it—you're acting like the situation's hopeless, and it's all our fault. Mine and Becky's."

"Ladell, I know I'm frazzled, but, shit, this isn't making any sense."

"You've got a very bright young woman in her tent back there, probably bawling her eyes out because she thinks she's the reason Cisneros was injured and her squad leader got into serious trouble."

The dots started connecting for Meyers. "This is about Starling?"

"No! Oh my—" Barlowe threw his hands up in the air. "No, it's not about Starling! It's about you. It's about you making every complication about me and her. It's about you acting like you're my commander."

"You're my IB asset. How the hell am I supposed to treat you?"

"Like a peer. Like a professional. Like you used to treat me when Jack ran things."

Spots danced across Meyers's vision. "Ladell—"

"You sent messages to Becky while she was supposed to be sleeping."

"Just a couple—"

"Twelve. She showed them to me."

"She should have had her earpiece in sleep mode."

"No, you should have queued the messages until she was back on duty or at least sent them low priority so they wouldn't buzz her in case she was sleeping."

Meyers wondered when his role as commander of ERF had changed to babysitter. "I just wanted her to think about any possible solutions to the Turning Point Grid problem. I can't get any meaningful data out of there. We need that data or this is going—"

"And I told you, she has a solution, and you should hear her out, and you should give her credit for it. And then maybe you should quit riding us like this is all our fault."

"Okay, now wait a second." Meyers checked to be sure no one had come out of the tents to listen in. "I'm not saying it's all your fault. Just stop right there."

"That's good, because the real problem is your team isn't ready for this."

"Don't." Meyers shook his head. "Don't say something you're—"

"You had a sniper who couldn't take a shot to save my life and another one talking all kinds of racist shit, and their sergeant acted like there was something wrong with us to even need extraction."

Meyers wondered where Barlowe had gotten his information. McNutt? Starling? Had he eavesdropped over the Operations Center's systems? "I've dealt with those problems. And the snipers were the last recourse."

"That doesn't change what happened."

"Fine, but I've got other problems, okay? I didn't bug you about them, because you're going into the city, and that's more important. Maybe. So it's not like I'm treating you two any worse than anyone else."

"Maybe that's not a good thing, either. You ever think of that? Just pushing your team until something breaks?" Barlowe's arms seemed locked across his chest now, as if they might never come undone.

"Shit! We're in a fucked-up situation here, and you want me to coddle people?"

"Not coddle, maybe just treat them with respect."

"Respect. Sure. What's that? Is that, like, call off the whole operation? Shut it all down and go home? We got our nose bloodied—time to give up?"

Barlowe glared.

"Okay, answer one question. Just one question, and if you do, I'll apologize and shut up. Will you do that?"

Barlowe closed his eyes, squeezed his lips tight, and blew out through his nose. "Fine."

"One-Six-Three suddenly develops flight system problems at the same time our BAS begins to act up. What's the common thread?"

Barlowe's arms unlocked, and confusion replaced the angry look on his face. "What do you mean?"

"I talked with Nunoz and Hassan, had them check their own flight systems logs. The Javelins had some odd readouts during the atmospheric entry, like the systems software wanted to compensate for turbulence that wasn't there, same as what seemed to be going on with One-Six-Three. But there's a secondary safety system on the Javelins, a redundancy system that was installed once they were delivered to Plymouth. It's a system built on Earth, for the ERF, not something delivered by the metacorporations. Hassan thinks it's possible One-Six-Three didn't have that system re-enabled after the software upgrades were loaded to match the Javelins. They probably didn't have time."

"One-Six-Three had software upgrades?"

"We wanted all the birds to have the same things running on them. When we couldn't be sure we'd get the third Javelin ready in time, we decided to bring One-Six-Three. It made sense. This is a small operation. We need everything to be at its best. The software was the latest and greatest. Just like the BAS software we're running. The latest and greatest, freshly delivered by the same people who sent us to Bellar looking for Waverley. The same software that shut off transmission from the survivors and on your systems when you went into Turning Point."

"You're saying this is deliberate? The metacorporations set us up?"

Meyers held up a hand. "I'm not accusing anyone of anything. I'm just saying it seems awfully convenient to me that the metacorporations made all the concessions they did, gave up the CEOs behind their little war to avoid big financial penalties, and then gave us new hardware and software at a nice price to show that they agree that the ERF can function as a responsible extension of the Special Security Council. And then here we are, down one ship full of people and everything fucked up because nothing we count on is working right."

"Yeah, that's a lot of convenient. A lot."

"So that's what I wanted to talk with you about, but I didn't want you distracted by it, not until after you got back. Starling, though, I want her working on things in parallel. Sure, I fucked up sending her those messages. And I've been pushing you two too hard. I'm new at this."

"But you're not new at this. You used to run operations. I've seen your records."

"I used to run small operations."

Barlowe threw his hands up again. "Didn't you just say this was a small operation?"

"Don't be like that. You know what I mean. It's a small operation, but it has huge implications. Everything's riding on this. We screw this up, we don't come back—it changes everything. The ERF broke the metacorporations. We ended the war. If we fail, if we get shut down, they have all the leverage."

The wind howled, and Barlowe hunched over as sand blasted them. Finally, the wind died back to where it had been, and he straightened, one eye cocked open.

"I know you're under a lot of pressure," Barlowe said. "And I want to support you. It sounds like way too many things are going wrong to just be coincidence. But you've got to trust the people on your team."

Meyers wondered if the problem was trust. He knew Barlowe and Banh and Dunne. Paxton had been with ERF long enough to be considered a reliable resource. Most of the others were unproven or were too new to ERF to simply be trusted without question. Meyers knew that wasn't true, of course. Most of Banh's squad had fought in the Metacorporate War. McNutt's squad was made up of survivors from the Plymouth resistance. The team was solid.

"I'll work on it. I promise."

"That's all we can ask."

"So, can you tell me about Starling's idea?"

"No. It's her idea. Let her explain it to you."

Meyers knew what Barlowe wouldn't say—it was something Meyers owed to her. "I guess I need to apologize."

"That would be a great start."

The wind kicked up again, and they stood between a pair of dust devils that climbed five or more meters into the darkening sky. When the wind settled back down, Meyers slouched toward the camp, and Barlowe crunched along a few steps behind. Apology or not, the reality was that they needed a miracle, the sort of trick or idea that had always been there when Rimes was involved. Meyers had been part of a few of those, but now his brain felt numb and drawn off into a million different concerns.

He stopped outside the tent that Starling shared with Hassan and Barlowe. The empty spaces left by all the losses had been converted into storage, an attempt by everyone to hide the reality of death.

Meyers opened a channel to Starling. "Private Starling? If you have a moment, I'd appreciate a chance to talk with you."

The tent flap opened almost immediately. Starling's eyes were still visibly puffy and red. "Yes, sir?"

"Why don't we head back to the Operations Center? I think I owe you an apology, and I'd like to have you walk me through your solution for the Turning Point Grid problem."

Starling's eyes lit up. "Oh, you don't need to apologize, Colonel."

"Let me be the judge of that." He smiled, and it felt good. "So, we'll start with that: I'm sorry if I was pushing you and Agent Barlowe too hard. I'll work on improving that. You two are doing great."

She seemed to blush. "I understand all the stress you've been under."

"We all have." He pointed toward the Operations Center. "Now, about that idea?"

She explained as they walked, and Meyers sensed he still had a long way to go to rebuild her trust in him, but at least he'd gotten it to the point where she could share her idea—and it was a solid one—with him.

He hoped it would be enough.

7

12 December 2174. Karpov Desert, South of Turning Point, Bellar Frontier Colony.

As Turning Point was revealed in the grainy video displays, Meyers paced the length of the Operations Center, thumbs rubbing palms, eyes jumping from the displays back to the floor. Paxton and Starling seemed mesmerized by the video Barlowe and Cisneros were sending back over the feed. Everything in the city had a gray, washed-out feel to it in the approaching dusk.

"How're we looking?" It was Barlowe, a casual question asked to Cisneros.

"Really good," Starling said. She looked up to Paxton, who nodded.

"You're coming through fine, Agent Barlowe." Paxton glanced over his shoulder. "Colonel?"

"Fine." Meyers stopped, feeling the heat he was working up and the pounding of his heart. His mouth was dry and sticky, his breath rotten. He gave the video feed a hard look and told himself to see what his men were seeing, appreciate the risk they were taking without stressing over it. "Good resolution. Private Starling's idea looks like it's going to work. How far in are you so far?"

"Past the worst, I think," Barlowe said, and there actually did seem to be a calm in his voice that wasn't present earlier. "This is apparently Theater Street, for whatever that's worth."

The hum of the electric motors of haulers on the roads was a receding sound, nearly drowned out by the propaganda playing incessantly from the huge rooftop displays. Cisneros turned so that his camera caught one of the displays. A muscular man in a muscle shirt shook a coppery fist at the viewer. With his dark hair, a handsome face dominated by full lips and a thick nose, and intense brown eyes, the man seemed as if he might have been created by a computer.

"Runs around the clock, I guess," Cisneros said. "Name's Reyes, apparently."

People strolled casually on the street ahead, calling to each other, assault rifles resting dangerously on shoulders. There was no sense of discipline or purpose among them, and more importantly, there was no hint of imminent violence. The look and demeanor of the men on the road had changed since the last checkpoint—dark-skinned, broad-faced, skinny, with loose-fitting clothes. Huddled on the road ahead of them were brown-skinned men, with straight, dark hair. Some wore kaffiyehs, others caps. They had prominent noses. Meyers thought they might be Arabs, but Turks seemed more likely. After all the wars in the Arab-controlled parts of the world, he was surprised there were still enough alive to be represented on Bellar. Then again, it wasn't like there was a shortage of political incarceration, even when populations were small.

The black men stopped to talk with the Turks, exchanging cigarettes and what looked like paper money and pointing down the road, toward the checkpoint and the haulers that bristled with militia men and heavy weapons.

"*As-Salaam-Alaikum,*" Barlowe said as the men looked toward him.

Meyers grunted. He'd been in Arab-influenced lands enough to know the greeting, something like, "Peace be upon you." It always felt ironic given the chaos he'd faced.

The men pulled cigarettes from their mouths and said, "*Wa-Alaikum-*

Salaam"—"Peace upon you, too"—in a mix of accents, although Meyers was sure he heard a couple simple English greetings. He wished the audio was better, but Starling's idea of placing one of the Javelin communication systems halfway between camp and the city had at least made things manageable. The app she'd whipped together to manage conversions and encryption was beyond clever.

"You travel with only pistols?" One of the Turks painted a glowing arc between Barlowe and Cisneros with the burning tip of his cigarette. The video was sharp enough that Meyers could see it wasn't hand-rolled. It had to be something locally manufactured, meaning the tobacco almost certainly was locally grown. "Did Savoy make a deal with Reyes?"

Barlowe laughed and looked back down the street. "I thought Theater Street was free territory at night."

The Turks and black men laughed.

"Since when Reyes honors that?" asked the tallest of the black men. "Reyes has no respect for territory. He take whatever he want, whenever." He pointed to the northeast. "You know Farmers Road? Mattias's territory. Buildings we will one day use to hold what we make with our hands. Reyes take all of them, say he want to be sure food come from farmers without theft, but he is the only one to ever steal."

"Sounds like he's a big problem," Barlowe said.

The tall black man snorted. "Just the two of you? And you think you go back through his territory? Might as well turn now and go through Mattias's territory. We honor our word. Can you pay?"

Barlowe held up a wad of bills, local currency he'd gotten from an exchange with a gun-toting pre-teen in Savoy's territory. The tall black man put the cigarette into his mouth and waved long, bony fingers, taking the wad of bills and peeling off about half before handing the rest back.

"You stay with Beniam, all will be fine." He jerked his head, and the entire group headed up the street, speaking a mixture of English and Arabic.

Meyers's stomach felt like it was full of concentrated acid. He rubbed at his gut as the video disappeared in a wash of static, then came back stronger than before.

He leaned in to be sure the image was still live. "What the hell was that?"

"Probably an area where the Grid doesn't have good coverage, Colonel." Starling didn't even turn from the displays. "I'll check the logs later."

"Barlowe, you passed through an area where we lost your signal." Meyers grunted when Barlowe just gave a thumbs-up. "Mattias controls the eastern Farmers and Cáceres Roads, right? See if you can get this Beniam to get you a look at those."

Paxton glanced back at Meyers curiously, but the look wasn't challenging.

Meyers muted his connection to Barlowe. "Who'd that checkpoint guard say ran the northeastern sector?"

"Mudar Badran." Starling just rattled it off like it was nothing. "I read up on him. Political dissident against all the fighting over the bones of Saudi Arabia and Yemen. Tortured by three different Arab warlords. He can barely walk now." An image of a middle-aged, olive-skinned man with a disfigured right cheek filled one of the displays.

"Sounds like he's liked, but he's not well-liked." Paxton chuckled but stopped when no one else joined him.

"The Turks," Meyers said. "Cemal..."

"Bey." Starling seemed caught up in an interaction with a virtual interface to her earpiece for a moment, fingers swiping and tapping at the air. An image appeared on one of the displays: A frighteningly skinny man, sunken cheeks covered in silver stubble, a crown of white hair, a bushy white mustache beneath a bulbous nose. "One-time Socialist, accused of assassinations, cleared, but kept jailed for another five years. Failing health. I can't remember what it is. One of the cancers without a readily available cure."

"And this Mattias?"

Another image replaced Bey's. The man had a long face, dark skin, and a prominent nose. His dark eyes stared intently out of the display.

"Asfaw Mattias. Ethiopian." Starling's eyes moved rapidly left and right, as if she was reading something. "Christian. Descendant from a powerful militia leader that fought in the last of the Muslim incursions. Spent a lot of his teen years in prison, family executed. Suspected of retaliatory strikes against former Muslim strongholds, spent twenty-two years in prison for that. Exonerated and released from one of the Delacourt Prison systems as they were being shut down."

"Arabic, Cuban, Ethiopian, Turkish, and American." Meyers rolled his eyes. "That's not a powder keg, I guess."

The group stopped outside a single-story building, dull gray in the twilight. Fires burned in metal storage drums at what appeared to be the corners of the lot. Men sat around tables spread across the front and sides of the building. Women in short shorts and crop tops moved among the tables with trays, serving alcohol, cigarettes, and what looked like a variety of drugs. The women seemed to be the same racial and cultural mix as the men, and they endured the men's groping with a smile, so long as money followed. Overhead, canvas flaps stretched and whipped like waves in the wind, so that the anchoring poles bowed and shivered. Music blared from within the building, and lights strobed—white to gold to green. The light show was enough to reveal dancing women, most wearing little, some wearing less. Men seated at tables inside waved cigarettes and wads of bills, and somewhere between the flash of lights and waves of darkness, the women moved closer and the gifts disappeared. The men laughed, apparently satisfied with the transactions.

Starling looked up just in time to catch the imagery, then looked away from the display, brow wrinkled, eyes hard. Barlowe's feed turned to catch the men seated beneath the canvas; Cisneros moved closer to the building entry and the dancers.

"We have enough left to get in?" Cisneros sounded half-serious.

Beniam laughed. "It takes little to get in, but you leave with nothing if you want to touch them. You are new to Turning Point, yes? From the farms?"

"Actually, from Daughtrey, just outside Ardennen." Barlowe's voice was smooth, convincing. "Researchers. We came down with some friends who wanted to visit family."

"In Savoy's territory?" Beniam pulled the dying cigarette from his mouth and pointed it south. "You come up from there? You staying?"

"In Savoy? We were hoping to, but no one told us Reyes didn't honor the open road."

Meyers sighed and squeezed his jaw. He had no idea where Barlowe had learned to bullshit so well but assumed part of it had to be Intelligence Bureau training. He'd gotten inside a genie-sponsored militant group back on Earth years before, so he had to be good. The story about friends in Savoy's territory sounded completely authentic, but as far as Meyers could tell, it was being constructed on the fly.

"Reyes, he is big man now, all the big guns. Big guns, means big control." Beniam puffed up. "He controls the harbor, the Farmers Road, and he gets stronger. Very dangerous. Madman."

"When did he get the big guns? Those look like they're military grade."

Beniam lit another cigarette, then he rattled off something in Arabic at a man standing next to one of the storage drums. In the light of the fire, the man looked old, his face wrinkled, his hair white. Even when his hands waved wildly and his voice rose, his eyes seemed dead, blinking rarely and slowly.

"He say it was just before the last barge was stolen," Beniam said. "Some people think the first barge had the weapons on it, but the people upriver, up in Ardennen, they never have weapons. Not like that. You have those, at your researcher station?"

"No."

"They talk about Lancers up there, spend big money for a small army, come and take back the barges. Reyes laughs."

"Lancers?" Barlowe's point of view shifted from Beniam to Cisneros, who shrugged.

"Freelancers." Beniam waved his cigarette in the air, like a sparkler. "Mercenaries. Desperate people. Savoy was one. Came here with three others, tried to talk settlement and law, for people in Ardennen."

"Didn't work out?"

The men gathered nearby laughed, but the sound was nervous, not mirthful.

"Savoy's friends, the Lancers," Beniam said. "What is woman's name?" He waved off a few muttered offerings and one man's cupping of large, imaginary breasts. "Reyes does things to one. She go. Kills another. Right in there." Beniam waved toward the building. "Savoy and his other friend, they surrender their guns. Savoy moves down south, soon becomes leader there. Now his territory. Bad blood with Reyes."

"We don't have anything on Savoy, do we?" Meyers asked. "If he's a mercenary, we should have his name somewhere."

Starling looked off into space and flipped her fingers, apparently working through her earpiece's interface. "There are a couple, sir. The way he's describing it, I don't think he's some sort of registered professional."

"Well, it sounds like there might be some pretty strong lingering hostility between him and Reyes, and it looks like Reyes is the main power here." Meyers paced again, stopping after a few steps. "Can you put up an overlay of what we think Reyes's territory is based on the checkpoints recorded so far? See how that compares to the power and Grid data consumption..." The display showed exactly what he was looking for. "Good. So Reyes is the big footprint we were looking at. And he has the heavy weaponry."

"Yes, sir."

Meyers came off mute. "Ladell, any chance they've seen Waverley or might know where he's hiding out? Could he be in Reyes's compound?"

Barlowe's view shifted west, toward the river. "Beniam, did Reyes always have the harbor?"

"He has it for a long time, but only recently he has cut off sharing of foods and supplies."

"Is someone helping Reyes, maybe? Supplying him guns?"

"We all have guns!" Beniam held up his assault rifle and stuffed his cigarette into the corner of his mouth. He raised the assault rifle over his head and shouted, "Freedom!"

At tables all around, men raised their weapons and shouted back in various languages. The meaning was lost.

"The big guns, those big haulers. I didn't see anything like that in Savoy's territory." Barlowe's view turned more southerly, now capturing the glow of the towering displays. "Except for all that armor, they look like construction equipment."

"Ah! Those! Yes!" Beniam's eyes widened and he clenched a fist so hard, the bones of his hand stood out. "To have one of those! He uses to show strength!"

"But if they didn't come on the barge, and the Lancers didn't bring them down, doesn't that mean he has someone else supplying him?"

A few of the closest seated men looked toward Barlowe, eyes white glitters in the settling dark. Meyers shivered as a tingle ran down his spine. People running around with assault weapons, women selling themselves for cigarettes and cash, alcohol and drugs flowing freely, but they'd finally found the taboo.

"I think we've found all we're going to find out about Reyes," Meyers said.

Beniam sucked on his cigarette and blew out a long tail of smoke. He waved a woman with a tray of bottles over, traded some bills for bottles, then jerked his head for Barlowe and Cisneros to follow; they did.

"Such a question is not a good idea," Beniam said, his pace picking up as they cleared the borders of the gathering place as indicated by the burning drums. "Reyes, he has spies. Maybe you are his spies—maybe some of the people there are spies. No one knows. But a man, if he seems like he might be a spy, he is likely to be found with his throat slit and his tongue cut out."

"I'm sorry. I was just curious about those big guns." Barlowe sounded like he was having a hard time with the pace. His earpiece picked up the scuff of rocks ricocheting away. "It doesn't seem right for Reyes to have so much power."

Beniam cut through a dark alley and turned onto a street. Prefab buildings rose on either side. They were heading east, and the black shapes of buildings seemed to disappear in the distance.

"Let me say, researchers should learn this: What happens here in Turning Point, it will change one day. Reyes has all the power now. He rules by fear, and it is a real fear. Very powerful, those guns. But there is no man here who has not thought once or twice he will die in prison and not see his woman or child again. Fear can only go so far before a man, he rises up."

Barlowe and Cisneros turned, and shadows slipped from the alleys behind them. Beniam quickened his pace, and they started to jog. The forms followed, still walking for the moment.

Meyers opened a channel to Zacharowski and Banh. "Team is moving east on—"

Starling pointed to the display where two green dots moved east on a blacktop street labeled Farmers Road.

Meyers nodded. "Farmers Road. Track position and move."

"Rolling," Zacharowski said, and the drone of the Rover kicking into gear and accelerating came through the connection.

"On our way, Colonel," Banh said.

"Stay outside of the city for now." Meyers wished Barlowe or Cisneros would turn around again, just to see whether or not their pursuers were trying to keep up. "I can't tell if they're in imminent danger, but I'd rather be ready to respond."

"Understood," Zacharowski said. "We should be in position in ten minutes."

Meyers closed his eyes and rested his chin on his chest as he tried to think the situation through logically. Ten minutes sounded like an eternity. It was long enough for the locals to overwhelm Barlowe and Cisneros and to cut their throats. It was long enough for Beniam to spin around and shoot them. Meyers thought about sending the Rovers straight in through the city, abandoning the idea of minimizing their presence. Even if he was willing to do that, it would be a useless gesture. The Rovers weren't built for anything more than quick transport. Reyes's haulers were full-blown vehicles, the biggest over six meters long, probably more than three tons fully loaded. Going in on the Rovers would be suicide.

"Colonel?" Starling sounded panicked.

Meyers looked up. The video feeds were the silver of static.

8

—————

12 December 2174. Karpov Desert, South of Turning Point, Bellar Frontier Colony.

FOR A HEARTBEAT, then another, the Operations Center was lit in a silvery glow, then video came through again, choppy and uneven. It showed shadows in shadows, simple building facades, alleys, and Farmers Road's empty, cratered blacktop. Barlowe was falling behind, keeping Cisneros back, and Beniam seemed unwilling to abandon them. Meyers found himself leaning toward the video displays, leg muscles tensing, hands clenching, his body heating up from the tension. He wanted to shove Barlowe forward, to shout encouragement or threats, but the Operations Center was quiet except for his and Paxton's breathing; Starling was holding her breath.

An icon on the display to the right of the main one flashed; Zacharowski's Rover was three minutes out from the edge of the city, its power below fifty percent after being pushed hard.

"We're on Farmers Road." Zacharowski's video feed was an extremely low-resolution image of the black road heading west toward the edge of the city. "Permission to head in."

Meyers considered the possible outcomes: rescue, engagement, death. "Hold position."

Cisneros's feed cut out, followed a moment later by Barlowe's.

"We need to know what's going on with these interruptions." Meyers meant it more as a reminder to himself, but Starling seemed to snap out of her frozen state. She began interacting with her earpiece.

"Looking at the logs now, sir." Tears welled at the corners of her eyes, but they looked like they came from eye strain and stress, not crying. She didn't even seem to notice. "That street looks like it's nothing but warehouses. No power drain to speak of."

Meyers recalled Beniam saying something about Reyes seizing the area.

Paxton shifted slightly. "Might be time to introduce ourselves to the locals, Colonel."

"Let's give it a moment." Meyers wasn't sure what he was waiting for. The last time Barlowe had twisted to look behind him, his pursuers were definitely closing. A freeze-frame capture put their numbers at eight.

"Sergeant Zacharowski, get as close as you can without giving away the presence of the Rover. Sergeant Banh, keep a fifteen-meter gap but do the same. Be prepared to proceed into the city on foot."

The image of the black road coming from Zacharowski's feed slowly changed on the display. There were shallow depressions and scrub on either side that could hide the Rovers well enough, but heading into the city would leave them exposed. Even if their BAS chameleon systems were working, it was risky.

"Well, shit." Paxton stomped as Cisneros helped Barlowe up from the street. "He's losing what little giddy-up he had."

"Barlowe, we've got people moving into position. Dig. Push yourself."

Barlowe ran again, but there were people close now. Moonlight broke through buildings, revealing more than just shadows—eyes, knives, some assault rifles. The situation was ripe for escalation. Beniam turned, held his assault rifle up, and shouted something, then he fired into the air.

The pursuers scattered, disappearing in alleyways and in the recesses of entryways.

"And there it goes," Paxton said beneath his breath.

Gunfire broke out, muzzle flashes lighting up dark alleys and building fronts. Beniam waved Cisneros and Barlowe into an alley just as bullets cracked against the building front and deposited chunks of the prefab materials at Barlowe's feet. Beniam returned fire, but all Meyers could see of it was muzzle flash and more bits of the composite that made up the walls spraying into the alley like sand.

"Watch the back," Beniam shouted.

Meyers felt reassured by at least the slightest hint of tactics. Cisneros moved down the alley, pistol drawn.

"Next time we send someone in, they go fully armed," Meyers said. He felt like kicking himself for countering Paxton's suggestion that they at least give Cisneros his CAWS-5 carbine.

Paxton tapped his nose.

"Two hundred meters out," Zacharowski said. Someone flashed in front of his suit's camera, and in the next frame sent, two others passed him, one of them fuzzy. "Heading in."

Meyers almost ordered Zacharowski to stand down, but it didn't feel right. One of his squad members was in danger. Barlowe was in danger. They had to take a chance. They'd already lost too many people.

"Sergeant Banh, be ready to back Zacharowski." Meyers told himself to stay calm.

"We are dismounting now, Colonel. Moving toward the city."

Zacharowski's squad was spread out, carbines locked on their backs. With the chameleon effect running, the camera captured vague distortions in the dark. The BAS outlined those distortions in green.

Cisneros reached the end of the alley just as a man came around the corner. He seemed surprised by Cisneros, who quickly disarmed and pistol-whipped the man. Gunfire tore up the corner where Cisneros had been, and he fell back, holding the stunned man as a shield. More gunfire, and the stunned man twitched and groaned. Cisneros looked down, and his camera caught blood spurting from the man's thigh. Cisneros dropped the man and fell back, ducking low. The firing stopped, and a moment later, a gunman popped his head around the corner, then pulled back.

"Ladell, give Cisneros some cover fire, damn it!" Meyers felt like reaching into the display and grabbing Barlowe's hand, forcing him to fire.

Finally, Barlowe brought the pistol up and fired three shots. It was enough to drive the gunman back. Another person flashed past the end of the alley, more fully revealed by muzzle flash, and Cisneros dropped as the bullets tore up the wall around him.

"Cisneros!"

"Fine, Colonel. Got some debris in my eye, but I'm fine."

Barlowe took a shot at the person who'd been firing, and the man pulled back behind cover.

Meyers checked the display tracking Zacharowski's movement.

"Reinforcements fifty meters out," Meyers said. "Stay calm."

Beniam's assault weapon went quiet, and Barlowe turned in time to see someone tackling Beniam as he tried to clear a jam in his gun. More forms closed from across the street. Knives reflected moonlight. Screams echoed from somewhere nearby. Barlowe brought the pistol up, and one of the men at the end of the alley sighted in on Barlowe with an assault rifle.

And then the imagery of Zacharowski's camera and Barlowe's earpiece merged. Someone crashed into the gunman, and his shot went wide. More of the gunmen tumbled to the ground, and their heads jerked right and left from rapid blows delivered by blurry shadows.

Barlowe's video feed showed the green outlines and distorted images as he moved to Beniam, who had a cut across his scalp. "He's alive." Barlowe stuffed the rest of the cash wad into Beniam's pants and patted his chest.

"Let's go!" Zacharowski yanked Barlowe up.

Barlowe and Cisneros ran down the black road in the moonlight, flanked by ghostly forms. More ghosts huddled at the side of the road ahead, carbines pointed toward the edge of the city.

Meyers clamped his hands together and ran his tongue along the insides of his mouth. "I need a drink."

"Maybe you'd settle for a hot shower, Colonel?" Paxton snorted, but his eyes were serious. "Something tells me, we got a bit to discuss when folks return."

~

MEYERS DID his best not to show his impatience at the crawl of data over the displays. The personal network he'd created from the BAS resources of everyone gathered in the Operations Center was struggling under the load he was putting on it. It was just part of the cost of losing One-Six-Three, a cost he knew he would feel even more intensely when he finally crashed from the stims.

And he was going to crash soon. His tongue felt thick, and his breath smelled terrible, a warning he'd been relying too heavily on the stims. The room was so hot that, even standing, he was having a hard time keeping his eyes open. He scanned those gathered, eyes dwelling on the squad leaders long enough to catch the frustration in their posture, then looked to Barlowe and Starling, both of them caught up in their own system challenges.

Finally, Meyers caught Paxton's curious stare. It seemed to say, "I hope you got something good, Colonel."

But Meyers didn't. They weren't much better off than they'd been before coming planet-side.

"I think that's as good as it's going to get, Colonel." Starling looked up from whatever she'd been trying to do to the network through her own earpiece. "We just have too much data to deal with. Without the systems on One-Six-Three, we're not gonna get anything better. This is all one big, shared workspace, so we're pushing the limits of available resources."

"Okay." Meyers shot a look at Barlowe, who finally seemed to be coming around to the idea something was up with all the upgraded software. "Ladell, could you..."

Barlowe stood and faced the displays. "Sure." He began rearranging images on the displays, then leaned forward. "It's a lot of data, and I think it's revelatory. We've confirmed the city is broken into five districts. We've also confirmed the most powerful of those is Adrián Reyes. Former Cuban Socialist dissident, spent ten years in prison on trumped-up charges. His family managed to buy his way out of the worst of his sentence. He probably made a lot of connections while doing time, and we think that's where a lot of the guns we saw in Turning Point come from."

Sergeant Banh raised a hand. "They had military-grade assault rifles."

"The metacorporations love selling weapons. The ammunition is a constant revenue stream. It doesn't matter who's buying." Barlowe defocused for a moment, as if reading from his earpiece display. "His family has connections to Cytek, and LoDu has a history with militant Socialists, especially those who have people in the prison systems. Really, with a little time, we could confirm the source, but it doesn't change what we have here: One of the five powers in Turning Point is probably the source for most of the weapons. Which presents a problem, because he's also the person with the most strategic holdings."

The harbor lit up on the display, and not too far from it, the compound Barlowe had identified earlier lit up. Static images of both blew up to fill the screen.

"Reyes controls the harbor, and as far as we can tell, anything other than food comes into the city that way. Most of the food comes in from the north and east, through Cemal Bey's territory—here." The northwestern sector lit up. "And Farmers Road in Asfaw Mattias's territory." The southeastern sector lit up.

Meyers pointed to Farmers Road. "Your guide said something about—"

Barlowe nodded. "Yes, Reyes apparently laid claim to that area where the warehouses are."

Zacharowski craned his neck to look at Meyers. "These are all criminals?"

"Prisoners," Starling said. "Most of the charges were junk, thrown out and records expunged when the UN shut down the private prison systems—"

"Yeah, I heard all that." Zacharowski glanced at her just long enough to flash a dismissive smirk. The bruise on his jaw almost glistened purple. "My point is that they aren't a real military force. They're punks with guns."

"Those punks with guns are undergoing classic power transitions." Barlowe tapped out a few areas and drilled down, revealing burned-out shells of buildings. "According to two sources we talked to in the Savoy district, there were three smaller factions, all wiped out in the last several months. And Savoy himself replaced another faction leader who was killed by Reyes. Transfers, consolidations—classic power transitions."

Zacharowski snorted. "Let's just fly in with one of the Javelins and blow Reyes's haulers up and turn him into a greasy smear, then we broker a deal with the rest of these criminals." He looked at Starling. "I mean, misunderstood victims."

"Yeah, that's gonna sit real well with a bunch of people spent time behind bars on trumped-up charges, don't y'think?" McNutt had been sitting on a cargo case, face buried in his powerful hands, but he looked up now. One of his dark-blue eyes was squinted, the other open wide beneath a cocked eyebrow. The small scrape he'd suffered earlier was a red, slightly swollen and scabbed patch of flesh. "Come flying in, show your intent to take control through violence, then sit down and start dictating the new power structure. Didn't your country do enough of that in the last couple centuries? How'd that work out? Banh? You got any thoughts on that?"

Banh shook his head and looked away.

"Yeah, well, some people got long memories," McNutt said. "We weren't sent here to play kingmaker, were we, Colonel?"

Meyers hesitated, then said, "No, we weren't. We may have to at some point, but it wouldn't be ideal."

Zacharowski threw up his arms. "So, we just let him bully everybody else around?"

Paxton seemed on the edge of saying something until Meyers shook his head.

"Sergeant Zacharowski, there are more than two options here," Meyers said. "If Waverley isn't inside Turning Point, then we're going to have to find him. That's going to take time, and every day we're here increases the odds of being discovered and compromising the mission."

"We cannot use the systems to track him, Colonel?" Banh looked at Barlowe. "Track his identity maybe or something like that?"

"Unfortunately, no. First off, our BAS systems and earpieces are all the computing power we have right now. Those resources, plus what we can pull off the Javelins' systems. That's not enough to do this sort of search quickly, not with everything else we're trying to do." Barlowe ran a hand over the display of the various sectors. "We're still sifting through data from every centimeter of this place, but so far, there's no indication he's been inside this Grid. It will probably be another couple days before we complete that sort of sifting."

"Days?" McNutt turned to Paxton and Meyers. "We got that sort of time?"

The frustration was palpable, and it wasn't just McNutt and Zacharowski. Banh shifted and glanced around, obviously uncomfortable. Barlowe screwed up his face, and Starling stared at the ground, as if losing most of the intelligence analysts and system resources was somehow their fault. Everyone had been briefed at the start that the odds of success dropped with each day they were on-planet.

"We don't have a choice right now," Meyers said. "That's why I brought all of us together. You know what we know. I want your thoughts."

The Operations Center was quiet except for the wind whistling past the entry.

"All right. So that's where we are. Two more days of data sifting, then we start building out the next step in our plan."

McNutt's jaw muscles stood out as he clenched his mouth shut. "And if we get nothing?"

Meyers looked around the room, saw the way they were all looking at him, hoping, expecting. It was the sort of situation Rimes had always excelled at: finding something good in something terrible. He could probably transform the situation in Turning Point without violence. That probably was the right course, but Meyers couldn't see a solution.

Starling seemed on the edge of saying something, but then she looked away.

"If we get nothing," Meyers said, "then we play kingmaker and see if that flushes Waverley out."

9

12 December 2174. Karpov Desert, South of Turning Point, Bellar Frontier
Colony.

FRUSTRATION WAS apparent on the faces of the squad leaders as they exited
the Operations Center. Meyers felt the same way, but he couldn't show it.
He wanted to stare at the pale, aqua sand that had collected on the floor,
hear its crunch beneath their retreating boots. That would have been the
easy way out. He nodded at each of them and thanked them for attending.
The wind blowing outside was cool and carried more sand in through the
entryway.

Paxton scraped to a stop at Meyers's side and stared into the night.
"Bitch of a thing, telling men they're going to have to learn to get along
under new leadership."

Meyers felt the sting, whether Paxton meant anything personal or not.
Taking command of ERF had been Rimes's idea. Meyers knew it was a poor
fit. He'd never had a chance to truly use Rimes as a mentor. There'd been
opportunities for observing and inferring, but the pace of operations had

never allowed them to sit down and actually train together, leader and future replacement.

"You think I'm talking about you taking over, Colonel?" Paxton chuckled.

"It crossed my mind."

"This place, how long has it been around? Not even eleven years? And I'm willing to bet, these fellas in Turning Point, all they've known since coming here is violence. Probably all they've known most of their lives."

"So taking out Reyes is a bad idea?"

Paxton squinted an eye. "Maybe he's all that's holding that place together."

"There, um, there might be an alternative, sir?"

Meyers turned. "I thought you were going to say something during the briefing, Private Starling. If you've got something, I'd love to hear it."

"It's those spots where we lost signals." Starling stood next to the display that showed the city broken into districts. She tapped the display, and circles appeared. "I've been checking the logs, and those aren't areas with bad coverage. They're areas with saturated relays and collectors."

"Saturated by what?"

Barlowe settled onto one of the cargo cases. "They don't have load balancing?"

Starling turned to Barlowe. "They have load balancing, but there's something operating in those areas that's overwhelming even that. I think it's overriding it. And, Colonel, that something might be Waverley."

"In..." Meyers edged closer to the display. "Is that Mattias's territory?"

"I don't know that he's in there, sir, but that's where this big load on the Grid is taking place." Starling tapped the circles she'd set up earlier, and they broke out into a crude animation showing data flowing. "I think someone just did a bad job of trying to do their own load balancing, maybe to try to hide the real flow of data, but in the process, they've created these areas where the network just can't handle the load, to the point we couldn't get our signals onto it."

Meyers tapped his chin. "Makes sense that it wasn't credentials."

"We were on the Grid everywhere else. I don't think it had the capacity to even handle our spoofing, sir."

"Sloppy, but it sort of makes sense. Master Sergeant?"

Paxton's forehead creased. "A man with billions to spend can't get a Grid to hide his traffic? No disrespect, sir, but that smells like bullshit."

Barlowe shook his head. "Actually, just think about it. He brought a limited staff with him. What did SunCorps estimate? He has in the range of six to ten bodyguards, a personal assistant, and some robot assistants. He's probably used to being on a Grid that can handle millions of heavy users. Who's going to do the technical work for him? That network's so crude, he probably doesn't even know that he's leaving an imprint on it."

The idea had real promise, and it had only been possible because Barlowe and Cisneros had taken the risk of going into the city.

"What can you do with this?" Meyers's voice rose with excitement.

"Well, I'm still pulling down logs. Those systems are so saturated, just requesting the logs took a while to get through. We've got enough data downloaded now, I think I can start building out a trace. It won't be pretty, sir, but what I can start doing is eliminating things."

"Eliminating things?"

"Yes, sir. It's, um, it's like Shadow Zone."

Meyers cocked an eyebrow.

"It's a game I played a little bit back."

Meyers bit back the urge to say something about comparing their predicament to a game. He actually understood the value of a lot of the entertainment options his people pursued. "Go on."

"Well, um, this game had an invisible opponent in it. If you tried to kill it using regular tactics, you'd fail. So when I knew the thing was around, I laid down some phosphorescent dust. I could see it with UV goggles after that."

"So what's our phosphorescent dust with Waverley?"

"Well, it's kind of knowing where he isn't, sir."

"Where he isn't?"

"For instance, we know some of the buildings are empty. Ladell and I ran through or looked into some of them. If they're empty, they can't be part of the load on the Grid, so we can take those out of any—"

"You can take them out of any trace that says they're part of the load on the system," Meyers said, an index finger tapping more quickly on his chin.

"Right. And you could start from there to work backwards. See what isn't there, what can't be there."

The odds of Waverley being inside Turning Point seemed very small. They'd already figured that much out. But maybe he was somewhere else, and knowing where the load on the Grid wasn't coming from meant eventually knowing where it was coming from, or at least possibly where it was coming from.

"That's good, Private. That's real good."

"Thank you, sir." Starling smiled and looked away. "It's something. Maybe it goes nowhere, but it might be better than dealing with Reyes."

"How long you reckon?" Paxton asked. "We're up against time, right, Colonel?"

"We are. We'll have to act at some point, but maybe this is the piece we've been missing, the thing we can keep in our pocket."

"Well..." Starling looked at Barlowe. "Without more processing resources, it's going to go slow. Really slow."

"Did you give the gear recovered from the crash site a look?" Meyers felt ghoulish asking someone else to dig through all the twisted debris McNutt brought back, but they were in an ugly situation.

Starling winced, as if she'd seen more than broken machinery while going through the debris. "Two or three pieces could be salvaged, but they'll need to be repaired."

"How long?"

"A day, sir?"

A day! The mission was already too far along without anything to show. Another day on a maybe, and that maybe from someone he had no track record with. The idea grated on Meyers.

"Any way to speed that up?" Meyers caught Barlowe's glare and saw the message clearly: Don't push too hard.

"I'll see if there's anything I can get John—Corporal McNutt—to help me with, sir."

"Good. Weigh the time spent on repairs against the added processing." It was basic troubleshooting, but Meyers couldn't afford to be sensitive about everything. They needed to make progress, and if he stepped on Starling's feelings, he would have to apologize later. Barlowe was just going to have to accept that.

"Probably a net gain, sir."

"So let's get that going. I can help."

Paxton coughed. "Actually, Colonel, there was the discussion we had earlier about you not taking any more stims? I think Private Starling can handle this herself. Private?"

"Easy enough, Master Sergeant." Starling seemed to straighten proudly.

Meyers knew better than to argue with Paxton on the point. Running on stims was getting to be a real problem. A nap, maybe some real sleep, was overdue.

"I'll swing by first thing," Meyers said. When Paxton coughed, Meyers added, "After I get up."

Paxton looked around the Operations Center. "I'll escort the colonel to his tent. Agent Barlowe, Private Starling."

Meyers gathered up his helmet and gloves, and then he followed Paxton out. They were immediately hammered by the wind and had to close their eyes and mouths to keep the sand out. Meyers was happy for that. Any reprieve from having to chat with Paxton was fine.

When they reached the tent Meyers shared with Nunoz, Paxton stuck his head inside. Meyers hadn't unpacked anything other than his shaving kit and the fresh undergarments he'd pulled out for his shower. His cot was still made. Paxton stepped into the room and sealed the entry behind them.

"Good to see you taking a rest, Colonel. You are taking a rest, right?"

Meyers set his helmet down next to the cot and pulled his backpack off the smooth covers. "I think I could cut her work time in half."

"At no risk to your decision-making, sir? No lives put at risk because you refuse to get some sleep?"

"All right. What about One-Six-Three? Were you able to salvage anything useful?"

Paxton pulled his helmet off and scratched at the thinning, brown hair that covered his scalp. The right corner of his mouth hitched up in a grimace, making his already hard-looking face even uglier. "Not much to salvage. Some flash-bangs, a couple CAWS-5 ammo cases. Found some CAWS-5s. McNutt's gonna see what he can do to salvage them. Don't look like most anything else made it. Figure some of the ammunition and ordnance blew up."

"Distribute the flash-bangs."

"You gonna be okay?"

Meyers set his elbows on his knees and clasped his hands. "It's a bust."

"How's that, sir?"

"This mission. It's a bust. A failure. We were supposed to get in a quick, clean kill and disappear. It's not happening."

"Probably not."

"This Waverley, he's a criminal. How many people died because of him? Millions? At least that, but we'll never know. And he's just the start."

"You losing your confidence about this mission, Colonel?"

Meyers looked up, ready to tell Paxton to take that question back, but there was no accusation in his face. It was as if Paxton sympathized.

"Hasn't been a war in history where all the criminals paid for what they did, Colonel. Often as not, some stupid kid got turned into a scapegoat and faced time, maybe even a firing squad while higher-ups were shuffled or at worst allowed to retire."

"We've got a chance to make a difference with this. People can't just ignore what happened. They want to demonize Jack for what he did, but no one wants to look too hard at what the metacorporations did."

"Colonel Rimes was a good man. His reputation's gonna be all right. But what he did..."

Meyers remembered the fights he and Rimes had had. Nuclear weapons, killing enemies who'd surrendered. Rimes had been right, though. None of the mercenaries who'd committed atrocities were being prosecuted or even pursued yet. None of the security chiefs from the metacorporations were being brought up on charges. CEOs were being offered up as sacrificial lambs, but none of the senior people who'd executed their war plans were facing penalties. The only justice had been what they'd faced on the battlefield.

"Some other time, Master Sergeant. Six months ago, I would've agreed with you. Now?"

"I understand. And my concern's not for that war. It's about this mission."

"Have I lost confidence in it?"

Paxton's eyebrows went up, seemingly asking, "Well, have you?"

"This mission is just. It's the only sort of justice we're going to get. And despite everything being thrown at us, I know we're going to succeed."

"That's all I needed to hear, sir."

"We'll get him."

Meyers twisted and pulled the covers on the cot back, and Paxton unsealed the entry, apparently content. Outside, the wind howled, throwing sand against the tents and camouflage netting. Meyers pulled off his uniform and settled under the covers. His eyelids were heavy, and in no time, he was yawning, and his breathing was becoming deeper. As he drifted off, he told himself everything was going to be okay. They were going to get Waverley.

But when sleep came, it brought with it troubling dreams. Pitched battles, death. Even in sleep, the truth couldn't be escaped. They had lost their advantage and were facing a long, painful struggle.

10

13 December 2174. Karpov Desert, South of Turning Point, Bellar Frontier Colony.

SHORTLY AFTER SUNRISE, Meyers crawled out of his cot and blew out a tired, rancid breath. He pulled on his uniform, then his armor, surprised at the twitch in his fingers. The CAWS-5 that was locked into place in the armor's brace along his spine seemed to calm him a little, but the real problem was the stims still in his system. He would need to drink a lot more water and let some time pass before the stims would be fully out of his body. His head felt like it had been stuffed with cotton, and his mouth tasted like it was lined with rust, but he was otherwise rejuvenated. It was too hot to sleep, though, even with the tent's built-in heat exchange system working to keep the temperature under control. Halfway through brushing his teeth, someone knocked on the tent frame.

"Come in." The words came out muffled, but it was enough for Paxton to understand. He let himself in, stepped away from the flap, and pulled off his helmet.

"Colonel." Paxton looked as if he'd just returned from a three-week vacation at an island resort. He always reminded Meyers of an old, sun-dried, leather jacket—weathered, worn, cracked, but reliable. Paxton was the oldest among the ERF soldiers by far, and he generally showed it. What little hair he let grow out was brown but beginning to go gray around the fringes.

Meyers rinsed, then he opened the flap and spat, squinting at the bright sunlight. He let the flap close, but the heat had already slipped through. "What's up?"

"I wouldn't bother you if it wasn't something important, sir. You do look better, though."

"I feel better." He squeezed cleanser into his palm, then scrubbed his face.

Paxton glanced toward the flap. "Private Starling's been scraping data. She set up a bunch of crawlers and filters earlier."

Meyers toweled his face dry. "And?"

"It seems word gets around pretty fast in the city. The rescue operation last night is all over communications. Sounds like the locals are worried there might be some sort of invasion going on."

"I see." Meyers set the towel on the end of the cot to dry. "Sounds like they're a little paranoid, doesn't it?"

"Yeah. A couple of the warlords are talking about—"

"They're warlords now?"

"Well, Colonel, that's what they'd be called back on Earth. They aren't elected representatives, and they seem to be holding their positions by right of force."

Meyers couldn't argue that.

"Anyway, they're talking about sending people out to see if there're tracks."

There would be; Meyers was sure of that. "Anything else to report? Waverley?"

Paxton looked down at his boots. "Not yet, sir."

"We need something, dammit." Pressure built behind Meyers's eyes. He tried to calm himself. "Okay. We run things in parallel."

Paxton cocked a bushy eyebrow.

"Starling and Barlowe keep looking for Waverley using the idea she had, see if they can find where he is, or at least where he isn't. At the same time, we make our presence known to the warlords. Officially."

"How were you thinking we'd do that, sir?"

"Is there enough of a trail being left on the Grid for us to contact one of them?"

"I'll check on that."

Meyers scooped up his helmet. "I'll come with you."

The wind had died down overnight so that it felt less like a blast furnace crossing the camp and more like a simple oven. Sweat trickled down Meyers's forehead when they stepped into the Operations Center. The far left corner of the building was piled with charred debris, most of it pried open to reveal cracked and stripped component cards. The stench of fried electronics and worse stung his nose.

His stomach growled as he came to a stop in front of the displays. Data crawled across four of them, and video played on two others. The video had text scrolling next to it, keywords highlighted in bold yellow. Meyers saw *military*, *invasion*, *Lancers*, and *Ardennen* in several of the flashing text boxes. Starling stared into the distance, caught up in something only she could see. Barlowe was seated below a blank display, legs crossed, hunched over as he stared at the display. He suddenly straightened, then stood. He looked wobbly, ready to collapse.

"Lonny." Barlowe rubbed his eyes. "You know about the chatter?"

"Yeah. I'm going to take a team in, meet with Reyes and the others."

"Really? You think that's a good idea?"

"Do you have Waverley's location?"

"N-no."

"Then we don't have a lot of options. If they send people out to search, they'll find Rover wheel tracks. They may not be able to follow them back to here, but they'll at least suspect something's out in the desert. I think it's best to give them some answers—maybe we can solicit help from them."

The corners of Barlowe's mouth twisted down; he didn't think it was a good idea.

"I'm open to alternatives, Ladell. Right now, I'm not seeing any. If we leave it to rumormongering, it's only going to get worse."

"I thought the Special Security Council directed us to not antagonize?"

Meyers's stomach grumbled, and it shot a hint of acid onto the back of his throat. "I think we're past that point, aren't we? Whether we let them slit your throats or rescued you, we were committed."

Barlowe reeled slightly, as if the comment had been a slap. "Sorry."

"Don't apologize. I don't think this is anyone's fault. There haven't been any good choices from the start, have there?"

Paxton stepped past to examine Barlowe's display. "These the warlords, Agent Barlowe?"

"Yes. I'm pretty sure. We've been trying to do meaningful image searches, but with the processing limits we're up against…"

"Can you get a message to them?" Paxton tapped the one that was labeled "Reyes," an angry looking, middle-aged man with long, black hair, a broad nose, and dark, coppery skin. "Especially Reyes. He's the one from all those propaganda videos? Colonel wants to pitch to them all, but the ringleader's what matters."

Barlowe settled back onto the cargo case a little unsteadily. "What's the message?"

No more argument, Meyers noted. He didn't like it when Barlowe just caved, but there was no changing his behavior. "So, I'm thinking we go with a UN pitch. Something along the lines of, *We would like to meet with Turning Point leadership to discuss a proposal from the United Nations Special Security Council about the Bellar Colony joining the United Nations as a probationary member.*"

"No mention of Waverley?" Barlowe's tone fell just short of challenging.

"Master Sergeant Paxton, what do you think?" Meyers saw that Starling was now paying attention as well. "Private Starling?"

Paxton crossed his arms and stared at Starling.

"Well, um." Starling blinked. Her eyes were red, and she looked about as frazzled and drained as Barlowe. "I think that was sort of the original mandate?"

Paxton grunted. "I think it's good, Colonel. To the point, and like the private said, it's not introducing a bunch of lies that'll bite us in the ass."

Barlowe winced; he didn't agree, but he wasn't going to challenge.

Meyers didn't want to antagonize his only I.B. Resource, but there wasn't much choice. "Please send that message, Ladell. And feel free to log your concerns in your report. I'll take McNutt and Zacharowski with me. Have Banh and McNutt's squad in position along the Farmers Road, ready for extraction. There's a large building north of that club you and Cisneros went to."

"I think that's the theater the road's named for."

"Good. Propose that as a meeting place."

"You want me to send that now?"

"I don't want to give them time to plan. Suggest an hour from now?" Meyers caught Paxton's approving tap of the nose. "I think that's more than enough time. Oh, and let's keep representation down to the warlord—or whatever you want to call them—and three bodyguards. Master Sergeant Paxton, could you get the squads moving?"

Paxton slipped his helmet over his head as he strolled out.

"I'm sorry about not having Waverley's location yet, Colonel." Starling's face tensed as she spoke. "We were able to salvage some processors and memory. That oughta help some."

"What you two are pulling off with these resources is amazing, Private. Thank you for your hard work. Take a break—maybe see if you can get a nap before the meeting." Meyers looked at Barlowe. "Both of you. We'll need you watching out for us."

He forced a reassuring smile, the sort Rimes pulled off naturally, then headed for the Rovers. As he waited for the approaching squads, he checked the Rovers' power supplies. They were both below sixty percent, which wasn't ideal. If they kept their speed low enough, the charges would hold about even in the sunlight, and there was always the option of transferring power from their armor, if necessary.

McNutt threw a casual salute as he approached. "Heard we're starting up negotiations, Colonel."

Meyers returned the salute. "Just trying to control a situation gone bad."

McNutt settled into the driver's seat of the closest Rover and looked at Meyers from beneath dark, heavy brows. "Situation gone bad. Wouldn't be here otherwise, would we?"

"No." Meyers slipped into the passenger seat beside McNutt.

Banh waited until Paxton was seated in the passenger seat of the other Rover, then took up the driver's seat. Zacharowski popped up the seat on the flatbed immediately behind Banh, then stretched out the leg rests and relaxed while the rest of the soldiers settled elsewhere. Once everyone was seated, Banh accelerated away from the camp; McNutt followed a short distance behind.

A few minutes north of the camp, McNutt turned. "These folks don't particularly sound like a weak group of pacifists, Colonel. You have a plan to make them all civil?"

"Something short of guns blazing but more than offering chocolates and roses." McNutt's soft snort was justified. Meyers wasn't sure there was an approach that would make a significant difference. With a population armed to the teeth, just getting people to come together to talk rationally would be a challenge.

They stopped three klicks out of the city, the Rovers hidden behind clumps of scrub. Meyers strode to the center of the road, back turned to the others, and waited until Paxton joined him before heading toward the eastern edge of Turning Point. McNutt fell in behind them, and a moment later, Zacharowski.

A klick out, Meyers closed his faceplate and tapped the CAWS-5 to be sure it was locked in place in the brace. "Seal up. I'll open a tight channel, but keep it clear."

Four soldiers in environmental armor were sure to be an intimidating sight. He hoped it would be enough to manage the delicate balance between preventing attack and not making it seem like an attack of their own.

The first to notice them were children. Black, olive-skinned, and several shades in between, they seemed to represent a broad mixture of the populace rather than just the area, which Barlowe and Starling had designated Mattias's territory. Then Meyers remembered that the section of road had been claimed by Reyes. Some of the children seemed young—maybe five years old—while others seemed a few years out from teenager. They mostly laughed and ran around Meyers and the rest, but a few just trailed and watched quietly. Meyers hoped that meant there was some level of peace beneath all the guns and posturing. That hope slipped away when men began drifting into view.

With assault weapons casually settled on shoulders, the men appeared from alleyways ahead and to the rear of the group's position, easily hidden by the towering, empty warehouses. They were black, probably Mattias's people. One of the men shouted, and the children froze. Another shout from the man, and the children ran.

"We're here to speak to your leaders," Meyers said. The suit amplified his voice without significantly changing it.

The men ignored him, or at least it seemed that they did, but then he saw they were continuing forward, flanking him and the others, leading them southwest. It was the direction he wanted, or at least it was for now. They crossed a modest road, and a bit later, another. Ahead, Theater Road, which marked the eastern edge of Reyes's territory, loomed. The displays were dull, barely visible in the daylight. Reyes shouted down on the people below from the display, but Meyers could only catch bits and pieces—promises of rewards for unity, threats about betrayal, reminders about how they were all treated on Earth.

Three haulers, the ones with what looked like light machine guns mounted, sat behind the checkpoint, on Reyes's side. Men leaned casually against the length of the flatbeds. Meyers couldn't sense any change in the escorts' pace, which he took as an indication things were all right. Even with the escorts, they didn't have the numbers to stand against Reyes's force.

"Agent Barlowe, those haulers—"

"I've got them down. AMARMI."

"Amar-what?"

"AMARMI. Apollo Minerals and Resource Management, Inc. SunCorps' biggest mining corporation. The larger ones are Cougars, the smaller one's a Devil Cat. They're modified versions of vehicles designed for HSI by Global Motors' Heavy Machines Division."

"HSI as in SunCorps' HSI?"

"Yeah."

"And *the* Global Motors?"

"Yes, part of True Transportation. Another of SunCorps' corporate structures. Heavy Machines does specialized haulers for the rest of the SunCorps entities."

Meyers squinted. "Why would Waverley flee to a planet where

SunCorps is selling expensive haulers to warlords? Does that sound like something a fugitive sold out by his peers would do? This is going to show up on a report to the SSC at some point."

"I-I don't know. Is there really any place SunCorps wouldn't have a presence of some sort?"

"Good point. What about those machine guns?"

"Alexander Arms."

"Shit. That's run by GDS."

Barlowe sighed. "There aren't that many heavy weapons manufacturers, Lonny."

"So it's pure coincidence Reyes's men are driving around armored haulers built by SunCorps entities, mounted with military-grade weapons manufactured by another SunCorps entity? The assault weapons?"

"MKEK."

"Also run by GDS, Ladell. Dammit. When were you going to tell me all this?"

"I don't see how it changes anything."

"You don't see—" Meyers groaned. "Are you serious?"

"Addis Ababa Street," the leader of the escort said. He waved his free hand at the checkpoint guards. "We go to the theater."

One of Reyes's men waved them north. Meyers wasn't sure what to make of that until his escort turned off the road and into an alleyway. Their pace picked up, and before long, they were jogging, with Reyes's men and the haulers becoming visible, paralleling them, whenever the group came out of alleys and had to cross streets.

"Looks like someone's not keen on your plan, Colonel," McNutt said over their internal channel.

Zacharowski chuckled. "You mean besides me?"

"Colonel said to keep the channel clear, you knuckleheads." Paxton's voice was calm, but the no-bullshit tone was impossible to miss.

Meyers appreciated it. There was a time for cockiness, and there was a time for caution. Every time he got a good look at the haulers, he felt surer that even their environmental armor would be tested by the sort of weapons they had mounted. Even the best armor transferred some kinetic energy to the wearer, and what they wore was a compromise between protection and mobility. A well-placed round might penetrate. Enough hits in the same general area, and the armor's integrity would fail. He wondered where the big hauler was, the one with the heavier gun on it. It looked like a mobile anti-aircraft weapon, something meant to take out armored vehicles. If the hauler and the gun were SunCorps, that would seem to seal the deal.

The open lot of the club appeared ahead of them. Turkish and Arabic-looking men stood there, gathered in two groups, many hidden behind what little cover there was in the lot: the tables, the storage drums. Their escort sprinted, and on Theater Road, the haulers came to a stop. Beyond the lot, the larger building rose, gray and ugly in the morning light.

Beniam stepped from the front of the building, assault rifle on his shoulder, a cigarette dangling from his mouth. A bandage stood out on his forehead, stark white against his black skin. He waved them forward, and the escort didn't slow until Meyers reached Beniam's position.

"You are safe," Beniam said. He looked past them, toward Reyes's forces. "Come."

They followed him inside the building, which had what appeared to be a lobby with a sealed-up concession stand and two double doors that were open to reveal auditorium seating that sloped down to a stage. Three men leaned against walls there, what appeared to be a representative from each of the other factions—two men who could be Arab or Turk, and a tattoo-covered white man. Several men were gathered at the foot of the stage. Beniam led the way down the sloped floor, and the other three men fell in behind Meyers's team.

"The United Nations arrived," Beniam said. He laughed, and his deep voice filled the vast, open space.

Meyers gritted his teeth and opened his faceplate. Paxton, McNutt, and Zacharowski did the same.

The men at the base of the stage moved forward, much less entertained by the situation than Beniam was. Meyers recognized Mattias, Bey, and Badran. Savoy was harder to recognize. His hair was dyed almost white and pulled back into a ponytail. Each of the men was flanked by two bodyguards. One of Savoy's bodyguards was Asian; the other appeared to be a multiracial mix.

The Minor Four, Meyers thought to himself.

Mattias stepped away from the others, and Beniam stopped, the smile now gone. "Beniam say you come last night. It is good to see his cut was worth the trouble. You speak for the United Nations?"

"We do." Meyers extended a hand. "Colonel Lonny Meyers, Elite Response Force."

Mattias glanced at Meyers's hand but didn't shake it. "We been here for nine years. Why is it you come now?"

"Maybe they want something they find up in Ardennen." That was Bey, the Turk. He looked sickly, shaking. His cheeks were sunken, and his dark eyes were watery, but they were alert.

Badran waved toward Meyers dismissively. "The United Nations always wants something."

Savoy drew himself up with a deep breath. "And maybe they're here to make an offer. Let's hear them out."

Meyers nodded slightly at Savoy, then turned to Mattias, who seemed to speak with the most authority. "We are here to make you an offer, yes." Meyers took everyone—even the bodyguards—in with a quick look. "When Reyes arrives—"

Mattias laughed. "Reyes has no reason to hear UN speak."

"He doesn't," Savoy said. He turned so that the left side of his head was better exposed, revealing a disfigured ear and severe scarring along his neck. "But maybe we do."

Bey wheezed and licked his lips, then said, "Let him talk."

"We should probably wait for Reyes." Meyers looked for support from Savoy and Bey, but they both shook their heads.

"He will not come," Badran said.

Gunfire erupted outside, then shouting. Beniam and the guards who had been waiting out in the lobby ran toward the front, crouching when gunfire came from the lobby, splintering the tops of the door frames. Several men sprinted through the doorways and fanned out along the wall that separated the theater from the lobby. There was more gunfire, and the shouting outside died. Moments later, six men strolled in casually, as if they'd just won a battle. They were heavier armed than the others, with assault rifles dangling from shoulder straps and pistol holsters strapped to their legs. Most of them pointed submachine guns toward the people gathered near the stage.

"*Amistades*," said the man in the front of the pack. Reyes. "I come all this way, and you were meeting without my arrival? That is not how things work in Turning Point, is it?"

Meyers stepped forward and extended his hand. "Thank you for joining us, Mr. Reyes. I was just—"

"You can shut your fuckin' mouth, United Nations." Reyes pulled a large revolver and pointed it at Meyers's head. "Or I think I might just blow your head off."

11

13 December 2174. Turning Point, Bellar Frontier Colony.

EACH STEP REYES TOOK CLOSER, his finger seemed to curl tighter around the gun's trigger. Meyers imagined there might be a slick spot or a hole in the floor, something to turn the ridiculous act of bravado into a deadly mistake. Reyes's boots scraped on the hard floor. For his part, Meyers held still and hoped his team would do the same. Reyes seemed to need the theatrics to establish or reinforce his dominance, and meeting that with some smart-ass, macho comment would only escalate matters.

Finally, Reyes came to a stop just in front of Meyers. The revolver's barrel was pressed just beneath Meyers's nose; all he could smell was gun oil and metal. The barrel was warm and hard and pushed so tight it hurt.

"Why don't you explain why you even came here, United Nations." Reyes pushed the barrel in tighter. "Hm?"

Meyers licked his lips and tasted blood. "The UN is looking to bring the frontier colonies into protected status. They don't want another repeat of the Metacorporate Wars. That's all."

Reyes snorted. "And you have them eating this *mierda* out of your hands?"

Mierda. Shit. Bullshit. Meyers knew enough Spanish to catch the occasional slang. "It's the truth. It's better for everyone all around if we have a broad umbrella protecting against undue influence."

"You see my people? We got guns, *puta.* We don't need your protection." Reyes lowered the revolver and turned toward the other leaders. "And you *cobardes*, you should know better. Nothing changes on Bellar, not without me saying so."

Meyers turned his head slightly to see the reaction of the other four men.

Mattias cocked his head. "And so now we are cowards? For listening to an offer?"

"Maybe the time is now to hear them out," Bey said. His watery, deep-set eyes showed no fear of Reyes or of the guns his men had trained on everyone else.

Reyes brought the revolver around to Bey. "Careful about embracing death, old man."

Bey seemed to straighten. "Death embraced me without asking for my embrace."

"What if this is about Ardennen?" Savoy asked. "That's what we're worried about."

"You know not to worry about them," Reyes said. He seemed ready to pistol whip Savoy. "We don't need United Nations telling us what to do. You forget already what happened to us when we let governments push us around? Huh? Every time? You forget already what I done for you?"

Meyers looked at the submachine guns of Reyes's men. They were good weapons, with recoil compensation enhancements, extended magazines, and what looked like smart targeting systems. They weren't on par with the CAWS-5s and the BAS, but they were definitely high-end, better than anything the Minor Four had.

The superior weapons didn't seem to matter to Bey and the rest. Their faces reflected frustration and anger, as if they were ready to take the matter forward. It was an ugly stand-off, with both sides staring, evaluating.

Paxton twisted slowly, casually, like he wanted to see what Beniam was doing. Meyers caught Paxton's eye; he was thinking the same thing, that this could go very wrong at any time. Meyers kicked on the BAS's combat enhancement system and ran that over the private channel he'd opened with Paxton, McNutt, and Zacharowski. That got McNutt and Zacharowski's attention. In seconds, their systems were feeding data over the channel, and the theater was being turned into a virtual battlefield inside their armor—Reyes's men were outlined in red wireframes, Meyers's team was outlined in green, and everyone else was in amber.

Reyes laughed suddenly. "Is this about the barges?" He looked at Meyers. "Hey? Did Weidmann go to the UN? Did they send you?"

Weidmann. Governor Weidmann.

The revolver slowly shifted to Savoy. "Maybe you should ask Savoy here what we did to the last group Weidmann sent down."

Reyes's men laughed, but their guns never dropped from their targets.

"The ERF reports to the United Nations Special Security Council, not to Governor Weidmann." Meyers activated the BAS's targeting priority system with a careful blink and started ranking Reyes's men. Those with submachine guns were one through five, then the ten men lined along the wall near the doorways. Reyes was sixteen, despite being the biggest pain in the ass. Meyers shared the targeting priority with the others. "We did come here seeking your assistance, though."

Reyes holstered his revolver and scratched at the soul patch beneath his full lips. A scar was visible at the edge of the whiskers. Compared to the rest of his men, Reyes was wiry, no more intimidating in purely physical terms than Savoy or Mattias. Reyes's eyes—so dark they were black in the theater's weak light—glistened, and he still seemed more entertained by the situation than angry. "So what could we do for the UN, *jefe*?"

"It's more about what we could do for you."

Reyes shrugged his shoulders and twisted his lips down, mock hopeful. "Go on."

"We're looking for a man by the name of Waverley."

"Waverley?" Reyes again shrugged, now opening his eyes wide. He seemed caught up in his own theatrics.

Meyers wanted to punch Reyes, to blow him away. "Chad Milton Waverley. Former CEO of SunCorps. Wanted for war crimes."

"Ah!" Reyes continued with the theatrics, now turning to his men clustered behind him and throwing out his arms. "*Jefe* wants us to help him with a *desperado*!"

"We're just looking for any tips you might have. Did he ever reach out to anyone? Did he offer to pay for protection, that sort of thing? The reward for assistance could be substantial."

"How substantial?" Savoy asked.

Reyes bolted past Meyers and backhanded Savoy. When Savoy grabbed Reyes by the shirt, Reyes pulled his revolver and pushed it up into Savoy's face. Savoy released his grip and slowly raised his hands out and up.

"That's right. That's right, fucker. You don't mess with me." As Reyes spoke, spittle flecks flew into Savoy's face. He didn't even flinch. Reyes turned on the rest. "Who gave you your guns, huh? Who gave you your freedom? Hm? Adrián Reyes! And who put you in prison? Who had you rotting your lives away? Who took your families from you?" Reyes jabbed the revolver at Meyers. "Those mother fuckers. The ones who want to offer you money right now to be their little *putas*."

"You won't find a person here who thinks those corporate jails were a good idea," Meyers said, fighting to keep his voice even. He couldn't afford to have things slip away. "Turning the justice system into a for-profit operation was a huge mistake. Every single person knows that now."

"That's right, *pendejo*!" Reyes waved his revolver. "A huge mistake! And it was people like me who suffered." He pointed at Bey and Mattias. "People like them! How many times we had cigarettes ground out on our flesh? How many times someone break our bones or crush our balls or make us go days standing in our own filth? But, hey, where was United Nations then?"

"That wasn't the UN. That was bad leadership. It was presidents and premiers and assemblies and congresses that spread corporate for-profit prisons across the world, not the UN."

"It was government." Reyes turned back to Savoy and the others, once more stopping in front of Savoy, this time to pat him on the cheek. "Now look what we got, eh? We got Lancers. We got guns. We got power to tell you to get the fuck off our planet."

McNutt's suggested targeting priority came in. He had Reyes tagged as one. Zacharowski's suggestions followed. They also showed Reyes at number one.

Meyers raised his hands slowly. He didn't want to provoke anyone, not with tensions so high. "The problem with might makes right is that there's always going to be someone bigger. If the metacorporations want something on Bellar, then they're going to blow through your defenses—"

"The metacorporations won't come here." Reyes relaxed and turned on Bey. "They want something from Bellar—they'll buy it. Ain't nothing here worth stealing, isn't that right?"

Paxton's targeting priorities came over the channel. He had Reyes at sixteen. Meyers locked down his priorities for all of them, then he flagged a hold to end the discussion. Initiating a gunfight would lead to a power vacuum. It would hinder the mission, not help it. They needed Waverley. The situation in Turning Point wasn't their concern.

"Okay." Meyers shook his head. "So, we made a mistake. We overstepped our bounds. I'm not a diplomat. I was probably the wrong person to send for something like this."

Reyes smiled, apparently pleased by the concession. "That's right. And you know what? I'm gonna let you live. I'm gonna let you live so that you can tell those sons of bitches back on Earth to stay the fuck out of our business." He waved toward the front of the theater. "You tell them we're building an army here. Anyone stupid enough to come to Bellar, we fill them full of holes and dump their bodies in the ocean. You hear me?"

It wasn't just bravado, Meyers realized. Reyes sincerely believed he had the forces to drive off anyone. There weren't even 20,000 men in Turning Point, and most weren't Reyes's to command, but he thought he could withstand a serious assault.

And then it made sense. Reyes was in with Waverley. That had to be it.

"I hear you." Meyers shot a look at Paxton, McNutt, and Zacharowski: *Follow my lead.* "We all hear you."

"Then get the fuck out of my city."

Meyers took a slow step forward, then stopped. Reyes had a hand held up, a finger raised.

"Leave the guns." Reyes pointed to a spot on the floor.

Meyers's tongue felt dry. Surrendering their weapons…it was meant to humiliate, that much was obvious. But it was also meant to give Reyes an advantage. He'd already done plenty to humiliate everyone. Meyers wondered whether Reyes had someone technically skilled enough to crack the BAS network through the CAWS-5 interface. It seemed unlikely.

Unless, Meyers realized, Waverley had brought someone of that caliber with him.

Meyers pulled his CAWS-5 from the brace and set it on the floor where Reyes had indicated. A few seconds later, Paxton did the same. Meyers glanced back at Zacharowski and McNutt. Their faces were flushed, and their fingers twitched, but they weren't reaching for their weapons.

"Sergeant Zacharowski?"

Zacharowski shook his head. "Fuck this asshole."

Reyes turned and stepped closer to Zacharowski, revolver slowly coming up.

"Best put that little toy down," McNutt said. It was so quiet, Meyers could barely make out the words, but the utter calm in McNutt's voice, the challenge—that came through loud and clear.

Meyers couldn't understand what they were doing. It was an unwinnable situation.

Reyes froze, then he squinted and brought the revolver up to a few centimeters from McNutt's face. "You think this is a toy, *pendejo*?" He placed the barrel just below McNutt's left eye. "You think?"

"Adrián," Meyers said. "Wait! Please. We had a deal."

Reyes's lips twisted into a snarl. "You leave your guns. That was the deal. Your little *putas*, they don't listen so good."

Meyers clenched his teeth. All the tension he'd worked so hard to drain from the theater was back now. Zacharowski had challenged Reyes, and now McNutt had taken that challenge to an entirely new level.

"They're just kids, Adrián. Punks."

McNutt's eyes narrowed.

Paxton twisted around. "McNutt, Zacharowski, surrender your weapons. Now."

Zacharowski slowly removed his CAWS-5 and set it on top of the others. A moment later, McNutt reached back and slowly pulled his from the securing frame, then he set it down on top of the other weapons.

Reyes snorted and holstered the revolver. "Get out. Now. Before I change my mind."

Meyers led the way to the lobby, doing everything he could to remain calm or at least to appear so. He was sure his cheeks burned red as he passed through the men who had escorted them. Those cheeks surely glowed brighter when he saw one of the Arabs on the ground outside, dead. That was all Meyers needed to see to remember what was at stake. He kept his hands up and his eyes looking straight ahead until they were past the haulers and their black-barreled machine guns and the copper- and caramel-skinned men with their assault rifles and Spanish-tinged insults. When he was across the club's lot, he listened, struggling to hear past the blood pounding in his head.

"Master Sergeant Paxton?"

"Right behind you, Colonel."

"Corporal McNutt? Sergeant Zacharowski?"

"Behind the master sergeant."

Meyers let out a sigh. "Don't ever do that again."

And then he let it go. When they were through the nearest alley, he sealed his faceplate, lowered his arms, and began to jog. He didn't stop until he saw Banh, who had the team deployed wide.

"They took your weapons, sir?"

"They did." Meyers settled into the passenger seat of the nearest of the Rovers and stared down at his hands, shaking inside the armor's gloves.

The Rovers quickly filled with the others, and then they were moving. Meyers was sealed away by then, burning with fury and humiliation. They'd lost more than just a bit of pride, but he couldn't figure exactly what it was. One thing he was sure of: The puzzle was something he had to resolve. Quickly.

12

13 December 2174. Karpov Desert, South of Turning Point, Bellar Frontier
Colony.

THE ENTIRE RIDE back to camp, Meyers wrestled with the meaning of what
had happened in Turning Point. By the time they pulled into camp, all he
had was a sense of certainty that he'd played into Waverley's hand. If there
were people within the metacorporations willing to deliver faulty software
to the ERF, there were also people willing to pass along intelligence to a
fugitive from the United Nations, especially someone as powerful as
Waverley.

It was all a set-up, he realized. Start to finish. The only thing that wasn't
obvious was how deep it went.

Meyers pulled off his helmet and jumped from the Rover. He wanted to
get out of the sun, to be alone. Instead, he waved for McNutt and
Zacharowski to follow, and then he walked between the camouflaged
Javelins, stopping halfway down their lengths. He stood in a sliver of shade,
listening to the wind whistle and feeling it dry the sweat from his face.

"Colonel?" McNutt stood at parade rest, hands behind his back, legs spread shoulder wide. His eyes were squinted, challenging Meyers.

Zacharowski was also at parade rest, but he stared straight ahead.

"At ease." Meyers ran his fingers along the edge of his helmet. He had to get out of the armor. He had to feel the world through his own skin. "We're going to complete this mission, all right? We've had some setbacks. Every mission does." McNutt's eyes twitched, and Zacharowski's shoulders shifted—message received. That was all that needed to be said about the theater incident. "If, for some reason, we have a need to go after Reyes, I want you two to know, it's going to be full-on. Understood?"

McNutt smirked. "We'll get another crack at him."

Zacharowski nodded.

"All right. So, listen up. First thing, Corporal McNutt, were you able to recover any CAWS-5s from the crash site?"

"A couple. Plus the ones from the wounded."

"Get those operational. We need to replace what we lost. Second thing, I think we've got a problem. A big problem. I can't figure out yet what it is, but my gut tells me our systems are compromised."

"Systems?" That finally shook Zacharowski.

Meyers held his helmet up. "Javelin systems software, BAS, everything."

McNutt looked at the ground. "You think that's why they wanted our CAWS?"

"I think so. One-Six-Three crashing wasn't an accident. I'm sure of that. Some of the other oddities, the way our BAS has behaved...I'm sure we're looking at significant sabotage. I think the only thing that's kept us alive so far has been just how primitive the infrastructure is in Turning Point."

"So whatta we do?" McNutt tapped his chest plate. "No BAS, this armor's useless."

"We see if there's a way to back out the software. In our suits, in the Javelins, maybe in the CAWS."

Zacharowski shook his head. "All we've done so far is sit on our asses, Colonel. If they know we're here, we're giving up valuable time."

"I know. But we've been operating in the dark. We didn't have a choice until now."

McNutt glanced over his shoulder, toward the tents. "Want us to tell the others?"

"Soon. I need to hear from Barlowe and Starling whether this is feasible." Meyers could already hear the protests. Falling back to older versions —if it was even possible—would mean giving up capabilities, giving up precious processing resources. Most importantly, it would take time. "Until we know, check with the others. Don't let on what's up, but see if anyone has noticed strange behavior in their systems—comm glitches, targeting problems, issues with networking."

"Some targeting problems don't have anything to do with software," Zacharowski said, eyes drifting to McNutt, whose golden skin darkened.

"Drop it. Both of you. I don't need two of my NCOs facing charges."

McNutt relaxed slightly. Meyers hoped calling McNutt an NCO got the message across: He was filling a vital position. Promotions were at stake.

"Talk to your squads. Talk to Banh. If anything jumps out to you, bring it to me. Not over the comms. Personally."

McNutt spun and headed for the tents. Zacharowski hesitated, as if he was ready to say something, then he followed McNutt. Meyers took a couple deep breaths, then he headed for the clearing and turned for the Operations Center.

When he entered, Barlowe and Starling looked up. Paxton didn't react; he seemed absorbed in the displays.

"They could hack the interface of the CAWS," Barlowe said. "They could get into our network. This is bad."

Meyers shook his head. "I don't think they can, but Waverley can."

Paxton didn't take his eyes from the display, but he said, "Colonel feels Reyes is working for Waverley. Private Starling, maybe you could provide an update?"

Starling's big eyes seemed to bug out. "I think we found him, sir. Waverley."

Meyers smiled. "Show me."

Starling turned back to the displays, and after Paxton stepped away, she seemed to slip into her own world—staring, swiping, and tapping at nothing. The familiar data imagery popped up: network blind spots, the representation of data flows, and then a new flow along Cáceres Road.

"We started by running all the filters, eliminating possible hiding places, and we tagged those as false readings. After that, we turned to where traffic was coming from that tried to point to those false readings. Some of that's coming from Reyes's district. Mostly, it was from his compound. But then when we dug deeper, we saw there was a concentration of traffic here, at the main relay on the edge of the city."

"Sending traffic down Cáceres Road?"

"Yeah." Starling smiled, enthusiastic despite looking like she was days overdue for a break. The smile faded slightly. "I mean, yes, sir."

"What's down that road?"

Starling sent the map display speeding east, stopping on an image of overgrown, abandoned buildings. Most were small, probably storage and utility sheds, but one was large. Very large.

"The Cáceres Compound. It's an old research facility. The first thing erected on Bellar. It was set up for a lot of automated work, but there was a research team, too. When Bellar was tagged as an ideal colony site, the compound was abandoned. All the serious research moved up to what became Ardennen."

"If he's hiding there, wouldn't that put too big a footprint down to hide? How many square meters would you estimate that is? Looks like it would put a huge draw on power, even if he was careful about it."

Barlowe pointed to the main building. "It would have been constructed to run off its own power source, maybe a small reactor. If Waverley brought a big enough ship with him, he could be using its reactor to cover most of their needs. Maybe with a surplus."

Meyers studied the image. "That's a big compound. He could hide a small army there. Why didn't someone else move in?"

One of the displays brought up new images, men with heavy tattoos, ritual scarring, and disfiguration. They were huge, and not in a way that just a little steroid use could manage. They stood over bloodied corpses or were engaged in combat with others. Rather than the ubiquitous assault rifles, these men wielded hatchets, machetes, and wicked-looking bladed weapons.

"It took a little bit of digging, but we found references to a gang known as the Zombies," Starling said. She drilled down on one of the images, and the self-mutilation became more evident. It was the sort of thing that was prevalent in certain drug communities back on Earth. "Cannibals, or at least that's their reputation. True or not, they were a big enough problem that Turning Point kicked them out. I mean Reyes. They still harass the little settlements outside the city—farmers, prospectors, and loners."

"More prisoners?"

Starling stared at the image in silence.

"Private Starling? Were these prisoners also?"

"Hm? Oh, yes, sir. Probably colonial. Not political types."

"So, even Reyes is put off by these guys?" Meyers stared into the eyes of the man on the display. They were black and dead, like a shark's. "How many were there?"

"Over 200 at one point."

"Waverley's instant security force?"

Paxton squinted. "Not if it was me. Couldn't sleep with something like that nearby."

Meyers couldn't either. "How old's the imagery?"

"Almost a year. Sir. But there's older." Starling's focus came back to the Operations Center. "We could get a Condor out there. To the compound."

Meyers turned to Barlowe. "I thought most of the Condors' control and surveillance components were in One-Six-Three?"

"This one's hacked together. Just video, not even very good, and a laser range finder. Oh, and limited flight time. You could probably do better. You know me and tools. Becky's pretty good with hardware, but she's been busy with this."

"I'll give it a look. Anything's better than year-old imagery. Anything else?"

"Food prices," Starling said. "Nothing significant, but one of the things we caught in some of the chatter we listened in on was complaints about farmers raising prices."

"Waverley?"

Starling shrugged. "There weren't reports of crop problems."

Paxton chuckled. "Must've converted those cannibals to vegan."

"Or he brought a larger force with him than we were told." Meyers wondered how delicate the system would have to be for ten, maybe twenty new consumers to affect it. Unless the farmers were simply extracting more because they could. Because they didn't like Reyes. "Great work. Both of you. Private Starling, were you in the Systems specialty before you joined the Rangers?"

Starling looked away, and it appeared she was trying not to smile. "Explosives Ordnance Disposal, sir."

"EOD?"

"Got a thing for the boom, sir." She covered her face with a hand, as if embarrassed. "I mean, that's what my supervisors said."

Paxton rubbed a knuckle against his nose. "You want a special package built, Private Starling here knows what you're looking for."

She looked away again, and Meyers could almost hear an "aw, shucks" in his head. "So, where'd you learn computers and systems, then?"

"My mother taught me the basics of software. Just the basics. My grandma, she taught me how to see systems differently, y'know? To really use them. Sir."

"Well, you're working with the best hacker I've ever met. But we have a new problem for you two to deal with, and I think it's too big to put off any longer."

"The flight systems?" Barlowe bit his lip.

"All the systems—BAS, flight systems, even the Condor and Rovers if they were connected to upgraded systems."

Barlowe waved his hand, casual, dismissive. "The Condor and Rovers are easy. We have stand-alone firmware modules for those. I can run a parity check against the original copies of their systems to see if anything's changed. The Javelins and BAS, that's going to be a problem."

"And our CAWS-5s."

"Once we get the BAS fixed, you can push the new version from your systems to your guns. But getting the BAS back to the old version?" Barlowe sighed. "Not easy."

Starling looked worried. "We've been using the BAS resources for most of our work, Colonel. If it's compromised, we've—"

"I know. I don't think Waverley or Reyes has the resources to make use of what they have available to them. Or at least I didn't think that before."

He nodded at the compound on the display. "Maybe they do. Let's assume so. Maybe they just haven't figured out what's going on yet?"

"That means they know we've probed the compound. Right?" Starling looked to Barlowe, who screwed up his face.

"Maybe. For now, the important thing is to get the BAS systems functional. We damn near got into a crossfire in Turning Point. I don't want to guess how that would have gone if they have access into our systems."

"But you don't think they're in," Barlowe said. "Not yet, right?"

"I think that's why they wanted the CAWS-5s. They must be missing something. Maybe the upgrades created a back door that they can pick out through the CAWS-5s. Whatever the situation is, our operational integrity isn't going to be worth a damn for much longer, not if they can get in easily."

Barlowe closed his eyes. He wobbled, unsteady.

"Ladell?"

He raised a hand, palm out. "I'm just trying to think..." His eyes opened. "Lieutenant Oppert!"

"What?"

"She was a last-minute addition, right? You weren't going to bring her along originally?"

"We needed someone who could handle One-Six-Three. She knew the Arrows better than anyone."

"Her BAS wasn't upgraded."

"No, just the squads'—" Meyers grimaced. "She's...in pieces."

Barlowe shook his head, excited now. "The BAS system software is distributed. Find enough pieces of her armor, we can extract the modules and reassemble them. I'll take the Rovers off the network, clean them back to a base system, create a virtual cleanroom, and rebuild her system software there. That's your baseline."

Someone would have to sort through the common grave McNutt's squad had put everyone into. Even if the armor still had enough power to transmit its owner ID, it would be gory, horrific work. "Start on one of the Rovers. I'll take the other out to the burial site."

Paxton scratched at his nose. "Not very safe going out there alone, Colonel, not if Waverley or Reyes might be watching everything we do."

It wasn't. "Get me two volunteers. Make clear what we're doing."

Paxton slid his helmet on and headed out at a jog.

Meyers wondered if there were two people up to the task. He wasn't even sure he was. But there wasn't really a choice. The mission had no chance without rebuilding the BAS software, and a failed mission would doom the ERF.

13

13 December 2174. Karpov Desert, South of Turning Point, Bellar Frontier
Colony.

BY THE TIME they reached the common gravesite, the winds had picked up,
and visibility was down to twenty meters. Sand scratched and scraped
against Meyers's faceplate. Something had finally gone their way, and he
intended to take advantage of it. When the Rover stopped, he jumped out
and checked the BAS display. There were still faint readouts coming off
Oppert's BAS—her ID and location. McNutt raised his faceplate, spun
around in the driver's seat, and plucked one of the entrenching tools from
the flatbed. Private Perkins handed Meyers one of the other tools, then
trudged toward the signal. Meyers raised his faceplate and squinted against
the sandstorm.

When McNutt walked past, Meyers cupped his free hand over his
mouth so that only McNutt could hear, then shouted over the wind, "You
sure he's up for this?"

McNutt's nostrils flared slightly. "Ain't a coward, if that's your meaning."

"What's this job he's planning to do when he gets back to Earth?"

McNutt shrugged. "Some sort of technology service."

Meyers considered Perkins's form, already hunched over, digging. Committed. Capable. Unaffected by the idea of digging up the dead and sorting through pieces. "You don't think there's any chance we can get him to change his mind?"

"Way this is going, may not be anything for him to change his mind about."

It was surprising to see McNutt thinking beyond the moment. Meyers sealed his faceplate and followed McNutt's guidance on where to start digging. It looked like the wind had already scooped away a lot of the sand. The closest signal wasn't even a meter beneath the surface, but it was tricky, blinking in and out, probably pulsing to conserve power.

About halfway down, Meyers's BAS registered another blip: Oppert's ID, weak, about five meters out from the gravesite. It wasn't something worth confronting McNutt over. Expecting his team to find all the body parts would be ridiculous.

Meyers thrust the entrenching tool into the sand and followed the signal. He stopped when something stuck to his boot. At first, it looked as if a snake had bit his boot sole, but then he realized it was just sand sticking to something long and coiled. Whatever it was, it had stuck to the bottom of his boot. He grabbed the thing—pliant—and pulled it free.

And then it hit him: intestines.

He tossed it away and wiped his gloves in the sand. The wind cleared more sand from a mound, revealing the outline of viscera. It was too much to have been missed by McNutt's squad.

The signal from Oppert's armor blinked on his screen again, and he headed toward it, unsure what to make of the pile of guts. A decent chunk of armor—a chest plate—jutted from the sand. A helmet fragment, also Oppert's, protruded from the sand. Something flapped from the chest plate, pale, sand-covered, and blood-stained. He dropped to his knees and leaned in close to examine the armor and the flapping cloth, brushing away sand from both sides, then freezing when he recognized part of a dark, ornate symbol. He brushed at the blood and sand more quickly, revealing more of the symbol.

A tattoo. A hawk, tail flared, wings spread so that their tips touched the back of Oppert's hips and the bottom of the tail disappeared in the dark of her...He remembered the way she had of moving so that the wings looked like they were catching the wind.

What were the odds, he wondered, of a piece of flesh being stripped away so completely and cleanly by a crash? Not good.

He reached for his CAWS-5 and found the brace empty. They hadn't replaced their lost weapons yet. He brought the BAS's sensors up to full and looked around, spotting more assorted pieces of armor.

And movement. He marked the moving forms—five of them, closing.

"We've got company," he said over a channel to McNutt and Perkins.

Meyers fell back at a sprint, pulling the sidearm from its thigh holster. He was qualified with it, but compared to the CAWS-5, it was a desperate option. He jumped into the depression next to his entrenching tool.

McNutt belly-crawled to Meyers's side, knife in one hand. "Reyes's men?"

"Zombies. At least I think they are." In his peripheral vision, Meyers saw McNutt's head twist around. "Cannibals. Drugged-up lunatics kicked out of Turning Point for being too much trouble."

"Nice to hear that sort of information, Colonel?"

Before Meyers could reply, the forms rushed them. He got off a shot, center mass, dropping one, but only for a moment.

Then they were on them.

BAS or not, their armor was effective. The Zombies had axes and swords, heavy things that could easily sever or break limbs or tear open guts. Meyers's armor turned the blows into bruising, numbing impacts. McNutt dropped his first attacker with a powerful, disemboweling slash, but then he was taken down by two others. As Meyers was taken to the ground, he saw the disemboweled Zombie get back to his feet. There was no time to be amazed by that, though. The two who had taken Meyers to the ground, rolled off, and began hacking at him hard enough to knock the wind out of him. Meyers wondered if Perkins had run, and a second later, he got his answer, as Perkins stepped out of the fog of sand and wrapped an arm around the face of one of the Zombies, pulling it back and off balance before slitting its throat. Dark blood arced out until the wind caught it and sprayed it over Meyers and the second Zombie.

Perkins disappeared, invisible on Meyers's display.

The attack left the remaining Zombie confused. Meyers whipped a kick into the Zombie's knee. Amplified by the armor, the kick buckled the knee and completely snapped the leg until it was bent backward close to sixty degrees. The Zombie fell, but it didn't scream or even clutch at the leg. That was fine with Meyers, who rolled over, grabbed the Zombie's greasy, matted hair, and rained punches onto its face. Memories of Oppert's flesh—no doubt cut away like an animal's—pushed Meyers through the numbness and soreness until the Zombie went still, its face a bloody ruin.

Meyers retrieved his sidearm and sent two rounds into the head of the disemboweled Zombie that was still staggering around, finally dropping it. Finally, he hauled the last one off McNutt, which was just a formality. The thing was gushing blood from multiple chest wounds. Meyers watched it bleed out, twitching. All five of the Zombies were smaller than in Starling's images.

Emaciated, or on their way to it.

"Any serious injuries?" Meyers looked from McNutt to Perkins.

"Nah."

Perkins shook his head.

"Get what you can from the grave," Meyers said, as he ran for Oppert's chest piece and helmet. Those would probably be enough to rebuild the BAS system, but every part counted. Still, if there were Zombies to contend with, it might be better to rely on "good enough."

He pulled the chest piece and helmet from the sand, then looked around. All the bits and pieces of armor spread around him, the half-hearted effort to cover the grave...and only five Zombies. Starling had put their numbers at 200 or more. They had a reputation for raiding Turning Point and the surrounding settlements with impunity. He looked toward the Cáceres compound, more than twenty klicks to the northeast. There was no way someone could have seen One-Six-Three's crash, not from Turning Point, and not from the old research facility.

Meyers jogged back to the Rover and set the armor pieces on the flatbed, locking them down with bungee cord anchored inside the flatbed. McNutt set a mangled arm and thigh piece down next to the cord, then secured them as well. Perkins added what might have been a glove and a lower leg piece. All told, it was nearly a third of the armor.

McNutt settled into the driver's seat and opened a private channel with Meyers as he buckled in. "What was that about?"

"Something's not adding up."

"Yeah, you could say that. Colonel. Zombies?"

"Local name. You've seen the types—steroids, a bunch of tailored drug cocktails, instant monster." Except they'd been attacked by five of them, and they were heading back to camp with nothing worse than bruises. He remembered back to Perkins's attack while setting up the perimeter sensors. Something had knocked him silly and scraped his armor, and Meyers was pretty sure it wasn't the sensor.

When they were close enough to camp, Meyers opened a channel to Paxton. "Get Banh's men out on perimeter patrol. Have Zacharowski's squad ready the other Rover. McNutt's squad, too."

"What's up, sir?"

"That's what we're going to find out."

A few minutes later, the Rover skidded to a stop in a spray of aqua sand. Perkins ran the armor pieces to the Operations Center while McNutt gathered the rest of his squad. Zacharowski's squad was already mounted.

Paxton and Starling came out of the Operations Center, carrying the Condor. Even with the wings folded up so that it could fit on one of the flatbeds, the wind tugged at its surface area and pushed the two of them around. Meyers knew better than to offer help if he didn't want to lose the good will he'd built up with Starling. McNutt didn't seem to have any concerns in that regard. He moved in tight alongside Starling and helped secure the Condor, then handed Meyers a CAWS-5 before settling back into the driver's seat. McNutt's squad squeezed into their seats, heads ducked forward to avoid the fuselage.

"Bad weather to send that bird up in, Colonel." Paxton jerked his head back toward the Operations Center. "Agent Barlowe says you'll be pushing its limits."

"That's all we've done so far," Meyers said. "Have Banh's team double-check the perimeter sensors. Patrol in teams of two, stay well within the perimeter. Constant comms checks."

Paxton grunted. "You got something you want to share, Colonel?"

"We ran into some Zombies. They'd been into the gravesite."

"Don't say."

"Five of them. Looked like they'd lost a lot of weight."

"The men in those images Private Starling showed could handle losing some weight and still be a problem."

"No. A lot of weight."

Paxton scratched at his nose, but he didn't say anything as Meyers washed his gloves clean. Sand quickly clung to the water beading the gloves' surface, but Meyers told himself it was clean sand.

"Master Sergeant Paxton, I need you to keep the camp secure. Maybe this is nothing, but…"

"We'll be here, sir."

Meyers slid back into the passenger's seat, and a few moments later, the Rovers crawled into the desert. Their power was below fifty percent due to the use they'd seen and the sandstorms obscuring sunlight. Meyers had the team plug in and transfer some of their armor's power, just enough to keep the vehicles' power levels stable.

Sunset painted the sky a strange umber and ochre when they headed into the light woods south of the Cáceres Compound. It was jarring to see the sudden transformation from desert to muddy stream twisting through low hills, and then trees. Most of the trees were scrawny, like fresh-planted palm trees, but there were thick patches of scrub and once in a while, a decent-sized tree. Most of those larger trees had sponge-like leaf and branch structures that started about two meters above the ground in an inverted cone. Meyers had them park the Rovers beneath one of those sponge trees, about five klicks out from the southern edge of the Cáceres Compound.

While McNutt's squad wrestled the Condor back toward a clearing, Meyers shared the map imagery with everyone.

"This is the latest we have, and it's nearly a year old." He highlighted areas of interest. "Sometime in the last year, a gang of Kimmies took over the place."

Gerhardt snorted. "Looked like a lot of those boys in Turning Point were juiced or hopped up on something. What makes these guys special?"

Meyers looked at Zacharowski, who shot Gerhardt a warning look, but neither said anything about the boy comment. "These are special. By the look of them, real Kimmies, serious chemicals. There were 200 of them."

"Armaments, Colonel?" Cisneros asked.

"Mostly hand-to-hand; we saw machetes, axes, and things like that."

Zacharowski and Gerhardt exchanged a look that seemed to say it sounded like a clown operation.

A loud hum filled the air, even over the wind, and McNutt broke into the channel. "Condor's away, Colonel."

Meyers brought the Condor's controls up, fought off the dizziness of dealing with its crippled optics, then brought it under control. He sent it away from the facility on a steep climb, then he punched in a path for it to follow, a low spiral down for a full sweep of the area without ever coming close enough to be detected. Outside of the desert, visibility improved significantly, and it would only get better as the winds died down.

Meyers waited for McNutt's squad to return, then said, "I know this sounds like a real joke, but keep in mind Reyes's men were intimidated enough by this gang to evict them from Turning Point. Not wipe them out, but send them away. And it sounds like there was an implicit agreement to turn a blind eye if they preyed on the smaller settlements. You don't do something like that unless you're concerned about your enemy."

Zacharowski and Gerhardt still seemed unimpressed. It had always been that way dealing with the Delta operators. Nothing else was allowed to scare them.

The Condor reached its programmed altitude and began its downward spiral, and its imagery feed quickly took on more meaningful value. Meyers overlaid the imagery on top of what Starling had given him.

The facility had changed dramatically.

The main building was lit up like a carnival. Camouflage netting covered what had been a large clearing, maybe a motor pool or some sort of open storage. A large, crude roof connected the main building to two smaller buildings. The Condor's optics were good enough to pick out what might be small vehicles beneath the roof. Everything—vines, scrub, the dark, blue grass native to Bellar—had been cleared back to the edge of the wood.

"What's this?" McNutt highlighted an area west of the compound that looked like a garden, recently tilled.

"Good question." Meyers wished there was more light coming from the main building. Without the Condor's infrared optics, they were left with a lot of guesswork.

Zacharowski highlighted the camouflage netting and the roof addition. "Need to see what's under the hood here."

They did need to know. Normally, specialized snake drones would handle recon of the sort they were looking at, but the only drone that had survived was the Condor.

"No sign of those Zombies, Colonel." Perkins tapped a trail to indicate several dark forms moving around the main building. "I count six. Looks like a pretty good perimeter patrol."

Meyers watched the forms for a while. "Yeah. Not something you'd expect a bunch of psychotic cannibals to handle." He estimated numbers based off the patrol: twenty, conservatively. If the camouflage netting was hiding a ship, it could be big. Big enough for twice as many people.

McNutt sent an enhanced image of the vehicles that were visible beneath the crude roof. "Why the roof?" He traced more details into the enhanced image. "Those are crawlers. Big ones. Look like junk, right? Up-armored junk." He sketched a few more lines until segmented armor became more visible—or believable—in the imagery the Condor was sending. "But this here, looks like extended fuel cell storage."

"Flyers," Meyers said.

"Looks like. Wouldn't've brought that with them, right?"

"Not likely. Looks like the doors are opened up. I wonder why."

"Pilots can get in faster? Dunno." McNutt drew a circle around two more areas, blurry shadows beneath the two vehicles that were most visible. "If they're armored flyers, what d'ya think this is?"

"Shadows?" Gerhardt looked around, but no one laughed.

Perkins enhanced the image, drawing the outline of a barrel. "Belly guns."

A cold chill flared in Meyers's gut. "We need visual confirmation."

McNutt raised a hand. "I'll go."

Zacharowski snorted. "This is Delta work. Colonel, I got it."

"You're not in Delta anymore, Sergeant Zacharowski." Meyers ran his eye over the Cáceres Compound again. He tapped a structure the Condor had identified that hadn't been on the grounds a year before. It was probably four meters on either side and seemed about as high. "There's this shed, too. See the way the perimeter patrol swings wide to pass close to it."

"Ammo dump," McNutt said.

Perkins leaned in, as if he were looking at the image projected on the ground instead of inside his helmet. Music floated out of his open faceplate. "Too close to the main building. If it's got ordnance. Maybe those are railguns and it's all just metal rounds?"

Four areas that needed to be checked, three of them in the path of a patrol of six men. Rimes would have taken the task himself. Meyers reminded himself he wasn't Rimes.

"Sergeant Zacharowski, you and Gerhardt, you think you can get a look under the hood?"

A smile spread across Zacharowski's face. "Easy."

"Corporal McNutt, this garden or whatever. You up for that?"

McNutt nodded. He didn't seem bothered by drawing the easier assignment.

"Sergeant Zacharowski, if you can get a look under that roof without drawing attention, I'd love to know what's in that shed."

Zacharowski smirked, and his eyes twinkled with that annoying cockiness.

Meyers turned to the squads. "So, that's how it is. Numbers. Armaments. We can only estimate the enemy's capabilities, even if this works. Put your BAS into passive mode. I don't want any inadvertent signal leaks. Keep an encrypted laser channel open to the Condor. Line of sight. We'll pull your comms down from there."

McNutt looked skyward. "That'll be a delay, won't it?"

"We don't have a choice. Line-of-sight, encrypted...it's as safe as comms get right now. Private Perkins, I want you on high ground, eyes out for Waverley. If you get a chance to take the shot, do it."

Perkins looked away. Meyers hoped it was to search for a good sniping position.

McNutt pulled Perkins aside for a chat, then headed north, toward the edge of the wood. Zacharowski and Gerhardt were already moving east, positioning themselves closer to their targets before moving north. Meyers waited until the four of them were gone before waving the rest to follow. As he assigned them positions along the edge of the woods, he wondered just what Waverley and the metacorporations were up to. The bad BAS and flight system software, the heavy weapons on Reyes's haulers, the up-armored flyers...

Whatever was going on, he didn't have the firepower to pull off what he'd been assigned to do. More than ever, he was sure that they'd been set up to fail.

14

———

13 December 2174. Cáceres Compound, East of Turning Point, Bellar Frontier Colony.

CORPORAL GERHARDT'S microphone was cranked up to the point that every breath and grunt came through, filling Meyers's audio channel. The camouflage netting shivered in the remaining breeze, teasing a look at whatever was behind it without ever actually revealing anything. Sweat trickled onto his lip, salty. He licked it away and rubbed his elbow where Gerhardt had just banged his own elbow against a buried rock. Gerhardt would barely have felt the impact, but Meyers couldn't help imagining he was there, crawling on his belly across the open field, trying to reach the camouflage net.

Exposed. Vulnerable. Defenseless.

But that was Gerhardt, Meyers reminded himself. Gerhardt was at risk. Meyers thought about that: one of the soldiers under my command, not me.

He shivered and switched to Zacharowski's feed. His audio was quieter, but it wasn't as crisp, even though his video came through clean. He was almost wriggling like a snake through low grass. His path was shorter than Gerhardt's, but it ran closer to the patrol than the others. The flyers were visible in grainy profile from his current position. Perkins's speculation about belly guns was looking more and more likely the closer Zacharowski got.

Meyers switched to McNutt. He was working hard, crawling on forearms and thighs, moving faster than the other two. It made sense, since he was the least likely to be spotted. A short distance from the edge of what looked like tilled soil, he paused and unsheathed his dagger, then he crawled forward again.

"At the edge of the garden," McNutt said. "About six meters north of the road. No sign of sensors. No one's been out here for a while."

The image became grainier as McNutt moved fully into the darkness. He looked to his right, revealed a line of low scrub between him and the main building. He crawled closer to the scrub, then onto the tilled earth. His gloves plunged into the dry dirt, then he inspected them for a moment before digging into the ground with the knife.

Meyers flipped back to Gerhardt's feed. He was frozen, eyes locked on the shoulders of two of the guards, standing fourteen meters away, partially hidden by the camouflage netting. They seemed to be talking.

"Private Perkins, can you get an angle on Corporal Gerhardt?"

After a few seconds, Perkins said, "I see him, Colonel. Two security guards standing just inside—"

"Good. Keep an eye on them. Don't fire without my say."

"Yes, sir."

Seconds ticked by, then the guards disappeared behind the camouflage netting.

"Private Perkins, Gerhardt lost visual on the guards."

"I've got them. They're coming out of the camouflage netting on the far side. Wait a second. They stopped again."

Gerhardt's view shifted right, as if he were rolling onto his shoulder and craning his neck. The guards were nowhere to be seen. Meyers imagined being in that position. The Commandos always cautioned to use patience, to wait for the right time, but Delta's training was—

The view shifted. Gerhardt was crawling forward.

"Private Perkins, can you—"

"They're still in position. If Titan keeps moving, he'll come out right where they can see him."

Meyers muted and let out a string of curses. Titan—Gerhardt's—suit was in passive mode, shut off from the BAS network Meyers had set up for the rest of the ERF team. Even if Gerhardt could receive a message, any transmission so close to the facility would be risky with the BAS likely compromised.

Gerhardt accelerated.

Meyers looked around, desperate for any means of contacting Gerhardt. Short of running across the field to get within whispering range—

The Condor's rangefinder!

Meyers shrank Gerhardt's view and filled the main display with the Condor's interface, and then brought up the optics interface. With most of the sensitive guts in little pieces spread across the desert, the interface only had a few options online. That made it easy getting to the rangefinder. He swiped through the options, selecting ultra-violet pulse and then searching for the interface to the camera system.

It was offline, too.

"Colonel, he's almost to the netting."

"Working on it." Meyers brought up the camera system and derived Gerhardt's coordinates from the Condor's internal positioning system, then he did the same for the edge of the netting. He copied both values into the rangefinder.

"Colonel—"

"Thank you." Meyers split his view, Gerhardt's feed filling the right half, the Condor's feed filling the left.

He activated the rangefinder and the Condor fired off a pulse of UV laser light at the netting coordinates—just as Gerhardt looked off to his right, in Zacharowski's general direction. Gerhardt reached for the netting; Meyers triggered the rangefinder again. This time, the beam showed up on Gerhardt's display, an almost white dot on the back of his hand.

Gerhardt froze. "What the fuck?"

"Come on." Meyers gritted his teeth and willed Gerhardt back.

Nothing.

Meyers fired the pulse again, but he tracked it down Gerhardt's side, back to the original coordinates Meyers had copied into the rangefinder. Gerhardt's view captured the rangefinder's movement. He was watching it, but he didn't move otherwise.

"Anybody seeing this?" Gerhardt asked.

Meyers repeated the pulse.

"Colonel, I think something's up." Perkins's voice was loud. "They're moving toward Titan's position."

"Okay."

Meyers fired off the pulse again and closed his eyes. Gerhardt wasn't getting the message, but what Meyers was doing was pretty close to the Concord's limits. No, he realized, there was more that could be done.

He went back into the optics, found his own coordinates, and copied those into the rangefinder, then fired off a pulse that ran from Gerhardt's hand, along his side, across the open field, and into the tree line. Gerhardt's view showed him twisting around to follow the pulse, then looking back at the netting.

"Is that you guys?" Gerhardt pulled his hand away from the netting and slowly reversed back into the open field.

"They're at the netting, Colonel." Perkins swallowed hard. "Do—do you want me to take a shot?"

Gerhardt's view was focused on the netting. When the security guards came around the edge, his view shifted to the ground.

"Hold fire. What are they doing?"

"Looking out into the field. Shit, they looked right at Titan."

"Did they see him?"

Perkins whistled. "Negative, Colonel. They're walking away."

Meyers nodded. "Thank you."

Meyers waited until Gerhardt looked up again, then reversed the rangefinder burst to move toward the netting. This time, Gerhardt understood immediately; he crawled toward the netting. After looking around, as if searching for the rangefinder, he pulled back the netting and looked.

Lights reflected off the hull of a ship as big as the yacht Meyers had seen on Sahara. Bigger, Meyers thought. It could hold thirty or more, depending on how uncomfortable people were willing to live.

Waverley's security force, Meyers thought.

He switched to Zacharowski's view. The image was inconsistent—one moment clear, the next choppy. He was moving beneath the roof, crawling under the bellies of the flyers. In some of the images that came through, the armor and belly guns on the flyers were clear. Most appeared to be machine guns, but Meyers thought he saw a railgun on the largest of the flyers. It wasn't a very practical weapon on a flyer unless there were dedicated batteries in the extra space, and even then, the gun would chew through power quickly.

For show, Meyers thought. Or to punch through armor the lighter machine guns couldn't handle. No matter what, it had limited application.

One vehicle stood out from the others—larger, lower to the ground, with heavier armor. Its doors were closed. From what Meyers could see of it, he thought it was a small hauler rather than a flyer. It seemed even more limited in use than the large flyer.

Zacharowski crawled clear of the roof and held up eight fingers. "If you're listening, eight flyers, seven with light machine guns, one with a pretty hefty railgun. And a big-ass crawler or small hauler. Like an armored security car. They're all up-armored. Mostly ablative plex-armor. Good enough to stop what we've got. For a bit."

Eight flyers. One with a railgun, seven with light machine guns. Up close, the flyers looked even uglier, as if they'd been sitting in a junk heap for a while or had been scavenged from parts.

Up-armored and burdened with guns and ammunition, their range would be reduced. Zacharowski's images at least gave them a starting point to make estimates on threat level.

Meyers switched back to McNutt's feed in time to hear him snort. "Well, Zombie mystery solved." He tugged something out of the hole he'd dug with his knife: a pale, beefy hand with modified nails—thick and pointy like claws. "Smells like they've been dead for a bit." He released the hand and scooped dirt back into the hole. "A garden this size, you could easily plant a hundred Zombies."

McNutt's view spun right abruptly, and Meyers caught lights sweeping over the top of the crude roof where Zacharowski was checking out the flyers.

"Something on the east side of the facility," McNutt said. "Lights moving."

"Private Perkins, we've got something on the east side of the facility. Lights, something—"

"I see the lights, Colonel. There's something out there, but it's...it's projecting something that's flooding my scope. I think it's UV."

"UV?"

"It must be. Trying thermographic imaging."

Meyers switched to Gerhardt's view. He was looking east as well, and he was close enough to pick out more details. Whatever the lights were attached to, it was moving, and its top rose above the roof.

Meyers repeated the rangefinder pulse for Gerhardt, running it from his position back to the trees.

"Heading back," Gerhardt said. He turned and crawled toward the open field.

Gerhardt passed through an area bathed in reflected light from the research facility's exterior floods. He moved much slower and more cautious than before, or at least it seemed to Meyers's eyes.

"I don't know if you can hear me, but sons of bitches got machine guns. Heavy ones. Automated. I saw two under the netting." Gerhardt's voice was shaky. "Covering this field. Fuck!"

Machine guns. Probably tied to sensors. Meyers wondered what sort of sensors and how far out they covered. Not good enough to catch the intrusion so far.

When Gerhardt was deep in the shadows again, Meyers switched to the Condor's feed. The east side of the facility was darker than the rest, the only light coming from the research facility. And the shed. The door had been rolled up at some point.

"Private Perkins?"

"I'm pretty sure there's something moving down there, sir, something big, but it must have some pretty good thermo-baffles. I can make out a vague shape sometimes, but that's it."

Thermo-baffles. Big. Not something they were armed to deal with.

Meyers went back into the Condor's optics interface and searched for Zacharowski. He was out of sight, no longer transmitting, somewhere under the roof again. Meyers spent a second considering whether to run a rangefinder burst from the edge of the roof to the trees, but couldn't see how that would help. On top of that, Zacharowski was far enough under the roof that he couldn't be seen by the Condor, so the odds of him seeing the laser pulse were negligible.

Meyers switched to McNutt's position and copied the coordinates over Gerhardt's, then ran a pulse from McNutt to the tree line.

"Was that you, Colonel?" McNutt looked skyward. "Something's going on at Zacharowski's position. Gonna check it out."

"No!" Meyers repeated the rangefinder pulse.

McNutt froze. "That's got to be you, Colonel. Repeat it again if you're ordering me back; otherwise, I'm checking on Zacharowski."

Meyers repeated the pulse.

"Yeah, I get it." McNutt headed for the trees.

Meyers filled his display with the Condor's video and tried to bring up a smaller window with Zacharowski's feed. The image came through choppy, the audio slightly better. He was somewhere under the roof, but close enough to the edge or a gap that his signal was getting through.

"You're gonna love this one, Colonel." Zacharowski held a hand up, but before Meyers could make out what was in the hand, the signal cut out.

Meyers went into the optics interface and took the coordinates for the southwestern corner of the roof. He pasted that into the rangefinder and prepared to fire a pulse from the roof to the woods, but at the last second, he stopped.

Something taller than the roof, capable of moving up near the flyers without Zacharowski hearing its approach and flooding UV and defeating thermographic optics. That sounded like the sort of thing that would probably be able to see UV laser pulses.

Zacharowski's feed kicked back in. He was holding a brick of plastique. "—small case of this. Probably enough to take out this little fleet. What do you say, Colonel?"

"Get out of there," Meyers whispered. "Move, dammit."

Zacharowski stuck a detonator into the brick. "Little surprise for our friends, huh? I know you'd want me to. Just like this." He held the brick up so the detonator was visible, then dropped it into a satchel filled with more bricks, all of them blinking. "I think they were making improvised explosives. Maybe for us."

Floodlights washed over the hoods and roofs of the flyers, and Zacharowski's video feed caught the thing. It stood three and a half meters high and was half as wide at the shoulders, then tapered down to maybe a meter at the midsection. It had two arms and legs, and was blockish, with exaggerated human dimensions. The arms ended in human-like hands. Instead of a head, it had a bump with mounted floodlights and what were probably UV projectors. Mounted below the right arm was a heavy machine gun, complete with large ammunition drum.

"Fuck me," Zacharowski whispered.

Meyers nodded. They were all fucked.

15

———

13 December 2174. Cáceres Compound, East of Turning Point, Bellar Frontier Colony.

MEYERS'S WORLD was static and hiss, indecision and fear. Zacharowski's feed was gone, cut off. Meyers switched to the Condor's view. Wind brushed the tips of the low grass, more static, this time moonlight gray. McNutt and Gerhardt were black specks among the gray outlines of dark blue, visible only because he knew what to look for.

"Private Perkins, I've lost connection to Zacharowski." Meyers switched to McNutt's view, instantly falling into his world, blinking, disoriented, then rocking slightly in time with McNutt's crawling motion. He was moving quicker than Gerhardt, who seemed to have switched to an even slower pace.

"He's under one of the flyers, Colonel," Perkins said. "That thing, I can see it."

"It's a proxy. I think a mining chassis. Modified." Probably built by another of SunCorps' hundreds of corporations, Meyers thought.

"Well, it's moving along the eastern edge of the covered area."

"Looking for Zacharowski. How's he squeezing under a flyer?"

"There's, uh…" Perkins swallowed. "There's a big one, and the gun's pointed out the back. There's people coming. The guards."

From bad to worse.

McNutt's audio—mostly his steady breathing up to that point—hissed to life. "Colonel, if you're listening, looks like Gerhardt might be wounded. He's moving slow." McNutt's view raised above the low grass, and Gerhardt's slow progress across the field became apparent from a side view. "Didn't hear any weapons fire earlier."

Meyers squeezed his eyes shut, but he couldn't stop imagining the automated machine guns. "Get your head down."

"Feeling all alone out here," McNutt said.

Meyers started to switch to Gerhardt's channel but stopped.

McNutt had stopped. His head was down again, swiveling toward Gerhardt, then looking down. "If I should be moving slower, how about a signal?"

Meyers accessed the Condor's optics system, swiping and poking so fast he missed his target. He pulled up McNutt's coordinates, then he copied and pasted them into the rangefinder. A distant groaning sound came over the audio feed.

"Colonel?" Perkins's voice was raised, tense. "That thing's tearing the roof off."

Meyers triggered the rangefinder. It pulsed white in front of McNutt.

"Perkins, any clear shots on that proxy? Antenna, video, sensor array—anything?"

"Negative. The guards are fanning out."

Meyers switched back to Zacharowski's view.

"—ucking all over the place." Zacharowski sounded cool, but it came across as a disciplined, false calm. He was looking up at the interior of a gull-wing door. The armor—clear, probably fifteen or more millimeters thick—stretched beyond the edges of the door. There were gaps on the chassis where the armor would fit when the door was pulled back down. "I've got an idea."

"Perkins, what about the guards?" Meyers couldn't see anything other than the flyer through Zacharowski's view.

"Six right now, but it looks like…" Perkins sucked in air. "More exiting the main building, sir."

"Send me your scope's video."

Six guards, more coming. With its gun and armor, the proxy would have been enough. From the quick look Meyers had gotten through Zacharowski's camera, it didn't look like something the CAWS-5s would be able to damage. Maybe sniper rounds could, but those were at a premium after One-Six-Three went down. Zacharowski could surrender and risk immediate execution or torture followed by execution. Or maybe Waverley would keep Zacharowski as a hostage. What mattered was that any doubt the ERF were on-planet would be gone. Charging the compound wouldn't change a thing.

Zacharowski pulled himself up and slowly crawled into the flyer. Perkins's scope video popped open in a corner of Meyers's display. He expanded it to fill the top third of the view, then half when Zacharowski's signal cut out again.

He was inside the flyer, his signal blocked.

The proxy moved around the edge of the lot, pausing to wait for the guards to get out of its path, then moving along the north side. It was ducking, looking beneath the flyers, moving with remarkable agility for something so big. Whoever was running it was very comfortable with its interface.

The guards fell back, giving the proxy more room and spreading into a semicircle. They had assault weapons, the same base design as Reyes's tricked-out submachine guns. Meyers finally realized where he'd seen them before: Tholen Armaments, a specialty arms manufacturer owned by EuroSekur, one of SunCorps' corporations.

EuroSekur. Tholen Armaments. Waverley's connection—or at least SunCorps' connection—to Reyes was becoming more obvious.

Zacharowski's video feed flickered back to life. He was lying down in the flyer, looking up at a panel that had been pried open. A circuit card dangled through the opening. The flyer's interior glowed dimly, the electronics displays kicking on but staying low. The flyer's roof opened, a dull, barely audible hum over Zacharowski's audio channel. Shouting, the whir and whine of the proxy's movement—Zacharowski had his faceplate up and microphone at full sensitivity. The outside noise quieted as Zacharowski's faceplate closed. Zacharowski patted something hidden in the shadows beneath the console.

The satchel full of explosives, Meyers realized.

"This is how it's going to go," Zacharowski said. "I hope you're hearing me. This won't make sense otherwise. Fuck. Never should have agreed to go in without comms. I ought to—" He reached toward his chest.

Don't do it, Meyers thought. Waverley's security team had to be monitoring the flyers now. Turn on the BAS's active systems, and they would have his location nailed down in seconds, with or without proper functioning systems software.

Zacharowski lowered his hand, then he slowly started sliding into the pilot's seat. "I'm taking this little baby to town. It's fully charged, the railgun's loaded. I'll get out about halfway to town and turn my BAS back on. This satchel? I'm tossing it out the roof. Good-bye, flyers."

Meyers looked up at Perkins's scope display. The proxy was at the west end of the lot now, looking down the length of the cleared area, shifting north, then shifting south, probably watching for a leg or arm sticking out.

The proxy froze.

"C'mon, c'mon. Get out of there."

Zacharowski was now looking through the front windshield. The plexarmor created a slight distortion, worsened by the proxy's bright lights, which were shining through the windshields of the flyer between him and the proxy.

"Oh, fuck," Zacharowski said.

He'd noticed the proxy's change in behavior. His hands flew across the console, which lit up fully. Control panels popped to life on the flat plastic. The doors dropped, and he turned as the security guards ran south, weaving between the flyers, stopping once they were in the field, then opening fire. Their bullets scuffed and cracked the armor, but nothing penetrated. The fans beneath the chassis roared to life, and the flyer rocked beneath Zacharowski slightly. As he swiped through the navigation system, the proxy crab-stepped back and to the south, just off the path that ran to the road. More importantly, Meyers realized that the proxy was clear of the lot.

Meyers found himself mirroring Zacharowski's moves—swiping the map, tapping the center of Turning Point, fast-tapping the liftoff sequence once the miniature gravitic drive came online, craning his neck to get a look at the proxy.

The flyer kicked suddenly, the fans pushing up with the vehicle's mass no longer working against them. Meyers and Zacharowski both grabbed the controls and thrust forward.

The explosives had been forgotten.

Gunfire—distant, dull—came through Zacharowski's audio, and light showed through the bottom of the flyer. Zacharowski looked down. His right thigh had a palm-sized hole in it; light, coming from the floor beneath, showed through muscle and shattered bone.

The proxy's lights.

Zacharowski gasped. "Okay, okay."

Then he turned his attention to the controls, which seemed to have a mind of their own, hauling hard to the left.

Meyers grunted. The fans. Bullets punching through the floor. They'd go through the fans first. "Hang in there, Ski. You can do this."

Zacharowski scanned the console. He was twenty-three meters up, but losing altitude, sixteen meters west of the other flyers, but drifting south.

Toward McNutt and Gerhardt. And the trees.

The controls stabilized, and Zacharowski got the flyer back on track, heading west. More gunfire, armor and plastic shattering, the sound as if they were a million kilometers away. The console blinked out, then it cycled from a black, dead display to static, before settling on a series of amber and red warnings that twisted and flickered. The chassis seemed to vibrate, and Meyers picked out a slight grinding sound beneath Zacharowski's labored breathing.

"Goddammit!" Zacharowski slapped the console, then he reached down and pulled the satchel onto the seat beside him. He poked a gloved finger through a hole torn by one of the rounds. "Must be depleted uranium or something, punching through like I'm in paper—"

The display and audio feed went dead for a second, then came back. The front windshield was shattered, covered in gore. Zacharowski looked down. There were two holes in his chest. Fist-sized. A piece of a rib poked out through the larger of the holes, dangling something—flesh, muscle, guts.

Zacharowski wasn't breathing now so much as sucking in shallow, wet gasps.

Meyers checked Perkins's scope display. The guards were running after the flyer, a string of maybe fifteen men stretched from the side of the main building to about half the distance of the camouflage netting. The proxy, its front lit by the machine gun muzzle flash, had taken several steps and was now halfway between the front of the main building and the netting.

There was no way the automated machine guns could fire. He opened the channel to the rest of the team.

"Fall back to the Rovers. Now."

Then he closed Perkins's scope video feed and ran into the field. Hunched low, weaving as much as he could, angling for an imaginary midpoint between McNutt and Gerhardt. Waving. Trying not to show up on whatever sensors Waverley's team had put up, but trying just as hard to gain McNutt and Gerhardt's attention.

"F-f-fuck this," Zacharowski said, or at least it sounded like what he was trying to say. His right hand hooked the straps of the satchel, and he pulled it onto his good leg. He swiped at something.

The detonator controls, Meyers realized.

McNutt rose up and ran toward Meyers. A second later, Gerhardt followed. Meyers turned and ran for the tree line. They were hunched low, like him.

McNutt opened a channel. "What's going on, Colonel?"

Meyers glanced at Zacharowski's feed in time to see the flyer plow into the ground. Zacharowski let out a weak groan, then the flyer's console went dead.

An explosion popped in Meyers's earpiece a millisecond before he heard it in the air around him. He spun around and saw pieces of the flyer tumbling through the air. Little tongues of flame crawled around the twisted pieces of what remained of the flyer's frame, now spread wide across Cáceres Road. The security guards were shadow silhouettes, most still lying on the ground, some slowly levering themselves up. The race with the flyer was over.

Meyers dove in among the trees and turned back to watch. McNutt dropped to the ground at Meyers's left, Gerhardt at the right.

"Was that Zacharowski?" McNutt asked.

"Yeah." Meyers felt numb.

The proxy advanced toward the smoking debris. There was still no indication the sensors had ever picked anyone else up.

Gerhardt pulled out his CAWS-5 and got up into a crouch. "What the hell happened?"

"I don't know," Meyers said. "That shed. There was a proxy in it. Some sort of combat version, a modified mining or construction model, I think."

Gerhardt leaned forward. He seemed on the edge of running back toward the facility. "How the hell did they spot him?"

"I don't know. It could've been pure luck." Bad luck.

Gerhardt spun around. "Why didn't you pull him out?"

"He was under the roof. I couldn't use the laser to get his attention." The Condor. Meyers brought up the command console and ordered it to head back to its launch point.

"We can't leave him out there." Gerhardt swayed back and forth.

"Not much left of him," McNutt said. "Not normal, that sort of explosion."

It was a neutral tone, and his eyes were locked onto the wreckage, but Meyers caught Gerhardt glaring, lips peeled back.

"He had a satchel full of explosives in his lap," Meyers said. "Corporal Gerhardt, he knew what he was doing. The only chance he had was to get out of there in that flyer. It just didn't work out."

"The only chance..." Gerhardt lowered his head. "You sent us out there with no communications. You could have gotten us all killed."

McNutt finally looked at Gerhardt. "We didn't sign on for the beer and sunbathing, did we? It's a bit of a thrill ride. Ski just punched his ticket today, that's all. Could happen to any of us, any day."

Gerhardt looked back toward the research facility.

"Let it go." McNutt jerked his head back toward where they'd left the Rovers. "You've got a squad to run now. You want to show Ski some respect, make sure the rest of his team goes home alive."

Meyers gave Gerhardt a few more seconds to cool down, then said, "They're waiting for us."

They headed back to the Rovers. During the entire drive back to the camp, Meyers replayed the recon operation through his mind, trying to figure out how Zacharowski had been discovered by the proxy while McNutt and Gerhardt slipped through the security perimeter unnoticed. There was something important in that, Meyers was sure, but he couldn't figure out what. It was one more mystery that had to be solved, and they were running out of time to solve them.

16

———

13 December 2174. Karpov Desert, South of Turning Point, Bellar Frontier Colony.

No matter how hard Meyers stared at the displays on the Operations Center walls, the details from the Condor's surveillance never improved. Everything—the cargo cases, his armor, the walls—was washed a dull, blue-gray from the displays' output. The silence inside the structure was broken by boots scraping on sand as someone entered, carrying in their wake a bit of the chilly wind blowing through the camp. Meyers imagined the air was just a little bit cleaner as a result. He wanted to walk in that wind, to let it cool him and carry away his guilt and confusion.

"Find what you're looking for, Colonel?" Paxton's tone was calm, neutral, absent any hint of judgment.

"Not yet." Meyers wasn't sure what he was looking for. Forgiveness? Justification? Understanding?

He blew out air that smelled like death, and then he blinked and stared harder. Enhanced with overlays from Perkins's sniper scope and McNutt, Gerhardt, and Zacharowski's feeds, they had a more accurate three-dimensional model of the compound, but it wasn't worth the loss of a soldier.

Nothing ever was.

Meyers wondered how Rimes had managed to stay sane after losing so many during the Metacorporate War. Some would have argued he hadn't stayed sane, but Meyers now understood the sort of pain that must have driven Rimes. He'd been sane. In retrospect, his decisions had been the only sane solution possible.

"How's Gerhardt?" Meyers didn't turn from the display.

"Pissed off. Had a little incident. We came to an understanding."

Meyers knew better than to ask for details. "They're definitely in with Waverley."

"SunCorps? You really thought they'd just give up the most powerful man in the…?" Paxton snorted. "Whatever we are now."

"I thought the Special Security Council—"

"Ah, hell, Colonel. It's all they can do not to piss themselves talking to SunCorps. No one wants another war. Talk big all you want, but we're all they got, and we got the shit kicked out of us last time around. Weren't for greed and turning on each other, they could've wiped us out."

Meyers finally turned from the displays. "We were wearing them down."

"Can't wear down a metacorporation. They went months surviving on nothing but sales to the colonies and each other before they attacked. They gave up billions in revenue, all to punish Earth economically. Because they could. Sure, they lost twenty, thirty people for every one of us they killed, but they could afford to." Paxton sighed and sidled up to the display. "You're a smart man, sir. Educated. You already knew all that. Just like you knew you'd lose people on this mission."

Casualties are a part of war. Meyers had told himself that too many times to count. It was something he'd learned long ago, when he was just an infantry private fresh out of training.

Paxton flicked a glance at Meyers. "You just got to accept it."

Meyers walked to the opposite wall. Slow. Deliberate.

Paxton turned and said, "Gun emplacements that don't open fire. Explosives stuffed in with a bunch of vehicles. Sloppy security, sir."

"Very." Meyers rubbed his hands together, now cold. "You can be sloppy with…"

"Superiority, yeah. So, you think this was just arrogance?"

"No." Looking back on it, the gun placement seemed more a matter of tight focus. Or bad planning. "I think they've got their priorities: protect their yacht and their fleet of makeshift assault craft. But there's more to it. There has to be."

"Maybe we weren't what they were looking for."

"You think they were watching for Zombies?"

Paxton tapped his nose. "And things like that."

Meyers returned to the display and pulled the view back. The gun emplacements covered the west and south. Nothing to the north or east. The shed held the proxy, and it had somehow been triggered by Zacharowski's approach or presence. Or maybe McNutt or Gerhardt's actions. Gerhardt had actually touched the camouflage netting. He'd been in close to the gun emplacements.

"So, limited resources, just those two machine guns, perimeter sensors that give them a look over a small arc and distance, probably a limited set of parameters—motion. Big motion. Numbers, people standing upright." Meyers rubbed his thumbs against his forefingers. "Those are rebuilt flyers, probably reclaimed from junk heaps. I'm surprised they had so many in a place like Turning Point."

"Who said they're from Turning Point?"

Meyers thought about that for a moment. "Okay, so maybe somewhere else on-planet. That's still a lot of flyers for a population of, what, a hundred thousand? But the guns, those had to come from off-world."

"Same as the guns Reyes has on his haulers."

Meyers tried to remember how far back Beniam said Reyes had gotten the guns. It sounded like about the same time frame as Waverley becoming a fugitive. "Okay. Gun shipments come to Bellar ahead of Waverley's arrival. He packs the yacht full of twenty to thirty security and support people and that proxy. That leaves room for food, ammunition, weapons, and gear. Not a lot more than that. Not for someone who's used to a life of luxury."

"Want me to get Agent Barlowe and Private Starling?"

"Let them sleep. They need it. And we'll need them. Bring McNutt and Banh in."

"Not Corporal Gerhardt?"

"We can't risk leaving the camp unprotected."

Paxton turned his head to look at Meyers. "You got something in mind already?"

"I don't think waiting works to our advantage. It'll make it feel like we failed, and we're afraid." Meyers watched Paxton for a reaction. The leathery face was still, almost impossible to read, but there seemed to be the slightest hint of approval in his eyes.

Paxton looked away. "Corporal McNutt, Sergeant Banh, report to the Operations Center. Sergeant Banh, have Corporal Gerhardt's squad replace yours on perimeter." Paxton turned his attention back to the display. "They're on their way, sir."

"You're not sold on acting right now?"

"I guess I'm concerned about not knowing enough about the enemy."

"I'm not talking about an assault."

"You think a sustained assault would win through, sir? If we did go that way."

"Well, if we had something that could take down that proxy and keep those flyers off of us, sure. We could flank way around to the east, get up on the north side, send the bulk of the force in from there, where they don't have any defenses, keep a modest-sized group in the woods to the south where we were last night. Yeah. But we don't have anything that can handle that proxy. Not until we get the Javelins operational again."

Paxton cocked an eyebrow curiously.

"Barlowe said he can get our BAS rebuilds done quicker, and that's a couple days out."

"You sure we're compromised, Colonel?"

Meyers thought about it for a moment. "Yeah, we're compromised. We have to be. Waverley's team didn't pick up on the BAS because Zacharowski and the others were in passive mode. If Waverley could pick up our location, I don't think I'd be here right now. They would've come at us with the flyers while we were in the woods or on the drive back."

"So they aren't two steps ahead of us."

"Maybe a half."

Meyers rotated the view of the Cáceres Compound, marked the gun emplacements and fields of fire, and then marked the paths taken by McNutt, Gerhardt, and Zacharowski. After considering the sequence of events, it seemed obvious what the likely sensor positions and coverage would be.

Crunching sand announced McNutt's arrival. He yawned as he pulled his helmet off, then came to a stop in front of one of the cargo cases. "Something up, Colonel?"

"Not yet. I wanted you and Sergeant Banh in on our discussions."

McNutt stared at the display for several seconds. "Thinking about hitting the compound?"

"We'll have to do something eventually."

Banh stepped through the doorway and pulled his helmet off. A fine rain of sand fell from the creases of his armor. "Colonel?"

"Thank you for joining us, Sergeant." Meyers waved Banh forward.

So close, Banh smelled like recycled air, his own body odor and breath, filtered. His armor radiated coolness, but with his helmet off, there was heat bleeding off as well.

"That is the research compound?" Banh pointed at the displays.

"Yes."

Banh nodded—rapid, energetic—and his eyes rapidly blinked.

Paxton tilted his head toward the display. "The colonel's been describing what he thinks is going on with this Waverley. I think he's got an idea about our next step but wants your thoughts about it."

McNutt cocked a thick eyebrow. "What about Corporal Gerhardt?"

Paxton crossed his arms. "I want him focused on camp security."

That seemed enough to satisfy McNutt, if not to convince him. He jerked a thumb at the display. "You put all this together from the video feeds?"

"And some guesswork." Meyers wished he could project more confidence.

"These things here, they are gun emplacements, Colonel?" Banh ran a finger over the arcs indicating fields of fire and the circles around the machine guns. "Just these two?"

"That's all Gerhardt saw."

Banh closed his eyes and bowed his head, then he looked at McNutt and Paxton. "Nothing protecting the north? This is their security?"

"That and a proxy." Meyers circled the shed to the east. "I think it's a mining model, with a heavy machine gun mounted. No way to be sure, but it looks like it's being kept in this shed. Plus twenty to thirty security specialists."

McNutt snorted. "Not top-shelf ones, either."

Paxton leaned forward until he was inches from McNutt's face. "A twelve-year-old kid can fire a gun well enough to kill the best-trained soldier, Corporal."

"I like my chances against that kid and these rent-a-soldiers about the same."

"Okay." Meyers shifted and paced anxiously. "We're talking about how they got to this point. Rent-a-soldiers, just two machine guns, sensors that didn't detect the three of you crawling in."

Banh looked at Meyers, eyes wide and staring intensely. McNutt shrugged, noncommittal.

"What would you think about this: Waverley comes here knowing the board of directors is going to sell him out." Meyers sucked in his breath. That seemed less likely with each discovery and inference he made. "No. Scratch that. Let's assume he's made an agreement with the board. It's not selling him out at all. It's a…high-risk set-up. Most of these directors are on other metacorporate or corporate boards or they're retired senior executives with huge stakes in the metacorporations."

"Colonel?" Banh raised a hand. "Then you are saying that the United Nations told this Waverley we were coming? Is that right?"

"Not directly. But SunCorps could have someone on the inside. It wouldn't be the first time."

"Thank you, sir."

"So, Waverley's the lure. Satisfy the United Nations, let them send the ERF in to kill him, cooperate, and provide upgrades. Smile and shake hands and talk about peace."

"And this is SunCorps now, Colonel?" Banh's brow was wrinkled in concentration. "They are the ones smiling and shaking hands?"

"Yes. And they're talking with the SSC. The Special Security Council."

"Thank you, sir."

Paxton cleared his throat. "Colonel, this is what we assume or what we know?"

Meyers smiled. "Good point. Let's stick with assume. Waverley starts shipping weapons ahead of his departure. Off the books, or at least not through legitimate channels. He secures that yacht, hand-picks his team and gear. Maybe he ships more gear along with the weapons."

"Gear?" McNutt cocked his head. "Sensors and such?"

"Exactly. He—Waverley—reaches out to the locals, finds out about this old compound."

"The locals," Banh said. "Reyes?"

"Governor Weidmann, I guess." Meyers couldn't see Reyes having enough control of everything that would be needed to sneak weapons shipments in. It didn't even seem likely he could cooperate fully with Waverley. "Let's assume Weidmann for now. So Weidmann tells Waverley about the compound, and Waverley figures that's the perfect place to hole up and wait for the assassins. Us."

McNutt snorted. "Did a piss-poor job planning, if that's what he did."

Meyers shook his head. "No. Something went wrong. The weapons and sensors weren't waiting for him. He has to work with what he brought with him."

"Reyes?" McNutt scratched at a chest pocket. "Double-crossed him?"

"I can't see that. I have a hard time even seeing Waverley trying to cut a deal with—" Meyers snapped his fingers. "The barges."

Paxton's face creased in confusion.

"Barges, Colonel?" Banh seemed as confused as Paxton.

"Yeah," McNutt said. "Waverley's not working with Reyes at all, then? He's working with Weidmann? The governor?"

"Or at least someone high enough up in power to make promises and push things through." Meyers opened a view of Turning Point and drilled down to the docks where the barges were tied off. "And Reyes either lucks into the weapons when he seizes food, or he's got his own special someone in Ardennen."

Banh held up a hand. "Then Reyes does not know about Waverley, Colonel?"

Meyers tried imagining Reyes being completely oblivious to Waverley's presence. It would be like an apex predator not sensing another apex predator in its territory, unlikely for any length of time. "I think he probably knows about Waverley at some level. He acted like he didn't know anything about him when I asked for help, but it was all show. I think they've had at least enough of an interaction for the two of them to form...mutual respect. Waverley wiped out most of the Zombies. He has the proxy. I don't think either one has enough to take out the other, but they both have something the other wants."

"Well, that's a sweet mess of shit," McNutt said.

"It is." The more Meyers thought about it, the more it made sense. "I don't think Waverley would willingly give so much firepower to someone he didn't have control over, and I think we've seen now that Reyes isn't someone you control."

McNutt sneered. "More like a mad dog needs put down."

Meyers switched his attention back to the compound. The weak security made more sense if someone intercepted some of the intended gear. Better sensors, the armored bubble turrets...Waverley would have been equipped to slaughter the ERF, even if they hadn't lost a third of their people during descent.

But even without sensors, someone had triggered something that brought the proxy into play. That meant something was working; the defenses weren't completely ineffectual. And for the proxy to have responded so quickly, the operator had to either be staying plugged in most of the time or be near the control rig. Taking the proxy down would weaken Waverley, probably even more than wiping out the flyers. The up-armor wouldn't protect the flight controls and fans from CAWS-5 fire, so their threat didn't match what the proxy presented.

"So, Waverley's a lot less protected than we thought," Meyers said.

Paxton glanced toward Banh and McNutt. "Still assuming, Colonel?"

"Yes. And I'm not ready to gamble everything on that assumption. For all we know, he could be planning to attack the camp at sunrise, and he could take the Javelins out, even if we tried to launch them. But I don't think that's the case. I don't think the plan Waverley and SunCorps had in place quite panned out, or we would already be dead. In fact, I don't think he even knows we're here yet."

McNutt stiffened. "They've got Ski's body."

"As big as that explosion was, I don't think they'll be able to put anything more together than some pieces of armor. Maybe. I'm betting they're more suspicious of Reyes than the ERF at the moment."

"What about imagery, Colonel?" The way Banh sounded, he seemed to be asking himself the question as much as Meyers. "Or do you not think they have cameras?"

"I don't think they got a look at anyone who went in. The problem is, everything we talk about right now is conjecture. We need to develop hard data, and the only way we can do that is by—"

McNutt pivoted. "You want to go out there again?"

"You have any other ideas?" Meyers looked from McNutt to Banh, and then to Paxton. "Any of you? Because the way I see it, we have a narrow window to act, and that window keeps shrinking. So either we take this opportunity to see what's going on inside that compound, or we wait for Waverley to figure out we're here and deal with what he sends our way. I don't know about you, but I'd rather be the one taking the chance, acting instead of reacting."

He waited, but no one said anything.

"All right. Then here's what we do."

17

——————

14 December 2174. Cáceres Compound, East of Turning Point, Bellar
Frontier Colony.

MEYERS ROLLED a stim across his tongue, letting the metallic bitterness
draw out saliva until he couldn't stand it any longer. He swallowed and took
a pull from his water bottle. To his right, Paxton gave a questioning look,
then he turned his eyes toward the compound again. It was almost cold
now, but the winds from earlier were a gentle breeze, not enough to move
the wispy grass of the field between them and the main building. According
to Meyers's system, they had just over two hours until sunrise.

He turned to his left. "Sergeant Banh, thoughts?"

"I would like to check security to the east and north, Colonel. I worry
they might have something we are not seeing."

From the tree line south of the compound, the east was just more open
field that turned into light woods several hundred meters beyond the main
building. The trees—small, low—were black shapes in the midnight blue
of pre-dawn. Work lamps had been driven into the ground every few
meters from the western edge of the camouflage netting covering the yacht

to the point where Cáceres Road turned into a dirt trail, about 160 meters west. The lamps gave off circles of silvery light that overlapped. Two of Waverley's security team patrolled that path, black figures walking east to west, weapon at the ready, then spinning at the edge of the light and returning east.

"Stay in the woods until you're opposite our position. You need to be back here in ninety minutes. If you want to move in close, you have to put the BAS into passive mode."

Banh closed his eyes, then he opened them and nodded. "I can do this, Colonel." He crawled back from his position and disappeared into the woods to the south.

Paxton watched the woods over his shoulder for a moment. "He a good scout?"

"A better medic, but good enough. He survived the attack on Plymouth and the campaign on Roarke. Rimes trusted him. I trust him."

Paxton grunted, apparently satisfied. "What're we looking for?"

Meyers squinted as he scanned the compound. "Honestly, Carl, I don't know."

An uncomfortable silence settled, and Meyers turned to see that Paxton was glaring, his face twisted—sour, disapproving. To Paxton's right, McNutt was scanning the compound, absorbed.

Meyers sighed. "Corporal McNutt, you didn't just hear me refer to Master Sergeant Paxton as if he were a peer."

"Don't have to tell me, Colonel." McNutt never took his eyes from the compound.

The sour look on Paxton's face didn't go away. "It's about the discipline and morale, sir."

"I understand. Losing nearly a third of our forces and vital supplies because of budget cuts and sabotage—that doesn't impact morale and discipline. Having our supposed allies feed us patently false data—that doesn't impact morale and discipline. It's all about whether or not we address each other appropriately."

Paxton shook his head and turned his attention to the compound.

"Shit." Meyers rested his face in his hands. "Sorry. I'm way out of line."

"Don't know there's a line right now," McNutt said. "Like you said, Colonel, we don't know who we can trust but each other."

Trusting each other seemed to be a challenge for some of the team, Meyers thought. He turned his attention back to the compound. "Looks like they've increased the patrol."

"Temporary. Rent-a-soldiers like those, discipline breaks down quick if they're pushed too hard." McNutt pointed to the spot where the Cáceres Road became a dirt path coming east into the compound, not far from where Zacharowski's flyer had crashed. Earth had been visibly turned over there. "Looks like they just buried the debris."

Paxton squinted. "Or they left some surprises for future visitors."

McNutt scratched his neck. "IEDs, you think?"

"It's what I'd do. Just a few. Don't need much."

Meyers hadn't considered that possibility. Zacharowski had guessed Waverley's people had been trying to rig bombs with the explosives. If they had more, mining the road would make sense.

"Don't think I'd use the same route twice, personally," McNutt said after a moment. "But maybe that says all you need to know about the security team. Assuming they really think it was Reyes."

Meyers had been lowering his faceplate; he stopped. "You don't think they're worried about Reyes?"

"Makes sense." McNutt seemed to stare off into the distance for a second, as if he might be seeing a different reality. "But I'm thinking this Waverley and Reyes, they're two of the same kind. Been living as big boys on top of the hill for a long time, right? They see everyone as a threat. Maybe they aren't at each other's throats just yet."

"So, Waverley doesn't think this was Reyes?" Meyers thought about that. "Someone from Ardennen?"

"Could be. Lancers, like Reyes mentioned." McNutt looked back into the trees to the south. "Could be Zombies. Even with that proxy, what're the odds he got them all? We ran into a handful. You think that's all there is?"

"A Zombie who stole a flyer and explosives?" Meyers wanted to believe they still had a chance at operating without Waverley knowing the ERF was onto him, but McNutt's Zombie idea seemed hard to swallow.

"Just because they're drugged and cut up don't mean they can't think.

We had gangs like that, domestic terrorists. Took a lot of hostages in Auckland once. Desperate, brutal, but I wouldn't underestimate them."

"How many would you estimate were in that grave?"

McNutt blew out through his nose, as if he needed to clear a bad smell. "Plenty. I didn't have to go deep to find mismatched pieces."

"Fifty? One hundred?"

"Could be. Could be there were more Zombies than we guessed, too."

Meyers clenched his hands beneath his chest. He needed more data, not more uncertainty. "What about your squad? If Banh sees an opening to the north, and we end up making an assault, we'll want to leave a squad or a part of a squad here. It could be the safest position, it could be the riskiest. You think your squad would be ideal for this or for the assault?"

"Honestly? After what we went through together, I wouldn't want a different group around me. I've seen them do the impossible. Sergeant Devoe—most of us were in his squad—he knew how to build a team."

Paxton nodded, but his focus was on his faceplate, which he had halfway down, probably to use its optics. "Devoe was an exceptional soldier."

McNutt's nose crinkled, as if he might be fighting off a sneeze. Or tears. "He was."

Meyers recalled Rimes talking about Devoe as someone they could groom to be a platoon sergeant, but the only interaction Meyers could recall with Devoe was an administrative issue. Devoe had covered for one of his soldiers—a known screw-up—rather than let that soldier face punishment. It had cost Devoe his first chance at platoon sergeant. Meyers wondered if McNutt had the same sort of self-destructive protective instincts.

"So, Corporal, would you want your squad here, or on the north, leading the assault?"

"Full squad, Colonel?" McNutt fixed his dark-blue eyes on Meyers. "Because I've got Private Starling with her face stuck in system guts nonstop and Cho playing medic. Neither one's had enough rest to be worth a damn in the field. And Perkins..." McNutt looked away. "He's got a baby on the way and a wife questioning all the killing he does."

"You managed to get them to find the nerve during the war."

"It's not nerve." McNutt's voice was gruff. His lips were stretched, and his right eye ticked. "Colonel." He straightened. "What this squad did in Widowmaker…" He shook his head. "Two squads went in—Devoe and Zimmer. Lots of body bags come out of there. Anyone survived, they earned it. They changed."

Meyers wished he'd had time to watch the full series of debriefs. Other than knowing it was a rescue operation gone wrong, he was vague on the details. "Pearson sent you in to rescue someone."

"Patharawarin Timkul, yeah. Former prime minister of Thailand. Powerful family, loads of money and more influence. Come to Plymouth to negotiate with Governor Burkhalter for the Special Security Council. Earth reaching out to the colonies for better relations, if that sounds familiar. The metacorporations got wind of it, apparently. Downed her shuttle over Widowmaker."

"And Pearson only sent in two squads?"

"Major Pearson didn't know the shuttle'd been downed. The mayday call just said they was going down. Widowmaker's a mess for systems. Our Dart lost power. Nearly crashed. Just before the Brotherhood attacked."

Meyers remembered the war crimes committed by the Brotherhood of Arms, the main mercenary force used by the metacorporations during the war. "They'll face prosecution."

"We'll never find them."

"We take care of business here. We'll have the clout to hunt them down. Trust me."

McNutt smirked. "Yeah, well, we didn't wait. We gave them a justice of our own."

Like Rimes, Meyers thought. "You still haven't answered. Would you want your squad positioned here or on the—"

Paxton held up a hand. "What was that? Sounded like a—"

Meyers heard it. A wailing, to the east. Banh?

Gunfire drowned the noise out.

"Get back!" Meyers lowered himself off his elbows and began belly-crawling backward, into the woods.

"That's not a CAWS," McNutt said. "Sustained automatic fire. Panicked."

More guns fired, a continuous growl, distorted by distance and the intervening woods.

"Maybe they spotted him," Paxton said. He glanced back toward the compound, then lowered his head again. They weren't deep enough into the woods to get off their bellies.

Meyers couldn't imagine Banh getting into a firefight with Waverley's forces, but there was no doubt the gunfire was coming from where Banh had been planning to pass through.

"He triggered something." Meyers tried to think of what Banh might miss. Security manufacturers were coming up with new devices all the time, but they were generally variations on a theme. Waverley might have had access to something new, something unexpected. "All that gunfire, are they chasing him?"

"Those assault rifles, unless he's got a lot of cover or they're terrible shots, he's dead by now." McNutt stood and turned east. "I'm gonna see what's going—"

Meyers got to his feet. "Negative. Sergeant Banh knows what he's doing. He's either going to meet us back at the Rover or not." And if he doesn't, Meyers, thought, then their choice was already made for them, and they were coming back with everyone.

Paxton cocked his head, as if he might be able to make out what was going on just by listening to the gunfire. "It's dying off. It's over."

And then the gunfire went silent.

"Let's get to the Rover." Meyers craned his neck and strained to listen, but the woods were silent now. "Weapons ready, double-time."

They jogged through the woods, instinctively hunched low, heads on a swivel, fingers on trigger guards. Halfway back to the Rover, Meyers fired up their BASes' private network and kicked their armor's sensors up to maximum sensitivity. One hundred fifty-two meters from the Rover, McNutt's system picked up a form closing on them from the east.

"Disperse!" Meyers leapt over a fallen log and took cover behind a fairly big tree. Paxton was hidden behind the fallen log, and McNutt was somewhere off to the left, out of sight. The target was still coming at them. Fast. "Wait for visual."

The target suddenly turned into a green wireframe, and Banh's ID flashed on Meyers's display.

"Hold fire! It's Banh!" Meyers held his position and watched the woods.

Banh broke from the trees, left arm dangling limp, slowing. He waved his right hand. "Colonel?"

McNutt circled around Banh, then stopped. "Clear."

Paxton jumped from his position and ran to Banh, ducking under his good arm to support him. "He's got a big scratch over his left shoulder."

Like Perkins had while setting up the sensors, Meyers thought.

"Zombies," Banh said. He gasped. "I ran into a patrol. Waverley's men. Six of them. Circling around from the north. I hid, but that patrol, there were Zombies following it, Colonel. One of them ran right into me. He hit me before I could get back up. He had a big ax. I think he dislocated my shoulder."

A patrol. Meyers tried to fit that in with the compound's security. Was that how they compensated for the lack of sensors and weapons, or was it a reaction to Zacharowski's attempt to steal the flyer?

"Corporal McNutt, check back along Sergeant Banh's path. Sergeant Banh, did the Zombie pursue you?"

"No, Colonel. The gunfire started, and one of Waverley's men ran right toward us. The Zombie, he chopped the other man's head off. I ran. I did not hear the Zombie chasing."

"Let's get that shoulder rigidified."

"I can do it, Colonel." Banh went off-channel for several seconds. When he came back on, he was gasping softly. "I can move now."

They walked through the woods slowly, speeding slightly as they approached the Rover. McNutt joined them shortly after Meyers had secured Banh in the passenger's seat. Meyers settled into the flip-up seat on the flatbed directly behind Banh.

"No sign of pursuit." McNutt slid into the driver's seat. "Looks like they sent the proxy out to finish things up. That thing's got to be a scare even to a drugged-up freak show."

"I think the Zombies must have a camp to the east," Banh said. "I saw a trail. They probably ran back there. Colonel, I do not think we can assault the compound. Too much trouble in the woods to the east, and those patrols, I think they are not new."

"Then we'll have to come up with something else." Meyers wondered what Rimes would do. There were no obvious weaknesses in Waverley's defenses to exploit now. "We need to draw them out. Ambush them away from their defenses. It's the sort of thing Colonel Rimes would have done."

Paxton leaned back in his seat. "Colonel Rimes is dead, sir. This is your battalion now. Might want to remember that."

Meyers's cheeks grew hot. He hadn't realized he'd mentioned Rimes until Paxton pointed it out. Command meant getting the guilt and uncertainty under control. The battalion was his to command, Colonel Lonny Meyers. He needed to be the one in charge.

McNutt twisted to look at Meyers. "Colonel?"

"Yes?"

"You think Waverley would leave that compound without all his toys?"

Meyers couldn't imagine a reason Waverley would do that. "No. But we have to find some way to turn that to our advantage."

McNutt chuckled. "That'll be a good one."

The woods gave way to the desert, gray in the twilight. Meyers stared at the low dunes. He thought of the Cáceres Road and Turning Point. There weren't any good ambush points. There were no obvious means to trick Waverley. If someone didn't come up with something, they were looking at a very bloody battle they could very easily lose.

18

———

14 December 2174. Karpov Desert, South of Turning Point, Bellar Frontier Colony.

THE MONITORS of the Operations Center were split between Turning Point, which was displayed across the middle two and the two on the left, and the Cáceres Compound, which was displayed on the two to the right. Barlowe, seated on the cargo case closest to the displays, yawned as he updated data on the Turning Point monitors. To his right, Starling stared into the distance, hands waving and tapping at nothing. Meyers turned as shadows passed over the Operations Center entry. Gerhardt hesitated at the doorway, pulling off his helmet and staring at Starling.

Meyers felt a surge of heat, and it wasn't from the sunlight. "Corporal Gerhardt, if you could take up your position over here, next to Sergeant Banh?" Meyers pointed off to his left, a meter back from the displays.

Gerhardt trailed powdery sand that drifted down from his armor. His steps were loud and scratchy. Paxton glared at Gerhardt's back, then shot a glance at Meyers before crossing to his side and leaning in.

"I don't think the message got through to him yet."

"Doesn't seem like." Out of the corner of his vision, Meyers watched Gerhardt, all angry glares and smug snarls. "Let's pull him aside after the meeting."

Paxton seemed to chew on that. "All right, sir. What about you?"

"What about me?"

"You ready for this? Did the message get through to you?"

The message. Rimes was gone; responsibility for the ERF fell to its new commander, brevet rank or not. Meyers puffed out his cheeks. "Yeah. The message got through. I'm in command."

The right corner of Paxton's lip ticked up in the slightest of smiles. Shadows passed over the doorway again; Ensigns Hassan and Nunoz entered. Paxton let them pass and returned to his position.

"All right," Meyers said. "I think we can get started. I've created a private network for everyone. Please let me know if you're not receiving the imagery and appropriate data." He waited for Hassan and Nunoz to settle at the back of the room, then did a quick scan of the faces of each person who had gathered—his squad leaders, Paxton, the intelligence team of Barlowe and Starling, and the pilots. "Good. I'm sure you all know at least a little of where we're at. If you need to review, I've made the AARs available. Please give them a good once-over. We've located our target..." The Cáceres Compound flashed. "And, at the moment, he's beyond our ability to reach."

Hassan raised her hand. "How long before the Javelins are ready to go?"

Meyers turned to Barlowe. "Two days after we get the BAS rebuild done. Ladell, did you want to speak to that?"

Barlowe blinked. "There's, um..." He turned to look at the pilots. "It's a problem of resources. We just don't have enough processing power to get their systems rebuilt faster than that."

"Two days?" Hassan shook her head.

"Maybe less." Barlowe looked at Meyers. "It's hard to tell with new hardware and—"

"That's too long." Nunoz crossed his arms. "We're glorified nurses right now."

"I'm pretty sure Lieutenant Oppert would have been fine with the option of a delay instead of what happened if she'd been given a choice," Paxton said.

Hassan and Nunoz cast their eyes down.

"We'll get the birds up as soon as possible," Meyers said. "Air superiority erases most, if not all, of the disadvantages we're facing. But without our BAS, it's a non-starter."

"Understood, Colonel." Hassan looked to Nunoz.

"Yeah, understood."

"Okay." Meyers sighed. He needed the pilots behind him. "How are our patients?"

Hassan rubbed her forehead. "Lieutenant Genêt's having a lot of problems, sir. Infections. It looks like local lifeforms. Most of the medicine was lost in the crash, so Corporal Cho's trying a few ideas out. Corporal Torres and Private Lumley are stable."

"Thank you for all you've done. Both of you."

Banh raised his good hand. "Colonel, I would like to consult with Corporal Cho when the briefing is over."

"Please do." Meyers turned so that he was looking at the displays showing Turning Point. "So, let me get to that briefing. Since we can't reasonably take the fight to Waverley, we need to have him bring the fight to us. And that's where our earlier recon into the city comes into play."

Buildings at the eastern edge of Cáceres Road lit up.

"These buildings are prefabs." Meyers tapped each one. "Empty, or used for storage. Most are three-story. They're located in Asfaw Mattias's territory, at the edge of the city, as far from Adrián Reyes's territory as we can get while still having a chance to draw Waverley into the city."

Mattias and Reyes's territories lit up. Animated haulers appeared along the north-south road separating the two territories.

"These represent Reyes's biggest threats. Haulers—flatbeds, two Cougars, and a Devil Cat—with machine guns attached to them. The Devil Cat has what appears to be a fairly light machine gun. Still a threat to our armor. There's another hauler. We don't have any good imagery of it yet, but Agent Barlowe thinks it might be a Leopard—bigger, meant for heavier loads, more rugged, and more importantly, it might have a railgun mounted on it. A quad-barrel."

Banh shifted and looked around.

"I'm confident it could even take down a Javelin." Meyers held up a hand when he saw Nunoz's face. "Assuming it could track the Javelin. I don't doubt you could take it out. I'm just talking about the power of that gun. For infantry, it's a huge problem."

"Then let's wait for the Javelins," Nunoz said.

"So, the reason we bring all this up is that we believe Reyes and Waverley have some sort of relationship. It could be purely antagonistic. It could be partly cooperative. They could be strong allies. Whatever this relationship is, we've already seen that Reyes isn't someone we can recruit."

Muscles bulged along McNutt's jaw. Meyers felt the same tension coil in his gut.

"That means when we draw Waverley into this area in Mattias's territory, we have to engage aggressively. Snipers need to take the shot if it's there. The faster we eliminate Waverley, the faster we can wrap this mission and go home. Until we get Waverley, any of his assets—his hardware or his people—need to be destroyed, whatever the cost. To include civilian casualties."

Meyers looked around at those gathered. Grim faces stared back, some accepting the requirements, some challenging. McNutt in particular seemed ready to say something.

"Corporal McNutt, did you want to share something?"

"I'm not used to hearing someone say civilian casualties are acceptable. That's all." McNutt shrugged, and the stiffness in the motion ruined any attempt at appearing casual.

Paxton's eyebrows shot up, but Meyers shook his head, just enough for Paxton to get the signal.

"There's certainly no intent to go hunting civilians, Corporal. If we could get a clean kill right now, I'd take it. I'd take a clean capture for that matter. But Waverley knows he'd be facing the death penalty. He's not going to surrender, and I'm not going to lose a single soldier to give him a chance to think about it. He's a fugitive war criminal. The case against him is airtight." Meyers highlighted the buildings in Mattias's territory again. "That's why we need this ambush. Control the battlefield. Minimize risk. Maximize firepower." He walked to the displays and ran his finger along Cáceres Road. "This is our best chance. Cut off some of their maneuverability, give us overlapping fields of fire. Do it around dusk—maybe our chameleon systems provide the edge we need."

Banh raised his good hand. "Target priorities, Colonel?"

"We'll firm that up, but, broadly, Waverley is target one. Take him down; they lose their reason to fight. You get a clean shot at a pilot or the fans on those flyers; you take it." Meyers looked at Hassan and Nunoz. They didn't react. It was war.

"What about the proxy?" Gerhardt looked around the room. "I saw the video. That gun it has mounted punches right through our armor. It's a lot more maneuverable than the haulers, and it's got heavier armor."

"The proxy's our biggest problem," Meyers said. "I don't know that we have anything that can penetrate the armor. We're still looking at the imagery Private Perkins's scope captured. I'm not very confident, but there's a chance we might find something we missed."

"So what're we supposed to do against it?"

Meyers fought back the urge to remind Gerhardt about protocol. He was still hurting from Zacharowski's death. Raw emotions were normal. "We think there's a chance we can at least slow it down. Overwhelm the sensors, maybe damage some of the joints. The operator still has to see to fire, so smoke and other obscuring agents might be worth a try."

"We're supposed to go up against something like that on a might and a maybe?"

"No. Those are all just part of a delaying action. Rather than take out the proxy, our best bet is to take out the pilot."

Gerhardt's head reared back. "The pilot."

Meyers tapped the main building inside the Cáceres Compound. "In here. The second Waverley brings his forces into Turning Point—you and Agent Barlowe need to get into here. That's where the pilot's going to be. Kill him, and the proxy is no longer a threat."

"The perimeter sensors..."

"Private Starling." Meyers looked over his shoulder at her. "How are we doing on the attack bots?"

"I've got five done, sir." She seemed to try to meet his gaze, but she broke out in a smile and looked away. "A-another one should be ready before long. They'll take about four hours to get through almost any security. Undetected. Agent Barlowe showed me how to get past almost any detection sys—"

"Wait, I'm leading an operation with them at my back?" Gerhardt swept a hand around to indicate Barlowe and Starling. "I need people I can count on."

McNutt lunged toward Gerhardt.

"Corporal McNutt!" Paxton stepped in McNutt's path. Despite McNutt's size and power advantage, he froze. "Stand down."

Once it was clear McNutt was under control—shaking with rage, but under control—Paxton stepped into Gerhardt's personal space.

"Look around this room, Corporal. Tell me what you see. No, I tell you what. Let me tell you what I see. A uniform. One. I see a patch. The ERF patch. I see a badge. The UN badge. You understand me? One team. All of us going after one objective. Now you tell me: What do you see?" Paxton about-faced. "You see gender, Corporal? You see skin color? You see people from different nationalities? Because if you do, you're the dumbest son of a bitch I have ever met."

"It's not that, Master Sergeant—"

Paxton spun back around. "I'm not finished, Corporal. You think a bullet gives one shit about what color someone is? You think it matters when a bomb goes off if you've got something swinging between your legs? War does not care. It's impersonal. And when you make something personal, you diminish the team you're supposed to be a part of. You understand?"

Gerhardt's face was beet red at that point. "I understand, Master Sergeant."

"You better. Because there might come a day when your ass is saved because your comrade is colorblind. Remember that."

Gerhardt lowered his eyes. "I won't forget, Master Sergeant."

Meyers waited a few seconds for the silence to deepen without isolating Gerhardt fully, then pointed to the displays again. "The BAS system software rebuild is close to completion."

"Sixty-five minutes," Barlowe said.

"Thank you. Once that's done, we'll push it out. With our BASes back to where we can trust them, we'll be able to operate freely, whether in

Turning Point or at the Cáceres Compound. It won't make up for all the gear and people we lost, but it's the one thing we'll have that no one else does. If there aren't any other questions, prepare your squads. We launch in..." He looked back at Starling, who seemed mortified. "Private Starling? The bot attacks?"

"S-s-sending them now, sir. Countdown's on the display." She looked up uncertainly.

"I've got it in my earpiece. Everyone see it or hear it? Good. Thank you, Private Starling." Meyers looked around the room, trying to assess just how much damage Gerhardt had done. Hassan's head was down, and she was watching Gerhardt out of the corner of her eye. Nunoz was making a point of looking away from Gerhardt. Barlowe's hands shook slightly, and McNutt looked ready to make it physical again once he had Gerhardt away from the others.

So much work had gone into bringing everyone together, seeing the way forward, accepting the challenges before them, and now...

Meyers listened to the timer. It was approaching four hours out from ready.

"All right. Everyone sync up on the network. Once we get the BAS update, this will automatically reset. At three, two, one..." The countdown gave a reassuring ping in Meyers's ear. "That's it. Be sure to have your squads sync up as well. We launch this operation in three hours, fifty-nine minutes, three seconds."

A strange tone—like a command override—hummed in Meyers's earpiece. Paxton's brow wrinkled, as if he might be hearing something similar.

"Colonel, I'm getting something." Hassan tapped her earpiece.

Nunoz pulled his earpiece and shook it. "Me, too. Like a command—"

"Hello?" An unfamiliar voice echoed over the network.

Meyers blanched. The private network had been hacked. Someone had been listening in the whole time. The planning and shared intelligence had been compromised.

"Good, thank you. I'm reading the network just fine," the voice said. It was an Indian accent with a strong British influence. "Then if I can hear you, and you must be able to hear me, let me start by saying that you will belay that order. You understand? Hello? You are not to proceed with your attack plan."

Meyers saw the same confusion that he felt on everyone else's face. He tried to shut the network down, to boot the unknown person. Nothing worked. "Who is this? Waverley?"

Barlowe shook his head. "It's coming from off-planet."

"Off-planet?" Meyers rolled his eyes. The radio silence they'd observed flying in, all the precautions they'd taken since arrival, all for nothing. "Is it at least ours?"

"That's an ERF command code. It's the..." Barlowe looked up, stunned. "It's your code. Battalion command—"

"Yes, I'm receiving you," the Indian voice said. "Excellent. So it sounds as if you, too, are receiving me. Colonel Meyers, your ID is showing up now. And it looks like most of your staff. Very, very good. If you could bring the rest of your staff onto the call, please?"

"Excuse me." Meyers's heart raced. He felt slow and stupid and in desperate need of sleep. He'd left his command code vulnerable somehow, and now an attacker was in his private network. "Who the hell are you, and how did you get access to my command code?"

A few seconds passed in silence. "Ah, yes. I understand. You did not hear my first transmission? Colonel Meyers, that is unfortunate. This is Colonel Abhishek Ramawat, ERF Battalion Commander."

"Battalion..." Meyers clasped his hands behind his back to hide the shaking he was sure everyone could see. He wanted to scream into his earpiece and tell the jackass the game wasn't funny—Lonny Meyers was the commander of the ERF.

Except he wasn't. He was a placeholder. It was all Rimes could have hoped to pull off. It was more than Meyers had ever wanted to have to deal with.

"Please have all personnel report to station. We are tracking you now. It seems you have some people quite some distance out. Our ETA is...eighty-five minutes. We will discuss the next operational plan once I am settled into my office. Please have a thorough SITREP prepared for me. I heard you mention the After-Action Reports. Please attach those, also. I believe we can delay the change of command ceremony until our return to Plymouth."

Change of command ceremony. Meyers squeezed his hands together. Ramawat. The name was coming to Meyers now. The person being considered to run the ERF after Rimes put the whole thing together. A decorated Indian Marine Commando—MARCOS. He finally got what he wanted. A laugh, high-pitched and short, escaped Meyers's throat.

"Colonel Meyers?" Ramawat didn't sound amused.

"We'll make preparations for your arrival, Colonel Ramawat. We've been operating with an eye toward subterfuge and stealth up to this point."

"Yes, of course. We'll analyze that decision once I've had a chance to settle in. Do be sure to have your entire staff gathered."

"This is my entire staff."

Ramawat was silent for a moment. "We can discuss more once I've settled in. Oh, and do have an honor guard at my landing, please. Colonel Ramawat out."

Meyers felt like the room was falling away, leaving him alone on a slip of sand, surrounded by darkness.

"Colonel? Colonel Meyers?" Hassan's face was in front of him, tilted, confused.

"I think we've got our orders," Paxton said from somewhere far away. "Time to move out, get your areas up to snuff, get your squads briefed. Let's go."

Someone clapped, shattering the spell. Meyers looked around. They were all leaving, their backs to him. Paxton stood at the entry, waving them on, eyes squinted, as if he were trying to break down a complicated equation.

"Lonny?" Barlowe set a hand on Meyers's shoulder. He turned, saw the sympathy there. "Go get some rest, okay?"

Meyers stumbled into the bright daylight, staggered toward his tent, watching the backs of his staff retreating into the golden light. Leaving him. Reports. He needed to get reports assembled. He needed a shower and a shave. The new commander was coming.

The new commander was coming, and Meyers had no idea what that meant for him.

19
____

14 December 2174. Karpov Desert, South of Turning Point, Bellar Frontier
Colony.

THE SUN WAS a brutal torch held close to Meyers's face, a light that burned
away his sight and leeched his will to live. Sweat dripped into the neck of
his T-shirt and spread along his back and chest. As miserable as he felt, the
honor guard had it worse. Detailed to wear their armor without sealing it
up, they were slowly cooking, hair matted, faces dripping. For whatever
reason, the wind that had harassed them since their arrival had gone quiet.
Even the grit of sand in their faces would have been worth the relief of a
cooling breeze. White salt tracks stood out on most faces, and Meyers could
smell that salt as he stood next to each soldier as well as he could taste his
own sweat.

Ramawat moved down the ranks slow as a snail. His small eyes squinted
as he looked down his nose at those who were shorter than him, and he
reared his head back to do the same at those taller. Thin streaks of sweat
trickled into thick eyebrows and down light-caramel cheeks. He chattered
in whispered tones with his XO, a large, dark-skinned man introduced only

as Captain Singh. Ramawat and his team had come in Zero-Zero-Three, one of the ERF's new Javelins, but they still wore MARCOS uniforms and insignia and carried a MARCOS kit, including the distinctive T-Corp Tiger-claw assault rifles.

With cartoonish stiffness, Ramawat moved to the third rank. Someone behind Meyers—it sounded like Perkins—muttered a curse.

Ramawat froze and stepped back to the second rank.

"Was there a question, Colonel Meyers?" Ramawat stood straight and stiff.

"I was complimenting Private Perkins on his boots."

Ramawat stared, unblinking, untouched by the heat. He didn't even squint. Finally, he returned to the third rank, and McNutt shot Perkins a withering, threatening glare.

An eternity of whispers and one comment about Private Luong's armor needing polish, and the inspection mercifully ended. The soldiers were dismissed, most no doubt headed off to peel off their soaked undergarments, leaving Meyers to deal with Ramawat and Singh. The XO barked orders to the MARCOS who were still standing at parade rest along the bottom of the Javelin's ramp. The MARCOS broke up, most of them quickly running into the ship to retrieve the rest of their kit. A few jogged out, heading past the edge of the camp in three different directions.

Meyers rendered a crisp salute, and Ramawat returned it before waving for Meyers to follow.

"This was the location of your Operations Center, was it not?"

"It is," Meyers said.

Ramawat slowed as he strode past the covered Javelins, then he continued on to the Operations Center. "Good job on the camouflage. From above, you are quite close to invisible."

Meyers wasn't sure what to make of that. Ramawat had been tight with comments, and what commentary he'd offered so far had been biting. Singh turned and bowed toward Meyers; he returned the bow.

At the base of the entry ramp, Ramawat spun and surveyed the interior.

"I think it'd be a good idea to bring Master Sergeant Paxton in if we're going to discuss our next move," Meyers said.

"I have found that discussions of the nature we are about to conduct are best limited to the more educated and sophisticated. There is a greater appreciation for the subtleties of professional military and diplomatic matters among those appropriately trained." Ramawat tilted his head slightly and craned forward. "You are something of an oddity in my own experience, at least as portrayed by your record—no academy training, no history of military service in your family prior to your own, a technical education. Failed aspirations to find employment with a metacorporation. And former enlisted? Is that all correct?"

Heat flashed through Meyers's face. "I didn't have the family connections to gain an academy position, but I have a PhD. in Applied Physics and graduate degrees in engineering and physics."

"Hm. Yes. Well, not to worry. I have more than enough experience for both of us. I should almost certainly be able to compensate for whatever shortcomings you present." Ramawat pointed to the displays lining the east wall. "This is all of your equipment?"

"We lost a lot when One-Six-Three crashed. Equipment, ammunition. People."

"Yes, the Arrow you chose to bring along. I saw in your SITREP where you blamed the crash on malicious systems software?"

"We're confident the upgrades that were offered to us before we headed out on this operation were compromised. We're pushing out BAS software rollbacks now."

"Mm-hm. Your record indicates you're quite accomplished technically. Do you think you might be too quick to look for technical reasons for failures in your command?"

Singh bowed his head, but before he did, Meyers caught a hint of embarrassment.

"Lieutenant Oppert was an excellent pilot. She experienced problems with her vessel from the second we left the *Valdez*. Agent Barlowe has worked with Ensigns Hassan and Nunoz to turn the black box data into useful data. That data points to bad flight control commands under stressful conditions. We checked our Javelins and saw the same exact commands being sent to the flight controls."

Ramawat smiled, and his face suddenly looked soft and pampered beneath the thin layer of black whiskers. "I saw the report, Colonel. And yet, we made it fine from the task force."

Singh raised his head, but he focused on the entry, not on Meyers.

"Then you understand that the only reason you made it down safely is that your Javelin has software the ERF techies loaded that overrode those bad commands."

"Ah, but we also brought one of your smaller craft with us, and it gave us no problem whatsoever!"

Meyers still couldn't believe the MARCOS force had loaded an old Dart with gear and brought it with them. "That's Oh-Seven-Two. It just got back from depot-level maintenance a week before we left. It has the old software in it."

"Colonel Meyers." Ramawat shook his head, and he somehow made the smug smile he'd flashed a moment before even worse. "Let us not quibble over matters like this."

Meyers wondered for a moment if he'd brought up the accusation that Oppert had crashed.

"What concerns me is the sequence of events that has brought us to this point we face now." Ramawat dusted sand off one of the cargo cases, then he sat. "And that situation has me assuming command of a significantly diminished unit in quite the hostile territory. At least now that you have seen fit to invade Mr. Reyes's territory and destroy one of Mr. Waverley's flyers. Unprovoked."

"Unprovoked?"

Singh's focus returned to the room, and his mouth opened as he looked at Meyers, then glanced down at Ramawat before returning his attention to the entry.

"The way the MARCOS operate, we rely on good sense to seize the minds of the enemy and to bring them around to the realization they are best served reconsidering whatever it is they happen to have done to bring our attention to them."

"This isn't the Indian Ocean or Bangladesh, Colonel. This is a frontier colony."

"Are you saying fear and respect are beyond the comprehension of someone like Mr. Waverley? Or that Mr. Reyes cannot bring himself to see the wisdom in negotiations when the alternative is an engagement with a clearly superior force? Is that your honest, professional assessment?"

"Did you look at the imagery we sent from Turning Point and the Cáceres Compound?"

"I did. A few up-armored flyers and a hauler with an anti-aircraft gun are hardly reason for concern."

Meyers struggled to keep his breathing even. Ramawat had to be running some sort of test—stress, human insight, mental agility. Something. There was no way a commander of such a prestigious force could be so clueless. Rimes would have seen through whatever it was Ramawat was doing. Rimes would have eaten it up and found a clever path to a solution where Ramawat got whatever it was he wanted and Rimes got the mission done. Meyers felt like an imbecile, a sloth trying to solve a timed puzzle while blindfolded. "Reyes has hundreds—thousands—of people armed with assault weapons at his disposal."

"Ruffians and thugs, Colonel Meyers."

"Waverley has a proxy that I seriously doubt our weapons can damage."

"Your CAWS-5s are carbines. Our Tigerclaws have the sort of punch to handle a proxy."

Meyers had handled a Tigerclaw before. It was a good weapon, but it offered nothing more than downrange accuracy over the CAWS-5. Ramawat had to know that. He had to. His behavior was beyond irrational. It was childish, petty.

"Colonel Ramawat, it's great that you've arrived. Your men and supplies give us the numbers we need to pull off a much better range of operations. Our options now are much better. We can take Waverley at the compound."

Ramawat clapped. It was loud and dramatic, a big motion that he ended by rubbing his hands together. "I'm afraid not. Instead, what we are going to do is to reach out to Mr. Reyes and get him to understand who Mr. Waverley is, what crimes he has committed, and that we have been sanctioned to bring Mr. Waverley back to Earth to stand trial for such crimes as we described. Once Mr. Reyes understands who it is he is dealing with now, he will certainly agree to render whatever assistance we see fit to ask of him. Perhaps we will even borrow his anti-aircraft platform to dispense with the proxy that has you so troubled. Such a show of force will be enough to bring Mr. Waverley to the negotiations table."

"I already tried to reach out to Reyes. It's in the SITREP—"

"Yes, Colonel Meyers, you did. I am quite capable of reading your reports. What I saw was a very crude and ill-informed effort, the sort of weak posturing that attempts to project strength but instead hints at vulnerability. In two decades of service, I have brought pirates, terrorists, and separatists to surrender. We have only needed to engage in combat situations seven or eight times, and those engagements ended rather quickly. It requires knowing your enemy and treating them with some level of respect while also making it clear that their choices are really rather obvious."

"Reyes is a petty dictator. He's a bully. He isn't going to back down to anything other than a clearly superior force."

Ramawat smiled up at Singh, who seemed to sense what was expected of him. He straightened and said, "Colonel Meyers, the MARCOS are the deadliest combat unit in the world. In the galaxy. Our training is superior to any you might know. With Colonel Ramawat leading us, we have broken terrible people—criminals and tyrants."

Meyers sucked in a breath, then blew it out and slowly counted to ten. It was something Rimes had used to control his emotions. "Captain, I respect the hell out of the MARCOS. The ERF would have loved to bring MARCOS members onboard during formation, but Colonel Rimes's offers were rebuffed."

That seemed to rock Ramawat.

"The problem is, you don't carry any clout here." Meyers pointed at the displays showing Turning Point. "Those people spent years in prison, sealed off from the outside world. They know what's gone on in the last ten years, most of that here, on Bellar Colony. They're not pirates in the Indian Ocean or Tamil separatists who have seen what your people can do. They've probably never even heard of you. You can't intimidate them."

Ramawat shot up from the cargo case. "Now see here, Colonel Meyers, that will be quite enough of your misinformed and dangerous nonsense. What I am describing to you, the plan that I have set out for our operations going forward, this is based on history. It is not something plucked from the imagination of a child. Even if these people have not heard of the MARCOS' history, they will see the greatness in us. They will realize the wisdom of listening to what I offer them."

"So, just like that, you're going to convince Reyes to turn over resources to you?"

"No reasonable man would do otherwise."

"Reyes spent too many years of his life wrongly incarcerated to be truly re—"

"That is quite enough." Ramawat stepped closer, until he was looking Meyers straight in the eye. "You would do well to remember you are a brevet colonel. Your position here is at my discretion. If I were to see you as undermining my command, I could return you to captain's rank, or I could send you back to the *Valdez*. It is a courtesy I have extended to you, this meeting, and it is a courtesy I extend at significant strain. Your incompetence as a commander has been proven out in the few short days you have brought your sad, little ensemble of miscreants to face unremarkable opponents. That incompetence will be reflected in my own reports, so you would be best served learning from a professional soldier while you have the chance. Is that ambiguous or confusing in any way, or am I making myself clear?"

Wind howled at the entry suddenly, but it couldn't pull away the stuffy heat pressing against Meyers. Even Singh—eyes wide and mouth barely open—seemed to feel that heat.

Meyers cleared his throat. "I understand completely, sir."

"That is quite refreshing to hear. You are dismissed."

Meyers exited the building at a fast walk. He clenched his hands to stop their shaking. Ramawat's words were white-hot coals burning in Meyers's gut. Whatever chance there had been to pull off some Rimes-like miracle diplomacy had been missed. Ramawat's mind was made up. He was going to give Reyes a chance to cooperate with the great and powerful MARCOS, and Reyes was going to quiver in fear and excitement and throw his lot in with the new ERF.

It was suicide, and all that remained to be seen was who else Ramawat was going to get killed.

20

14 December 2174. Karpov Desert, South of Turning Point, Bellar Frontier Colony.

Soap filmed the water that slushed in Meyers's washing bowl. He stared at his hygiene kit: the tube of soap, another of shampoo, a comb, the razor, a stick of antiperspirant, toothpaste, floss, and toothbrush. All laid out on his cot. The towel resting on his shoulder smelled fresh. It was soft on his face as he dried away the last of the water and soap. A shower would have been better, more complete, a chance to wash away the rest of the filth clinging to him after meeting with Ramawat, but he'd already had his shower. Even with the water harvesters that had been in the Javelins, self-discipline was called for, especially with twenty-four more consumers, none of them properly outfitted for desert conditions.

Meyers opened the entry flap, leaned out, and tossed the water into the sand. It darkened the sand. Before long, the sun would heat it, and it would evaporate, and then it would be drawn into the condensers.

"You're letting all the heat into your room, sir."

Meyers looked up, saw Paxton's form taking shape in the sun's glare. He pulled off his helmet, tucked it under his left arm, slicked back his hair with his right hand, and flicked the sweat into the sand.

"I'm not really up for conversation," Meyers said.

Paxton snickered and shouldered his way past. "Figured not."

Meyers sealed the flap and toweled the bowl dry, then he set the towel out to dry and put the hygiene kit away. "What's the mood like?"

"Oh, it's downright cheerful. Didn't you hear the big dance earlier?" Paxton looked at the cot. "You planning to get some rest? Long overdue, if you can manage in this heat."

"I might."

"Since I wasn't invited to the big shindig in Ops, you gonna tell me what happened? I'm feeling pretty useless right about now."

Meyers set the hygiene kit under his cot. "I'm not sure I even know what happened, Carl."

"Give it a try."

"Okay. Ramawat seemed to call me a liar and an incompetent. He definitely brushed aside all my assessments and suggestions. And then he dismissed me. I think he's putting together his plan right now for how he'll recruit Reyes to help us arrest Waverley."

Paxton laughed. "That's good stuff. Pull the other one."

"I'm not kidding." Meyers sat on the cot. The nausea and weakness he'd felt earlier weren't completely gone. "He thinks he can intimidate Reyes, like somebody 600 light years from Earth even knows who the Indian Marine Commandos are. Oh, I should mention that. I definitely got the sense we'll be observers from now until any firefight happens. Ramawat doesn't expect there to be any resistance, though."

"About what I figured. I had a chance to talk with my...replacement. Rao. Looks like he's still getting used to being a Master Sergeant. Straight shooter. Asked for roster turnover, looked it over, told me he'd contact me if he needed anything else."

It was painful being displaced, but Paxton seemed to be holding up well. Better than me, Meyers thought. "He's the commander. It's his right to build out his staff as he sees fit."

Paxton grunted. "I was thinking, maybe it's time to look for a new position. I'm not getting any younger, and I've got an open invitation to join

General Zapata's staff in Manhattan. That'd be a promotion, and it sure beats jumping from hot spot to hot spot."

"I don't know what I would do. Jack always told me I was meant to be an officer, but..." Meyers looked at his hands. They were still nimble, the flesh unbroken by the scarring Rimes's hands had carried. "He had a way of always finding solutions to impossible situations, like some crazy, fucking magic he kept stored away until he needed it. I don't know how he pulled it off."

"He was a good soldier."

"Yeah."

"And so are you. Look, you don't have to be Colonel Rimes to be a good commander. You're not him. You don't need to be. He wasn't perfect. He made mistakes. Hell, half the UN's still trying to figure out if he's a hero or a war criminal. Ramawat probably wouldn't be marching around the Operations Center if not for what Rimes did."

Meyers couldn't argue that, not in good conscience. "So, what? Give Ramawat a chance? See if he gives me a billet somewhere?"

"Seems like an ambitious guy. Maybe he does a few years running the battalion and returns to Earth to go into politics. His family's influential, right?"

"I think that's what Rimes said back when this all floated up the first time."

"Those sorts don't tend to stick around long. Punch your card, salute sharply, move on to the next stepping-stone."

Meyers tried to picture himself running an administrative position somewhere, maybe as a liaison on the *Valdez*. He wasn't so sure he had the makings of a toe-the-line, wait-your-turn careerist. Then again, he hadn't ever thought of a commission until Rimes had pushed the idea in the first place.

Paxton scratched at his nose. "Just don't do anything that limits your opportunities. Options are nice to have."

"I'll keep an open mind." Meyers felt the fatigue weighing heavy at that point, as if accepting the idea of a potential position had removed stress he hadn't really thought was present.

He jumped to his feet at the boom of a knock, and the thought of sleep faded.

"Come in."

The flap rattled; Paxton barked out a warning to step back, then he cleared the snaps securing the flap and stepped aside to let Singh in.

"Colonel, Master Sergeant." Singh shuffled to the center of the room and looked around before regarding Meyers. "If I am disturbing you, I can go, Colonel."

"Not at all, Captain." Paxton took up a position against the wall opposite the cot.

"We were just discussing the future." Meyers almost chuckled at the way Singh sucked in a breath and straightened. "Don't worry, Captain. It's not some sort of coup or whatever you're thinking. Speculation about staffing and options for new positions, that sort of thing."

"Yes, of course, Colonel." Singh's voice was low and raspy, and it was quieter than when he had been around Ramawat earlier. The left side of his face ticked, and he stretched out his lip and revealed a gap where the upper canine should have been. His lip and the flesh above were scarred in the same area. "I think you will find a place in the ERF, Colonel, once Colonel Ramawat has had a chance to truly evaluate what faces us."

Paxton cocked an eyebrow at Meyers, either amused or surprised.

"I didn't come out of that meeting feeling like a warm welcome had been extended. Did I miss something?"

"Miss something?" Singh seemed to consider the question. "Maybe I do not understand?"

"Colonel Ramawat implied that I was incompetent. Or maybe he was implying that I was lying. I don't know."

"Oh, okay, yes. I understand now." Singh shook a finger. "That is not it. No. The colonel, he is very thorough, very intelligent. He is assessing. You do the same?"

"Assess personnel? That's part of being a commander."

"And that is what he is being: a commander."

Once again, Meyers wondered if the whole exercise in the Operations Center had been a test. It still didn't feel like it. "Are you sure there's not something more personal behind all this?"

Singh sucked in a breath and straightened again, completely missing

Paxton tapping his nose. "Colonel Ramawat, he is very capable." Singh seemed to force himself to relax. "The greatest officer in the Indian Navy. He could be a commander of a fleet in the new combined military, but he has to prove himself now. He is under quite the scrutiny, with many watchful eyes upon him."

"And a lot of help," Meyers said. "The ERF command position is very high profile. There were a lot of people older and more experienced trying for it, weren't there?"

"Oh, yes. But not as capable. The world understands the accomplishments of the MCF—the Marine Commando Force, the MARCOS. They know we are the greatest force in all the world. It is only right that the colonel, he is given this position. When he was passed over, even by our own delegate to the UN, it was very bad. Our country suffered quite serious damage to our status in the world."

Meyers didn't think Singh would be open to the reasons given for passing over Ramawat and his competitors within the Indian army. Just as the Intelligence Bureau had caused the marginalization and eventual elimination of Delta Force, T-Corp's role as the greatest economic power in the Indian region had led to undue influence in the Indian government and military. The Special Security Council had been almost prescient by passing over potentially compromised officers.

"I think every nation has suffered damage to its status as the world changed," Meyers finally said. "It's time we stopped looking at things through the prism of pride and prestige and started looking at how we work together to survive."

Singh nodded enthusiastically. "And that is Colonel Ramawat. It is how he wishes to lead—together. And you will see, he is an exceptional commander."

Paxton cleared his throat and stepped away from the wall. Opening the flap twice in the heat of the day had let a lot of heat in, and having three bodies squeezed into the small space wasn't helping. Paxton dabbed sweat from his brow with the sleeve of his free arm. "How long have you served under the colonel, Captain Singh?"

"For many years. My entire time in the MARCOS."

"And you think you're a good judge of character?"

"I like to think so, yes. I am."

"Do you get the sense there might be some sort of payback at work here?" Paxton pointed his helmet at Meyers. "Maybe Colonel Meyers here is being punished for his association with Colonel Rimes?"

Singh seemed to struggle with the question for a moment, then his face lit up and his thick brows curled over his eyes, like wings in flight. "Ah, I understand! No, I do not—"

Meyers's earpiece chimed.

It was Ramawat.

"This is...Meyers. Go ahead."

"Colonel, is Captain Singh with you?"

Meyers fought not to roll his eyes. A quick check of the BAS should have been enough to show Singh was in close proximity. "He is, Colonel."

"Please have him accompany you to the Operations Center."

Meyers looked at Singh's curious face. "We're on our way."

"Very good." Ramawat disconnected.

"Colonel Ramawat wants to see us in the Operations Center."

Singh smiled. "This is good! He must have reached a decision."

"That was quick, wasn't it?"

"He already had a very good appreciation for the situation on the ground, Colonel."

Meyers wondered exactly what qualified as a good appreciation of the situation. He pulled his helmet from beneath the cot, shook it, and pulled it on. Paxton opened the tent flap, and Singh fell in behind and to Meyers's right. There was still very little wind, and the sun seemed hotter than Meyers could remember it since landing. He glanced at his helmet display: sixty-five Celsius.

Ramawat was facing the wall opposite the entry to the Operations Center, staring at nothing, arms crossed behind his back. The displays were powered off, leaving nothing but the sunlight coming in through the entry to light the interior. It was much cooler than outside.

Meyers stood next to a cargo case and looked at Singh, who stood at attention. When Ramawat didn't respond, Meyers said, "You wanted to see us, Colonel?"

"Yes." Ramawat turned. He frowned when he looked at Meyers as if expecting something, maybe for him to be standing at attention. "I want you to gather your men."

"They're your personnel, sir. I'll have them fall in, though."

"Very good."

Meyers turned to go. He hoped this wasn't for a formal open ranks inspection or some ridiculous ceremony, but he didn't want to challenge Ramawat's decisions.

"Do you not wish to know my decision, Colonel Meyers?"

Meyers turned. "Decision?"

"I thought over what you said earlier. Although I believe you are incorrect in your assessment about the system software, I consulted my pilot. He said that there were quite surprisingly bad flight control data in the logs. That has led to my decision to support deploying the old BAS software to your armor. My MARCOS will remain on the version they are running until this matter is fully sorted out."

"Will they be compatible with ours?"

"Compatible enough. We can continue to communicate, and my men are more comfortable with what they've trained with for the last few years. As for the Javelins, please have your systems people expedite the deployment of the old systems software. We cannot afford the failure of things so vital."

"I'll ask Agent Barlowe and Private Starling to get on that immediately."

Ramawat looked at the displays. "Do you think someone as...young as your Private Starling can be trusted with such a sensitive task?"

"Agent Barlowe says she's more than capable. If he says that, then she is. This is about her age, right?"

Ramawat jerked his head back around. "Of course. Once they have started the Javelin work, please inform Agent Barlowe that he is to accompany us."

"Us?"

"Oh, yes. You and your Master Sergeant Paxton will be accompanying Captain Singh, Master Sergeant Rao, and myself into Turning Point. I wish for the three of you to see how this is done. I will do all the speaking, of course. Mr. Reyes will be given the opportunity to surrender or to cooperate with us in the arrest of Mr. Waverley. After consideration of your

AARs, I have decided to offer Mr. Reyes immunity for his crimes as an enticement."

"And assembling the ERF personnel?"

"I wish to express to them how this operation will impact them, of course. We should prepare to tear down camp, officially gather and stow the dead, and so on."

Meyers looked around the Operations Center interior. He realized now that the systems had been powered down not because they offered no value, but because Ramawat considered the operation on the verge of completion. It was a certainty in his mind that Reyes would sign on and that would be enough to bring Waverley in.

Singh was wrong, horribly wrong. Ramawat wasn't just incompetent, he was delusional, and he was going to get everyone killed.

21

______

14 December 2174. Turning Point, Bellar Frontier Colony.

TURNING Point was lit by the peculiar amethyst and puce of Bellar's late sunset. Master Sergeant Rao pushed the droning Rover to its limits, guiding it expertly along the road leading north into Savoy's district.

Castro Street. Starling had determined the names of all the streets, dirt, and blacktop. Meyers doubted that would interest Ramawat.

Meyers traced the breadth of the bay up to the glittering river and then turned to admire the way the sunset gave at least a little personality to the prefab buildings. Soon, the long shadows would disappear in twilight, and the city would be caught up in the darkness of another night. He glanced to his left, at Barlowe—rigid, wide-eyed, staring straight ahead—and Paxton —eyes half-closed, staring at nothing, seemingly resigned and reflective. Meyers understood their mood. It felt like they were being driven off to a firing squad, especially when cigarette smoke drifted toward them from the small buildings that marked the beginnings of the city.

Dirty children laughed and darted across the road as the Rover approached. Rao never slowed or swerved, and beside him Ramawat rocked side to side with each rut and pothole strike. The Rover bounced as the packed clay rose up to the blacktop, still cracked and holed, but slightly smoother. Women shouted for the children to get out of the way, and men watched from behind the glowing tips of cigarettes.

The homes whipped past, and then the Rover had them in the city proper, larger prefabs rising up on either side, plunging them into alternate shadow and light. The smells of the city with night approaching hit Meyers: food cooking, sweat-soaked people cooling in the shade, the first smoke from barrel fires.

People leaped out of the Rover's way, and it sped forward until the first checkpoint came into view.

Rao slowed, and then he came to a stop when it was clear the gate wasn't going up.

Two guards approached, guns at the ready. Two more watched from the gate, alternating attention from the Rover to the checkpoint three meters farther up the road. One of Reyes's haulers kicked up dust somewhere to the north, out of sight. Meyers thought he could hear the motor whining and gears grinding, as if it were quickly maneuvering.

The guard on Rao's side looked the Rover up and down, and a perplexed half-smile drew the edges of his mouth up. "You have any idea where you're going?" He was as dark as the Ethiopians, but his accent placed him from somewhere in the American southeast.

Rao stared straight ahead.

Ramawat turned his head slightly and smiled. "We are on our way to see Adrián Reyes."

The guard on Ramawat's side, a pale, freckled man, looked toward the checkpoint. "Bobby, see if they're expecting visitors!"

One of the guards still at the checkpoint—a short, deep-chested, Hispanic man—shouted something in Spanish to the other checkpoint. It sounded like a harmless question. Reyes's men didn't take it well. All four of them glared back toward Bobby, weapons raised but not pointed.

"Don't look like they know you was coming," the black man said.

"Please feel free to pass along to them the imminence of our arrival."

Meyers set his hands on his knees and squeezed. If he could have pinched himself through his armor, he would have.

"Oh, shit," the freckled man said. He was staring back down the road, past the Rover.

Meyers turned. A dusty, banged-up crawler was approaching. Two motorcycles flanked it. He thought he could make out Savoy in the passenger seat of the crawler, white ponytail visible as he turned to talk to someone in the backseat.

The crawler slowed, and the motorcycles drove past, coming to a stop shy of the checkpoint. Meyers recognized Savoy's Asian bodyguard as one of the motorcyclists but couldn't recognize the other. The doors lifted, and Meyers turned in time to see Savoy and the multiracial bodyguard from the amphitheater get out.

The black checkpoint guard jerked a thumb at Ramawat. "These guys say they want to go see Reyes, but he ain't expecting them."

As Savoy walked past Meyers, there was a flicker of recognition, and then disbelief. Savoy walked around the front of the vehicle and stopped a meter away from Ramawat, but looked past, at Meyers. "I didn't think we would see you back here again after what happened." Savoy turned his attention to Ramawat. "Or am I talking to the real commander now?"

"Very good, very good. I am Colonel Abhishek Ramawat. You must be Savoy."

"Yeah, Teddy. You really want to head up into Reyes's district? It's gonna be dark before long." Savoy stepped closer to the Rover; looked it over. "Things get uglier at night."

The hauler Meyers heard earlier sped down the street toward the checkpoint on Reyes's side. The hauler was huge, and the gun mounted on its flatbed was the quad-barreled, anti-aircraft piece. Dust caked the armored bubble. Meyers thought the armor might be a little thicker than what the up-armored flyers had, but not by much. He caught Barlowe looking the hauler over.

"Leopard," Barlowe whispered. "That's a Cobra railgun. Alexander Arms."

SunCorps, Meyers thought to himself. "Thanks."

"We should be able to conclude our business quite rapidly," Ramawat said to Savoy.

Savoy looked from Ramawat to Meyers. "And what is your business?"

"We are going to give Mr. Reyes an opportunity to cooperate with us."

Savoy's brow wrinkled, and his eyes seemed to ask Meyers whether or not Ramawat was serious. "Colonel…" Savoy looked back at Ramawat.

"Ramawat."

"Colonel Ramawat, I hope you'll reconsider. Your man there nearly got his head blown off the last time he talked to Reyes, and things haven't calmed down since then."

"Mr. Reyes will appreciate the strength I bring to the negotiations."

Meyers fought back a chuckle, saw Savoy's look of disbelief. Meyers shook his head, and Savoy walked to the checkpoint. His men raised the bar, and Savoy slowly crossed to the other checkpoint, hands raised away from his body. He stopped short of the other bar and slipped into a fairly casual tone, a few times motioning back at the Rover. Meyers wasn't sure what to expect. Savoy had seemed like someone they could negotiate with, but there was obviously something between him and Reyes, possibly going back to the incident Beniam had mentioned, when Savoy had been a Lancer.

Paxton leaned past Barlowe, who didn't react. "Colonel, how far you figure this goes before it turns into a total clusterfuck?"

"Not too much longer." Meyers was actually surprised things had gone so easily. It made him reconsider the dynamics with Reyes and the other warlords. Maybe the haulers and their big guns weren't quite the edge they appeared to be.

Savoy returned and stopped next to Ramawat. "Reyes will see you. You're to follow that hauler. If you want my advice, you take your little dune buggy and head back to the desert. Cross into Reyes's territory…" Savoy shook his head.

"Thank you, Mr. Savoy."

Ramawat waved for Rao to drive on, and they sped toward the Leopard, which was still maneuvering. Rao slowed until the hauler was parallel, then he accelerated. The Leopard's driver glared down and seemed about to shout at Rao, but he stared straight ahead. The anti-aircraft gun spun so that its barrels were pointed at the center of the Rover, and the man inside the armored bubble laughed. His black hair was greased down, shaved on the sides, combed over left to right on top. Something sparkled every now and then in his ears, and Meyers realized there were studs from tips to lobes. The gun operator seemed a little small for one of Reyes's men, yet Meyers couldn't stop thinking that they were seconds from being turned into shredded, pink slivers. Ramawat wasn't just trying to negotiate with lunatics; he was provoking them. Worse, he was ignoring their reactions, which was certain to irritate them even more.

But the anti-aircraft gun never fired. It pivoted and rotated, and the operator laughed, but that was all that happened.

They headed northwest, taking them closer to the river, and a few minutes after the checkpoint, Meyers got a decent look at the harbor. It was shielded by a chain-link fence, just like Starling had said, but the gates seemed to be open, and there were no guards or haulers in sight. With night coming, Meyers wondered if people might already be headed home.

The hauler slowed, and Meyers twisted around to look past it. A walled compound came into view. The wall was crude, possibly adobe. Rather than a gate, the entry was blocked by another checkpoint, but the bar was already raised.

Rao sped ahead of the hauler, and the anti-aircraft gun tracked hard on the Rover's flatbed. The checkpoint guards sighted with their weapons, but they didn't fire.

Meyers couldn't help feeling impressed by Reyes's estate, which was much nicer than the overhead imagery had indicated. The house—a mansion, really—was constructed from what appeared to be local materials, mostly brick, but with elements of wood visible. There was real craftsmanship in the design and construction and an undeniably pleasing aesthetic about it. Even the smaller buildings within the compound—large sheds and smaller living quarters—had the look of professional workmanship. The north courtyard held a garden, and a few people seemed to be wrapping up their work, raking and watering what appeared to be rich, dark soil.

The Rover stopped, and Rao hopped out, running to Ramawat's side, as if there were a door to be opened. Meyers waited until the Leopard came to a stop before unbuckling and sliding out of his seat. He moved deliberately, keeping the railgun in his peripheral vision. The front door to the mansion opened, and three men with assault rifles stepped out.

They spread out on the porch, dark baseball caps pulled low over their eyes.

Ramawat glanced back at Meyers, then looked at the men. "Lead us to Mr. Reyes, if you would be so kind."

Rao skipped up the steps ahead of Ramawat and stood among the men. Reyes's men looked at each other, chuckling and shaking their heads, then one of them waved the Leopard away and casually headed back through the doors. The other two brought up the rear. No one asked for their weapons.

Meyers was surprised when he glanced right and saw Singh, who seemed pleased with the moment. Singh smiled and said, "You seem surprised we are here, Colonel."

"I didn't expect we'd make it this far." Meyers craned his neck so that he could admire the paneling and other aspects of the interior. "Master Sergeant Rao seemed to enjoy antagonizing our escort."

"It is how Colonel Ramawat prefers to operate, and it is effective, don't you think?"

"No denying the results."

They passed through a foyer, and beyond that, an open room with a set of stairs. Polished wood and marble floors, furniture that had to have come from Earth or one of the colonies, a chandelier—Meyers couldn't begin to imagine how much the mansion had cost to construct and furnish. Everything looked and smelled new. Most impressively, the air within was cool. The place had an air conditioner.

They entered a hallway running north, and the man who had been escorting them opened a set of double doors on the west side of the hall. Through the doors was a huge room. They entered, stopping in front of three tables arrayed in front of the north wall. Reyes sat behind the center table, an older man to his right, a beautiful, young woman to his left. To the right and left of each of them sat two younger men. Trays of food were piled in front of them all—meats, vegetables, bread, fruits. It was more than Reyes and his entourage could possibly eat.

Ramawat came to a stop a meter in front of Reyes, and Meyers stopped a meter behind Ramawat. The last light of the day shone through a pair of beautiful French doors on the wall opposite the doors they'd entered through. Meyers glanced outside, saw the garden there and a huge fountain that had been hidden from the front approach. At the top, three cherubs spilled water from buckets into a bowl that was probably a meter and a half across, and that water bubbled and splashed into a larger basin below. Gunmen herded the gardeners out of the courtyard.

Meyers couldn't recall seeing the gunmen from the driveway, either.

"Mr. Reyes," Ramawat said as he slipped into a parade rest posture. "I am Colonel Abhishek Ramawat, commander of the ERF Battalion. I appreciate you agreeing to meet with me given such short notice."

"Of course." Reyes sounded smooth, calm, as if it were a minor inconvenience.

"Since we have interrupted your dinner—I apologize—I will proceed expeditiously to the point."

Reyes and the older man to his right exchanged a look. Meyers thought it might have been mock-surprise. Or mock-impressed. It was definitely mockery.

"I have come to you with a proposition I believe you will want to hear."

Reyes waved a drumstick at Meyers. "I think your little *puta* already made your offer."

Ramawat didn't even look at Meyers. "This is a new proposition."

"I am a businessman. I enjoy making deals." Reyes smacked as he ate, mouth open.

"Your mansion is quite amazing, by the way." Ramawat looked around the room, nodding.

"You know how much I paid for this? The plans, the materials? Fifteen million."

"Very nice. It would run more on Earth."

"Those doors." Reyes waved greasy fingers at the French doors. "Imported from Earth. Twelve thousand."

Meyers glanced at the doors again. The laborers were gone, the gunmen out of sight. He wondered if the money Reyes was rattling off was real or part of some trade. If the mansion was even a year old, it didn't show it. Trade or outright purchase, Reyes's money had to have been coming in before Waverley. With no visible manufacturing or other sources, Meyers couldn't figure what was generating that money.

"If I had a place like this," Ramawat said, "I would very much want to protect it."

Reyes set the drumstick down and wiped his hands with a towel, eyes squinted slightly.

"And that is why I am here."

"You come to protect my home?"

"To help you protect it, yes, that is correct. You see, my task is to arrest Mr. Chad Milton Waverley. You have heard of him?"

"Yeah. Your *puta* said he was going to assassinate Waverley."

"The ERF will be run different now. I bring with me years of operating the MARCOS, and I intend to see to it that my experience is most fully exploited."

"Marcos?" Reyes chuckled and looked at those seated at the table, who smiled back. "You don't look like a Marcos."

Reyes's people laughed.

Singh straightened and gritted his teeth. To his right, Rao seemed ready to charge Reyes. Meyers looked around the room. He counted eight gunmen, not including Reyes and the others seated at dinner. There was still no sign of the gunmen who had been in the garden, although Meyers thought he'd seen movement in the gray of dusk out of the corner of his eye. Just the eight in the room were a problem, even if that was the entire force available to Reyes. They had their guns at the ready, and they were positioned at the back.

Finally, Ramawat laughed along with Reyes. "The name. Yes. I see. That is a Spanish name? MARCOS. It is short for Marine Commandos. The deadliest force on Earth. And in space."

"Oh yes, of course." Reyes took an apple from the bowl nearest him and bit into it, producing a little pop as he tore away a piece. Juice rolled down his fingers.

"And that leads to the unfortunate need for us to interfere with your operations here on Bellar, Mr. Reyes. In order to arrest Mr. Waverley, we need to draw him into negotiations. The best way to do that is to use that hauler that escorted us, you see. A show of force."

Reyes dabbed at his face. "The Leopard? But that's mine."

Barlowe, who had been staring at the floor the whole time, looked up suddenly. He looked at Paxton, then at Meyers, mouthing, "Crazy."

Paxton nodded. Meyers wasn't sure what to make of Ramawat. Crazy didn't seem accurate.

The gunmen at the back of the room shuffled closer, a subtle move that Singh and Rao didn't react to if they noticed it. Paxton noticed. His eyes jumped from Meyers to the area behind him. Meyers could feel the man there, the gun pointed low, maybe for a shot into the back. It was a bad idea, what with Reyes and his people sitting at the table.

"We would return it to you, of course," Ramawat said. "Once we are done with it. But there is a problem of some of the criminal activities you have been engaged in, and the best solution to that problem is to grant you a pardon. And that is within my power."

"A full pardon?" Reyes finished off the apple and set the core down, then he wiped his hands again.

"Yes. In exchange for your hauler and assistance bringing Mr. Waverley to justice."

"That is very promising. Enrique, it's promising, right?"

The older man nodded. "Very promising."

"And that way," Ramawat looked at the ceiling and the walls, "there is no threat to all the hard work you have put in."

"Well, I am certainly not one to enjoy threats to my hard work." Reyes set down the towel he'd wiped his hands on, then folded it. "As a business-man, though, I feel I have to counter-offer."

"I am afraid those are the only terms—"

Reyes held up a hand. "Please. I heard you out. Thank you. Now, the way I see it, you are the commander of the ERF and the most dangerous force in the galaxy. That makes you very valuable to the United Nations. Right, Colonel?"

"They value my insight quite significantly."

Shoes squeaked on the tile behind Meyers. With his own team, with even a few more men, he would have signaled a strike before Reyes's men were ready. There was no way of knowing how the MARCOS would react. They had no training as a force working together. They had different soft-ware. It was the most ridiculous situation Meyers could imagine a commander leading his people into, and there was nothing to be done about it.

"So, my counter-offer is that I take you and your men hostage and sell you back to the United Nations for twenty-five million dollars." Reyes sneered. "What do you think about that?"

Rao snapped into action at that point, spinning, grabbing the assault rifle of the surprised man behind him, striking, sending that man to the ground, then pulling the assault rifle up, sighting, and snapping off a short burst into the chest of the next gunman to the right. Singh started to turn, but he was knocked to the ground by a quick burst into his back. Three more bursts, and Rao dropped, his face a gory mess leaking from the front of his helmet.

Meyers held out his hands, signaling no intention to attack.

Reyes pulled a pistol from under the table and shoved it into Ramawat's face. "Maybe thirty mill—"

The French doors shattered, and shapes arced through the air.

Flash-bangs.

The gunmen behind Meyers spun and fired at the doors. Meyers took Barlowe to the ground, shielding his head, eyes shut, arms covering ears. The flash-bangs detonated, and everything became a roaring ringing. It sounded like the gunfire might have continued, but it could have been the ringing.

Someone helped Meyers up. Through the spots dancing in front of his eyes, Meyers recognized Calderon. His copper skin glistened with sweat.

"You okay, Boss?" Calderon was shouting, but his words were distorted, distant.

Meyers nodded. He looked around the room. Reyes's men were dead. Reyes was bleeding from a shoulder wound, and the pretty young woman's right hand was clamped over her left bicep, which was bleeding. She was in shock. Someone stood between them, an ERF uniform. Ramawat looked dazed. One of McNutt's men, his name escaping Meyers at the moment, was helping Singh up. Starling was helping Paxton. Barlowe was sitting up on his own.

"Let's move!" McNutt came into view, slinging something over his shoulder. Rao's body.

They were rushed through the $12,000 French doors—kindling now—and into the garden. Soft lights glowed from the bottom of the fountain basin, and water spilled and splashed, but Meyers couldn't hear it. Bodies lay throughout the garden. Reyes's gunmen. Meyers counted three, but there was so much blood, black in the near-dark. There had to be more dead.

"Exiting Reyes's place," McNutt said as he set Rao down on the flatbed. His helmet came free, and blood and brains flopped out of a hole in the top of his head. McNutt worked two bungee straps free and secured Rao.

Calderon helped Meyers into a seat, then helped someone else buckle Reyes into the next seat to the left. Starling helped Barlowe into the seat to Meyers's right, then buckled in behind the driver's seat. Reyes looked around, disoriented. He seemed to be cursing. Or trying to.

McNutt was there, suddenly, slapping Reyes, soft on the cheeks, holding up an earpiece. Reyes's. "Hey! Listen! You need to tell your—" He slapped Reyes hard. "Listen up, yeah? Tell your men to clear Castro all the way south. Open all the checkpoints. Or we'll blow your fucking head off and sink your fucking barges." McNutt held up a detonator. "You understand? Yeah. Explosives. All over the harbor. Set you back more than this pretty little shack you call home, right? Make the call."

Reyes shouted into the night. "I'll fucking kill—"

McNutt punched Reyes. Blood gushed from split lips. "Last chance. Make the fucking call."

Reyes seemed even more disoriented, but he took the earpiece and mumbled something in Spanish. Meyers picked up a few words; Reyes was relaying McNutt's message.

Ramawat had gotten out of his seat at the front of the Rover. He wobbled next to McNutt. "You are out of line, Corporal. Your irresponsible behavior got Master Sergeant Rao killed. I will have you up on charges."

"Save it for later, Colonel. We need to roll." McNutt shoved Ramawat back into his seat and buckled him in, then made sure everyone else was strapped in before getting into the driver's seat.

The Rover jumped to life and spun around the driveway. The bar was lifted already, levered up by two corpses.

Meyers's head began to clear, and sounds and shapes became sharper.

"Clear of Reyes's place," McNutt said. "Two minutes out."

They cut west a short distance from the Reyes property, off Castro Street, shooting between buildings rather than sticking to the roads. It was a bumpy ride, the sort of thing the Rovers were built for. The gate to the harbor came into view. It was turning dark now, the moon not yet bright.

McNutt pushed the Rover hard, once getting the wheels beneath Meyers off the ground. "Approaching the gate. Clear."

McNutt looked back after they passed through the harbor gate and cut south along the quay. Meyers looked behind them, saw the other Rover and forms slipping from the shadows. The other Rover fell in a short distance behind them.

"Cut him loose," McNutt shouted over his shoulder.

Cisneros unbuckled Reyes. "End of the line, *jefe*." Cisneros shoved Reyes free of his seat, laughing as the surprised warlord screamed before tumbling into a stack of crates and going silent.

Ramawat swung around in his seat at McNutt. "That is not how you treat a prisoner! Your career is over, Corporal!"

"Yeah, Colonel, look, I wake up every day stunned to still be in uniform. I've been expecting a court martial since the day I signed on. So just shut it for now."

Starling smiled and shook her head, and Meyers found himself laughing. They passed through a gap in the fence and before long were approaching the blue-gray of the desert. Wind blew across his face, and the smell of the sea came to him. They were alive, at least more of them than had any right to be. Everything was a mess, but they were alive.

At least until Ramawat came up with his next hare-brained scheme.

22

———————

14 December 2174. Karpov Desert, South of Turning Point, Bellar Frontier Colony.

THE WINDS BLEW HARD, and Meyers wondered if they had seen the worst of it yet. Sand rattled against the exterior of the Operations Center and curled in through the entry, now mostly sealed. The camouflage netting scratched and thudded against the roof. The cooler air did nothing to calm Ramawat, who stared at the wall opposite the entry, hands gripped behind his back. His legs were shoulder-width apart, and those shoulders were thrust back stiffly. But Meyers had seen those shoulders shudder, and he knew Ramawat was struggling to control his anger.

Ramawat suddenly turned, sand crunching beneath his boots, his right lip curled in a snarl. Controlling his anger was apparently no longer a concern. His eyes were bloodshot, the lids twitching. Sweat and tears mingled on his cheek.

"Did you authorize Corporal McNutt's operation?" Ramawat's breath stank, as if he'd been breathing in fumes from some underworld while he seethed.

"The operation that saved our lives? That operation?" Meyers wanted to throttle Ramawat at that point, to smash his head against one of the cargo cases. "I wish I had authorized it. But I didn't. He's a smart soldier. He assessed the situation, saw the risk, and came up with a solution on his own. That's the sort of initiative the ERF wants in its personnel, and it should be awarded."

"He went against my orders."

"You told the ERF personnel that their duties were to focus on preparing the camp for breakdown. Sergeant Banh did exactly that. You've seen the plan he submitted when we returned."

Ramawat shook his head, and his shoulders shook along with it. "This was freelancing. McNutt exhibited a lack of discipline and control. This is exactly what the Special Security Council feared, both under a rogue like Colonel Rimes and then from his understudy."

"Maybe the SSC should review the records of the Metacorporate War."

"We are not here to debate the outcome of a foolish war!"

"You brought up the SSC's supposed concerns about Colonel Rimes."

"Because it was the foremost concern expressed by the delegates!" Ramawat swatted at the air, as if he were imagining swatting at Meyers, then returned to the back wall. "You are unfit for command."

Meyers took a step forward, hands balled into fists, then he stopped himself. "Tell me how incompetent I am that I ignored the SITREPs and AARs and recommend—"

Ramawat spun around again, eyes bugging out. "I ignored no such thing!"

Meyers jabbed a finger at the floor. "That I ignored the SITREPs and AARs and recommendations of the officer I was replacing mid-operation. Or maybe you could tell me how incompetent I am that I took six soldiers into the heart of territory controlled by someone almost certainly aligned with my target."

"Your reports in no way made a clear connection between Reyes and Waverley."

"Bullshit!" Meyers stepped closer, and he found himself wondering how much he valued his career, if it was worth letting the egomaniac off the hook when an ass-kicking was the least of what was called for. "You fucked up, Colonel. You let your arrogance and twisted perspective drive you into a hopeless situation, and that cost you a platoon sergeant. And now you want to pin this mess on the man who saved our lives? Fuck you!"

Veins stood out on Ramawat's forehead and along his neck. He leaned forward and brought his hands up, and Meyers heard a little voice in his head saying, "Come on! Come on!"

But Ramawat only snorted, and then he lowered his hands and straightened.

Meyers waited, hoping Ramawat was bluffing, that he was waiting for Meyers to drop his guard before charging. Ramawat took a deep breath and turned around to stare at the wall again.

"This mission is going to be seen to its conclusion, Colonel Meyers. We are going to bring Mr. Waverley to justice, and we are going to do so by capturing him alive and sending him back to Earth to face trial. Your cowboy ways are obsolete and destabilizing. This is the new era, the era where the American way is shown for the sad failure that it is."

Meyers opened his hands, saw the way they shook. He'd been close. "This is an international force. We've trained together for years. Our operations have seen us on every single colony world, and now we're on a frontier colony. I don't think the SSC gave you carte blanche to dismantle that proven model. Did they?"

Ramawat shook out his shoulders. "We are discussing Waverley now. Please do stay on subject."

"Fine. How do you plan on pulling this off? Waverley's no idiot. We know he has some knowledge about the goings-on in Turning Point. Maybe it's not Reyes, but someone is getting information out to the Cáceres Compound. You're not going to trick Waverley. You're not going to intimidate him. Any engagement you have with him will turn violent, and when it does, he'll use his superior firepower, and there will be more casualties. Lots more. Your only chance is to take him down."

"We are not assassins."

"No? We left at least ten of Reyes's men dead in his compound and at the harbor. That's how these sorts of operations work. We don't deal with saints. Reyes is a murderer. If the people of Turning Point can be believed, he's a rapist. That's probably just the beginning. How did he pay for a mansion like that? All those weapons? His people are clearly juiced up on something. All of that takes money."

"Our assignment had nothing to do with Reyes."

"You just got one of your men killed for the hell of it?"

Ramawat turned, this time slowly.

"You can't have it both ways." Meyers let his anger form a smile that shook at the edges. "And it sounds like you're forgetting our role of assessing and cultivating potential diplomatic ties. Reyes is terrorizing the rest of the people in that city. Removing him would probably establish a lot of goodwill between Earth and Bellar."

"Even in your interpretation of instructions, you cannot help inserting your American expansionism and colonialism."

Meyers snorted. "How the hell did you even get considered for this role?"

"I earned this position. I earned it by putting together a career that is second to none." Ramawat looked Meyers up and down and sneered. "I did not have some...mongrel hand it to me."

And there it was, Meyers realized. If not the root of Ramawat's problem, then a significant contributor. "What, was Colonel Rimes too black for you? Hm? Like Private Starling? How many of those soldiers out there aren't brown enough for you or are too yellow? Hm?"

Ramawat blinked. "Mongrel was a poor choice of words."

"No. It was a consistent choice of words. It was perfect. It finally let me see what's going on here. You got passed over for the most prestigious job you could imagine, and the job went to a mongrel. Worse, it was one of your own people who passed you over. And now you're going to show everyone how wrong they were."

"You are showing an unhealthy irrationality, Colonel Meyers."

Meyers ran his hands over his uniform shirt. The shaking was gone.

"As I said, it was a poor choice of words, nothing more." There was a different tension in Ramawat's voice now. Rather than angry, he sounded shaken, nervous. "Now, we will proceed with my plan. The way to bring Waverley down is to use exactly what you said: his access to information inside Turning Point. More specifically, we are going to disable that access, take him off the Grid completely, and wait for him."

"Where?"

"On the Cáceres Road, in the area controlled by Mattias."

Meyers wondered if Ramawat had talked to someone about the details of the plan he'd ordered canceled. "You have to be careful which place you set up. Some of those buildings are occupied. Children play in that area."

"Of course. And that is exactly how we will eliminate Waverley's air superiority. Those roads are too narrow to bring the flyers down low. Even if he were foolish enough to bring them along, what with women and children in the area, so he surely will not. He cannot use them to engage us. Without air superiority, he will surrender."

Although Meyers had thought of knocking Waverley off the Grid, or at least degrading his access, the idea of using that to lure him into the city seemed weak. "It's a pretty big assumption he won't use his flyers because the conditions will be unfavorable or because he's afraid of hurting civilians. He's wanted for the murder of tens of thousands of civilians during the war. Why would he care about killing more? He's a fugitive. He's facing life imprisonment."

Ramawat shrugged his shoulders. "This is the difference in how we lead. I have assessed the enemy and the battlefield. I have no doubt of my plan."

"You have to have doubt. It's part of being a leader."

"Doubt makes you weak. Perhaps this could explain why your Colonel Rimes had to resort to..." Ramawat chuckled. "Everything he did."

"I was thinking I might be able to stay on with your staff, maybe learn from you."

Ramawat's shoulders shot back, and his chin rose. "Of course. That is very wise."

"Now I realize I would only have to unlearn everything you taught. When we get back to Plymouth, I'll put in a request for transfer."

"To where? Who would even have you? Things are changing very rapidly on Earth."

"I'll have to see."

"We will." Ramawat stared at Meyers for a few heartbeats. "Go to Captain Singh. I have sent him the deployment information. See to it your men are briefed thoroughly and that there is no misunderstanding. There will be no mistakes this time."

Meyers peeled back the entry's flap and let himself out. He left the flap twisting in the wind, figuring it was Ramawat's Operations Center to care for now. After swinging by the Javelins to check on the wounded, Meyers trudged to the north edge of the camp, where the MARCOS had set up their tents. They were simple, lacking the insulation, energy capturing, and other technologies of the ERF tents. That meant the MARCOS forces were drawing on ERF resources—water, power, even computational power.

Once again, Ramawat's refusal to take on anything other than the MARCOS ideals and technologies was putting a load on everyone else.

Singh stepped from the west-most tent and pulled on his beret. He somehow got it to stay attached and managed a crisp salute, all in a sharp, continuous motion.

"Colonel Ramawat sent me to—"

Singh waved to the dunes north of camp, then he took off in that direction, ignoring the sand slamming against him. Meyers fell in at Singh's side. He kept up a good pace until they reached the closest dune, then he got on the leeward side and slowed, finally turning to glance at Meyers.

"You seem upset, Colonel."

"How's your back?"

"Bruised. It will heal. My armor is being repaired as we are speaking. I will request a new set when we are returned."

Meyers thought about that. He wasn't sure returning was a good idea for him. Maybe just waiting for the next flight to Earth was the way to go.

"Colonel?"

"Sorry. You have the troop deployment and battle plan?" Meyers waited while Singh stared off into the distance. A communication from outside Meyers's BAS requested approval for opening a shared workspace. Meyers sighed and approved. "Your commander sure knows how to introduce unnecessary complications."

"The battle plan is—"

"No, I haven't even looked at it yet." Meyers glanced at his display. "Fuck. Okay, yeah. So this is a problem, too. I was talking about keeping your team on a separate version of software and network, but..."

Singh stared off into space. "You do not approve."

Meyers turned his back to what little wind whipped around the dune. "Ritesh, right? Your name?"

"Yes, Ritesh. Thank you."

"I know he's your commander, and I know there's a lot of pride in your organization. And I saw you and Rao in action against Reyes's men. You're more than competent. Under different circumstances, I think your team would make an exceptional addition to the ERF. We could all learn from each other. But Ramawat, he doesn't get it. The day of racism and nationalism and classism, it's dead; it's over. It has no place in the ERF, and he's going to destroy a great man's dream by pushing things backward a century."

Singh's eyes focused on Meyers. "Colonel Ramawat, I think you misunderstand him."

"Yeah? I don't think so."

"But if you look at his deployment and battle—"

"He's ignored everything we learned the hard way. What's with the Dart? Why even have it involved? It has no weapons."

"It is to be airborne. For intelligence gathering and combat control. Agent Barlowe and Private Starling, they will provide a better view of the battlefield. For coordination."

"Yeah, that's bullshit. It's risky, and it's unnecessary. We have the Condor."

"But the Condor, the report said it is not functioning at full—"

"It can give you an eye in the sky without risking any lives. And if you guys were running the same BAS as we are, you could integrate the data feed we can put together—a complete battlefield awareness." Meyers was worried that Singh was even arguing about the matter.

Singh made a sound, maybe a "Hm."

"Look, Ritesh, I have to ask, has he always had these problems?"

"Problems?" Singh looked around, as if he thought someone might be watching.

"Ramawat. The way he doesn't listen to anyone. The subtle racism." Meyers wasn't sure if calling Rimes a mongrel was subtle, but giving Ramawat the benefit of the doubt because of language and cultural differences seemed fair.

Singh looked down at his boots, partially sunk in the sand. "It is compli-cated. The cultural differences, the historical problems."

"I get it. My country wasn't even four centuries old when all these changes hit, the borders disappearing, the idea of a national identity evapo-rating. India goes back...?"

"Millennia, yes. In one form or another, in some parts. Very complicated."

"Well, we had plenty of problems of our own in our short run." Meyers thought of Gerhardt's behavior. "We still have problems. But it's up to people in our positions—leaders—to show what sort of behavior is accept-able, not to..." He sighed, annoyed that he even had to voice such concerns.

"Colonel Ramawat means well. He does, I am telling you." Singh lowered his head. "It is very hard on him, these changes. Five years ago, it still looked..." He sighed. "His family has expectations, you see? Genera-tions of officers, and the colonel, so promising, so decorated and successful. But the military, there is so much change, so few positions left. Even the brilliant and great, they are facing premature ends. They will not do as well as those who came before. Very disappointing. Those who would enter politics, like the colonel, maybe rise to head a party. It is not likely. The nation, the people, so much change, and the pride is lost."

Meyers wondered if he was being too sensitive, maybe expressing concerns that were rooted in biases of his own. He looked at the battle plan again. "Maybe he does mean well, but this plan is for shit. It introduces unnecessary risk."

Singh's eyes defocused. "How would you change it? Show me. Please, Colonel Meyers."

"All right, but keep in mind there isn't a good solution, just less terrible ones."

"Okay."

Meyers drilled down and moved icons representing the troops around. "So, it starts by waiting until sunset, getting the sun at our backs, moving to the east end of the town, using what little cover we have available to us..."

23

15 December 2174. Turning Point, Bellar Frontier Colony.

MEYERS ROCKED in the seat of the Rover, straining to see the first glow of the sun in the eastern sky but seeing only darkness. Dawn was approaching, bringing with it the heat and brightness that would wear everyone down, sapping endurance and resolve. It was peaceful at the moment, the desert winds dead, nothing but the drone of the Rover's drive system, the sand spitting out from the back of the tires, the fresh air, the stars pale flecks splashed across the black sky. Some of the lights weren't stars at all but those of the Dart, circling Turning Point high overhead.

Meyers hooked a hand in the front of his armor, reminding himself it was there, keeping him cool, keeping him safe. He caught movement to his left: Ramawat, turning in the passenger seat, throwing an arm over the seat back, his earlier anger gone.

"I reviewed Captain Singh's input," Ramawat said. "Have you seen it? Quite good, don't you think? Very good, making use of what cover the battlefield offers. It also hides our true strength. Smart. You would agree with that, wouldn't you, Colonel?"

Meyers wished the engagement were over and he could be done with Ramawat. "I think his ideas made the best of this situation. Why are we moving into position so early?"

Ramawat just stared for a moment, apparently unsatisfied with Meyers's response. "I did change a few things. Yes. You will see when I send the final plan. Basically, though, I do not agree with the idea of engaging at the entry to the city. We want them west of this road you call Guevara Highway."

Meyers pictured the area. Guevara was the first north-south road as you traveled west into Turning Point. Blacktop. Two lanes. Big enough for even the Leopard. The prefab buildings—mostly empty at the edge of the city—became apartments after Guevara. There was an open lot between it and the first apartment. A playground. Children, mothers.

"Can you believe they bother with road names?" Ramawat being conversational.

"Kids play on that open lot. The one west of the highway."

"Yes. I mentioned before, it will affect Waverley's thinking. More reason to surrender."

Meyers looked down at the sand passing below his feet, a deep blue-gray in the darkness. To his right, McNutt, helmet sealed, stared straight ahead. Meyers wanted to seal his helmet and block Ramawat out, but Ramawat was in a talkative mood. He would just open a comm channel and keep blathering.

"I have seen the whole thing as it will transpire," Ramawat said. "I have already spoken to Waverley and accepted his surrender."

Meyers looked around, confused. "What? Then why are we driving to Turning Point?"

Ramawat chuckled, but it was crafted, part of the conversation he'd put together, his way of bringing Meyers around. "In my mind, you see. Think it, see it, make it true. Do you believe that?"

"No."

"I sent him a message just now, just before I talked to you. An offer to meet with him and discuss the terms of his surrender. I even offered to put in a good word for him at trial if he should make this easy for all involved."

What sort of idiot would give even a second of thought to that? Meyers wondered. Certainly not the most powerful businessman ever.

"You think this won't work," Ramawat said.

"It won't. He's negotiated deals worth billions and billions of dollars. This is trivial to him. He'll see through the offer."

"I would be quite disappointed if he didn't. But he will show up to turn me down, and to re-institute his Grid connection. Your Private Starling is taking it down now, eliminating all of his access points and disabling his ID. And, you see, when Waverley shows, it will be with force. We all project strength, even a businessman. Intimidation is a powerful tool, whether getting pirates to see the futility of their situation or getting a small corporation to accept a buyout at a lower price than they wish. As you said, he has negotiated deals worth billions of dollars, and this is trivial to him."

"Have you ever seen what proxies can do?" Meyers couldn't imagine the sort of people the MARCOS went against fielding that sort of technology, not as expensive as it was.

"Of course. We have had many offers from weapons suppliers. T-Corp has shown us their products. Human shells, much larger shells, big and indestructible, quite the same as you describe this one. Were you aware that there are people in India who have completely given up their human bodies? Ah, so you're familiar with this? Left their old flesh behind, and you cannot tell the difference. Many worry about what this means for the journey of the soul." Ramawat squinted his eyes. "Is this what frightens you and your men? The proxy?"

"My soldiers." Meyers emphasized soldiers. "It's not fear—it's respect."

"Fear. The ERF fears them. Not my MARCOS. You'll see soon enough."

Meyers wanted to let it lie, but he couldn't. Fear—irrational and inexcusable—wasn't what he felt. "We went up against proxies in the war. Telepresence, run remotely, and like what you're describing, entirely new bodies. I saw one once. It survived a burst of plasma that destroyed people in armor like mine. These were human-type bodies. What he's got..."

"It is a single weapon. We have many more."

"That single weapon can't be damaged by the sort of weapons we're using, and it packs enough punch to get through our armor. Easily."

Ramawat chuckled, and it was once again a practiced sound. The Rovers turned onto Cáceres Road, and he turned enough that he could see the walls of the large buildings on the eastern edge of the city.

"Colonel Meyers, this explains so much about your failures here. When you let fear control you like you have, you simply cannot be effective. My men understand that fear is the enemy. They don't give it the slightest foothold."

My men. Meyers wondered if Ramawat could hear himself. "What about Reyes?"

Ramawat's eyes narrowed. "Reyes? What about him?"

"Those haulers of his are an even bigger threat. What if he comes to Waverley's rescue?"

"Or comes seeking revenge for your man McNutt murdering his men? Isn't that more likely?" Ramawat snorted. "It won't happen any more than Waverley bringing in the flyers. We'll remain in Mattias's territory, and there are too many civilians in the area, and those big machine guns can be quite indiscriminate when firing."

"You think Mattias's forces are going to try to stop Reyes if he brings those haulers in? Seriously? With what?" Meyers was becoming more unsure by the second about Ramawat's sanity.

The Rover passed between the buildings on Turning Point's eastern edge. Meyers looked at the eastern sky and caught the first hint of sunlight, finally. He could feel Ramawat's eyes burrowing. Moments later, the Rover crossed Guevara Highway. To the right, the open lot where kids played was a broad square of dirt. The lot spread northwest, crossing a dirt road and connecting to a soccer field. On the opposite side of the dirt road stood smaller buildings. Beyond those, a few makeshift houses stood. Many more makeshift houses stood west and east of the soccer field. Everything was black in the first sunlight and the ever-present glow from the displays lining the edge of Reyes's territory. There was movement in the city already, indistinct forms among the houses and apartments, people stumbling from the alleys between the prefab buildings.

Meyers remembered Barlowe's flight from the city and Beniam's concerns about spies. Functional cameras still existed here and there inside Turning Point. They fed the Grid audio as well as video. They could be effective spying tools. It was only a matter of time before Reyes knew the invaders were back in his city. It wouldn't matter whether it was in Mattias's territory or not. Reyes was the type of man who would seek revenge.

The Rover stopped in an alley on the south side of Cáceres Road. Meyers unbuckled and slid out. The ERF forces—Banh's squad—formed up around Meyers as the second Rover arrived and dropped off McNutt's squad. Once everyone was offloaded, the Rovers sped off. It would be two more trips before everyone was deposited in the city.

"Colonel?" Banh looked around. "Mattias, he is a Christian? His people, too?"

"Yeah."

"Is there a reason they have been chosen over the others?"

Meyers saw the pain in Banh's eyes. He'd resented the ERF not having chaplains, an expense no one could have justified given how few requested them. "It's just the luck of the draw. They're located on the eastern edge, facing Waverley."

Banh nodded, apparently accepting that. "Where should we deploy?"

Before Meyers could answer, he received a message from Ramawat, who was standing in the middle of the road. Meyers scanned the message description: the battle plan.

He opened the file and quickly found himself grinding his teeth.

"What is it, Colonel?"

"Nothing. Take your squad to that building." Meyers pointed to a three-story prefab on the north side of the road, three buildings down from their current position. "Find whatever cover you can. Break your squad up over all three stories. We'll want to lay down overlapping fields of fire, so coordinate with Corporal Gerhardt, who will be in this building." Meyers pointed at the building that looked onto the Guevara Highway and Cáceres Road intersection. "McNutt's going to be here." Meyers pointed to the building across the alley.

"Both snipers on the south side, Colonel?"

"Maybe Colonel Ramawat's going to put some of his people on the northern rooftops. I don't know. This is his plan, not mine."

"Do you think it is a good plan, Colonel?"

If he were being honest with himself, Meyers didn't know how safe the plan was, but that wasn't the right thing to convey to the others. "I don't think there's a good plan for this situation, Corporal. We just need to do what we can to get through this."

People began stepping out of the buildings Meyers's squads were going to be occupying: mothers, children, men with assault weapons slung over their shoulders. They scanned the soldiers, squinting, brows knit in confusion. Their sense of being invaded would only intensify when the doors to their homes were burst in and soldiers took up position behind windows, windows where simple curtains were being drawn aside by wide-eyed children.

Banh edged closer to Meyers. "Colonel Meyers, we are going to take up positions inside the homes of these people?"

"Unless you can find empty apartments."

"This will endanger people."

Meyers sighed. "I know."

"Do you think Colonel Rimes would have done such a thing?"

Anger flared, and Meyers nearly snapped at Banh, but it was a fair question. It was a question Meyers had been asking himself nonstop. Rimes would have probably refused to bend to Ramawat's demands. But Meyers realized he wasn't Rimes. He needed to find his own way. "I can't guess what Colonel Rimes would have done. I can tell you that I've made it quite clear to Colonel Ramawat that this is a bad idea."

That seemed to be enough for Banh, who bowed his head and closed his eyes for a second before waving for his squad to follow him.

Probably praying for forgiveness, Meyers realized. He wished there were some way he might find forgiveness for what he was doing. Maybe there would be a god at some point who would allocate blame appropriately. Simplistic fantasy or not, the idea certainly had appeal to it.

Meyers waved McNutt over.

McNutt's gaze kept going from Meyers to Guevara. "What're we doing this side of the road?"

"Ramawat's plan. I tried getting him to move it back to the abandoned buildings."

"Said no, huh? What's he use that head of his for other than a hat rest?"

"Let's just do what we can to minimize civilian casualties." Meyers pointed to where Banh had his squad formed up on the north side of Cáceres Road. "Banh's got that building over there, you've got this one, Gerhardt's here." Meyers pointed to McNutt's building, then tapped the easternmost one. "Break your team up over all three stories—empty apartments if you find them. Put Perkins on the rooftop."

"Alone?"

"You think he'll run?"

McNutt scowled. "He'll be without support up there."

"Gerhardt's going to be on the roof here."

"This Waverley's got ordnance even a little better than the explosives Ski found, he could just bring these buildings down on top of us—make fast work of the whole thing."

Meyers thought about that. It didn't seem likely. "You threatened to blow up the barges. Did you find some explosives?"

"In one of the sheds on the quay, yeah. Mining grade, my guess. Kept a bit for Starling."

"Well, I think Reyes has all he needs without any more explosives. Did you get a sense he had something heavy hidden in his compound somewhere?"

"Nah." McNutt turned to look the building over, then thumped a gloved fist against the facade. "This material, it's not thick enough to stop the rounds of that proxy's gun."

"I know. Remind your men of that. Priority is those flyers."

McNutt sneaked something out of a leg pouch and began rubbing it. "This all Ramawat's idea?"

"Yes." Meyers tried to see what McNutt was rubbing. "Is that some sort of good luck charm?"

McNutt looked down at his hand. "Might say that." He opened his hand so that Meyers could see a polished stone small enough to hide in a man's palm. "My old man raised me after my mum died. Brought me up right, taught me to be independent and strong. A few days before I turn sixteen, we're out climbing. A section of cliff just gives way beneath him—takes him down twenty-five, thirty meters. I kept a piece of it, that cliff, had it smoothed. I figure it killed one McNutt, maybe it'll protect the other."

"Is that why you joined the Army?"

"New Zealand's no different than anywhere else now. You're born t' money, or your choices are pretty limited. I'm not quite what you'd call metacorporate material, if you didn't already see that." He kissed the rock and pushed it back into the leg pouch, then he wandered to where his squad was gathered and began waving at the building.

The sun was fully seated on the horizon when Gerhardt's squad arrived. Meyers passed along the battle plan, struggled to remain calm as Gerhardt challenged the plan, then headed over to Ramawat's side.

"Colonel, your men look so serious. They can't possibly believe Waverley would be so foolish as to attack, can they?" Standing ramrod straight, Ramawat managed to ooze an unfathomable confidence and calm.

"Where did you want me positioned?"

Ramawat pointed back and to his left. "Here. I will have Captain Singh with me, as well as Corporal Tavva's fire team."

"Are you going to have any people on the rooftops? At least on the north side?"

"Would that make you more comfortable?"

"Yes."

"Then we will assign our sharpshooters to those positions." Ramawat looked up and away, then he chuckled. "Excellent! Mr. Waverley has just informed me that he's en route to discuss this matter of surrender and to resolve this interruption to his Grid connection. Just sending the message seems to have upset him. He will become angrier once we shut off the last of the Grid connection. I will have Private Starling do that now."

Meyers looked up and down Cáceres Road. People had gathered along the fronts of the buildings. Children in simple clothes watched from the open lot on the north side of the intersection. A tall, slender, black man approached down Guevara Highway, turning west onto Cáceres Road. He was trailed by four other men, all of them with assault weapons carried at the ready. Backlit by the sun, it was hard to make out details about them. The tall man said something to the children on the playground, getting a laugh from them. When the man was ten meters out, recognition hit Meyers: Beniam.

"You come back, even after what has happened with Reyes?" Beniam looked Ramawat over. "You are the one told Reyes to help you?"

"Colonel Abhishek Ramawat." Ramawat clipped his heels together and bowed slightly. "You might wish to move your men out of the road as we have an appointment with Mr. Waverley imminently."

"Mr. Waverley?" Beniam looked around, then looked at Meyers. "Who is this? The fugitive?"

At the east end of the city, the Rovers came into view, trailing dust and whining loudly. Beniam scowled as they came to a stop and the last of Ramawat's men jumped clear. The squad leaders shouted out orders, and the MARCOS dashed into buildings. The Rovers crossed over the highway, and the drivers parked them against empty buildings. Beniam's scowl deepened.

Once again, Ramawat looked up and his eyes defocused. "Thank you, Agent Barlowe." Ramawat turned back to Beniam. "Yes, Mr. Waverley is a fugitive. You will have an opportunity to meet him soon enough, if you wish. My reconnaissance aircraft just reported spotting his approach." Ramawat pointed toward the slowly thinning sand cloud the Rovers had created east of the city.

Beniam turned and shielded his eyes. Sunlight gleamed off something. He turned and pointed to the buildings where Ramawat had positioned his soldiers. "These are our homes. Who said you could come here?"

"We are on United Nations business."

Beniam shook his head. "Reyes, he knows you are here. He will come soon. He will kill you all."

Meyers thought he saw the slightest flinching in Ramawat's face.

"We have concluded our business with Mr. Reyes."

"You do not conclude business with Reyes. Only he concludes business." Beniam turned east again and shielded his eyes. The sun was heating everything now, glinting off multiple objects. "The United Nations, it makes you do stupid things? Put your enemy's back against the sun?"

Meyers looked away and fought back a chuckle.

Ramawat drew his shoulders up. "It would be safest for you and your companions to get off the road on the slight chance there might be a short exchange of gunfire."

Beniam shrugged. "When you are dead, we will take the weapons from your bodies and drag you into the desert for the Zombies." He headed back toward Guevara Highway, this time stopping to shout at the children on the playground, who ran away.

"What an unpleasant man," Ramawat said.

Beniam glared back at Ramawat, then turned north on Guevara Highway. The sand cloud kicked up by the Rovers was completely gone now, and the morning sun lit up a shimmering mirage some distance east of the city. Meyers thought he could make out the flyers and beneath them, the proxy. They were minutes out. He looked west, saw the civilians fading into the alleys and buildings. Somewhere beyond the range of his eyes, he swore he heard the whine of haulers. Thanks to Ramawat's plan, their odds against Waverley were bad enough. If Reyes attacked, they were doomed.

"Sergeants, prepare your squads!" Ramawat stepped forward. "Corporal Tavva, hold your position. Captain Singh, Colonel Meyers, remain close on my flank. It is essential we present a committed and professional image."

Meyers stepped forward. The sound of the haulers became clearer, louder. There was no kidding himself it was just his imagination. Sweat trickled down his face, and his heart sank. They were about to be caught between two superior forces, and there was nothing he could do to stop it.

24

15 December 2174. Turning Point, Bellar Frontier Colony.

SAND CLOUDS TWISTED and swirled as they rolled up the length of Cáceres Road from Guevara Highway, knocking visibility down for those who were relying on naked eyes rather than their BAS overlays. Meyers was one of those, his faceplate up, just as Ramawat had ordered. The better to show the lack of fear in their eyes.

Flyers hovered overhead, their fans roaring, drowning out anything less than a shout. The air carried a rusty, dead smell, as if the flyers had been dug up from a cemetery that doubled as a junkyard.

Meyers desperately wanted his faceplate down, his helmet sealed. He wanted a private network with his ERF team. He wanted to lay down target priorities and watch the vitals of his team. He wanted Barlowe and Starling back at the Operations Center, running intelligence feeds through the Condor. Instead, Meyers breathed in sand and tried not to let it show just how pissed off he was.

Waverley's armored hauler—smaller than Reyes's vehicles, but with a serious plex-armor upgrade—rolled through the sand cloud and came to a stop three meters in front of Ramawat. Waverley sat in the passenger seat, blurry, distorted, but clearly smiling smugly. The proxy cast a shadow over him, the arm with the machine gun attached extended toward Ramawat's entourage.

If Reyes's haulers were indeed approaching from the west, the flyers drowned out any whine of motors.

"You must be Colonel Ramawat." Waverley spoke, but it seemed off. His lips moved, impossible to read behind the plex-armor, and after a small delay, his voice came from a speaker somewhere. Meyers realized it was from the proxy.

"I am," Ramawat yelled. "And you would appear to be Mr. Chad Milton Waverley."

"That is correct." Waverley managed to add about ten percent more smug to his smile.

Meyers wished he had even one person held back in reserve. Even one would have been enough to sneak into the Cáceres Compound. Blow the proxy operator away, turn the proxy into so much metal and composite materials, and the battle would be decided.

Ramawat wouldn't consider anything so dishonorable. Plus, it was unnecessary.

"It is my honor to meet you, Mr. Waverley." Ramawat clicked his heels.

"Let's keep this short, shall we?" Waverley looked at the flyers overhead. "I have no intention of surrendering. That must be obvious. And I will have my Grid access again, one way or another."

"You haven't yet heard my terms," Ramawat said.

Meyers wondered how his and Ramawat's teams were doing. Did they have targets? Did they have cover? Could Perkins or Gerhardt get a clean shot at Waverley—test the hauler's armor? Was there anything visible from above on the proxy's surface that could be damaged?

A shadow passed over the street, and the roar of the Dart drowned out the flyers' fans for a moment. Meyers tried to find the Dart without fully looking up. Sunlight gleamed off its wings, then it was gone, banking away.

The proxy's torso turned up and pivoted to follow, but its gun stayed on Ramawat.

A channel request pinged; Meyers opened it without checking to see who it was.

"Colonel?" It was Starling's voice, tinny, small in his earpiece.

Meyers lowered his head enough that he could talk without it being too obvious. "Private Starling, I'm pretty sure Colonel Ramawat asked Agent Barlowe to handle all communications, and they were to go straight to the colonel."

"I understand, sir." She sounded chastised. "This is a special connection. Private, off the normal network. Colonel Ramawat won't know. Agent Barlowe's trying to talk to him, but...I don't know if he's getting through."

"What is it?"

"Haulers, sir. They're coming in from Reyes's territory. It looks like Mattias's men have abandoned the checkpoints. Reyes's men are moving fast. He's got at least fifty people on or running alongside those haulers. Easily twice that coming in at a jog. Another group forming up in his territory still. The haulers are moving into the open market west of your position, barely slowing down."

Fifty. Maybe 200 more. Meyers's stomach twisted into a knot. "Tell your pilot to get some altitude. They've got a gun that can bring that ship down."

"I'll try, sir. He's following Colonel Ramawat's orders."

Meyers squeezed the armored segments covering his thighs, imagining they were Ramawat's head. He was going to get them all killed. "Keep this channel open, Private."

"Will do, sir."

Ramawat looked back, still confident, somehow able to put aside the absurdity of the situation he'd created. "Colonel Meyers, I was just explaining to Mr. Waverley that we would both be willing to testify at his trial should he surrender peacefully. You would agree to this, wouldn't you?"

Behind the armored glass, distorted, Waverley leaned toward his driver, laughing.

"Reyes is on the way," Meyers said. "Fifty or more men, plus the haulers."

Ramawat's face knotted up, brow wrinkling. "I am quite aware of the situation. We have the more pressing matter of Mr. Waverley's surrender at hand."

Meyers looked past Waverley's hauler. Children had returned to the playground to the east, watching. More people—women and children—had gathered in the alleys. Some leaned out windows in the apartment buildings. Overhead, the flyers slowly gained altitude, and their belly guns rotated, tracking to positions where soldiers watched from windows. Behind the distorting glass armor, Waverley waved a hand, a chopping motion. The smile faded.

He was tired of the game.

The proxy raised its gun slightly. Aiming.

Meyers lowered his faceplate and opened a channel to the ERF forces as he turned and dove. "They're firing!"

He took Singh to the ground as gunfire thundered. Meyers rolled and ran for the southern alley. The armor's audio receptors caught the sound of the proxy pivoting, and he dove again, then he rolled as the machine gun cycled, tearing up the street, the earth, the walls. A round grazed his thigh, creasing his armor, sending fiery pain through his leg. He got up and staggered into the alley, retreating as the proxy apparently followed to get a clean shot at him. Its rounds punched through the surrounding prefab walls easily. As Meyers neared the back of the alley, a door popped open, and a slender, young woman stepped into the entry. Her eyes were wide with terror, stark white against her dark skin. She waved for him to come inside.

"Hurry!"

The proxy fired, and the door burst into pieces. Behind it, the young woman did the same, her limbs falling away in pieces, her shoulders and head collapsing down, and then sliding off her shattered torso.

Meyers ducked lower as he staggered, caught a glimpse of rungs and rails—access to the roof—and when he reached the back of the building, he dropped and rolled. He peeked around the corner. The proxy was at the other end of the alley, trying to squeeze into it and failing. Behind the proxy, Meyers saw two MARCOS running for the opposite alley: Singh, pulling Ramawat behind. They were easy targets for the proxy if it turned.

Meyers pulled his carbine out of its harness and sighted on the proxy.

There were no obvious places to target and there was no chance his bullets would penetrate, but he hoped he wouldn't need to.

He fired a short burst into the area approximating a head, the area that had looked up to track the Dart. Bullets ricocheted, and the proxy backpedaled. For a moment, it seemed to just stand still, then it twisted right and left before raising its weapon clumsily and firing close to where he would have been if he were standing. Chunks of the prefab wall tore free and rained down on him. He rolled back behind the building and belly-crawled east, away from the proxy, behind Gerhardt's building.

Suddenly, a strange whining, grinding sound overwhelmed the gunfire. Meyers looked up just as one of Waverley's flyers flew over the top of the building.

Then Meyers realized that the flyer wasn't going to make it. Thick, white smoke was whipping around one of the forward fans. The flyer was losing altitude fast. Its rear clipped the building corner and more chunks of the prefab building material tore free, some of it rattling in a terrible series of ricochets in the alley he'd just left.

The flyer's motors all died at once, and it plunged, coming straight down toward him. He rolled up tight against the wall and braced for the impact, knowing it would be too much for his armor.

A fan kicked on, sputtered, shot out pieces of blades that embedded in the walls and the dirt road, then there was nothing but a grinding sound again. That was enough to kick the flyer into a horizontal position and send it into the street a little over a meter away, where it hit hard. People who had come out from the other building to see what was happening ran away as the gull-wing doors popped open. The pilot and passenger slowly began unbuckling from their seats.

Meyers sighted on the passenger and fired. Blood burst from the passenger's chest and sprayed the pilot, who looked around while reaching for a shoulder holster. Meyers fired again, splattering the pilot's brains into the street.

After listening for a second to be sure no other threat was imminent, Meyers crawled again, waiting for the hum of the proxy's guns. He sent out a private network request to all the functional ERF BASes within range. Immediately signals rolled in. He stopped crawling long enough to build out squad data, focusing first on vitals. He let out a sigh of relief when no red signals popped up; he hadn't lost anyone so far. He opened a channel to McNutt.

"Corporal McNutt."

"You all right, Colonel?" McNutt sounded amazingly calm.

"I'm fine. That proxy has a vulnerability. Have Perkins focus on its upper torso, where the head should be."

"Copy," McNutt said.

Meyers brought Gerhardt into the channel. "Corporal Gerhardt, that proxy's upper torso where the head should be. I think there's a sensor array there. Something. My rounds didn't penetrate, but they pissed it off."

"Fuck, Colonel, just what I need right now."

"When you can, Corporal."

Video started to roll in, and Meyers's BAS turned that into the beginnings of a shared view of the battlefield. Banh's feed revealed Reyes's forces. The haulers—the Jaguar at the front—were limited to entering the street one abreast unless they wanted to come in staggered, which would limit where they could fire. Already, the other haulers were backing up. Suddenly, the window of the third hauler—the Devil Cat—cracked, and blood sprayed all over the console and glass. The Devil Cat stopped until it was pushed back by the leading Cougar.

Meyers pulled his attention away from Banh and Reyes's forces. The flyers were still a huge problem or at least seemed to be. Meyers brought up Perkins's and Gerhardt's video feeds. Perkins was focusing on the proxy, popping off a shot, then ducking back and moving positions. Gerhardt was busy with two flyers, which seemed to be toying with him, chasing him around the rooftop.

Of this building, Meyers realized.

He crawled to the corner of the alley opposite the one he'd run into. Rungs ran up the side of the building, not two meters in, same as the other building. There were guide rails on either side of the rungs that ran all the way to the top. He got to his feet and holstered his CAWS-5, then he unlocked two silicone grips from the armor over his ribs. The grips were almost like little hands, but with balls embedded in the palms. He stretched the grips out from his body, revealing thin, yellow cabling. He played out enough that he could secure the grips to the guide rails. Once the grips were secured, he activated them, and they crawled up to the top of the guide rails and locked. He grabbed onto the guide rails lightly, pointed the tips of his boots so that they were wide of the rungs, and again activated the grips, letting the winch in his armor pull him up. His boots skimmed along the outside of the guide rails until he was at the top. He quickly set his boots on the rungs and deactivated the grips, which sucked back into his armor.

Both flyers were visible from his vantage point. They were actually getting in each other's way, fouling up shots and nearly clipping each other as they tried to get a clean shot at Gerhardt, who was rolling and feinting. His maneuvering shouldn't have been enough. The guns should have taken him out. Meyers looked back at the flyers and realized why they were having such a problem: both pilots were slumped forward, dead, their windows blood-spattered. The passengers—gunners now acting as pilots—weren't as adept.

Meyers sighted on the left front fan of the nearest flyer and popped off two quick bursts. The grinding sound he'd heard from the crashing flyer broke the steady drone of the fans, and white smoke started floating out from the underside. The gunner-pilot overcompensated, and the flyer tilted hard, driving the right front fan into the already chipped-up roof with enough force to crack the fan housing. Blade fragments shot out and over the roof even as the back end of the damaged flyer popped up and into the other flyer. Fan blades sheared through housings and screens, shattering fan blades until there was a terrible, deafening screech that Meyers's suit struggled to filter down to tolerable levels.

Both flyers fell to the rooftop, and their motors instantly died. Meyers sighted on the nearest copilot and squeezed off three short bursts. The first did nothing more than spiderweb the window. The second punched through, and the third burst caught the copilot in the throat as he was aiming a pistol at Meyers.

He turned to the other flyer, but Gerhardt had already dealt with the copilot.

"Thanks, Colonel!" Gerhardt loped to the north end of the roof and settled into a squat.

Meyers ran forward, hunched low, and settled against the north wall, waiting a heartbeat before looking over. The scene was complete pandemonium.

Corporal Tavva and his fire team were just segments of armor and puddles of blood. Meyers made out chest pieces, two helmets, and a foot before looking away. Civilian corpses, even more unrecognizable, littered the street and doorways. There were four flyers down; one of them apparently just crashed in front of one of the apartment buildings where the MARCOS were operating. Its gull-wing doors popped open slightly, then stuck. The occupants staggered and pushed the doors up, then gunfire shattered the glass of the doors, and both occupants dropped back into their seats.

The MARCOS marksmen had several of Waverley's bodyguards pinned down in alleyways, and McNutt and Gerhardt's squads had managed the same on the other side of the street. Considering how badly outnumbered and outgunned they were, the teams were holding up well.

"Colonel? Are you okay?" It was Starling.

"Go ahead, Private Starling."

"I'm sending you video through my BAS feed, sir. Those haulers are moving now."

Meyers flipped to the video from Starling, saw the dead driver beneath the Devil Cat; the Devil Cat backed up, crushing the dead driver's head. Meyers could barely make out the new driver, who was low in the seat, head barely visible over the wheel.

"The others are moving north, Colonel. Into the market. They're... plowing through people and stalls."

Meyers searched through the video, caught the big hauler—the Leopard—doing exactly what Starling had described, crashing into a stall of clothes and running over the woman inside. She managed to roll over what might have been a baby before she was crushed beneath the tires. Meyers squeezed his eyes shut, then he added Starling's feed to the private network.

"Any word on Singh and Ramawat, Private?"

"Agent Barlowe's communicating with the colonel now, sir."

"So, he's alive?" Meyers felt disappointment rather than relief.

"I think he's saying this is your fault, Colonel."

Of course he is, Meyers thought. Why start accepting responsibility now?

Meyers considered leaving it alone, letting Ramawat deal with things on his own the rest of the way. It was his disaster, and the ERF was holding up better than could reasonably be expected. Then Meyers realized it was only a matter of time before Ramawat called.

Better to own the problem, Meyers thought.

He sucked in a breath and opened a channel to Ramawat.

25

———

15 December 2174. Turning Point, Bellar Frontier Colony.

THE CACOPHONY of battle tested the limits of Meyers's BAS and earpiece. The grit of sand and pulped construction materials were a fine layer on his armor, a threat to clog the armor's intake filters. Already, he could smell breath and sweat building up in the recycled air of his helmet—a sure sign the armor was conserving resources. Gunfire, the drone of motors and whine of fans, even the crack of the prefab walls disintegrating beneath heavy caliber automatic weapons fire...it was all too much for the system to effectively filter and diminish. Meyers knocked all audio other than his direct line to Ramawat down to fifty percent of the Ramawat channel peak.

While waiting for Ramawat to accept the connection, Meyers scanned the battle zone again. Three of Waverley's men stood in the shadows of an alleyway across the street, one using a woman as a shield, the other two holding children—neither of them possibly older than eight—to their chests.

Meyers scanned west along the rooftops where Ramawat was supposed to have put sharpshooters. Only one was visible, crouched low, moving, apparently trying to get a better angle on one of the flyers while staying clear of its sights. While scanning back toward the east, Meyers spotted the missing MARCOS sharpshooters. One was bleeding out on the rooftop diagonal from Gerhardt; the other was part of a torn-up rooftop corner just across the street. The sharpshooter's head and upper torso were bloody ribbons dangling from the rubble.

Meyers opened a channel to McNutt. "Corporal, you've got a MARCOS sharpshooter on the roof across the street from you. Any chance you could help?"

"What's he need?"

"There's a flyer working its way east, about seven meters off the road."

"I see it."

"Have someone lay down fire, get the pilot's attention."

"On it!"

"Oh, and put your armor into chameleon mode."

"Music to the ears, Colonel, and it'll piss Ramawat off."

When McNutt closed the connection and Ramawat still hadn't accepted the open channel request, Meyers opened a channel to Banh. "Sergeant Banh, how're you holding up?"

"You are all right, Colonel?"

"So far. I've got a low-res feed coming from the Dart. Are you seeing it?"

"Yes, Colonel. Those haulers, they are moving to the north side."

"Can you have a surprise ready for them? They don't do so well without drivers."

"Or gunners, yes. I have half my squad on that north wall. They wait for the shot."

"Excellent. I want your people in chameleon mode now."

"But Colonel Ramawat—"

Meyers thought of Ramawat's dead sharpshooters. "That was to show our numbers. No need to give away our positions."

Meyers sighted on the bodyguards with human shields. There weren't any clear shots, but he couldn't leave the people hostages. Just being in the area would get them killed. He settled on the man farthest back in the alley, who only had a child raised to chest height, leaving the visible parts of the man's armored neck and head exposed. Meyers aimed for the neck, where the armor looked weakest.

The CAWS-5 bucked slightly, and the bodyguard dropped the child, then clutched at the neck armor. Blood flowed over the bodyguard's gloved hand, and he slid to the ground.

Meyers turned to check on Gerhardt, who was crawling back from the western corner just as gunfire shattered the wall there. "Gerhardt, have your men switch to chameleon mode."

"What about the MARCOS? They could fire on us if they don't see us."

"I'm calling Ramawat." Meyers looked up as his earpiece chimed. Ramawat had finally accepted the channel invite.

"Colonel Meyers?" Ramawat was agitated, shouting.

"One moment."

The bodyguard holding the woman up pulled her tighter as the other bodyguard squatted next to the fallen one. Meyers sighted on the standing bodyguard. There was a sliver of exposed armor where the bodyguard's right shoulder was higher than the woman's. Meyers put a round into the joint, knocking the man back slightly. The woman tried to pull away; the bodyguard had to twist to stop her. He was in profile for Meyers. He put a round into the neck area again, dropping the man to his knees.

"Colonel Meyers, what do you think you are doing?"

"Saving lives. Waverley and Reyes are showing clear disregard for civilians."

"You are part of my command staff! I need you to join Captain Singh and me immediately!"

Meyers tried but couldn't get a shot on the last of the bodyguards, who withdrew into the alley. "You may have one of Waverley's men coming your way, using a child as a human shield."

Ramawat was silent for a moment. "Singh will see to that. Where are you?"

"South side of Cáceres Road. Rooftop of the building you assigned to Gerhardt."

"What are you doing there?"

"Initially, running away from the proxy."

Meyers turned to check on Perkins the next rooftop over. He was still engaged with the proxy. There were two sections of the rooftop wall completely torn away, probably by the proxy's railgun, but Perkins was still up, still moving.

"Please return to my side immediately," Ramawat said.

"Colonel, I've got the best seat in the house here. I mean, seriously. Overlaid with the shared BAS network, I'm getting my people in the best position possible. We're—"

"I thought I told you not to use the BAS network."

"And not to use the chameleon functions of our armor, I know. But we're in battle now. We need those advantages."

"My men do not have those advantages."

They're all your soldiers, you idiot, Meyers thought. "You have a network of your own. I can send you basic targeting information, Friend-or-Foe, share our information through a secondary network. Your men can avoid firing on friendlies that way and get a look at the battlefield."

"They will still be without chameleon technology. That simply won't do. Have your people turn that off. We present ourselves as a unified force."

Meyers threw himself flat as one of the flyers climbed and opened fire on his position. The wall he'd been pressed against broke into fist-sized chunks that fell on top of him, rattling against his armor before sliding to the roof. He brought his weapon up as the flyer rose above the roof, its rear climbing so that the pilot could get a better look. The belly gun rotated, tracking Meyers as he rolled to his feet.

Gunfire. The flyer shivered.

The belly gun roared, but it was thrown off-target by the failing rear fans. Meyers risked a quick burst at the driver, but the windshield barely cracked, and then the flyer was spinning wildly away. Its rear end slammed into the roof edge the machine gun had just shattered. More chunks went airborne, and then the vehicle disappeared from sight.

"—hear me? Colonel Meyers?" Ramawat was even more agitated than before.

"I was under fire—" The connection died. Meyers heard distant machine gun fire.

The haulers! He ran to the roof's edge, scanning the building on the north side of the street where he'd last seen Singh and Ramawat. If they'd been out in the open when the haulers came around through the open-air market west of the apartment buildings, a quick burst would have torn through their armor.

Meyers reopened the channel to Banh. "Corporal Banh, status?"

A red light blinked in the corner where he had Banh's squad grouped. Meyers opened the window. The red light indicated Banh and his squad were offline. Another red light blinked: McNutt's squad. Meyers opened the window to confirm. He looked over at the building where McNutt and his were still firing. They weren't offline, at least not in the sense of being dead.

Meyers pulled back and brought up the BAS network information just as Gerhardt's squad went offline. He looked at the last place Gerhardt's green wireframe had been. A vague, shimmering form squatted there, holding a slightly more visible CAWS-5 with a sniper package.

Gerhardt's faceplate lifted as he turned. He motioned for Meyers to open his own faceplate. "What the hell? We lost the network, and Ramawat's ordering us to shut off our chameleon mode. He's spreading Banh's squad over two buildings, and he's trying to tell McNutt to do the same."

None of that had come through to Meyers at all, but Gerhardt had heard it, even after losing the BAS private network. For Gerhardt to have lost the network...

Meyers checked his network's status. Now it made sense. Someone had used his code to isolate his network. Not his code, he reminded himself, but the battalion commander's code.

"Unbelievable," he said. "Ramawat shut everyone out of the network I built."

Gerhardt's face screwed up, and then it seemed to dawn on him. "He cut you out of command?"

The move was impossible to comprehend. Meyers couldn't breathe. "Yeah."

"What is this guy's deal?"

Power, Meyers wanted to say, but that didn't capture the depths and twists of Ramawat's actions. "Stay in it. Keep hammering the enemy. Pass along to Banh and McNutt what's going on. I'm going to try to raise Paxton."

"And the chameleon mode?"

"See if you can delay him on that." Meyers headed toward the guide rails, then stopped and spun around. "Gerhardt."

Gerhardt turned around. "Yeah?"

"Try to stay respectful."

Gerhardt's face twisted into a bitter frown, which disappeared behind his faceplate.

Meyers stopped at the guide rails and squatted. Unarmored men were swarming down the street on the south side of the building. He counted seven, all of them running in a crouch, assault weapons raised toward the upper floors of the apartment building McNutt's squad was in.

Reyes's men.

Meyers activated his armor's chameleon mode and moved around the flyer wreckage until he had a clear line of sight on Reyes's men. They were moving into the alleyway where the proxy had nearly gotten him. Heading for...

He brought the CAWS-5 up and sighted on the lead figure as he approached the shattered doorway where the young woman's body lay in pieces. Meyers fired, dropping the lead figure as he waved the others forward, then shifted right. In the alley below, the other men looked up and around, searching. Meyers pulled a flash-bang grenade from his belt and tossed it into the alley. A couple of the men fired at him, others at the flash-bang. Their shots were off. The flash-bang detonated, and all but one of the men fell, groaning. Meyers fired a short burst into the standing man's chest; he fell, and his assault weapon clattered on the packed dirt of the alley. Meyers swapped out his magazine, then he finished off the rest and slapped in another fresh magazine.

The others needed to know about Reyes's men flanking them, but there was no way to get the word out. Meyers shook his head, still unable to see where Ramawat was coming from. It was ego, it was a crazy need to assert his dominance, and it was putting lives at risk.

Meyers attached the silicone grips to the guide rails, then he climbed onto the top rung before pinching the outside of the guide rail with his feet. He let the grips lower him at a safe but fast rate. Once on the ground, he ran to check on Reyes's men.

He stopped at the alley entry and looked west. The street was largely clear, but there were bodies. They appeared to be Mattias's people, maybe women. Possibly children.

Memories of Plymouth flooded back into Meyers's thoughts: the meta-corporations executing civilians, showing no respect for even the most basic rules of engagement. They were barbarians, and Reyes's men were no better.

After confirming Reyes's men were all down, Meyers jogged north through the alley, pressed tight against the wall centimeters below the holes punched into it by the proxy's railgun. The last he'd seen of the proxy, it had fallen back to Waverley's armored hauler, still being harassed by Perkins.

At the north end of the alley, Meyers peeked first to the right, then to the left. The last of the flyers were now hovering over the playground to the east and the open market to the west. Wisps of white smoke spiraled out from their bellies. Their fan assemblies were damaged and failing. A short burst echoed in the street—one of the MARCOS firing on the proxy. The proxy reeled, but it wasn't affected. It returned fire, tearing through the wall and window sill the MARCOS was using for cover. Clumps of wall rained into the street, followed a second later by clumps of the MARCOS.

The proxy had to go, or they were all going to die. Its torso had dents where there should have been a head, but the armor was still intact. It was still operational. The only way to take it down was a truly heavy weapon, like the one on Reyes's Leopard, or meaningful ordnance.

Meyers suddenly remembered McNutt saying he gave Starling the explosives he took from a building on the harbor. She had been in EOD, Meyers remembered. She had a thing for the boom.

He tried to raise her, using the private channel that she'd opened with him before.

"Colonel Meyers? You okay, sir?"

"Yeah. Alive. Colonel Ramawat shut off my access to everything. He's demanding I come to him, and let him run the show."

"That sounds dangerous, sir."

"It is. The most important thing is that we need to get the word out— Reyes has men infiltrating south of Cáceres Road, maybe north, too. They're trying to get into the buildings where we're deployed."

"I—I'll pass that along to Agent Barlowe, sir."

"Please do."

Sections of the wall fell away behind him, and Meyers realized the proxy had spotted him. He dropped and crawled back into the alley.

"Colonel?"

"I'm okay. That damned proxy..." Meyers paused and listened. His thigh still ached from where the proxy's round had clipped him and the armor was still somewhat deformed, but if it was necessary to run, he could. The proxy stopped firing. "Private, Corporal McNutt gave you some explosives. Did you ever get a chance to do anything with those?"

"I rigged up satchels for Private Perkins and Corporal McNutt, sir."

McNutt. Meyers looked back toward the doorway where the young woman lay in pieces. "Okay, last thing. I need the data feeds I was getting before. Can you and Ladell—Agent Barlowe—get me back onto the network somehow?"

"Doesn't Colonel Ramawat have the code to override, sir?"

"He does. But there's got to be a back door, something Agent Barlowe knows but he's never told anyone about? Maybe the older version the MARCOS are running has a vulnerability?"

"I'll check, sir."

"Thanks! I'll take whatever he can pull off."

"I've got to go, Colonel. We're swinging around for another fly-by."

The connection died, and Meyers wondered again what the hell Ramawat was thinking. Ego couldn't explain it all. There was a level of petty vindictiveness implied in a lot of what was going on. Even Singh seemed to see it, but no one was challenging Ramawat. People were dying needlessly. The ERF concept was being compromised.

It had to stop, and Meyers knew it was going to come down to him.

26

---

15 December 2174. Turning Point, Bellar Frontier Colony.

BLOOD POOLED on the packed dirt of the alleyway and in the shattered doorway that led into the apartment building where McNutt's team was deployed. The alley was quiet other than his own breathing and the faint scrape of his boots. He was alone for the moment, except for the dead. The room beyond the doorway was dark. Meyers tried to find somewhere to leap over the corpses of Reyes's men and into the room, but there was nowhere to land, not with the pieces of the young woman...

He looked away and sucked in a breath of his armor's stale, recycled air. That probably saved his life.

More of Reyes's men stood at the end of the alley, one already aiming.

Meyers dropped onto the corpses and lay flat as automatic fire—still loud despite his helmet muting the sounds—filled the alleyway. Bullets tore into the dirt, the walls, and the dead flesh around him. His left foot bounced off the ground, and a burning sensation shot through his heel. One of the bullets must have caught him in the heel, he realized, penetrated the armor. That wasn't so bad.

He popped up and fired a short burst into the shooter, dropping him, then twisted and sighted on another, this one running. The runner fired his assault weapon with one arm, and bullets bounced off the alley walls around Meyers. He fired a second burst, and the wounded man went to the ground, his gun arm hanging limp, muscle and flesh blooming from his biceps.

The rest of the men were gone, back west, out of sight.

Meyers checked himself. He was covered with blood, but only what was escaping the heel section was his. He got to his good foot and hopped through the corpses, into the young woman's ruins.

Outside, the wounded gunman screamed. Meyers leaned against the doorframe, saw the man getting awkwardly to his feet. Meyers sent a single round into the man's head.

Glass shattered, and Meyers realized there were small windows on the room's south wall. Reyes's men were there, firing, cursing. Bullets crashed into the ceiling and off to his right, high along the north wall.

Meyers swapped in a fresh magazine and hopped through the room, getting comfortable with what the ultraviolet imagery revealed. The room was longer than it was deep, with big sinks mounted to the west wall and tables built into the east wall. Cables ran the length of the ceiling, and three drains ran the length of the center of the floor. There was a door across the room, near the north corner; that was his access to the rest of the building.

He was in a common washing area, now with a burst pipe. Water swirled around the northernmost drain. He crouched and ran across the room, splashing through the water, turning his bloody bootprints runny rather than tacky.

The gunfire continued from the south wall, but it wasn't a threat. Outside the room, a hallway that ran west. Doors, some open, revealing apartments.

And corpses.

Meyers hobbled down the hallway, pausing at an intersection. An open doorway led into a room. He could make out the base of a set of stairs. He hopped up the stairs, leaning hard on the rail for support. His faceplate opened with a hiss, and he squinted against the lived-in smell of the building. It was dark, the stairwell unlit, the walls not yet punched through.

At the second floor doorway, he leaned into the hallway and called for McNutt.

Nothing.

On to the third floor, the wounded heel aching, he gasped.

Meyers hopped to the third-floor doorway. Gunfire, shouting. "McNutt!"

"Who the hell?" Someone came running, stopping at the corner, barely visible.

"It's Meyers!"

McNutt's head poked around the corner. "I thought you were dead."

"Feels like we're all on the way. Ramawat cut me out of my own network."

"He can do that?"

"Someone at the UN gave him the command codes."

McNutt snorted. "This guy, he's crazy." He tapped his helmet. "Took a round off the helmet, or I'd still be telling him to fuck off."

Meyers couldn't see any indication of damage to McNutt's helmet. "Starling said she made you a satchel charge?"

"Yeah?"

"I think that could take out the proxy."

Heavy, automatic gunfire roared from the north end of the building, and McNutt dropped into a low crouch. He looked back toward the north. "Keep your chameleon mode going unless I say otherwise. And stay in cover." He turned back to Meyers. "What's wrong with your foot?"

"A scratch."

"Yeah? Nearly fell when you tried to squat. Scratch do that to ya?" McNutt crawled closer. "Nice. Took off the back of the heel. Wipe away that crud, bet you could see bone."

"I'm fine."

"Make a deal with you. Watch over my squad, I'll get the proxy."

Meyers shook his head. "The proxy's mine."

McNutt banged his head with the heel of his hand. "Christ. That round to the head. Really shook me up. Can't recall a thing. You said something about a satchel, Colonel?"

"Fine. Last I saw the proxy, it was right next to Waverley's armored hauler. You get them both, we wrap this mess up and head home for our court martial."

McNutt chuckled. "Now that's a deal I can't pass up." He jogged out of sight, then returned a few seconds later, the satchel hanging from a shoulder.

"Reyes's men are crawling all over the place down there."

"Good. I'm getting tired of killing Waverley's men."

"Watch your back."

McNutt bounded down the steps recklessly, filling the stairwell with echoes. When those echoes were gone, Meyers headed to the north end of the building. The hallways were thick with dust, the floors covered with chunks of the prefab material, the walls punched through with holes. There were fewer corpses, but any corpse was terrible. McNutt had three casualties, but only one of them was out of action. Meyers stopped to check on the man, got a delayed thumbs-up. Meyers recognized the bloody face: Mahali Jasuli. A tough soldier, even as McNutt's squad went. The wounds were bad, but they didn't look lethal.

Meyers headed toward the window of an empty apartment. It looked typical for a prefab: one bedroom, probably a bath and kitchenette. He got through the door, saw a mother hugging a baby and infant to her in the southeast corner. There was nothing heavy enough to stop the worst of the munitions being used by the flyers, so he flipped her bed up in front of her, and in front of that he pushed whatever he could—crude furniture, bushels of food, a big pail of water.

His earpiece gave off a strange chime.

"Lonny?" Barlowe sounded even more stressed than the last time they spoke.

Meyers pushed an old entertainment console in front of the rest of the pile. His heel burned from the exertion. "Tell me you can get me back into my own network."

"Ramawat's got the command code."

"Are you saying there's no back door?" Meyers hopped to the windows on the north wall. Somehow, they were still intact.

"I'm really stretched right now."

"We're losing people, Ladell." He scanned the building fronts and alleyways. There were MARCOS corpses, ERF corpses. Civilian corpses. "Good people."

Meyers's system buzzed. There was an anonymous link waiting for him. He selected it, and it took him to one of Turning Point's relays, where a message was waiting for him. He opened the message.

A command code.

Meyers copied it. "Ramawat's code?"

"I guess."

"Ladell..."

"I don't know. It was sitting out there, unencrypted. Well, weak-encrypted. It could be a trap."

"It's not." Meyers brought up the interface to the BAS network.

"He'll know if you get back on the network."

Ramawat would, Meyers realized. He needed something, but he didn't want to get into a confrontation. Not yet, not with so much else at stake.

"I'll figure something out."

"Okay. Hey, you've got a squad on the west side?"

"Sergeant Banh's." Meyers wanted to say it wasn't really his squad anymore.

"They're getting chewed up. One of their guys is...there's not much left."

"They were going to lay down an ambush for the haulers. I heard Ramawat ordered Banh to spread his squad to another building." As good as Banh was, he wasn't known for standing up to bad orders. He respected rank too much.

"I've warned everyone about Reyes's men sneaking into the buildings. I've got to go."

"Thanks."

Meyers barely noticed Barlowe disconnecting. Already, the puzzle of the BAS hack occupied every thought. Flipping through the interface took several seconds. It was dense if the user needed to get deep into the settings.

Sunlight flashed in the window, and one of the flyers sped past, trailing curls of white smoke, firing its gun at something east of the building. Meyers thought about McNutt, moving through the alleyways and streets. No shared combat data, no one to provide cover fire or watch his flank.

McNutt could handle himself.

Meyers went back to the interface. He was about to abandon the networking configuration when he spotted an option that was ghosted out: Secondary Network. It was how he could have brought the MARCOS team onto the ERF network, if Ramawat had listened, a channel that could adjust to different bandwidths and protocols. It could be used to see into the ERF's BAS network without actually being seen on it, and since Meyers had the right software and the command code, he could activate the secondary network without giving away his presence.

Maybe.

He brought up the system administration menu, which prompted for his identification, then asked for the command mode to get onto the network. Instead, Meyers selected the manual network selection option and activated the secondary network.

His command interface lit up.

His old BAS network was a layer visible through a window. He closed his faceplate and filled its viewing area with the window, then he drilled down into the network he'd been running earlier.

McNutt's team showed up in the nearest part of the display, still locked in to the network, feeding their data up to Barlowe and integrating his feed into theirs. Gerhardt's team was doing the same thing, presenting an image of the north side of Cáceres Road. Only Banh had pulled off the network.

It was the north side of the road that mattered. Banh's people who were still in the building where they'd started were under heavy fire. The proxy and the flyer patrolling the east side were laying down persistent fire, tearing away large sections of that building's south wall. An ERF helmet would show up in a window, then it would disappear, and the wall around the window would shatter. The building sagged now, a good third of its lower floor damaged beyond repair.

Meyers thought about Ramawat's order, to spread out to other buildings. There was some value to it, but the cost was that they wouldn't have the firepower to deal with the flyers. They should have been moving MARCOS units into the buildings with them, keeping enough firepower to make the maneuver meaningful.

Not only wasn't Ramawat seeing the ERF and MARCOS forces as combined, he wasn't seeing them as part of the same operation.

Meyers tried to find McNutt on the display. He showed up as a green wireframe at the back of Gerhardt's building.

Not moving.

The only way they could take down the proxy was with the satchel charge.

Meyers backed out toward the doorway, stopping long enough to pop open his faceplate and wave to the young mother. "Stay low. Stay behind that cover until this is over."

She nodded, eyes wide with fear. Meyers wondered how terrible he appeared, blood-covered, heavy armor, gun at the ready. He was probably more of a threat in her eyes than Waverley's forces.

He hopped into the hallway and down to where he could hear the loudest cursing and gunfire.

"Corporal Chavez!" He shouted over gunfire and hoped Chavez's audio receptors would pick up the shout.

The gunfire stopped. "Colonel? McNutt said to watch over you, but—"

"I think he's wounded or pinned down."

"Hold one." Chavez was quiet for a few seconds, then he fired his gun again. "Yeah, pinned down. A bunch of Reyes's men."

"Tell him I'm on my way."

"Watch your ass. Sir."

Meyers chuckled and moved as quickly as he could to the stairs. He got there just as a couple of Reyes's men exited the stairwell entry. They had their backs to him, looking down the opposite hallway. Meyers put a bullet into the back of the head of the closest one, then switched to short burst and fired through the red mist. All three rounds caught the other man in the chest as he spun around; he fell hard but was still breathing. Meyers paused to finish the second man off, then headed down the stairs.

He found more of Reyes's men in the common laundry room, apparently killed by McNutt. Meyers swapped out his last full magazine and hopped over to the young woman's body, looking into the alleyway and listening.

The gunfire was clear now. Rapid, fully automatic bursts from nearby.

Wasteful. Sloppy. Barely noticeable beneath that noise: controlled, short bursts from farther away.

Meyers crossed to the southern corner of Gerhardt's building and braced against it. There were two of Reyes's men across the packed earth street, hidden in the alleyway, fiddling with their assault rifles. The crashed flyer was between them and their target. They were oblivious. Chattering, laughing.

He waited for another burst of automatic fire, then put a single round into both men.

After confirming it was clear to the west, he popped his head around the corner. Three more of Reyes's men, standing close to the wrecked flyer, assault rifles raised, posing as if they could kill someone with attitude, firing so that their weapons jumped in their arms.

Meyers dropped to a knee, sighted on the closest, and sent a round into his head. Meyers aimed a little lower on the second, who was turning and trying to rapidly slap a magazine into place. The bullet caught him in the chest, and he fell. Meyers put a round center mass on the final one, who managed to load a fresh magazine before pitching face first into the dirt.

That apparently got the attention of the rest of Reyes's men. Automatic gunfire roared, and chunks of prefab fell. Meyers pushed back into the alley and waited.

Someone shouted in Spanish, and Meyers thought it might be a flanking order.

Then a CAWS-5 fired, and the shouting stopped. Meyers peeked around the corner, saw one of Reyes's men staggering around on the packed-earth road, struggling to lift his gun. There were no other gunmen in sight.

Meyers alternately hopped and jogged east until he reached the opposite alleyway. McNutt was pulling himself into a seated position. His armor was dented along the chest and he was bleeding from a couple joints. His faceplate popped up.

"Nice little surprise party," McNutt said. He jerked a thumb down the alley. "Three of 'em waiting in that laundry room, a bunch more across the street."

Meyers glanced down the alleyway. The hum of the proxy's railgun was clear, so it had to be close. An entire section—rooms—on the second floor of the apartment building across the street gave way, spilling dismembered bodies into the street. Civilians.

"Give me the satchel."

Instead of arguing, McNutt pulled the strap over his head. Meyers took it.

Meyers tried to open a channel to Barlowe on the secondary network. He accepted.

"Lonny? We're in a mess up here."

"I understand. There are two flyers left, and we don't have the numbers to get clean shots on them. Can one of you fire up some basic bots and hit their systems? Those were junkers. They can't have sophisticated systems defenses."

"We really need to focus on Colonel Ramawat's orders."

"Ramawat's going down. When this is over, I'm going to relieve him of command."

"Shit. Lonny—"

"He's gotten people killed. Our people. Civilians."

"Even if you manage to get him relieved, your career—"

"Fuck my career. I need those bots. I'm going after the proxy in a second, and it has a flyer watching over it."

"I-I'll see what I can do. I think Becky still has her bots from earlier."

"Thanks. Signal me when it's clear to go."

Barlowe disconnected.

"You sure you want to throw away your career, Colonel?" McNutt looked concerned. "You seem like a career sort of guy."

Meyers snorted. "I used to be just like you, ready to fight the system, even when I knew it was right. I can't believe I made it this far." He owed Rimes for that.

"Well, whoever survives from the ERF side, we'll testify."

"Thanks. I'm sure his men will do the same. The UN really screwed this one up."

Meyers pulled up the BAS command interface and sucked in a deep breath. "Well, here it goes."

He tapped the network options and switched from the secondary network to the one he'd set up originally, then he changed the command code and degraded Ramawat's level of access to a basic user level before opening a communication channel to everyone.

"ERF forces, this is Colonel Meyers. I am taking command again. You are to disregard all orders from Colonel Ramawat from this point forward."

Ramawat sputtered. "Meyers? I demand you cease this foolishness! I will have you up on charges! Your career—"

Meyers muted Ramawat's connection. "Sergeant Banh, pull your squad back. If you have to, hook up with the MARCOS squad one building east."

"We are pinned down, Colonel! That quad-railgun—the Leopard hauler—it is tearing out the back of the building. I have two dead, two wounded. Many civilians. The MARCOS are worse."

"Give ground. We'll deal with it."

The signal came from Barlowe. The flyers were being hit with bot attacks.

"Perkins, Gerhardt, I want that east side flyer down. It should be vulnerable."

"Got it," Gerhardt said.

"Runnin' low on ammo, but I can take a shot, Colonel." Perkins was cool, not like someone conflicted over his job, not anymore.

Meyers got to his feet and moved as quickly as he could toward the end of the alley. The flyer on the east side of the street wobbled down toward the ground and past the alley front, the white smoke coming from its belly thick. High-powered shots rang out, and the clear canopy armor cracked. The pilot twitched, and the copilot slumped. The proxy lurched into view, railgun raised and firing. Meyers pulled the cord on the satchel, counted to three, and lobbed it up high, toward the proxy's chest, then he dropped to the ground and covered his head.

The world was swallowed by a boom that slid Meyers forward and pressed him down into the dirt of the alley. His armor's systems squealed and blinked and chirped, and he thought they might fail. He squeezed his eyes shut for a second, then tried to focus on the display, which was returning to normal. His audio system was a wreck, but the BAS was adjusting.

Paxton's voice came from somewhere far away. "Colonel Meyers?"

Meyers looked back at the street, where the proxy was staggering, just like Reyes's man after McNutt had shot him—dead, but not quite accepting it yet. The proxy's legs were warped, and each step produced a clicking and whirring sound that coincided with bits of armor and mechanical guts falling off. The gun arm and half the torso were gone, exposing servos and circuitry.

Meyers laughed. "What is it, Master Sergeant?"

"If Banh abandons that building, he'll take away the only support for a squad of MARCOS that's really banged up. They won't make it, not without support."

The laughter died in Meyers's throat. He couldn't leave soldiers to die. "Sergeant Banh, can you get over to that MARCOS squad?"

"We can. The quad-railgun, it has stopped firing. They have all stopped firing."

Meyers wondered if word of the proxy's destruction had already reached Reyes's men. "Be careful, but go. Sergeant Paxton, any idea what Reyes's haulers are doing? Are they trying to flank—"

A shadow passed over the alley, and Meyers looked up in disbelief. The Dart was close enough overhead that he could make out details along its frame.

"Lonny!" Barlowe sounded panicked. "He's sending his pilot in for a close sweep! He's sending us in low! I think it's to get back at you. I think—"

The hauler gunfire that had died down to the north opened up again, and Barlowe's connection went silent.

27

15 December 2174. Turning Point, Bellar Frontier Colony.

MEYERS WAS ALREADY HALFWAY across Cáceres Road before he realized how exposed he was. He glanced right, where the proxy still defied its inevitable death, staggering, remaining arm swinging. Beyond that, smoke drifted up from Waverley's armored hauler, the front windshield a vast spiderweb. Dead, Meyers hoped, but there was no time to check. He glanced left in time to see the flyer Perkins and Gerhardt had finished off crash into the front of the building McNutt's men held. The impact took out a large section of the wall, no doubt including support structures, but the building held. At the far end of the street, the final flyer was still airborne. It wobbled, but it wasn't down.

Corpses—mostly Waverley's bodyguards—littered the street and alleys. There were bodies, pieces of bodies, puddles of blood and viscera, and pudding-like remnants of what had minutes earlier been human beings. It was all so bright and vivid in the early morning sunlight. The stench was probably testing the limits of the armor's already laboring filters.

Meyers continued, trying to keep a meaningful stride despite the pain in his heel. His breathing sounded wrong—wheezy and desperate. It was all he could hear.

In the shade of the north alley, he nearly lost his footing in one of Waverley's bodyguards, who had been torn in two, apparently by friendly fire. Meyers had mistaken it for two separate corpses. It wasn't.

The channel came alive again, and Meyers stopped, straining.

"Colonel! Colonel Meyers! Um, shit! Mayday! Mayday!" It was Starling. "We're going down! The pilot's...gone."

Other sounds leaked through her armor's sensors—the Dart's engines, whining, static, the sort of popping that might be systems overloading. He imagined that the Dart's small passenger cabin was already filled with smoke, although he wasn't sure what to think when she said the pilot was gone.

"Private Starling, this is Colonel Meyers." He started running again, listening. "I've lost your positioning."

"Um...um..." Her audio was weak, cutting in and out.

"The Dart." He tried to remember where the comm antennas were on a Dart. "Switch to the aft antennas." It was a different frequency range, but the BAS could handle that.

"Colonel?"

"Good! You're clear now. Where are you?"

"We're...it's in a spiral. Agent Barlowe's unconscious. He banged his head hard. There's buildings below us. I see the soccer field off to..."

Meyers stopped at the end of the alley and glanced left, where Reyes's haulers had been. They were still there, seventy or eighty meters away, sitting at the southern edge of a clearing that led up to the soccer field with people scattered around in clumps. Civilians, most of them crouching, some lying face down. Reyes's men danced around the haulers, assault rifles raised high, as if they'd brought the aircraft down.

"Use your mapping. Where are—" He glanced right and saw the Dart, north of his position, probably 300 meters, just east of Guevara Highway, spiraling lazily, losing altitude. "I see you. Marking you now."

He brought up the battlefield map and tagged the Dart's location just as its engines stalled and it fell.

"Colonel!"

The Dart dropped, disappearing from sight. Meyers brought up the data Starling had managed to gather on Turning Point. The buildings in the area were warehouses, empty. Seized by Reyes, he remembered. Farmers Road.

The cheering of Reyes's men stopped, and the haulers' engines whined as the drivers backed up.

They were going for the Dart.

"No!" Meyers sighted in on the nearest clump of men and fired. One of the men fell. His comrades didn't even notice at first.

Meyers set his CAWS-5 in its back brace and ran as quickly as his heel allowed back down the alleyway. He searched among the dead, finally finding a serviceable assault rifle. Waverley's men had plenty of ammunition. He took five magazines, then headed back to the end of the alley.

"Colonel Meyers?" The voice sounded like Private Perkins. Meyers confirmed.

"What is it?"

"I-I thought I heard Becky. Is she okay?"

"The Dart's down." Meyers tagged the location and forwarded it to Perkins. "Warehouses up there, about 400 meters from my position. Maybe they landed on one. Farmers Road."

"Permission to head to that position, Colonel."

Meyers set the assault rifle to automatic and opened fire on the group of Reyes's men who were now looking down at their fallen comrade. That got their attention. "Those haulers are getting back onto Cáceres Road. I'm pretty sure they're trying to get up to that warehouse."

"I see 'em, sir."

"If you want to try..."

"I do, sir."

Reyes's men were gathering, building up courage. They crouched, became tough targets. Meyers waited until they charged forward, then he sprayed the group with automatic fire.

"Colonel?"

"Go. This area's crawling with locals." Bullets thudded into the wall around him, a sound too soft to be right. It couldn't be the lingering effects of the explosion, since he was hearing transmissions okay. Then he remembered—he'd cut back audio on everything but the communications channel. He adjusted the setting and returned fire. "Perkins, give me a full feed, audio, video."

Perkins's video came through crisp. He was dropping into the alley between McNutt's building and Gerhardt's, using the silicone grips on a section of wall that didn't look very sound. Gerhardt's voice droned in the background, an internal discussion.

"Just fucking cover me, Titan." Perkins slid over the side of the building, dropped at a dangerous speed, and thudded into the alley with a grunt, then he pulled down the grips and ran into the street.

Meyers struggled with a moment of disorientation as Perkins glanced west and sprinted ahead of machine gun fire from the last flyer, all while Meyers laid down another automatic burst on Reyes's advancing men. Meyers shrank Perkins's feed to about one-third display area and half opacity, good enough to track his progress. He was hugging building fronts, heading east, past the shivering proxy and Waverley's smoking hauler to Guevara Highway.

"McNutt, you still conscious?" Meyers swapped in a fresh magazine. With so many close-packed targets, he liked being able to just send rounds downrange, but he hated the speed he was burning through ammunition.

"Back on my feet, yeah. I'm pulling out of the sprint competition, though."

"The Dart's down. Perkins is heading to its position. I want you to redeploy your squad—" Meyers ducked back as bullets thudded into the ground centimeters outside the alley. "I want you to redeploy your squad to Banh's position. Tell him to hook up with Perkins ASAP, hold that building."

McNutt gasped, probably testing the limits of his body. "His squad any better off than mine?"

Meyers thought about that. Banh's squad had been chewed up badly by the haulers. "Master Sergeant Paxton? Carl?"

"I heard you, sir. Just linked up with Sergeant Banh's squad. They're under fifty percent effective. Colonel Ramawat and Captain Singh are here as well. The colonel's in a particularly pleasant way."

"Hold your position. I'll be there as soon as possible."

Paxton chuckled. "That's gonna please the colonel so very much."

"All right, McNutt, take your squad up to the Dart." Meyers tapped in the route Perkins had taken. "That last flyer's still up there, west side of the street, but I think they only have partial control of the flight systems."

"My wounded," McNutt said. His voice was raw and heavy with concern.

"Corporal Gerhardt, get a fire team over to McNutt's building—retrieve his wounded."

Gerhardt hissed something unintelligible.

"Corporal Gerhardt, did you—"

"I heard you. I've got people on the way."

Meyers set the assault rifle to burst fire and started testing its accuracy. He dropped two of Reyes's men with three bursts. The rest dropped to their stomachs and contented themselves with firing on his position at full auto. He fell back and swapped out the magazine.

"Colonel, sounds like your dance card's full, but just so you know, there's a lot of local boys who would love some time with you here." Paxton's audio carried a near-constant stream of automatic gunfire and other sounds of combat.

"Is it just Reyes?"

"Just, sir? There's gotta be a hundred screaming lunatics all around us. Not disciplined or bright, but there's a lotta lead flying."

"What's left of the MARCOS?"

"Ten, and that's being nice. Banh's men rescued three. There's a couple people ain't gonna make it, still trying to hang in there. Tough soldiers."

"Corporal Gerhardt, when that fire team returns with McNutt's wounded, send them over to Sergeant Banh's position." Meyers popped around the corner, sprayed some automatic gunfire toward the pinned-down men, then pulled back into the alley.

Static roared in Meyers's ears.

"Shit!" He tweaked the volume down slightly.

"Colonel Meyers?" Starling sounded shaky.

"Private Starling? Are you okay? Can you get me a video feed?"

Meyers filled half his display with Perkins's video feed, then when Starling's feed came through he put it in the other half.

Perkins was running north along Guevara Highway, only occasionally looking down and ahead at the cracked blacktop. He was glancing west, toward what looked like the soccer field. He'd been spotted by Reyes's men and was using the shack houses lining the western side of the highway for cover.

Starling's video took a moment to figure out. The orientation was all wrong, with what looked like a catwalk visible through a hole where the cockpit used to be off to her left. The view seemed to be almost parallel with the catwalk, maybe four meters down from a ceiling, but it was looking at the underside of the catwalk. Meyers suddenly realized the hole he was looking out of the cockpit through was in the floor. The Dart had to be upside down. It had fallen through a warehouse rooftop.

"I think I may have busted my leg, sir."

"Upper or lower?"

Starling gasped. "Upper. Left leg. It kind of hurts just breathing."

She would still be in her harness, he realized, so her thigh would be pressing against that. Any movement…"Okay, just hang in there. Private Perkins is on his way. McNutt's following as fast as he can."

"Ladell's breathing. I think I heard him groan." She shifted, gasped again, and her video captured Barlowe, across the cabin from her, definitely upside down in his harness, head lolling, blood trickling up his cheek and disappearing in his helmet.

Meyers couldn't see anything horribly wrong with Barlowe. "He looks okay."

"He's kinda pretty, huh, sir?"

Meyers laughed. "Yeah. I'm going to need you to hang on, okay? Can you promise me that?"

"Just hanging around, Colonel?"

That drew a smile. "Yeah. We'll get—"

Something in Perkins's feed drew Meyers' attention. He expanded it to fill his display, realizing as he did what it was: the flyer. Its shadow—zigging and zagging—flew past, then came back. Gunfire came through Perkins's audio, and the road ahead of him shattered into doughy clumps. The video jerked and darkened, and Meyers realized Perkins had dove off the road. A moment later, he was ducked down at the side of one of the shacks, screaming for everyone to stay low and out of sight. The machine gun fired again but quickly stopped. The shadow bobbed and twisted, as if the pilot were drunk. When it looked like the flyer had flown past, Perkins sneaked a peek.

The flyer was maybe twenty meters up. White smoke curled around all four of the fans, almost managing to obscure the belly gun, which seemed to be searching for a target, spinning, spinning. There was a definite wobble to the flyer, almost like what had happened with One-Six-Three, except the flyers had no wings.

"What's the matter, sir?" Starling asked.

"Private Perkins is having a problem with the last of the flyers."

"I got it, Colonel," Perkins said. He watched the flyer for a moment longer, then he ran out from between the shacks and sprinted up Guevara Highway.

"Okay, he's back on track." Meyers flipped from both videos to a clear display and peered around the building corner. Reyes's men had found their nerve again and were rising. He let them run forward before bringing the assault rifle up and emptying the magazine. Two of the men fell and didn't get up. The rest started crawling back.

Meyers shrank Perkins and Starlings's feeds to the top third of his display, then got up and limp-jogged south through the alley, dropping the assault rifle on the corpse that had been torn in two. What remained of McNutt's squad was forming up ahead of the opposite alley.

"That flyer's still up." Meyers tapped the location on the map. "Limited flight control, looks like, and I'm not sure how long it can stay up with the fans like they are, but keep an eye out."

McNutt waved in answer, then he led his team in a slow jog onto the street, past the finally still proxy and Waverley's smoking hauler. Meyers risked a quick glance, and he thought he might have seen Waverley and the driver slumped forward in their seats.

Meyers headed west, hugging the building fronts where he could, scanning rooftops and alleys, expecting one of Waverley's men to pop out at any time. There was no way to get a meaningful count of the dead at the moment. Had Ramawat agreed to put his people on the secondary network, they could have built out a full model of the battlefield. They could have marked the enemy and tracked each time they dropped one of them.

Every complication, every misstep had been Ramawat's. Meyers was sure of it. He had a case for relieving Ramawat of command. The ERF had nearly been destroyed on the mission, all because of his arrogance.

Meyers checked the display for Banh's location. His squad was definitely banged up, three flatlined, two with ugly vital signs.

Meyers entered the apartment building through a gap that had been created by heavy weapons fire. Inside, a foyer held several small bodies, some crushed by the collapsed wall, some torn to pieces by the same bullets that had torn the building front to pieces. They were young kids, maybe as old as Rimes's boys had been. Meyers stepped over the dead carefully and thought back to all that had happened in the last year, all the stupid deaths and the killing. He reminded himself this was about bringing closure to the Metacorporate War. It was about healing. That helped him get past the corpses.

The foyer connected to the hallway, where he stopped to listen. Sporadic gunfire. A break in the combat. He glanced down the hallway.

The back third of the building was a gaping hole.

Apartments, the common laundry room, a maintenance room—everything was visible to some degree. Someone had set up a crude triage where the two hallways met. There were MARCOS and ERF wounded there, on litters. And corpses. The haulers and their guns had ultimately proven to be as big a problem as Waverley's more advanced weapons platforms. And Reyes had a small army as well.

Paxton was a green wireframe stooped behind a wall a few meters away. Meyers approached, not seeing Ramawat until it was too late.

Ramawat drove his right palm into Meyers's sternum, which was effective only because of the surprise. "I will have you up on charges the second we return to the *Valdez*! Your career is finished, Colonel!" He waved his sidearm and slowly brought it around to point at Meyers's faceplate. "I should execute you now! I have every right!"

It barely registered for Meyers that Ramawat's armor was caked in dried, grit-heavy blood. His face was grimy, clear only where sweat trailed down it.

"Get your hand off me," Meyers said.

Ramawat just glared. His eyes wobbled, as if he couldn't focus.

Meyers slapped the pistol away and punched Ramawat in the throat. He reeled back, and Meyers followed, backhanding across the face, chopping at a shoulder joint. Ramawat crashed into the lower half of a wall, knocking a small chunk free.

Singh came from around another wall and inserted himself between Ramawat and Meyers. "Colonels, we are in the middle of an engagement!"

Meyers's head and neck throbbed. His throat constricted so that speaking and swallowing were a challenge. He opened his faceplate and sucked in the air of the ruined building, drawing strength and resolve from the stench of death. "You're relieved of command, Colonel Ramawat."

"I think not." Ramawat raised his pistol. "Your actions warrant execution!"

Singh turned. "Colonel, please." He twisted back around, eyes pleading. "Colonel Meyers, is it possible this could wait?"

Meyers relaxed, suddenly feeling foolish. "I'm sorry. All this death—"

"There will be one more," Ramawat screamed.

His pistol was a deafening crack in the momentary quiet of the battlefield lull.

28

15 December 2174. Turning Point, Bellar Frontier Colony.

THE SOUND of the gunshot was still echoing when Singh collapsed. His groan—weak and surprised—was nearly lost in the clatter of his armored limbs smacking against the stone-hard floor.

Paxton charged from his position and disarmed Ramawat, who shook his head in disbelief.

"Ramawat, what the hell—" The last of the fury left Meyers's body. He became aware of the heavy, acrid smell of gunpowder, tangy and metallic on his tongue, and he imagined he could sense it still coming off the pistol. He shook, but now it was with the realization that another person might have died because of Ramawat, and this time Meyers couldn't absolve himself of involvement.

He dropped to a knee and ran gloved hands beneath Singh's back, neck, and head. There was blood, but it was tacky, gooey with dust.

Singh still breathed, but his eyes were closed.

Meyers carefully flipped Singh over and searched along the back of his helmet. A discolored streak where the armor was deeply dented near the base of the skull revealed the likely impact point.

Concussion, Meyers thought. Maybe a cracked skull. Not immediately life-threatening.

"He's alive. I think he'll be okay." He looked up, saw Ramawat's shocked look, beyond him, the concerned faces of MARCOS and ERF personnel. "Let's get him on a litter."

Banh dashed from cover and squatted next to Singh, back toward Meyers. He pulled the thin poles at the edge of Banh's backpack out. He pulled a thin sheet of material from one and attached it to the other with slender rods at the top and bottom, then telescoped the poles out with Banh's help.

As Banh shifted to get his hands under Singh's shoulders, he said, "Careful, sir."

Meyers realized just how visible his shaking was at that point. He took a deep breath, shook out his arms, then looked at Banh. "On three."

They shifted Singh to the litter, then cautiously moved him next to the wounded. Banh pulled his gloves off and began examining Singh, checking his pupils, reaching slender fingers through the helmet opening to get a pulse.

Meyers looked up at the sound of booted feet coming from the entry; it was the fire team Gerhardt had sent. "Corporal Norman, deploy your men along that north wall. Keep to cover."

Ramawat stood a few meters away from where Banh was working on Singh. "I-I should resume command..."

Meyers's felt his cheeks turn hot. He stepped toward Ramawat, caught the slightest hint of a flinch. "I think you've caused enough damage."

"I'm the senior officer." Ramawat thrust his chin out, defiant.

"Look what you've done." Meyers pointed to the casualties.

"I quite nearly had Reyes as an ally—"

"What is wrong with you?" Meyers was ready to beat some sense into Ramawat. It didn't seem like there would be anyone to stop him, either. The MARCOS watched from cover, faceplates up, heads slightly bowed, as if in shame. "This isn't about rank. It's not about your pride or your family or some imagined slight to your nation."

That seemed to sting. Ramawat's eyes jumped from Singh to Meyers, and the curl of a snarl held for a moment.

Meyers sensed the wounded pride was too great for Ramawat to overcome. "I'll tell you how this is going to go. We're going to continue running things as two different operations. You command your MARCOS, I'll command the ERF."

"I was given command—"

"And you—" Meyers realized he was screaming. He lowered his voice. "And you blew that command. You treated my soldiers like they were unfit for duty. You ignored useful intelligence, and you demeaned my people. You didn't show the slightest hint of professionalism. How you handle this from this point forward is probably going to reflect on the ultimate outcome, but trust me on this, Colonel, you're done. You'll never command the ERF. You may have taken me down with you, but I'm not about to let you do any more damage to the ERF. You understand me?"

Ramawat's eyes twitched, but there was a hint of acceptance in the way he shifted his shoulders and reared back his head.

"Colonel?" It was McNutt, over the comm channel. "Slight problem."

Meyers turned away from Ramawat. "What's up?"

"That flyer's got his eye on us. We can't get a clean shot on his fans."

"Where's Perkins?" Meyers brought up Perkins's video feed, saw him crawling across a low rooftop. One of the shacks, from the look of it.

"We lost him, about 100 meters ahead."

"I've got him. He's on a rooftop, 120 meters north of you. That Devil Cat hauler is trying to cut across the soccer field, it looks like."

Perkins's video switched to his rifle scope. The magnified view threw a crosshair over a laughing driver behind shattered, clear armor that failed to cover a good portion of his upper torso. Perkins was sighting in on the driver's exposed neck. "Colonel, there's a hauler trying to take a shortcut. Big problem."

"I see it. Corporal McNutt's having problems with the flyer."

"I only have a couple rounds left."

"You're the shooter, make the call."

Perkins's CAWS-5 roared and bucked, the driver slammed backward, and the Devil Cat slowed, then stopped. Perkins trailed his sights along the side of the hauler, stopping on the gunner, who stuck his head out of the armored bubble protecting the gun. His mouth opened, as if he were shouting. The gun bucked again, and the top of the gunner's head peeled off. He slumped, spilling blood and brains onto the ground.

"All out, Colonel."

"Understood. McNutt, did you—"

"We'll handle it, Colonel." McNutt's voice was raised over the sound of heavy, automatic gunfire. "Perkins, get your ass moving."

Meyers filled his display with Starling's video feed. He couldn't see any change in the situation. "Private Starling, how're you holding up?"

"Okay, sir. I think I'm getting dizzy from the blood. Rushing to my head, I mean. The Dart shifted a little. I think we're hung up in cabling or something. I got one of the exterior cameras to work, and I think maybe there might be some sort of scaffolding under us, too, like they were working on this building or something."

Scaffolding and cabling didn't sound like enough to hold up an aircraft, even one as small as the Dart. "Maybe you're sitting on a support beam, or part of the roof didn't give way completely."

"Yeah. Sir." Starling hissed. "Sorry. I moved a little."

"Hang in there. Perkins is almost halfway there. McNutt's not too far behind." Meyers didn't want to mention Perkins was out of ammunition or that McNutt and the fire team were pinned down.

"I'll do what I can, sir."

Meyers switched to Gerhardt's feed. "Corporal Gerhardt, Corporal Norman's fire team arrived safe and they're in position."

"Good to hear. That proxy quit moving."

"Can you see anything beyond our position? Numbers, activity?"

"Nah. Well. Movement, yeah. You got people shifting around in the alleys northwest of you."

"Numbers?"

"I don't know. Twenty? Thirty? They must be planning something. Fuckers aren't staying in sight long enough to see their little brown faces."

"Corporal Gerhardt—"

"Shit. I know, sir." Gerhardt actually sounded contrite.

"What about the haulers?"

"They're..." Gerhardt drew in a sharp breath. "They're moving east on... what's two streets up from Farmers Road?"

"Um, Pilgrim?"

"Pilgrim, then. Accelerating, too. That big one's in the middle of the pack. I don't see the little one."

"Why aren't they on Farmers? Or Center Street?"

"Someone's set fires there. Looks like maybe garbage. Lots of smoke and debris."

"Both roads?"

"Yeah."

"Do you have a shot on any of the vehicles?"

"With all that armor? From this distance?"

"Driver or gunner, even any exposed riders."

Gerhardt's gun roared, and he chuckled. "Not many riders tagging along, but that's one less."

"Anything to slow them down or keep them away from that building."

"I can try against that lead vehicle. One of the Cougars. I'm running low on ammo."

"Perkins is out. Do what you can."

After several seconds, Gerhardt's gun roared again. This time he whooped. "Okay, front Cougar is out, and we have a pile-up. That'll buy us a little time."

"Excellent. Let me know if something changes."

"Oh, it's changing all right. They're jumping for cover and looking for me."

"Keep it up."

Meyers dropped into a squat and moved to Paxton's position. It was a wall that had once separated four apartments; now it was nothing more than the crumbling, corner support where all four apartments were joined. Coming off that corner support, a segment of wall ran east, sloping from just over a meter high at the corner support to twenty or thirty centimeters off the ground, then rising again to a solid wall on the opposite side. Paxton stared over the top of the highest point. Fragments of furniture and shredded clothing were piled around him like sandbags. There were two more walls similarly torn up in front of that position, the last one abutting the dirt road.

On the east side of the wall, Ramawat squatted next to one of the MARCOS Paxton had mentioned as fighting while mortally wounded. The man's armor above his left hip and up into the rib cage was gone, as was substantial flesh and bone that should have been there. He'd been bandaged up, but the bandages were soaked through and were almost black from all the dust and other things in the air.

The man busied himself with his gun, blinking slowly, breathing with effort.

"They're moving out there, northwest. Gerhardt put their numbers between twenty and thirty."

Paxton popped his magazine and screwed up his face. "If he can see thirty, there's got to be fifty. I wonder where the rest got off to."

Meyers examined the BAS display. With Norman's fire team, there were eight ERF in place. Meyers looked around, counted eight MARCOS, assuming Ramawat was going to contribute. Against fifty of Reyes's men. Without the Condor or Dart, there was no way to see the enemy deployment. They could definitely use a Javelin right about then.

"Private Starling?"

There was no reply for a few seconds, then, "Yes, sir?"

"You're not nodding off on me, are you? Getting too comfortable?"

"I don't mean to."

"Fight it."

"I am, sir."

"You have to stay awake. We're counting on you." He worried shock might be setting in. "Were you working with Agent Barlowe on the Javelin systems software rebuilds?"

"The software rebuilds?" Starling sounded disoriented. "Oh, yeah. I remember. Yes, sir. They were still running. There was bad software. Wait. You know that. I'm sorry, sir."

"No need to apologize. Can you check on the status?"

Starling went silent, and he worried she might have slipped unconscious. Then a shot rang out.

"Enemy!" It was one of the MARCOS positioned along the north wall.

Automatic gunfire suddenly split the relative calm, and chunks of the prefab building rained down from above. A round cracked near Meyers's head, and he ducked instinctively.

Banh crawled past, stopping when he was even with Meyers. "Captain Singh is alive, Colonel." Then Banh crawled to a spot on the shattered wall just ahead of Meyers's position.

Reyes's men were visible now, moving forward, hunched low, taking up positions at the corners of alleys and in doorways on the opposite side of the packed-dirt road separating the apartment building and the smaller buildings opposite. The MARCOS and ERF returned fire when they could, sticking to single shots and burst fire.

Then the firing stopped. Reyes's men had fallen back.

Meyers scanned the positions where Reyes's men had been. Only a few were down. It didn't seem right. They hadn't made a serious effort. And why push forward at all with less than half their numbers...

"They're flanking," Meyers said. "Corporal Norman, get your team back here. Now!"

Meyers ran to the wounded and laid down, facing the hall that led to the entry. He could hear them now, quiet steps, the scrape of debris beneath booted feet. He pulled his last flash-bang, waited until he saw the first shadow, then threw, banking the flash-bang off the hallway wall so that it might bounce into the entry foyer.

Gunfire, shouting, and the rush of bodies.

Reyes's men, assault rifles raised, raking the positions behind Meyers with automatic fire. The flash-bang went off, and the firing stopped.

Meyers got to his feet. One of Reyes's men was just ahead, blinking, disoriented. Meyers dropped the man with a butt-stroke that crushed his nose. Two more men stood in the hallway, leaning, trying to focus. He fired a round into each at point-blank range. The foyer was filled with more, most of them lying on the ground, arms and heads moving slowly. He dropped his CAWS-5, picked up one of the assault rifles that had been dropped, and began spraying the stunned men. When the magazine was empty, he tossed the rifle and picked up another. Norman and his team were there, then, hesitating at first, then executing the stunned men with single shots.

When they were done, there were thirty-two dead in the hall, foyer, and just outside the building front.

Norman and his men raised their faceplates; Meyers did the same. The air was foul with guts and gunpowder. Reyes's men were a carpet over the innocent who'd been slaughtered earlier by Waverley's flyers. Meyers raised his face to the ceiling and tried to clear his nostrils of the stench but couldn't. He looked at Norman, saw that he and his team were avoiding eye contact, as if they were ashamed.

"Listen up," Meyers said. He retrieved his CAWS-5, pulled one of his near-empty magazines, and began removing rounds. "These men were seconds away from shooting all of us in the back. You understand? We're not fighting some legacy military that honors established rules of engagement. There's no taking prisoners. There's no honor. It's kill or die. Get it?"

Norman looked at his fire team. "Got it, sir."

"Okay. Gather their weapons and ammo, return to your positions. It's only a matter of time before their buddies realize the plan didn't work."

Meyers stopped to check on the wounded, then he returned to Paxton's position.

Paxton turned enough to see who it was. "Trouble, Colonel?"

Meyers turned to check on Ramawat and saw that the wounded MARCOS was dead. "Not anymore."

Norman's fire team moved past, slowing to drop off an assault rifle and magazines for Banh.

"I think there may have been some confusion over the rules of engagement," Meyers said. "That's all cleared up."

"Rules?" Paxton chuckled. "When did these bastards go all gentlemanly on us?"

Meyers thought about that. He couldn't remember the last time war had been anything but brutal slaughter. "Let's just hope the politicians back home understand the realities if we survive this disaster."

"There's gonna be hell to pay, regardless."

"Enemy!" It was the same MARCOS as before.

There always is hell to pay, Meyers thought. He brought his CAWS-5 up and scanned the buildings and alleys across the street, looking for a target.

29

---

15 December 2174. Turning Point, Bellar Frontier Colony.

MEYERS froze when he saw Reyes's men. His guts twisted, and his voice made a raspy, guttural noise that filled his helmet. He suddenly felt feverish, unable to breathe.

Reyes's men were advancing from the alleys and out of the building fronts behind a wall of women, Mattias's people. The women were tied together at the waist by sheets and belts and cabling. They cried, barely audible over the gunfire, and their hands covered their eyes. Reyes's men were hunched down, some crawling, their guns poking out between the women's legs.

"Hold fire!" Meyers knew he didn't need to give the order, but he did anyway.

Reyes's men advanced, firing and taunting. They were packed tight behind the women.

They were nearly halfway across the narrow street already, and the constant stream of automatic fire now had the MARCOS and Norman's fire team pinned down behind cover.

"Flash-bang!" Meyers peeked over the wall "Anyone have a flash-bang?"

Norman banked a flash-bang off the low section of wall to Meyers's right. It fell on the far side of the wall. "That's all I have, Colonel."

Meyers lunged for the flash-bang, felt a round hit him in the ribs, then pulled back, gasping. He had the flash-bang in his hand, but his entire left side burned. He checked his armor, saw no indication he was bleeding, and risked a quick peek over the wall.

Reyes's men were more than halfway across the street. Meyers guessed there were ten women, most of them young, some not even old enough to be married yet. He gauged the distance. Because he had to get the grenade under the top of the northern wall where Norman's team were in position, the throw was going to be tough. It would almost be better to try to skip the flash-bang along the street, but Reyes's men were crawling. The grenade was more likely to get caught on one of them at the front than get back into the group. He needed it back in the pack to be most effective. He needed a better place to throw from.

The common laundry room!

There wasn't much cover between his position and there, but popping into the alleyway like he could from that room would give him a chance to lob the flash-bang over the women.

He slapped Paxton's shoulder. "I'm going for that laundry room."

"I can send some shots high, maybe scare them."

"Do it."

Meyers ran, cursing each time his wounded heel came down. He leaped over the wounded to reach the hallway, landing on that same heel, and his vision filled with black spots. Bullets cracked and thudded around him, and he thought one might have clipped his hip, but it wasn't enough to slow him. He leaned on the wall, ducking where it disappeared, and stopped at the entry to the laundry room. There were holes in the eastern wall, and through those, he could see more holes in the northern wall, facing the dirt road outside. Three of Reyes's men were visible there, wide of the main group, outside the human wall, possibly waiting for the right moment to charge the laundry room and dash through the hallway to flank.

Meyers stuffed the flash-bang in a pouch and brought his CAWS-5 up, then he crouch-ran into the laundry room. He kept his eyes on the flanking men through the biggest hole in the north wall, waiting until they sprinted toward him.

He fired, short bursts, unconcerned with ammunition at that point. The moment was too critical to worry about anything but dropping the enemy. The first two fell, but he missed the third, who ran into the alley. Meyers ran to the door and met the man there, knocking aside his gun, then punching him in the throat. The man gaped and fell back, eyes bugging out. Meyers swung the CAWS-5 and clipped the man's jaw, shattering it and sending him to the ground.

Meyers ran up the alley, pulled the flash-bang out, activated it, searched the road for his best target, then lobbed the flash-bang. It arced just over the head of the closest woman and bounced off the back of one of the crawling men at the front before disappearing from sight.

Two of Reyes's men saw the threat and pivoted on their bellies. They fired through the legs of the women, eliciting screams as bullets shattered bone and tore muscle. The women fell, and bullets bounced off Meyers's chest plate.

He stumbled back into the alley, unable to breathe, unable to appreciate the boom of the flash-bang or the whooping of the ERF and MARCOS personnel who jumped out from cover and ran among the stunned enemy, shooting and clubbing. Meyers looked down, saw blood trickling from a small hole midway between his left shoulder and hip.

Not lethal, he told himself. He staggered to the alley edge, saw a few of Reyes's men stumbling down the opposite alley. He brought his CAWS-5 up and dropped each of them, firing until the weapon only clicked.

The magazine was empty.

He limped back into the alley, tried to set the CAWS-5 back into its brace, then gave up. The man with the shattered jaw sat up, one hand clutching the jaw, the other waving Meyers away. Meyers guessed the man was in his early twenties. Unfairly imprisoned, probably even before adulthood. Most of his choices had been made for him, all of them bad. He wore the uniform of his warlord—grungy, tattered jeans and a muscle shirt. His arms were covered in tattoos—tribal allegiance, threats, declarations of triumph. His eyes were wide, terror-filled.

Meyers scooped up one of the dropped assault rifles, opened his face-plate, and waved the man away. "Get the hell out of here."

The young man ran, wheezing, groaning, spitting up blood.

Meyers headed back to the others, wondering why he'd suddenly felt compelled to show mercy. It made no sense whatsoever given the stakes and conditions.

As he rounded the corner, he heard a voice: Perkins.

"Colonel, they got a sniper out there somewhere." Perkins grunted, and his video feed showed him climbing onto a rooftop. "Not a great one, but good enough to nearly hit me twice."

"Gerhardt, you hear that?"

"Yeah. I thought you wanted me keeping those haulers locked down."

Meyers tried to gauge how far Perkins was from the Dart. It looked like it was less than 100 meters. "Perkins, how far out are you?"

"Seventy-five meters, maybe less."

"Gerhardt, you have those haulers locked down?"

"No. They've got a driver getting into the front vehicle. That Devil Cat's hooked back up with them. I don't have a clean shot. When they turn south onto Guevara, that'll change."

"Find that sniper. Perkins, any idea where he might be?"

"Got a hunch he's in one of the prefabs west of the soccer field, Colonel."

"Gerhardt, watch the—"

"I'm not deaf, Colonel. But I don't see anything. Sunlight should be reflecting off any sort of rig a local…thug would have. Hey, Perkins, how about giving him something to shoot at."

"How about you fuck off?"

"Just remember who ran out of ammunition first before you start bitching. Why don't you move? Just give him a little head. I promise he won't c—"

Meyers shook his head and sighed.

"Wait!" It sounded like Gerhardt was sucking air in between his teeth. "Reflection, third floor, southernmost prefab."

"Take the shot," Meyers said. Meyers heard a faint crack and Perkins grunting, then another, louder crack.

"Barrel tip visible," Gerhardt said. "Sniper eliminated. Checking on those haulers."

Perkins's video showed a rooftop wall, like the one Meyers had hidden behind.

"Private Perkins?" Meyers listened for breathing.

The video shifted. "Moving, sir."

Perkins was on the ladder, sliding down.

Meyers switched to McNutt's feed. The flyer was lower now, even more unsteady, and the smoke was dense. Meyers imagined he could smell the metallic, acrid stench and burning sensation that sort of smoke would leave in his throat.

"Corporal, Perkins is seventy-five meters out and moving again. You think that flyer is still a threat?"

"Not like the people who got us pinned down now."

Meyers realized he was hearing the roar of automatic weapons and the thud of bullets through McNutt's feed. Meyers scanned through the video, finally spotting two clumps of men. There were about fifteen, all told. They were crawling and low-running forward, one group at a time, the second providing cover fire. They either had some sort of formal military training or learned awfully quickly.

"I see them. Can you get to the east side of the highway, put some more buildings between you and them."

"Yeah, sir, that thought'd never crossed my mind," McNutt said with a sigh. "We tried, and that's when Mr. Flyboy decided to show us he still had ammo in that belly gun."

"I think we've broken Reyes's men here. I'll send Norman's team forward, see if they can't help out."

"That'd be seriously appreciated."

Meyers limped the rest of the way to the little triage area and settled against a wall, faceplate raised so he could breathe the comparatively fresh air. "Master Sergeant Paxton?" He leaned his head back and closed his eyes.

Paxton came to a stop a meter away, knuckling grime from his eyes. "Already sent them on, Colonel." He squatted. "That's not a particularly good shade of pale."

Meyers tapped his chest plate. "Cracked rib, I think."

"Banh's still got a couple painkillers."

"No." Meyers knew his injury paled in comparison to the other wounded. "It didn't go deep."

He blew out a breath, brought his faceplate halfway down, and then he brought up the overall battlefield map. "Any sign of Reyes's men?"

"Fell back. I think they had all the fight knocked out of 'em for now."

Meyers tried to imagine Reyes accepting defeat when he probably still had a couple hundred men and three or four haulers. "They'll be back."

"Colonel, this is Private Starling. You hear me?" Starling's voice was soft, slow.

"Go ahead, Private."

"It took me a bit. I-I don't know why. But I got into Zero-Zero-One. The Javelin?"

"Great!"

"It's done, but I just realized, we left the communication module. You remember that module? To amplify the signal coming out of Turning Point?"

Meyers remembered. He couldn't believe he'd forgotten. "I remember it."

"Yeah, so, we can't use Zero-Zero-One."

"What about Zero-Zero-Two?"

"Yeah." Starling went silent. "Yeah. Zero-Zero-Two. It's ninety- eight..."

"Ninety-eight percent done?"

"Yeah. Right? I'm sorry. I'm having a hard time..."

"Private Starling? Private Starling?"

"Colonel?"

"Can you go ahead and program Zero-Zero-Two to fire up when it's ready?"

"I can, sir."

"Good. Please do that." Meyers clasped his hands in front of his face and squeezed, then he tapped out a quick beat on his knees.

Paxton gazed out through the north wall. "Was that Private Starling?"

"Yeah. I think she's slipping into shock." Meyers opened a channel to

Ensign Nunoz. "Antonio? Zero-Zero-Two's going to be firing up in a little bit. The system software rebuild is nearing completion. I want that bird airborne the second it's ready."

"Yes, sir. Do we have a time estimate?"

"No. Soon. Once you're up and running, connect to my BAS network. I'll have an open invite out to you. It's still a mess here."

"How bad?"

Meyers closed his eyes. "Bad enough you'll be flying home with an empty Javelin if you don't get out here soon. You think you and Genevieve could get the Condor up while you're waiting? We need eyes in the sky."

"Sure! Give it a few minutes."

"I don't have much choice, do I?"

Meyers disconnected and sent an invitation to Nunoz to join the BAS network.

Paxton squatted and leaned in. "You're looking awfully worn out."

"How the hell did Rimes do all this? I mean, he was smart, but I'm smart, too. I can't keep up. We're spread all over the place, people dying, people wounded..."

"Maybe you're doing too much," Paxton said, leaning in closer, his breath a pungent mixture Meyers couldn't figure out. "You've been so caught up in untangling his mess..." Paxton jerked his head toward Ramawat's position. "...you don't even realize you're making the same mistake he was making."

The same mistake Ramawat was making; Meyers tried to figure that one out.

Paxton snorted. "Delegation. Trust. That's what sets a good commander apart from a bad one. You trained this unit to operate as a whole and to operate as individuals. Let that happen."

Meyers thought back over the engagement. He had been a little deeper into the weeds than normal. Choosing which squad would help out Perkins, watching Perkins's progress, specifying deployments. It was the same level of detail Ramawat had been getting into, the same sort of implied lack of trust.

"Shit, Carl. I'm sorry."

Paxton leaned back and waved the words away. "Typical reaction to things going to hell on you."

"So, did I get it wrong with Ramawat, too? Did I go too far?"

"Nah. You gave him enough rope—he hung himself. It's gonna be ugly, but I'll be there for you. I think if anyone makes it through this, they'll be there for you."

"Won't help much, will it?"

Paxton seemed to think about that. "Not usually."

"Didn't think so." Meyers slouched forward and opened Gerhardt's channel. "Corporal Gerhardt?"

"Yeah?"

"Please keep Master Sergeant Paxton up to date on Norman's progress. You two need to make sure we free McNutt's team up."

Gerhardt didn't respond at first. "All right, Colonel. Master Sergeant, I see Norman's team about fifty meters—shit!"

Meyers straightened. "What is it? Gerhardt?"

"The proxy!" Gerhardt's gun boomed. "It's moving again! I think it's going for the belly gun of that flyer that crashed—" Gerhardt's gun boomed again. Gunfire from nearby leaked into his audio.

Meyers got to his feet. They needed the other satchel charge. He racked his brain, trying to remember who had the second...

Perkins!

"Do what you can," Meyers shouted into the channel.

He stumbled forward, barely managing to reach the foyer before he had to stop and catch his breath. The dead seemed intent on dragging him down, but he finally reached the front door. He scanned the street, but the only movement he saw was the proxy, it's one good arm now holding the belly gun of the flyer that had crashed into the front of the apartment building catercornered from the one he was in. The flyer still rocked on its tires, the pilot and copilot's corpses moving in rhythm.

Meyers doubted the belly gun was still operational after a crash like he'd seen the flyer suffer. He wasn't sure the proxy could use the belly gun, even if it was operational. That didn't seem to be stopping the proxy, which was backing away from the building front on wobbly legs, raising the gun as if seeking a target.

Somehow, the gun fired; not completely—more like a halfhearted burst. It was enough to tear a section of the front wall away beneath the roof.

Meyers stumbled into the street, still trying to figure what he could do, when the proxy turned.

And slowly brought the belly gun around.

30

---

15 December 2174. Turning Point, Bellar Frontier Colony.

THE STREET WAS silent except for the clacks and whirs of the proxy and the strained whine of the machine gun's belt feed mechanism. The sunlight was a blinding halo around the proxy. Meyers froze for a second, unable to take his eyes off the gun, suddenly convinced that it would fire, and he would be killed.

The gun belt feed mechanism whined and sputtered, and the spell was broken.

He crossed the street as quickly as he could. The proxy pivoted, tracking with the gun, and the strained whine grew louder before degenerating into a series of grinding and popping noises. He ran into the alley just west of the proxy and leaned against the eastern wall. Sucking in the fresh air, thinking through everything facing him, he tried to compartmentalize the pain in his ribs.

He had to think. He had to plan.

Clacks and whirrs, and the unsteady creak of bowed, mechanical legs: The proxy was coming for him.

Meyers pushed off the wall and ran toward the south exit, where a dirt road awaited him. He was gasping and wheezing before he reached the end. Two teenagers stepped around the western end of the alley, assault rifles in their hands. He froze, too late seeing their mouths open in shock, the way they held the guns as if they'd never fired one before. Behind him, the grinding and popping again became a strained whine, then a grumbling, mechanical clicking. Meyers dropped, and the machine gun let out a terrible coughing sound that became a short series of booms. Bullets thudded into the ground to his right, then tracked up along the western wall, passing through as if the material were paper.

Blood misted around the boys, and their guns clattered to the ground. The boys dropped, one shedding an arm, the other his head.

And then the grinding and popping sounds returned.

Meyers got to his feet, fighting back screams of fury and pain. Tears flowed down his cheeks. He reached the end of the alley before another coughing sounded, but this time, it was followed by an explosion.

The south road was still littered with corpses. Reyes's men. Meyers edged east along the apartment building's south wall and stopped at the alleyway.

Several men stood in the alley, guns held at the ready. Meyers recognized Beniam.

"Get out of there." Meyers's voice was a hiss, his wave weaker than he intended. It got Beniam's attention.

"The robot." Beniam jogged to the back of the alley, stopping at the sight of the boys, then looking down, shoulders sagging.

"That gun it has, it can punch through my armor. Without armor..." Meyers shook his head.

Beniam wiped away tears, slow, resigned.

"You knew them?"

"My nephews, Abune and Yakob."

"I'm sorry." Meyers didn't know what else to say. Nothing would bring them back.

"What can we do?" Beniam pointed back up the alley. "You have nearly broken their spirit. We want to help."

"Reyes still has men out there. Keep them off of us. Get them out of your area."

"His gun-haulers, they will do just as this robot."

"They're trying to get to a couple of my people, up near Farmers Road."

Beniam looked at the other men. "Then we will drive Reyes and his men from our territory."

The other men raised their assault rifles. "For Mattias!"

"Northwest," Meyers said. "Go wide, take Addis Ababa, and stay off Cáceres Road."

He waited until they were beyond the boys' corpses, then moved into the alley, slow and careful. At the laundry room door, he stepped over the corpse. The water was still running from the broken pipe and swirling down the drain. He paused at the door to the hallway, listening. The proxy was still out there, somewhere off to the west, maybe still at the entry to the alley. Meyers caught his breath and tiptoed through the hallway until he could see the foyer. The street was visible through the hole the flyer had created when it crashed.

Meyers leaned toward the flyer. Despite all the damage it had suffered, the wheels on the flyer looked intact. In fact, the driver's side tires, which were all he could see from his position, looked like they might still be inflated. There was no indication the fuel cells or any of the batteries were cracked. He ran through some basic math, estimating the flyer and proxy's probable mass. It didn't look promising, but neither did anything else.

He hunched as low as his cracked rib would let him, then duckwalked through the foyer, stopping at the hole in the front wall. When he didn't hear the proxy coming closer, he craned his neck and stretched until he could see the proxy. It had the machine gun propped against the front wall of the next building over, the belt feed mechanism popped open. It seemed totally absorbed in whatever it was doing.

Meyers reached out until he could touch the side of the flyer, only taking his eyes off the proxy to search for the door release. He popped the release, and the door rose slightly.

The proxy didn't react.

Meyers belly-crawled under the door, grimacing from the pain, then he popped the belt lock on the driver. The mechanism had been damaged in the crash and refused to come free. He squeezed and punched and pulled until the lock finally released, then he caught the belt and fed it up into the receptacle.

The proxy still seemed absorbed in the machine gun's workings.

Meyers pulled the driver's corpse from the seat, marveling at the way the blood had mostly drained out of the corpse's back and pooled on the bottom of the seat. He dropped the driver onto the foyer floor, waited until he was sure the proxy wasn't aware of what was going on, then climbed into the seat. The blood sloshed and spilled over the seat edges as he settled in.

He pulled the belt down and tried to lock it. The lock didn't want to catch. After three tries, he simply slammed the belt into place, and the lock clicked. He let out a relieved sigh, checked on the proxy again, then examined the console. It was a fairly basic system, like the ones he'd flown before. A red light still blinked a warning that all fan blades were broken. He didn't need the blades for what he had in mind.

There was a physical gear shift to engage the mechanism that converted the fans to what amounted to flywheels. Gears and belts engaged beneath the chassis, and the flyer—now a simple crawler—rocked.

The proxy froze.

An indicator lit up, showing the vehicle was at twenty percent potential power. Batteries, fuel cells, solar collection...he wasn't going to get huge performance from the vehicle.

The proxy turned, slowly, awkwardly, but it still turned.

Meyers set the accelerator at maximum, but he didn't engage the gears to use the stored energy. Not yet. He needed the energy to continue building.

The proxy grabbed the machine gun by the barrel and held it up like a bat.

The indicator showed twenty-five percent. That was going to have to do. Meyers engaged the gears, and the crawler lunged forward, a ball shot from a cannon, throwing him back against the seat. The crawler sped over the five or so meters separating it and the proxy, until front end met knee joints.

Meyers was thrown forward against the belt, which surprisingly held. His arms slammed against the steering controls. Even through his armor, he felt the impact. The crawler's rear end lifted off the ground, then fell back, and blood flew up into the air.

He looked up. The last of the flyer's armor and windshield were gone, parts on the hood, most sprayed over the street. The proxy was on its back, meters away, one leg completely ruined, the other's mechanisms exposed. Its good arm lay at an odd angle beneath it.

Meyers fought free of the belt, then he crawled out of the vehicle, aching everywhere. The proxy seemed dead, but he'd assumed that before.

He reached back for his CAWS-5, remembered not being able to slam it into its brace, then headed down the alley to collect an assault rifle off the dead boys. He took what magazines he could find, then returned to the proxy, lining up for a clear shot at the exposed joint mechanisms. He fired three bursts into each joint, smiling at the sparks and the skitter of debris.

"Lonny?" Nunoz said something beneath his breath. "Um, Colonel?"

"Yeah, go ahead."

"Good and bad news."

Meyers shook his head in disbelief. "I could use some good news."

"The Condor is up. I programmed it to circle Turning Point at one kilometer until it receives other commands or runs down to twenty percent power, then to return here."

"Great." Meyers scanned for the Condor's feed. "And the bad?"

"Zero-Zero-Two. Software's done, but she won't start. It looks like we got a short at startup, fried the altimeter and inertial nav circuits. Could be a lingering effect of the bad system software."

"How long to fix it?"

"The module's behind a pretty tight panel, not one of the easier—"

"What about moving the communications module from Zero-Zero-Two to Zero-Zero-One? Take that altimeter module offline before you start it up, maybe prevent the short?"

"Yeah. We were thinking about that. It should be quicker. But if that doesn't clear the short..."

"Do it."

"We should be airborne in five minutes if this works."

"We needed you ten minutes ago."

Meyers stepped away from the building front and waved his good arm over his head. "Corporal Gerhardt?"

Gerhardt laughed. "Shit. Sounded like a crawler crash down there, Colonel."

"Just a little one. We should have the Condor in a few minutes. I'll push the feed out on the network when I get it."

"Could've used that earlier. Norman's team is pinned down. Walked right into a group of Reyes's men coming onto the soccer field."

"What about McNutt?"

"Still pinned down. I've picked off a couple of the shooters, but I've been focused on those haulers. They backed off after I took out the lead driver again, but they're getting two guys ready to run for the lead truck. Don't think I can get both. They'll be up on that building before too long."

Meyers connected to Perkins. His video showed he was standing in an alleyway, facing a building front. "Private Perkins, where are you?"

"Right across the street from the warehouse, Colonel. I can see the hole in the roof. They've got someone moving around. See him?"

One of Reyes's men came around the west side of the warehouse, gun slung over his back. He seemed to be looking for a way into the building.

"Those haulers aren't far away."

"I know, sir." Perkins held a knife up and leaned forward. "I was hoping I wouldn't have to do this again."

Meyers watched in silence as Perkins raced across the street, catching Reyes's man mid-turn, using the momentum of the run to knock him into the building front, then bearing him down to the ground. He was shorter than Perkins but muscular. Perkins used the angle and his weight until, finally, the knife blade scratched the man's throat. That brought on greater struggle, but the man's punches were ineffective against Perkins's armor. Perkins kept his weight on the blade. The man's desperate breathing became almost a whimper, then the blade sank into his throat and blood sprayed up. The desperation intensified, and the whimper became a scream, but a twist of the knife severed the trachea, and the screaming became a whisper of escaping air.

Perkins got up and cleaned the blade on the man's shirt with shaking hands. After a few seconds during which Meyers could hear deep breaths,

Perkins took the dead man's assault rifle and ammunition, then ran to the east side of the building. A few seconds later, his armor's grips were hauling him to the rooftop.

"Private Perkins, I need to check in on McNutt."

"I'm okay, sir. Heading for the hole now."

Meyers switched over to McNutt's feed. "Corporal McNutt, any good news?"

"Sun's shining," McNutt said. "I think I gave one of the bastards a face full of lead. That's about it."

"Perkins is at the warehouse. He's on the roof."

"We can't move, or we're dead."

"I know."

The Condor's feed finally showed up. Meyers took control of it and began tweaking its flight path.

"I've got the Condor now. It's flying in from the northeast, so I have to keep it up high, where those haulers won't notice it. I'm seeing them now. Okay. Looks like they're moving again. We've got a Javelin maybe three minutes out from launch."

"Too bad we couldn't transfer some of the weapons to the Condor."

Even one would have been worth it. Just a missile set for proximity, something the Condor could have dropped or even carried in. It would have been enough to finish off the haulers.

"I'll push the feed out to everyone as soon as I have good video."

"Thanks. Don't mind us. We'll just get our tans for now."

Paxton's request for a connection popped up, and Meyers accepted. "Colonel?" Paxton's voice was subdued and deeper. "Ramawat's gone."

"Gone?"

"I was checking on the wounded for Banh. When I came back…"

"Any ideas?"

"Didn't say a thing. Took three of the MARCOS."

"Shit. Mattias's men agreed to help us. They're going to come around from Addis Ababa Street. The way Ramawat talked about Starling—"

"You think he'd try to hurt her?"

Meyers thought about it. It didn't seem like it would accomplish anything. "No."

"I don't see it, sir. Ramawat's a different kind of problem than that."

Meyers flexed and relaxed his hands. Pain oozed down from his collarbone and shoulders. "I hope you're right." The Condor's video was exactly where Meyers wanted it. "I'm pushing the Condor's feed out. You should have it coming through...now."

The soccer field filled the left of the display. Meyers quickly tagged the two groups of Reyes's men. The haulers were turning off Guevara Highway onto Farmers Road. Meyers tagged them, and his heart raced. He searched around, found Norman's fire team and McNutt's team and tagged them.

Suddenly, he saw another group, a fire team, moving north at a sprint along the highway. He pushed the camera in as tight as he could.

"Carl, are you seeing this? On Guevara Highway, about twenty meters south of McNutt."

"Is that Ramawat?"

"I think so." Meyers brought McNutt into the channel. "Corporal, you've got—"

"I see them, Colonel. Reyes's men do, too. Taking our opportunity to say hello back."

Gunfire. McNutt's position. Two of Reyes's men flopping, then going still. McNutt and his team moving from cover, laying down fire. Reyes's men breaking, running. Norman's team, free of fire from the north, now able to return fire on Reyes's other team to the south. More gunfire, this from the west.

Meyers brought up the broadcast channel. "Check your fire on the west flank. Those are friendlies. Repeat, west flank of soccer field, friendlies."

Reyes's team broke and fled south. Only three made it to the buildings.

Meyers switched his attention to Ramawat, who was still sprinting north. Toward the haulers. And the Dart.

31

15 December 2174. Turning Point, Bellar Frontier Colony.

As if summoned, a wind blew in from the northeast, tossing up clouds of pale, blue sand, bitter and earthy on Meyers's tongue. The sky seemed to turn dark. Meyers caught a whiff of the sharp, ammonia smell of fertilizer blowing in from the farms outside Turning Point and closed his faceplate. Sealed up again, the world took on a different sound—duller and deeper, with more minutia leaking through. The BAS overlays were brighter and more vibrant. The Condor's images were deeper and lifelike. It felt like Ramawat and his men were pulling away in a race, leaving everyone else behind.

Meyers wondered what Ramawat was doing, then started jogging toward the highway.

"Sergeant Paxton, I'm heading for the Dart."

"Banh's got the wounded stable, Colonel. If you'd like, I could—"

"Hold that position. I need to handle this." Meyers wouldn't say it, but he knew Paxton could hear it: Things might get ugly with Ramawat. No one else needed to be around to witness that.

"Hey, Colonel?" It was Gerhardt's voice.

Meyers looked up and over his shoulder. Gerhardt had his faceplate down, too. "I need to reposition. I can't see shit up here now."

"Get the rest of your squad over there." Meyers waved Gerhardt to the building directly north. Imperfect, but it would have to do. Gerhardt disappeared from sight.

Meyers picked up speed, watching the Condor video feed at half opacity as he ran. McNutt was moving with similar sluggishness, fighting through wounds. Norman's fire team members were paired up as they ran, from the look of it, the two lesser wounded supporting the more wounded. None of them were going to keep up with the sprinting MARCOS, who were quickly approaching the Farmers Road turnoff.

"Private Perkins, what've you got?" As Meyers spoke, he switched to Perkins's video feed.

"I'm inside, Colonel."

Perkins stood on the bottom of the Dart's fuselage. He looked up, through the hole in the roof. The wire from his grips was a thin strand of yellow-gold in the sunlight, rattling in the wind. Sand rained down through the hole and hung in the air like dust. The tail and center of the fuselage were largely intact, but the canopy and nose were mostly gone, hollowed out. Dark streaks marked what may have been all that remained of the pilot. Perkins wiped his boots, smearing the fuselage a black red.

"Can you get in there?" Meyers rotated his head around, as if that might move Perkins or give a better view of what he was seeing.

Perkins squatted and pointed to the hole. "These edges look pretty jagged, sir."

Meyers stopped, thinking he might have seen or heard something out of place. He wasn't sure if it was something Perkins was looking at, or something in the world just outside, the Meyers-space. Almost too late, he saw it, moving through Perkins, or the image of Perkins: Waverley's armored hauler, reversing, speeding toward Meyers.

As he dove to the right, he shrank all other views to nothing. The hauler caught him in the thigh, whipping him around and smashing his face against the passenger side door.

For the briefest instant, he was face-to-face with Waverley, staring into his eyes, seeing the fresh scratches on his face, the dazed look of someone who'd experienced something terrible and unexpected and wanted out of it.

And then Meyers bounced off the hauler's cracked armor and was knocked away. The hauler reversed farther onto Guevara Highway, then it accelerated forward, wheels spinning, chirping, spitting up sand and smoke. He thought it might run over him, but it hauled hard left onto Cáceres Road, spraying pebbles and sand over him and heading east.

For the compound.

He lay still for a moment, filling his display again with Perkins's video. He was slipping through the hole in the Dart's bottom, and Meyers felt a part of that, and not really a part of himself. Below Perkins's boots, the hole where there should have been a canopy dropped into a tangle of scaffolding. Meyers heard something tear. He reached for the grip wires, exactly as Perkins did, gasping along with him. Meyers imagined falling through the hole, into the poles that made up the scaffolding.

"Shit. Thought my grip wires got cut," Perkins said. His relief bled through the connection into Meyers.

"What was it?" Meyers's voice was a raspy groan. He sat up with some effort, then was still, waiting for his head to quit spinning.

Perkins felt around his front, then reached for his back. "Okay, not the assault rifle strap. Oh. Becky's birthday present." Perkins twisted a satchel around for his cameras to capture. "I need to re-gift it before too long."

"You worry about our people first."

"You okay, Colonel?"

Meyers got to his knees, then, with another groan, to his feet. "I'm still trying to get the identification number of the hauler that hit me."

"O-Okay." Perkins grabbed onto what looked like the cabin door and detached his grip wires, then he hunched low and crawled into the passenger cabin. "I see them. Shit, Becky?"

"She probably passed out. Shock." Meyers checked Starling's vitals. She was okay. Barlowe, too. "Careful with her. Broken femur, she said."

Meyers tested his legs, wondering if anything had broken. Nothing complained too loudly other than his head. He began jogging again, realized he was veering to his right, and slowed.

Perkins was fiddling with Starling's harness, moving tentatively.

"She's either passed out completely and you won't wake her, or she's going to wake up screaming when she falls out of that seat." Meyers stopped and fought to keep his balance. "Rub the armor on her thigh so that it stiffens. That should help some."

"Um, which leg?"

"She didn't say." It occurred to Meyers how uncomfortable Perkins sounded. "Don't think of her as a woman—think of her as a soldier."

"Yes, sir. It's just, she's a...good friend."

A good friend, Meyers thought. He wondered what had happened between them back on Plymouth. He switched to the Condor view and tried to find the haulers and Ramawat. "You want to save her some pain, do what I said."

While searching through the view, he opened the channel to McNutt and Paxton. "Waverley's still alive, heading for the compound."

McNutt snorted. "Too evil to die."

"I think he was running the proxy all that time. Something about the way his eyes looked, like he'd survived something he didn't quite know how to handle."

Paxton cleared his throat. "You got a look at his eyes, Colonel?"

"His driver hit me with that hauler. I think I've got a concussion."

"Need Banh to come get you?"

"I'm fine—lightheaded, nausea, loss of balance. Just another day."

"Waverley's gonna get away."

Meyers winced. "I know. Nothing we can do about it."

Meyers blinked and tried to focus on the Condor's video feed, finally locating McNutt and Norman's teams. Ramawat's team was among the buildings on the south side of Farmers Road. Meyers ordered the Condor lower and focused on Ramawat and the haulers.

The Cougars were parked close to each other on the north side of the road, the Devil Cat bringing up the rear. The Leopard was slowly cruising down the east end of the street, the railgun bubble spinning in a tight, ninety-degree arc that covered most of the north side buildings. Gerhardt had managed to scrape off the last of the passengers, leaving only gunners and drivers.

Suddenly, the gunner and driver of the Devil Cat climbed out of their armored positions. The driver of the Leopard backed up and leaned out of his own armored cab to yell something at them. One of the Cougar drivers leaned out of his cab to listen. Meyers couldn't hear what was being said, but it looked like Ramawat could. He waved his people into positions on either side of the alley, then they all sighted in on the haulers.

The MARCOS opened fire, quickly taking down the driver and gunner of the Devil Cat. By the way the Leopard driver reacted—slouching, then jerking back into his cab—he must have been struck, too. The Cougar driver who'd been leaning out of his cab slid to the ground.

"Move," Meyers said.

Paxton grunted, then he said, "What was that, sir?"

"Ramawat. They just opened fire on the haulers." Meyers took a step, then another. "They're holding their position. Those assault rifles aren't going to get through that armor."

The railgun bubble swung around, and the gunner laid down fire along the front of the building half the MARCOS were hunched behind. The first shots were high, punching through the prefab building easily, then doing the same farther south on the building a couple meters to the west. The Cougar with a healthy driver was stuck, and the mounted machine gun's view was blocked by the Leopard. The railgun operator brought the weapon back around from west to east, this time tracking lower and splitting one of the MARCOS in half. One second, the man was firing on the armored bubble; the next, his midsection transformed into a red mist that settled on the wall and ground, and he went limp. There was a full meter between his upper torso and thighs. The other MARCOS next to the dead one rolled away, and it took Meyers a second to realize there was an arm still lying in the alleyway.

"That railgun's tearing them up," Meyers said.

"Almost there," McNutt said.

Meyers fought back nausea and tried to pick up the pace. "You don't have anything that can take that gun out."

"We'll come up with something."

"Perkins has a satchel charge." Meyers added Perkins to the channel. "Private Perkins, that Leopard is about fifteen meters outside your building, and it's shredding the MARCOS. McNutt's coming up on the west end of Farmers. Can you get that satchel charge to him?"

"Yes, sir. I got Agent Barlowe out of his harness, and I've nearly got Becky onto the catwalk. Sorry, Colonel. Private Starling."

Meyers thought of the sort of jump it would take to get across to the catwalk and nearly pitched over from the resulting vertigo. "Good work. Hurry."

He switched back to the Condor view. McNutt was leading his team along the road, staying low. When they reached the Devil Cat, McNutt waved his team north, into an alley, then disappeared beneath the rear of the hauler.

"Corporal McNutt, what do you think you're doing?"

"Shit, Colonel, might as well tag my location for them." McNutt's armor audio picked up the hum of the railgun and the scrape of something moving over blacktop. "I've got an idea. I sent Chavez up to help Perkins."

Gerhardt sent a channel request; Meyers just added Gerhardt to the open channel. "What is it, Gerhardt?"

"I can't see shit up where the Dart went down, Colonel, but there's a bunch of people massing over in Reyes's territory. I'd like to see if I can break them up."

"If you're sure they're Reyes's men…"

Gerhardt sucked in a breath. "Yeah. It's his men."

"Do what you can. Have your last fire team hook up with Banh, and call Norman back. His team's too banged up to be out in the open. Sergeant Paxton, you hear that?"

"Moving to the wall now, sir."

Meyers stumbled and slowed. There were huge holes in the blacktop, much worse than the cracks he'd come to expect. He looked around and realized he was moving through the spot where McNutt's team had been pinned down by the flyer. After looking around to get bearings, Meyers continued forward more carefully.

On the Condor's video feed, McNutt slid out from beneath the Devil Cat and climbed onto the flatbed, then he slid into the armored bubble of the machine gun.

"McNutt, what—"

"You give these haulers a good look yet, Colonel? Put together by a pack of wild clowns strung out on Synthacaine."

The bubble rotated, overshot the railgun hauler, and came to a stop just to the left of the cab. The bubble shifted slowly, lining up with the cab.

"Should've put the guns up on a raised platform," McNutt muttered.

The machine gun opened fire, tearing through the armor covering the cab, then shearing away the cab roof, which loudly crashed down and slid onto the street. McNutt kept firing, and the rounds tore into the armored bubble of the Cougar ahead of his, splattering the gunner inside. The lead Cougar's bubble pivoted toward the Devil Cat and opened fire, and the cab of the middle Cougar exploded in a shower of clear armor and plastic.

McNutt dropped out of the bubble just as the railgun twisted around and opened fire on the Devil Cat. He barely stayed ahead of the rounds that tore the vehicle in half. The railgun and machine gun bubbles turned on each other but held fire, then they swung around in semicircles. The Leopard accelerated west, braking as it approached Guevara Highway.

"That's got 'em spooked," McNutt said.

The railgun fired into the buildings at the end of the street, first the north side, then the south. At the same time, the final Cougar's machine gun spun and fired into the warehouse where the Dart had crashed. After a moment, the bubble on the Cougar pivoted right and opened fire on the next building over.

"Shit." McNutt sighed. "Too spooked. Gotta fix this."

Meyers closed all the overlays and video feeds and looked north on Guevara Highway. He could actually make out Farmers Road. If he strained, he could hear the hum of the railgun every time the machine gun stopped firing. His heel felt like someone was holding a blowtorch to it. His thigh ached where Waverley's hauler had struck, and it felt like vomit was going to come jetting up at any moment. Meyers told himself he still had a good arm, he could still contribute. That was enough.

He brought the video feeds back up.

Perkins crawled along the rooftop, assault rifle cradled on his forearms. McNutt was once again out of sight. The Leopard was firing into buildings on the south side of the street, slowly driving forward.

Meyers dropped, suddenly realizing a railgun round could easily reach him.

Perkins was at the edge of the warehouse roof now, sighting down the assault rifle's barrel at the Cougar's machine gun bubble.

"Private Perkins, that gun isn't going to get through that armor."

The assault rifle popped and jumped, and Perkins dropped flat on the roof, then skidded back.

The machine gun bubble didn't move.

Perkins's head rose. "There's a small opening on the door, Colonel."

McNutt climbed out from beneath the hauler, looked into the bubble, then stabbed a thumb skyward. "Clean shot. Got brains everywhere."

"Good deal." Perkins laughed. "That was my last bullet."

"Glad I was a little slow crawling—"

"McNutt, get out of there!" Meyers jumped back to his feet and nearly fell. He ran toward the sound of the railgun firing, easy to hear now that the machine gun was silent.

McNutt managed to drop just as the Leopard sped forward and cut to the south side of the street. The railgun fired again, this time tearing apart the last Cougar. McNutt had barely reached the alleyway when the Leopard driver slammed into the Cougar that had just been shot up, pushing the front end out of the way.

Perkins was at the edge of the roof, on one knee. "He sees you, McNutt. Run!"

"Can't." McNutt gasped. "Leg."

"Shit. Hang on!"

The Leopard reversed, then it slammed into the front end of the ruined Cougar again, pushing it even farther forward. Perkins ran back, then he leapt from the rooftop, landing on top of the railgun bubble. Immediately, he slid off and landed on the street awkwardly and fell onto his back.

Meyers could barely make out the shape of something sliding down the bubble and settling onto the flatbed. The satchel charge.

As Perkins got to his feet, the railgun bubble spun around, froze, and fired.

Perkins's torso and head disintegrated. The bubble shifted, and his legs became small chunks of flesh and armor, flying through the air.

The railgun operator jumped out of the bubble and tossed the satchel charge into the street, then he jumped back into the bubble. A second later, the Leopard plowed through the demolished cab, knocking it aside, then driving east before braking and turning around.

Meyers stared in horror at what remained of Perkins. The satchel charge, only a few meters away, still hadn't detonated.

And the Leopard was coming back.

32

---

15 December 2174. Turning Point, Bellar Frontier Colony.

PALE AQUA SANDS swirled across Guevara Highway as the winds picked up. Meyers was sure he heard a howl in the winds, a protest against Perkins's death, or at least against the satchel charge not detonating. That rendered Perkins's death more painful, pointless.

Vomit shot up into the back of Meyers's throat. He fought it back, but it was in his saliva and sinuses. He swallowed and stumbled forward, staring at the blacktop.

He was past the point where the road was torn up. Closer to the fight.

Nausea kicked in hard, and his vision blurred. He shivered, his gut cold, his head as hot as Bellar's sun.

There had to be a way to take the railgun out. A sniper to shoot the gunner or driver? The only sniper remaining was Gerhardt, and he was trying to keep Reyes's men from attacking again. Other explosives besides the satchel charge? They'd lost everything when One-Six-Three crashed. Meyers would gladly take a knife to the gunner if there were any chance of getting up to the Leopard fast enough. A desperate, pathetic laugh echoed in Meyers's helmet—he was barely upright, fighting blurry vision, and weak. He would be gunned down the same as Perkins.

They needed something. They needed the Javelin.

Meyers tried to focus on the BAS display, to search through for Nunoz's name, then gave up. "Channel to Nunoz."

The BAS sent a channel request. While Meyers waited, he flipped his attention to Farmers Road. The Leopard was back now, stopped in front of the warehouse where the Dart had crashed. After a second, the Leopard reversed, swinging south, probably giving the railgun a clean look at the alley and front of the warehouse. Meyers tried to anticipate what the gunner might be looking for: McNutt. He'd been in the alley, down, something about his leg. Meyers searched desperately, finally spotting McNutt and someone else at the back of the building, pressed tight against the north wall.

"McNutt, the Leopard—"

"Yeah, we can hear the motor." McNutt was breathing through his nose, hard. Probably fighting through pain.

"Who's that with you?"

"Chavez. Pulled my ass out of the fire."

"Not for long."

McNutt's breath whistled. "If I could get some sustained shots on that cab, I could probably do enough damage to finish that thing off. Immobilize it."

"They got Perkins."

"Thought they might. Fuck." McNutt sounded close to tears. "Shouldn't've—"

"I know." Meyer couldn't say anything more, but Perkins had gone out a hero, giving his life for the mission, trying to save squad mates. They owed it to him to finish the mission.

Meyers slowed. Farmers Road was just ahead. He got off Guevara and jogged toward the closest building, one of the ones the railgun had shot up after McNutt destroyed the other haulers. Light leaked through head-sized holes in the walls. Meyers peeked through, hoping to get a look at the Leopard. Crates blocked his vision. Dirt slowly leaked through holes the railgun rounds had punched, forming small mounds, black and sparkly, not like the pale, bluish sand or dirt from Cáceres Compound.

"McNutt, I thought these buildings were supposed to be empty?"

"Yeah, that's what Barlowe and Starling said."

Meyers looked around, saw more scaffolding and catwalks in the warehouse, same as the one where the Dart had crashed. Toward the southern wall, there were more crates, and a small forklift, too light to be of any use against the Leopard.

He shook his head, trying to clear it. Empty warehouse buildings filled with crates. A quad-barreled railgun, heavy machine guns—military hardware.

More to think about if he survived.

He leaned against the wall and advanced to the corner, then he peered around. The Leopard was pushing the ruins of the Cougars out of the way. The motor's whine, the cracking of the plex-armor: He could have located the Leopard from the noise, even with the railgun silent.

"That driver's trying to get the gunner a look at the other alley." Meyers closed his eyes and took a long, deep breath. "It's only a matter of time before they just go around the block and come up behind you."

"Not gonna be here when they do." McNutt groaned. "We're heading inside."

"Be quick about it. I don't think they could hear you if you had to make some noise."

"Sounds like a waste compactor going at it."

"You said something about your leg earlier."

"Lost a bit of it. One of those rounds slid along my thigh. It's got a nice little kiss, that bitch."

Meyers checked on the status of the call to Nunoz. It was still pending. There was no indication of a problem with signal strength or other elements of the armor. Comms were working.

"Bring up..." Meyers tried to remember his other squad leaders. Banh. Zacharowski? No. Dead. Gerhardt. "Bring up Gerhardt's feed. Full display."

A rooftop corner, looking down on a dirt road, smaller buildings. Alleys. Men rushing, tight against the walls, minimal targets, searching for someone too brave or stupid. A head pops out, neck craning, assault rifle coming up. Recoil from the CAWS-5, but it was a clean hit. Automatic gunfire. Ducking behind cover.

It definitely couldn't be the signal strength, Meyers realized. He had a strong connection and sharp video from Gerhardt.

Meyers tried to select Paxton's channel, had the same problem with jitteriness, and gave up. "Paxton channel."

Automatic gunfire, prefab walls cracking and crumbling, controlled fire. Shouting. Moaning.

"We're under a lot of pressure here, Colonel."

"I'm trying to raise Nunoz, Carl. That Javelin should be ready to go. Just hang in there."

Paxton grunted. "There's too many of the bastards."

Meyers remembered what Gerhardt was seeing, people thick in the alleys. Like rats. He brought up the BAS view of the area Paxton and Banh were holding. There were four active ERF signals and two green wireframe forms Meyers assumed were MARCOS.

"You're missing a fire team." Meyers looked around, confused. "Gerhardt was supposed to send—"

"They're pinned down, Colonel. You okay?"

"Yeah." Meyers stared at the video. "Yeah."

The wireframe and video of the building interior were incomplete. He tapped into the systems of the dead and wounded in the area, hoping to expand the view and details. The wireframe built out more behind Paxton and Banh, and the BAS quickly began rough interpolation to fill in the wireframe. Every wall had at least some damage to it, and most had sizable holes, worse than Meyers remembered. It was a testament to the design of the prefabs that the building hadn't collapsed yet.

Meyers shook his head, hoping to clear it. "I'll keep trying the Javelin. Do what you can."

He sent another channel request to Nunoz, then a simple text telling him people were dying. After one last glance around the apartment building, Meyers switched back to McNutt. "McNutt, add Chavez to the channel. Have him add to your video feed."

McNutt's channel expanded to a video feed. The BAS quickly built out a model of what it could sense through McNutt and Chavez's armor, first in wireframe, then filling it in with shades of gray.

"Adding Calderon, too," McNutt said.

More details filled out the warehouse's interior—the catwalk, the Dart, the matrix of pipes and beams that made up the scaffolding. Five green wireframes, McNutt and Chavez detailed out where their armor's cameras captured video of them. McNutt's gory leg came into view—a big hole in the armor; blood leaking around the sealant someone had sprayed over the wound, jagged pieces of flesh and muscle visible beneath the sealant, moving when he walked.

More video of the catwalk filled in, including Barlowe and Starling, captured from the memory of Calderon's gear. Barlowe lay flat on his back, his helmet secured to his armor for spinal stability. His right shoulder joint was rigid as well. Meyers figured a broken collarbone or dislocated shoulder. Starling had the same thing done to the opposite shoulder, and her thighs were rigid at ninety degrees, the same position they'd been at when Perkins got her out of the harness.

The Dart took on more detail, also drawing from BAS memory. Everything that wasn't a live feed had a faint shimmer to it, signaling for the eye not to trust it.

"Hey, Colonel?" McNutt sounded hopeful, almost. "That gun's been silent a bit. You think it's out of ammo?"

"No. Those things can carry a lot of ammo. No need for propellant, more room for rounds. Maybe they've pushed the power system too hard, though." It didn't seem likely. The Leopard was used in mining operations. A lot of its space would be dedicated to extra batteries and fuel cells, and the gun itself would have its own capacitors, possibly even a generator. "I think they're just trying to locate you."

"Yeah, well, it's personal for me, too."

For all of us, Meyers realized. He hated the Leopard. He hated the driver and gunner, and he knew that there was no way he would let either of them live, even if they surrendered right then. Making war personal was a mistake. He'd fought with Rimes about that exact thing, but lines had been crossed.

Paxton's channel opened; it was an urgent call. "Here they come!"

Meyers filled his helmet display with Paxton's feed. Reyes's men burst from the alleys like puss from a boil. Some stayed under relative cover, firing up at Gerhardt, two buildings to the east. Others fired at the building next to him, probably where Gerhardt's fire team was pinned down. The rest filled the dirt road, firing their weapons indiscriminately. Inside the apartment building Paxton and Banh were holding, bullets cracked and zinged off the walls. It was a constant sound, climbing until it was like a jackhammer gone mad. Paxton returned fire, using one of the assault rifles taken from Waverley's dead. Paxton was also firing on automatic, but Reyes's men were packed so close together, the bullets found plenty of targets.

But there were too many for it to matter.

"Fall back!"

Banh leapt over a wall, as did one of the other ERF forms; the last one didn't move, its vitals dropping. Paxton emptied another magazine, then he turned to jump back. His camera swept over one of the MARCOS, a man Meyers recognized as one of the mortally wounded who still fought. The man was prone, one leg gone at mid-thigh, a section of cracked ribs exposed beneath clear sealant and blood-soaked bandages. He was trying to reload his assault rifle, but his hands were shaking too violently to slide the magazine in. Bullets raked the area, tearing through joints in the armor, cracking the sealant, shattering the exposed ribs. The man went rigid, then he slumped. Paxton cursed, and almost immediately grunted. Meyers realized that Reyes's men were finding their mark now, too. The ERF armor could handle most rounds, but it wasn't invulnerable to small arms fire. A solid hit at the right angle or in the joints from a powerful enough gun, or enough impacts flipping the nano-fibers in opposing directions too quickly, or even simply hitting just right in the head—they could be killed or incapacitated.

Paxton crouched behind a wall and spun back to the street just as Reyes's men reached the outer wall. A few paused to fire on the ERF and MARCOS forms still against the wall, but most rushed in. Packed so tightly, they made easy targets for the surviving ERF and MARCOS soldiers. Automatic fire boomed, and the front rank of Reyes's men fell. More in the second rank fell, but they pushed in, stumbling over the dead and the debris. More gunfire, and it was down to the third rank, which broke.

Reyes's men ran, but several didn't reach the alleys.

"Cover me," Paxton shouted, then he crawled forward, checking first on the MARCOS soldier. He was clearly dead.

Paxton crawled to the wounded ERF soldier. "Son of a—" The soldier's armor was cracked, dented, and there was a hole in the faceplate, but the right hand moved. "He's still alive!"

Even with the armor on, the man was small and slim, and Paxton easily hooked an arm under the armored chest and retreated to the triage area. Banh followed, faceplate up, eyes jumping from one portion of the armor to another. He dragged his gloves off.

Without looking up from the wounded man, Banh said, "Mai, gather weapons and magazines."

Mai, the last of Banh's squad still standing, crawled to the bodies of Reyes's men and began collecting weapons and ammo. Paxton watched the street outside, gun raised.

"Master Sergeant, there are some survivors here," Mai said.

"If any look like a threat, you've got a knife." Paxton's voice was hard, cold.

Meyers switched to the Condor's view. Norman's squad was near the end of the soccer field, but they were on their bellies, crawling. Meyers couldn't see why at first, then he spotted a second clump of Reyes's men, maybe sixty strong, no more than fifty meters south. They were moving east, crouched low, apparently unaware of Norman to the north. They were probably hoping to flank the apartment building where Paxton and Banh were holed up. Or to get up on Gerhardt. Or his fire team.

"Join Gerhardt to Paxton's channel," Meyers said. "Gerhardt, you've got fifty to sixty of Reyes's men, south of the soccer field, between Norman and the buildings to your north. They look like they're trying to flank."

"Can't see 'em. I can see Norman's team."

"Add him to the channel. Have him engage them if he thinks he can pin them down."

"All right."

Meyers switched his attention back to the Leopard. It had moved the last of the destroyed Cougars out of the way and nudged up to the alley on the warehouse's west side. As it moved forward, Meyers spotted two MARCOS coming from the south side of the street. He recognized Ramawat's armor.

"McNutt, looks like you might have company." Meyers shook his head in disbelief. "Ramawat and one of his men, coming across the street toward your—"

Ramawat waved the other MARCOS wide, to the left, then started running along the street. They weren't heading for the warehouse.

"Hold on." Meyers looked around, trying to see if there might be something Ramawat could see that wasn't obvious. "Shit. Ramawat's got the satchel. He's got Perkins's satchel charge."

Would Ramawat kill the last of the ERF to cover up his errors and salvage his career? Meyers wondered. Was that what he was up to?

Ramawat slung the satchel charge over his shoulder, then he opened fire.

On the Leopard.

It braked, and the bubble spun around. It tried to track Ramawat, but he was already gone. And then the MARCOS south of the Leopard opened fire. The gun bubble spun again, and once again there was no target, as the MARCOS dropped behind the wreckage of the Devil Cat.

"They're drawing off the railgun," Meyers said. "I don't think they realize what they're doing."

The Leopard reversed onto the street, and the railgun bubble spun. The MARCOS that had been hiding behind the Devil Cat ran. The railgun tracked him.

And then the whine of the railgun filled the air again.

33

---

15 December 2174. Turning Point, Bellar Frontier Colony.

Even before the railgun fired, Meyers knew he couldn't just stand by and be a witness to more deaths. The MARCOS were trying to help, to save lives, and all he had done was watch.

He peeked around the corner just as the MARCOS dove behind the building next to the warehouse where the Dart had crashed. The railgun hummed, and sections of the south wall exploded. The air grew powdery thick with wind-blown sand and bits of the wall, but Meyers could make out the Leopard well enough. It was maneuvering, hunting the MARCOS down, just as it had with McNutt.

Meyers tried to find the hole in the armored bubble Perkins had mentioned, then gave up and fired. The bubble spun toward him, and he fell to the ground.

The railgun hummed again, and fragments of the prefab material rattled off him.

"Colonel Meyers, this is Ensign Nunoz. I just saw the channel requests. Sorry."

"Where've you been?" Meyers was shouting, even though he doubted the railgun's hum was being picked up by his armor's damaged audio sensors.

"I had my helmet off and earpiece out while I was getting the module plugged in. Engines are online. Everything's a go."

"Get airborne!" Meyers sent Nunoz Paxton's feed. "Master Sergeant Paxton's in the biggest mess. We've got wounded at risk, and there are only a few people there to protect them."

"We're launching now."

Meyers listened to the Javelin's engines, a mix of high-pitched whine and deep thrum, then he turned his attention back to the Condor video feed.

The hauler was speeding west on Farmers Road, coming toward him.

"Shit! McNutt, I've got trouble!"

"What's up, Colonel?"

"Leopard headed my way. Need a distraction."

Gunshots boomed from the north side of the street, east of the warehouse. Bullets cracked against the armored gun bubble, and the hauler braked hard.

"Disregard, McNutt. Ramawat's engaged. There're three of us now."

The Leopard reversed, the whine of its motor loud in the street.

Meyers got to his feet, leaned against the wall for support, then headed south. He needed to get to the alley east of his current position before he could fire again. The building front where he'd been firing from was dangerously chopped up. As he limped along the warehouse side, he watched the Condor's video. He stopped when the MARCOS who had managed to escape catercorner to his position popped out of the alley and opened fire on the Leopard driver. Even if he'd managed a clean shot on the driver, a break through the armor, a quick kill, he'd miscalculated. The gun bubble whipped back to the north and fired.

The rounds hit the MARCOS in the chest, punching through his armor as if it were paper, liquefying his upper torso. His head and arms fell to the ground, but his abdomen and legs stayed up, quivering. Finally, even those fell to the ground, and his guts spilled out in a dark, spreading pool.

Meyers hurried into the alley, leaning against the wall, grunting, trying to keep his footing. It was down to two people, Meyers realized: him and Ramawat.

A new channel request popped up...Ramawat. Meyers accepted.

"Colonel Ramawat, that hauler's too fast for us to keep this up for long."

"It is."

Meyers could see Ramawat, pressed against the wall of the building, squatting low. The Leopard accelerated toward his position.

"It's coming toward you."

"I hear it, Colonel." Ramawat peered around the corner. "Do me the favor of drawing its attention, please."

Meyers did his best to run, skidding unsteadily as he reached the street. He brought the assault rifle up and fired on the windshield. To his surprise, a section of armor splintered and fell away. The MARCOS' attack had actually done some damage. The Leopard stopped again. Meyers fired off another burst, then fell back and dropped. A second later, the wall above him blew out into the alley.

"Attention drawn," Meyers said.

"So I see. That gun's the sort of thing I'd expect on an armored vehicle. Very much military grade. Like these explosives in the satchel."

"I know. Something's not right. All that hardware—"

"Yes, just as you said. By the way, the detonator was knocked free of the explosives. That's why it didn't go off."

Meyers remembered when Perkins fell through the Dart, the tearing sound, the satchel. "Perkins fell."

The railgun fired again, and more of the wall fell onto him. The Leopard sounded like it was moving again, coming closer. He edged back on elbows and thighs, gritting his teeth against the pain where Waverley's hauler had hit him.

"I made some errors," Ramawat said. "Quite a few. The worst of them was showing the same disrespect toward you and your men that had been shown toward mine. Not by you, but by others. That's shameful, not right, not good. I feel obligated to apologize for that."

The Leopard was close enough for Meyers to hear the click-clack of something complaining in its drive system. He took some satisfaction from knowing they'd managed to do something against the impossible odds, but it wouldn't mean much if everyone died, and it was looking more and more likely that's how things were going to play out. He tried to push back deeper into the alley, freezing when the cab of the Leopard came into view.

Gunfire. A CAWS-5. From across the street.

"Got his attention, Colonel." Chavez, sounding cool.

Meyers froze. "Don't let that gunner get a good look at you, Corporal!"

The railgun fired, and this time there wasn't the accompanying rain of prefab building materials.

"Chavez?"

"I'm good. He's tearing up the building front. Holy shit! That thing."

Meyers flipped over to McNutt's feed. He was lying low about halfway into the warehouse, beneath the catwalk, behind one of its support beams. To his left, the scaffolding groaned and swayed as the railgun's rounds sheared through poles and cracked beams. A round shot through the warehouse's central support beam, which was still balancing the Dart on a collapsed section of roof. The beam splintered, and the entire structure groaned.

"Chavez, get to cover," McNutt yelled.

The railgun continued to fire, and the Dart's weight finally collapsed the weakened support. Chavez crawled clear just as the Dart slammed to the floor with a deafening crash that sent pieces of the scaffolding flying. As the clatter of all the debris settling to a rest quieted, a different, more ominous sound became more apparent: a creaking groan, as if the weight of the building were testing the rest of its support and not finding it adequate.

"I'm not liking that sound," Chavez said.

The groaning grew louder.

Chavez whistled. "Uh-uh. Not one fucking bit."

"Calderon, everyone okay up there?" McNutt asked.

"So far, but it feels like this platform shifted, Boss."

"Yeah, I think I shifted my pants," McNutt said, deadpan. "At least that fucking railgun's silent."

Meyers switched back to Paxton's feed. He was lined up where he'd been when Meyers had entered the apartment, just forward from the triage area. At his side, Banh was on one knee, watching the street where Reyes's men had charged earlier. Mai and the last MARCOS soldier squatted next to each other behind the wall to the right.

"Paxton, you have anything new?"

"They're moving again. Won't be long now."

Meyers flipped back to the Condor feed. Norman's team was spread out, lying flat. They were tracking Reyes's men as they moved west. A much larger group of men—more than 100--had filtered into the alleyways across from Paxton's position. Meyers switched back to Paxton's feed.

"Corporal Gerhardt, I think they're getting ready to attack."

"I see their...faces, sir."

"How're you holding up?"

"Ten rounds left, but I grabbed one of those assault rifles and a bunch of mags on my way up. They're not bad."

"All you need to do is hold out for a few more minutes. Ensign Nunoz has the Javelin in the—"

Reyes's men charged from the alleyway, and the cacophony of battle drowned out the channel. Automatic weapons fire, the crack of bullets against walls, the screams of the wounded...

Meyers pulled out of Paxton's feed and shook his head to clear it. The data was too much for him. Everything was too much for him at the moment.

"Colonel Meyers, are you still there?" Ramawat sounded concerned.

Meyers switched back to the Condor's feed, pulled his eyes away from the alleyway and the street overflowing with Reyes's men, and he focused on Farmers Road. The Leopard was crawling closer, as if the driver hoped to sneak up on Meyers's position.

"I'm here." Meyers pushed himself deeper into the alley.

"They seem to have chosen you for the moment. That works out quite well for me. I was mentioning before that these explosives are military grade. They could also be for mining. With the right connections, you can buy just about the same sort."

Mining. Meyers thought about Waverley's armored hauler, the Leopard. Even the proxy. All mining gear. But Bellar wasn't supposed to have any significant mineral deposits, at least nothing to justify all the expenses and regulation associated with safe mining if they wanted to do business with Earth.

"It couldn't have come with Waverley. His yacht's big, but it's not that big." Meyers continued deeper into the alley. "You'd want explosives like that broken out over a few cargo areas meant for just that sort of transport."

The front of the Leopard was less than a meter away from the alley.

"After what I've had the unfortunate opportunity to witness on Bellar, Meyers, my views about Waverley and the metacorporations have undergone significant..." Ramawat sighed. "Adjustment. I've logged an AAR and uploaded it to my Javelin."

Meyers brought the assault rifle up. "What does that mean?"

"It means that the time has come to resolve this matter with this horrifying vehicle and to set about cleaning up at least some of the mess I've made."

On the Condor's feed, Ramawat dashed into the street. He didn't have a weapon out, just the satchel in his right hand. He sprinted toward the armored hauler, leaning in.

"What the hell are you doing? Lure it in and throw that!"

The gun bubble spun, and Ramawat skidded to a stop, then he tossed the satchel. It arced through the air, to the right of the hauler. The railguns hummed, and Ramawat flew apart.

Suddenly, the railgun bubble spun, as if the gunner were trying to target the satchel.

It was too late. The satchel struck the street and bounced beneath the cab.

Then the charge detonated, lifting the hauler into the air and splitting the flatbed from the cab, flipping it onto its top, flinging the driver through the shattered windshield armor. He landed at the head of the alley, miraculously still alive and groaning.

Across the street, the warehouse seemed to echo the groan.

"McNutt? Calderon? Chavez?"

"All okay, Colonel," McNutt said, although he didn't sound very confident. "Just let it find its balance."

Meyers held his breath for a second, and everything seemed to settle. He looked at the Condor's video feed and saw Reyes's men, swarming outside the apartment building Paxton and Banh were trying to hold. Norman's fire team had the flanking group pinned down, but exposed and outnumbered, that wouldn't last long.

"Nunoz, our people are getting torn apart!"

"I see Turning Point, Colonel. You sure you want me to open fire on civilians?"

"They're killing my men, Ensign! What do you think?"

The Javelin roared into view, maybe ten kilometers southeast of the city, flying low, trailing a shadow off its left side.

Meyers switched to Paxton's feed. "Hang on! Hang on!"

Reyes's men were inside the building, taking cover, rushing forward. Just behind Paxton, Singh was up, weight fully pressed against cover, somehow managing to effectively fire his assault rifle. Paxton rocked backward for a second, reeling from a solid hit to the chest that was close enough to one of the torso cameras to knock it offline. Banh and Mai maintained steady, disciplined bursts, dropping man after man, but one of Reyes's men stood tall and sent several rounds into Banh, who dropped and disappeared from the BAS.

Meyers twisted around to look back toward the section of the city where the firefight was raging. He wanted to be there, to be with his men.

The Javelin shot past, guns quiet, no missile launched.

"Nunoz, I ordered you to fire on those men!"

"Negative, sir. There's another group moving in from the northwest. I couldn't tell who to fire on."

Meyers wanted to shout "all of them," but he bit that back. He drilled down in the Condor's video of the area and saw what Nunoz was talking about. Maybe fifty men were closing in on Reyes's men bunched in the alleys and street. A group at least as large was rushing toward the men Norman's team had pinned down. Both of these new groups opened fire, apparently unconcerned that they were exposed. Their gunfire was constant and deadly. Reyes's men, trapped in the open, tried to return fire. After a few seconds, realizing their positions were hopeless, and with so many already dying or dead, they broke.

Some of the gunmen who had come to the ERF's aid pursued, maybe seeking vengeance for some of Reyes's abuses, maybe realizing this was their only chance to break his strength. Meyers only cared that they were doing what he would have done, given the chance.

He slumped, realizing the battle was over. What little remained of his forces had won. All the dead, all the wounded, all the horrific wounds—it squeezed his chest until he couldn't breathe.

He muted his microphones, buried his face against his knees, and cried.

34

15 December 2174. Turning Point, Bellar Frontier Colony.

SOMETHING about the wind coming in from the northeast changed in Meyers's perception. It wasn't the color—still a pale aqua. And it wasn't the density of the powdery clouds or the taste or the texture—metallic and gritty on his tongue now that his faceplate was up.

The wind died down suddenly, and he stumbled toward Farmers Road, still trying to figure out what had changed. At the head of the alley, the driver looked up to him with pleading, dark eyes. His lips twitched, and his shattered jaw shifted, but he couldn't manage more than a gurgling rasp. Meyers looked the man up and down, seeing horrific pain and inevitable death in the twisted limbs, the ruptured and blackened skin, and the blood leaking onto the blacktop. The driver's eyes were bloodshot, seemingly lidless, and yet they managed a stunning level of expressiveness. Meyers realized the driver wanted to be put out of his misery.

Meyers looked up and down the street, now littered with wreckage both human and machine. He recognized the smell the wind had carried: death.

He squatted next to the driver and said, "I know you must be in terrible pain."

I am, the driver's eyes said. They all but glowed at Meyers's understanding.

Meyers shook his head. "It's terrible. All this death. All this...killing."

The wind picked up again, drowning out the gurgling. Sand settled onto the driver's eyes and into his tortured flesh. The eyes seemed to plead now for release.

Meyers stood and looked the destroyed body over again. "I think we've done enough killing for today."

He crossed the street, stopping only long enough to marvel at the work Starling's satchel charge had done on the Leopard. The bubble had been blown clear of the flatbed and split open. Lying inside one half, the gunner seemed at peace. His jeans were baggy enough that you could almost imagine the legs weren't impossibly twisted. His arms had lost any hint of definition and seemed almost serpent-like with the strange twists they had taken on in his final repose. His head lay awkwardly to the side, but his face seemed to have escaped significant injury. Meyers recognized the heavily pierced ears, the face that had laughed maniacally.

And then he realized the gunner had been a woman.

Meyers wondered what could have created someone so gleefully committed to killing in such a terrible way, but he quickly stopped once he realized the only difference between them was that the gunner seemed to have enjoyed doing what she had done. Whether that was true or not, Meyers would never know.

He fell against the doorframe of the warehouse, which shuddered with his weight. Chavez and Calderon were on the loft, lowering a litter with Starling strapped onto it. Barlowe already lay next to McNutt, who leaned against the west wall.

"Corporal McNutt," Meyers said.

McNutt's eyes opened.

"No dying on me, Corporal."

"Got too much vinegar in the veins to stop yet, Colonel."

Meyers nodded and looked around the interior. The place was a wreck, but it was still possible to get a sense of the layout. It looked a lot like the warehouse he'd been hiding behind, although there were no crates in this one.

"This place doesn't seem like it's going to stay up much longer."

Calderon and Chavez descended from the loft using their grip wires. Chavez twisted as he descended, and said, "We're getting out of here as soon as McNutt gets off his ass, Colonel."

"You two may have to take an electric prod to him." Meyers smirked when McNutt's eyes fluttered open again.

"Good way to get a broken nose, trying that."

"Okay. I'll leave the details to the three of you. If Barlowe or Starling wake up, tell them they're going to be okay," Meyers said, then he turned and headed back toward the warehouse, mind racing. He opened a private channel to Nunoz. "Ensign Nunoz, what're you seeing from up there?"

"Not much, Colonel. There's still the occasional individual or small group trickling back into Reyes's territory, but a lot of them are being gunned down."

"Okay. We'll need to put a stop to all that."

Meyers brought up the BAS interface and flipped through to the systems Starling had hacked before Ramawat ordered the assault. She'd left a relay in the Grid wide open. Meyers tapped into that.

"Citizens of Turning Point, this is Colonel Lonny Meyers of the United Nations' Elite Response Force. I would ask you to impose an immediate ceasefire. Hostilities should be brought to an end. Now."

He listened to the message, brought up a connection to the Grid, then transmitted it to all Grid connections, setting it to loop through a few times, pause for fifteen seconds, then loop through again. Off to the north and west, the message played over the meager public warning system. If it did the same to the south, he couldn't hear it, but he felt it should be enough to drown out Reyes's nonstop propaganda. When it had played through all the way, he brought up the Condor's video. There were crowds gathered all along Theater Street, Addis Ababa Street, and Center Street. The folk were a mix of Arabs, Turks, and Ethiopians, men and women, young and not so young. They held assault rifles over their heads. Occasionally, one would run into Reyes's territory to throw a rock or kick a corpse. It was the typical reaction of the downtrodden to a broken despot, played out over and over again as far back as Meyers could remember.

It didn't seem likely that he could say anything to stop the cycle, but he had to try. He leaned against the warehouse that had offered him protection earlier and started recording again.

"The United Nations wants to reach out to Bellar—"

He growled and erased the message.

"The United Nations wants to reach out to you, the people of Bellar, and to establish a relationship. I'm not a diplomat, so I'm in no position to describe that relationship. Then again, I think that's something you would want to think about. Maybe it's time you decided what sort of world you want this place to be. It's your home. Do you want it to be like this—a war zone where people live in fear for their lives? Or do you want something more?"

He played the message back, then sent it through the Grid. After a few seconds, he began another recording.

"I hope we can all find peace and—"

"Listen up!" Reyes's voice played through the same Grid, over the same public warning system.

Meyers stopped recording.

"You think I don't know what you've all done? Like I suddenly can't see what the cameras record, huh? I've seen every one of you and what you did to my people. Did you forget how we got here? All the lies that put us into prison? You forget about that? You forget about the betrayal from governments? Every time, the lies they told? I didn't!"

Meyers pulled up the interface into the Grid and frowned. He didn't have Barlowe's knowledge or skill with systems. There were no notes on how Starling had hacked into things. Figuring it out would take time. There was no brute force shutting down Reyes.

Not on the Grid, at least.

"Let me tell you something. This *pendejo*, he comes here and starts up a war, and he tells you, hey, it's all good now, why don't you kiss the United Nations' ass? And you listen? He got nothing left! His people are dead! You didn't turn on me, we'd be tossing his corpse out in the desert right now!"

"Colonel?" Nunoz's voice was tense. "You seeing the crowds?"

Meyers checked the Condor's video, then switched to the Javelin's hi-res imagery. The crowds were calm now, the weapons no longer thrust into the air.

Not calm, he realized. He looked closer. Fearful. They were afraid.

"I see it. The tyrant hasn't been knocked out."

"Yeah. It's like they've completely forgotten what happened a few minutes ago."

That, Meyers realized, was the power of tyranny.

He opened the connection back into the Grid. He couldn't shut Reyes out, but he could try to talk him down.

"—fought together, didn't we? Huh? And who got you guarantees of money when those jobs didn't come through?" Reyes still sounded angry, but now it was a worked-up, charismatic angry. He was taking the fear of the people and giving it a target.

The outsiders. The United Nations. The ERF.

"Reyes, listen," Meyers said. "We want to work with you and the leader—"

"No, you listen! We tried working with people. We gave peace a chance. We followed promises: a fresh start, a clean slate, a chance for a new life. Bullshit!"

Meyers's head throbbed. Even before he'd been tossed around by Waverley's hauler, there hadn't been enough history to understand Reyes and the people of Turning Point. There was no context to work from. They'd been done wrong, and now they were the ones doing wrong. "Let's talk this over."

"Talk? Like maybe you promise us jobs, huh? Security? Is that what you want to talk about?"

Meyers peered through the holes of the warehouse. The dark, sparkly dirt had collected in piles around the shattered crates. The crates were stacked to the ceiling at the back of the building. He tugged at the remains of the front door, tearing away most of the bottom half, then he ducked into the shadowy interior.

"I want to talk about stopping all of the pointless killing. Can't we at least start there?"

"The professional assassin wants to talk about peace? You think all these people can't hear how stupid that sounds? You think we don't know the smell of more bullshit after having it shoved in our faces our whole lives?"

Meyers found a crate with a functional identifier panel and tapped into it. It presented all the usual information it would to an unauthorized person: mass of the cargo, basic description, owner, source, destination.

"We never wanted conflict with the people of Turning Point," Meyers said. He glanced at the Condor's data feed. The crowd's earlier bravado was gone, and they were now looking up at the giant displays. At Reyes. Meyers was losing them.

"But you killed my people, huh? You talk big about peace, but you come in and assassinate. You come to us and ask us to help you assassinate. Or didn't you?"

Nunoz said, "Colonel, something's going on in that compound. Reyes's compound. They're moving around...I think it's a small hauler. Oh, shit. They've got another one of those anti-aircraft systems."

Meyers brought the Condor down and sent it closer to Reyes's compound. In the courtyard at the front of the mansion, maybe twenty men were securing a bubble to the back of a hauler, another Devil Cat. It didn't look like another railgun, but it didn't need to be. A heavy machine gun in an armored bubble would be enough to kill...everyone.

"Reyes, what happened can't be undone. It doesn't matter that your men tried to kill my people and we acted in self-defense. Right? And it doesn't matter that you've been living large while the rest of the people of Turning Point barely get by."

"Hey, *puta*, don't you—"

"What matters is I'm not going to allow you to threaten anyone anymore."

Reyes laughed. "You ain't got nothing to tell me what to do."

"I'm going to give you a chance to stop all of this, Reyes. I'm going to give you one last chance to be a part of the future of Bellar."

"Who do you think you're talking to, huh? I am the future of Bellar!" The sound of Reyes pounding his chest was a deep, bass thud. "I drove off the Zombies. I got us the food and water. That was me!"

Meyers squinted. He wanted to be sure the gun was the threat it appeared to be and not a bluff. Without sending the Condor or the Javelin in closer, that just wasn't possible. "Nunoz, get a lock-on. Two missiles. That hauler, and Reyes's mansion."

"Locking on."

Meyers blew out a sigh. He scooped up the fine dust of the sparkly dirt —dark, heavy. Nothing like the aqua sand blowing through the street outside.

"Reyes, this is your last chance." Meyers pulled the Condor back up, watched the crowd below. There was uncertainty there, mingled in with the fear. Everything came down to what happened next. He switched back to Nunoz's channel. "Nunoz, do you see any large concentrations of Reyes's men anywhere else?"

"Negative. Probably thirty in the front courtyard, half that elsewhere."

"I got a surprise for you, Mr. ERF," Reyes said. "You ain't in no position to tell anyone about last chances."

"Those men are moving away," Nunoz said. "I think that gun's active."

"On my signal." Meyers switched back to the Grid, but he stayed connected to Nunoz's private channel. "You were given a chance at peace, Reyes. I hope everyone will think back to that whenever they consider violence as the solution. Ensign."

To the naked eye, the missiles were twin contrails—fluffy, gray-white vapor. They didn't even track back to the Javelin, which was already headed south, over the desert and out to sea. The Condor recorded the reaction of the crowd, all the fingers pointing skyward, the heads tracking the trails down into Reyes's territory.

And the explosion. On the Condor's video, it was two white balls of smoke-wreathed fire, but to those on the ground, it would be a boom felt in the chest and head. They would close their eyes as the pressure hit them, a wash of warm air. And the fire and smoke would climb above the inter-vening buildings, maybe pull debris skyward for a bit before it spun back to the earth.

Meyers wondered if there could ever have been peace with Reyes involved. Then Meyers closed the Grid connection and began the long process of gathering what remained of his people.

35

18 December 2174. Ardennen, Bellar Frontier Colony.

THE BUILDINGS of Ardennen's main street were new, the tallest of them four or five stories high. Looking into the polished glass surface of one meant looking into the entire street, one reflection built upon another. It was cool enough that Meyers had the rear window of the long-body crawler down. He leaned out and glanced the length of the street, noting that they were a more durable concrete rather than Turning Point's cheap blacktop. The people strolling on the raised concrete sidewalks were clean and wore elegant, presumably fashionable clothing. Bistros and cafes were spaced among buildings meant for business and government. Many of the restaurants had actual human staff tending to nicely attired customers.

When Meyers closed his eyes, the aromas from the shops reminded him of home during the holidays. His head still ached, but not so much he couldn't appreciate the moment—the happy chatter of citizens, the smooth ride of the crawler, the fresh air on his face.

"Approaching Governor's Mansion." The automated driver's voice was refined and extremely human. It sounded like a French nobleman who'd spent half his life in the small swath of London walled off by the new aristocracy.

Inertia gently tugged Meyers forward as the crawler braked and emitted a warning tone to nearby pedestrians that it was turning. He closed his window and relaxed as it descended into the shade of the garage. The governor's mansion was a cube, the underground garage filled with the sort of expensive crawlers that were shipped, not printed up and assembled by local boutique fabricators. The long-body crawler came to a stop outside a bright, chrome-framed, glassed-in breezeway, and the rear gull-wing doors lifted.

"Governor Weidmann will see you in the Friesland conference room. Follow the green arrows. Please make yourself comfortable."

Meyers unbuckled and slid out, standing still to let the security systems confirm his identity. A pleasant chime announced approval, and the glass doors popped outward with a cool hiss of floral-scented, recycled air. His boots echoed off polished marble floors.

"Welcome, Colonel Meyers. Please follow the green arrows to the Friesland conference room. Governor Weidmann is on his way."

Meyers passed through the breezeway, and his eyes scanned up the length of the hallway. The green arrows were a faint glow floating on the surface of the east wall in his peripheral vision. He passed a break room that looked like one of the cafes on the street, an empty office with a wooden desk and other fixtures he associated with senior officers and managers, then he followed the arrows to the right. Around the corner, there were closed doors. A good-looking man in an extremely showy shirt and tight pants stepped out of a room, smiled pleasantly, and arched his eyebrows. Meyers nodded. Two doors later, the green arrows outlined a doorway, the door already open.

The Friesland had warm, almost red paneling, a matching table, a cube of displays suspended from the ceiling at the center of the room, and a glass wall currently dimmed against the afternoon light. There were eight chairs around the table, all of them empty.

Meyers settled into the seat at the near end of the table and checked his earpiece. He was four minutes late, almost perfect.

He heard an elevator chime, and seconds later, hard-plated heels clacked against the marble hallway floor. Meyers cocked his head, imagining the stride, considering the fact that the wearer had chosen a hard plate rather than something soft: a bold announcement. The shoes would be expensive; the need to be recognized would be paramount. He smiled when Weidmann breezed through the door, mouth open to voice a welcome and apology, then froze at the sight of his seat being taken. He tugged at the cuffs of his suit—it appeared to be authentic wool, a deep, grayish brown, with a vermillion tie and pale cream shirt. The shoes were black, almost glossy, and certainly expensive.

"Governor Weidmann." Meyers waved to the seat at his left. He didn't stand or extend a hand.

Weidmann cringed just enough for Meyers to catch the few wrinkles on a meticulously groomed face but otherwise didn't move. A single hair, dark-brown gone silver at the long tip, drifted free of the right side of the center part, breaking the perfect symmetry of an angular face covered in pale, soft, pampered flesh. "I was expecting different representation from the UN."

"I'm sure the UN will be sending someone more to your liking. Eventually. I'm not here as a representative of their diplomatic concerns." Meyers shoved back the chair he'd pointed to earlier. "Why don't you take a seat."

Weidmann's long nose wrinkled, and his thin lips pursed over his pointed chin as he seemed to take Meyers's measure, then he settled into the chair and relaxed, hands folded on the table, as if the meeting were going exactly to plan. "So, if you're not here for the UN, let's see how I might help you. What is it you want, hm?"

Meyers glanced up at the overhead display. It lowered and the displays came to life, prompting Weidmann to jump.

"Let's begin by completing our assembly," Meyers said.

The overhead display unfurled along the horizontal axis so that the vertical cube walls became a straight line. On each, a face appeared—Mudar Badran, Cemal Bey, Asfaw Mattias, Teddy Savoy. They wore the simple clothes of Turning Point. Sweat trickled down their faces, and their eyes sparkled with fury.

"What-what's this about?" Weidmann's brow furrowed as he looked from the warlords to Meyers. "I don't recall mention of—"

"Meeting with representatives of your citizenry?" Meyers frowned.

"Think of it as working a new muscle. It hurts at first, but it gets better with time."

Weidmann straightened, and then again relaxed and let his eyes drop to his hands.

"Mr. Reyes won't be joining us," Meyers said. "His people are still working out the details of electing a replacement."

Weidmann's eyes shot back up to Meyers at that. "Something happened to Mr. Reyes?"

"He failed to understand the new dynamics of the situation and had to be removed."

Weidmann nodded slowly. "I see."

"I wanted to go through those dynamics with you. That's why I contacted you and agreed to meet with you this afternoon. The people of Turning Point understand that things are going to be different going forward. Elections, structured government, a responsible and empowered citizenry..." Meyers looked toward the displays. "I think we have buy-in on these concepts?"

The warlords nodded or muttered agreement, but their angry eyes never left Weidmann's face.

"This is good," Weidmann said. He opened his hands and smiled at the displays. "We have always wanted the citizens of Turning Point to be more active participants in the political process."

"Excellent," Meyers said. "Because one of the other things we're going to implement starting today is full transparency. It's a cornerstone of effective representative government, after all."

Weidmann's hands folded again, and he cleared his throat. "Transparency?"

"Full disclosure. It's probably best understood through example. Here, let me show you." The four warlords' images shrank to fit the two center displays, and the outer displays took on two new images. To the left, a still image of the crates in the Farmers Road warehouses. To the right, data from the crates' ID plates. "How long ago were you brought on as Bellar Colony governor? Ten years ago? Eleven?"

"E-eleven years this coming May, Earth-reckoning."

"And at the time, you understood the colony's prospects weren't particularly good? Most colonies have maybe a fifty percent chance of real success, less than that out here in the frontier. Right? Most of the other frontier colonies have it pretty tough, even if they succeed. So far out from Earth and the other colonies, fewer people willing to take a chance, risk of economic collapse, miserable living conditions, maybe even death. Right?"

"Yes."

"The climate here's nice, really. Better than I expected. Especially here in Ardennen." Meyers glanced at the displays. "I'd consider it sort of cool up here, personally. Not uncomfortable, but not..." He looked back at Weidmann. "Not Turning Point, right?"

A smile ticked at the corners of Weidmann's mouth. "That is correct."

"How long ago did someone discover there were substantial rare earth deposits on-planet? Governor?"

"It was confirmed just...about a year after we began building Ardennen."

"A year." The image of the crate was replaced by the Cáceres Compound. "It may have been a bad decision putting Waverley up in the Cáceres Compound. He made it off-planet, by the way, but he did a terrible job cleaning up after himself. You remember the Cáceres Compound, right? The place where the exploratory committee ran colonization viability studies? Dr. Cáceres, one of the colonial committee board members? Ties to SunCorps through several of his businesses."

The image of the compound became a video. A tall, bronze-skinned man, balding, thick, dark mustache and beard. Cáceres. "There are numerous indicators of exceptional mineral deposits based on flyovers, cores, and samples. The odds of rare earth minerals deposits—and I mean substantial deposits—are very, very high. Based on that alone, I recommend an accelerated development endeavor. You'll need an exploitable workforce, of course, preferably unconcerned or uninformed regarding the effects of aggressive extraction efforts that would maximize profitable mining. I've highlighted the areas I feel would be best prioritized for this, based on available groundwater for convenient slurry conveyance and other favorable geographic concerns. All of this with the assumption we would operate with an eye toward minimal involvement of external regulatory efforts."

The image froze.

"External regulatory efforts," Meyers said. "Aggressive extraction efforts. Accelerated development endeavor. Those all sound...convenient? Like code words. If I were an educated man, I'd think they were referring to active avoidance, you know? Of the regulation and oversight you signed on to when you accepted zero-interest, fifty percent financing through the United Nations as part of the colonization contract. You remember that, right? Something about preventing the same level of exploitation and destruction we brought about on Earth? That's a big part of these colonization efforts getting off the ground."

Weidmann chuckled. "I think you might misunderstand the nature of—"

The image on the displays changed again, with all four of the warlords now on the rightmost display, and the others showing video of three sites where haulers and proxies moved with robotic precision across the bottom of large pits and ascended terraced walls via huge, blacktop-covered paths. The view pulled out, and the pits looked like horrific wounds in an otherwise pristine wilderness.

"You know, Governor." Meyers pointed at the mines. "I'm betting I could get access to your budget pretty easily. If not here, then when I get back to Plymouth. And I'm betting your entire budget for the ten years this colony has been around wouldn't cover half of the cost of one of those mines. Then again, I'm not sure how much of Ardennen could be accounted for." He looked at the display where the warlords glared. "This city really is beautiful. I'm betting this street—what is it again?"

"Ardennen Concourse." Weidmann forced a smile, but he didn't bother looking at the displays.

"I'm betting there's nothing on Ardennen Concourse that's older than three years. It all sort of reminds me of Reyes's mansion. New money, and lots of it." Meyers switched to a video of Turning Point. "But none of that really makes sense, does it? That kind of money, the outlays for all that mining equipment...that would show up on your reporting to the UN about the loan repayment. Wouldn't it?"

Weidmann's forced smile twitched.

"I guess you could get around that with loans from someone else.

Maybe someone like SunCorps? But why would they do that, unless they had some sort of sweetheart deal where they could buy the minerals without having to bid on the open market? That would work, wouldn't it? Governor? You don't have to answer. It's all sort of coming together for me, though. Especially when I consider the way certain members of the Special Security Council made such a big deal about not bothering you and minimizing our time on Bellar.

"And then there's the Zombies. Did you know them as that? No? I'm betting I could track back where they came from, but I don't have time to get into your ledgers right now. To qualify as an ideally exploitable workforce, I think they'd best be prisoners. The colonies can still send their prisoners off to orbital prisons, and someone can buy their release. Pump them up with growth hormones and stimulants, push them to work around the clock. I wonder how long you could go with a workforce like that. Maybe hire some Lancers to come in and shut things down when there's a problem. Does that sound like the sort of work Lancers would do on Bellar Colony, Mr. Savoy?"

"Yeah," Savoy said.

"And when that becomes too expensive or too unsustainable, well, you just bring a whole bunch of new exploitable labor in from Earth. Make promises of—what was it Reyes said? A clean slate, jobs, a chance at a new life? But before they had even settled in, I'm thinking someone offered you a better alternative. All those robots. So cheap in the long run, because they don't ask for raises or promotions or get sick. Does any of this sound at all like something you've heard before, Governor? No? Pretty outrageous stuff? I mean, you'd have a problem if you went with this series of decisions, right? Thousands of unemployed people, just sitting there, doing nothing. That's the recipe for disaster, isn't it: riots, crime, maybe even insurrection? So, you'd need an enforcer to keep control. All those Zombies roaming around, hungry for drugs, hungry for anything. They'd need to be controlled, too. Who could do that? Someone who maybe fancied himself a governor in his own right?"

Weidmann glanced at his hands, which seemed to be locked into place. "That really is a lot of speculation, Colonel. Very preposterous."

"I know. How many laws are we talking about being broken in something like this? How many billions of dollars are we talking about here? You wouldn't know it to see Turning Point, though. Maybe looking around up here. All those pretty people, all these beautiful buildings. And what if that little despot you set up down in Turning Point got tired of being your hired thug? What if he got it into his head to really start checking into all the money you were making shipping things through his little town? Down to that spaceport you have built about 100 kilometers south of Turning Point? What if he started hoarding your barges and the cargo crates? I bet that'd be a real problem, wouldn't it? The kind of thing a handful of Lancers couldn't handle. Mr. Savoy?"

Savoy leaned closer in the display. "Not without knowing what was really going on, no."

"But the Metacorporate War." Meyers bit his lip. "That would work out really nice, wouldn't it? Going down the way it did, with SunCorps suddenly in need of a place to hide their biggest embarrassment? And that embarrassment carrying around his own heavily armed security force, wouldn't that work out nicely? He ships you some heavy weapons, you send those weapons down to Turning Point to pick up. Maybe one dirty hand cleans another? At least, if it all goes well?"

Weidmann glanced up at the displays, rapidly blinking, licking his lips. "I'm assuming there would be more to all this speculation than discussions about transparency, or you would simply report the speculations to your superiors and let them investigate."

"Good point. In fact, I will be passing all my findings on to the Special Security Council. How they deal with that information..." Meyers shrugged. "You know how slow government moves. And then there's the one hand washing another, like I said. But between now and then, you have plenty of time to start turning things around. Open and fair elections might be a good starting point. Finding employment for the people you promised jobs would definitely be helpful. Fair distribution of the wealth you've been sitting on." Meyers pointed to the displays. "That would be one of the first things I'd look at. I mean, I didn't see a single armed constable the entire drive through the city. You probably don't need a large police force when everyone lives a comfortable life. Certainly nothing that could stand up to hundreds of very angry people wielding assault rifles."

Weidmann's eyes jumped from the displays to Meyers.

"We create some pretty hideous monsters when we don't think things through, wouldn't you agree, Governor?"

"That's it? Those are your demands?" Weidmann's face was strained. Clearly, the demands were already too much for him to accept.

"I want every piece of communication you have from SunCorps regarding Waverley. Every communique, memo, video, audio—anything they've sent in the last year."

"I couldn't possibly—"

"You have fifteen minutes, Governor. After that, I'm leaving. The data I've shared with you is queued up in the orbital buoy. If you hurry, I might be able to attach a positive report to it before it's sent along to Earth."

Weidmann's pale, gray eyes widened as he sucked in a deep breath, then he stood. The plates on his shoes clacked quickly down the hallway.

Meyers drummed his fingers on the table.

Mattias said, "What now, Colonel?"

"We should know in...fourteen minutes, twenty-eight seconds."

36

12 April 2175. ERF HQ, Plymouth Colony.

MEYERS ROLLED his shoulders and head, but he couldn't work the tension from his body. He glanced to his right, where Captain Singh sat straight, calm. To Meyers's left, Master Sergeant Paxton seemed even calmer, but his eyes jumped between the two men seated across the table, separated by coffee mugs and data displays. Those men seemed out of place in the small, low-ceilinged room that had been designated Conference Room One. The room took up most of the small trailer supplied by the construction firm managing the ERF headquarters reconstruction. That reconstruction was finally past the point of clearing away the last of the radioactive debris and laying down the new foundation for the sprawling campus. The drone of robotic construction gear and the strained rattle of an underpowered air conditioning unit filled the conference room as completely as did the heat of the morning sun.

The man Meyers knew as General Tyler V. Durban, one of the people responsible for getting the ERF concept approved, shifted in his chair and sighed, blowing coffee breath across the table. Durban wore a crisp, white dress shirt, a blue tie loosened below an unbuttoned collar. Sweat rings were visible around his armpits. He absently dabbed at his forehead and stared at the display propped up in front of him. It was a simple, small display, functional, like the table they'd hastily squeezed into the trailer. Durban's face was thinner than Meyers remembered, and despite the wrinkles that had settled, there was an even greater resemblance to Lieutenant Timothy Durban, the general's son, who had died on Sahara years before.

Durban looked up, then turned to his right, where a short, heavyset man sat. This man wore a similar white shirt but with a red tie. His round, brown face was sweat-drenched; his thick, black mustache, like the hair atop his head, visibly damp. Pudgy fingers tapped a few times at the display, then he too looked up, his narrow mouth pursed, his big eyes watery.

"General Durban, General Patel, can I get you anything?" Meyers pointed to the small tray resting against the wall next to the trailer's front door. Sweat dripped down stainless steel pitchers, which were surrounded by stacks of clear, plastic cups.

"Anything but coffee," Durban said as he rubbed his stomach.

The other man wiped his face with a handkerchief, limp with sweat. "Cold water, please."

Singh jumped to his feet before Meyers could move. Ice clattered and water splashed. Meyers smiled at Patel's look—inquisitive, analytical, maybe even judging. Singh returned with two cups, handed them across the table, and settled back into his seat. Paxton hooked his index fingers through the coffee mugs, then got up and a little later returned with cups of water for himself, Singh, and Meyers.

Meyers watched the way water condensed on the outside of the cup and leeched into the leather-like table cover, where it spread like blood.

Durban cradled his water cup as if it were a diamond, then took a swig. He tilted the cup and stared into the water. "Dinesh, I think I'm ready to begin."

"Me as well," Patel said. He took a long drink, and then he set the cup aside. "This humidity is as miserable as any I have felt." He shook his head.

"Colonel." Durban looked up. "We've seen the reports. We've reviewed the data. You're an educated man, by all accounts smart. I think you know we didn't come out here to shoot the shit."

"Of course not, sir."

"It takes a lot of coats of paint to cover up a shack." Durban pointed at the display in front of him. "How many coats did you lay down on this?"

Meyers glanced sideways and caught Singh's worried look. "We tried to be as accurate and thorough as possible in our reporting, sir. I'm sure you both understand how details become hard to keep up with in battle."

Patel leaned back and pulled the front of his shirt out of his pants so that it wasn't tight against his stomach. "The Special Security Council assigned us for more than fact finding, Colonel Meyers. I am sure this is also obvious? We are here for many reasons, but none of them are to hear a distortion of what events transpired on Bellar."

Meyers's back ached. "I think *distortion* is a hard word, General."

"Maybe it is," Durban said. "How would you describe a report that says a decorated colonel with years of experience running an elite military unit got himself killed in a blast that took out an enemy mobile weapons platform after suffering more than a fifty percent casualty rate with a force from his new command?"

Meyers looked down.

"Excuse me, sirs," Singh said. "We all agreed that it was preferable to show Colonel Ramawat's demise in a positive light, General Durban."

"A positive light?" The skin of Patel's brow bunched up. "May as well that this report had said the colonel was a fool."

"In retrospect, we felt it better to represent the colonel as...lost. Sir."

Patel cocked his head. "Lost? You mean what when you say that?"

Singh stiffened. "Confused, General. Unaware of the complexities of the situation."

Patel slammed his hands on the table. "Colonel Ramawat spent years dealing with pirates, terrorists, and separatists—the very worst people in the world."

"Begging your pardon, General, but there might be a level of sophistication in the sphere of politics and corporate intrigue that goes beyond what the colonel was used to." Singh swallowed hard. "The adversaries you mention have simple enough agendas. They have limited resources. What we encountered on Bellar was not understood until we departed."

"Actually, I'm not sure we'll ever fully understand everything that's gone on out there," Meyers said. "Governor Weidmann turned over what he wanted. We didn't have the resources to do a deep hack into his systems. I wouldn't be at all surprised to discover things went much deeper, assuming he hasn't destroyed all incriminating records."

Durban took another drink, then turned to Patel. "The biggest takeaway I had from the report was that it was a mistake to send Colonel Ramawat directly to the battlefield. That's a clusterfuck in the making right there. Dinesh, you recommended against that, didn't you? I know I did."

Patel tugged at his mustache. "It was very disappointing to see him ask for that. Very disappointing. The Special Security Council, they should have known better than to appease his ego in such manner."

Durban looked at Singh. "Blunt assessment, Captain: Was Colonel Ramawat simply over his head, or did he make this personal?"

Patel's wide eyes watched Singh from beneath heavy brows.

"Unfortunately, General, it was both."

Patel's eyes returned to his cup of water. "Very disappointing. Very."

Singh turned to Patel. "There was the stress of the situation, General. But there was also the stress of expectations. I should have spoken about things when I had concerns. The colonel, he was very upset over not receiving the battalion command. He was very worried that his career might end prematurely. Politics requires much more clout now than before. The competition was looking quite unfavorable."

"Yes, yes, I know," Patel said. He didn't meet Singh's eyes. "This command is very problematic. The Russians, the British, the Germans, the Chinese—they all feel they should have this position. So many careers about to be ruined." He shook his head.

Durban looked from Meyers to Singh. "The SSC has accelerated the drawdown. Ten years, fifty percent force cuts gone to five years, seventy-five percent."

Paxton turned to consider Meyers. "That's a lot of military folks thrown out of work awfully fast."

"The SSC thinks it'll be just fine, and, really, when you have half the world starving to death, it's hard to justify spending so much money on guns and soldiers." Durban dabbed at his brow. "But it's risky. We've already seen..."

Patel buried his face in his hands. "It will be a disaster, so many dangerous people with no job. They will feel betrayed and angry. This is very bad."

Durban shot a glance toward Patel that Meyers thought might have been angry, then the look was gone, and Durban finished off his drink. He looked around the table. "I'm not sure what's worse, Waverley escaping or SunCorps setting us up in the first place. And before you think I'm saying that all the losses you suffered weren't tragic, hear me out. With Waverley's escape, the metacorporations scored a victory. They showed that even with their cooperation, the ERF just wasn't up to the task. If you haven't already figured it out, that's a bad deal for you. But SunCorps being involved with Weidmann and covering for Waverley and us not having anything actionable to do about it?"

"Very bad," Patel said as he rubbed his eyes. "This governor, all he has to do is say he provided information under duress, and it is of no value."

Meyers felt heat in his cheeks. "No legal value, sir. There's not much likelihood he would have been prosecuted, regardless, right? It's a colony world. A frontier colony world. The UN wants to establish diplomatic ties. This is the sort of thing that gets swept under the rug all the time. If anything, they now have a negotiating tool."

Patel looked up and seemed to think about that. "Of course."

Durban poured a small piece of ice into his mouth and chewed on it. "That leaves us one big problem still."

Patel nodded. "The brevet. Very problematic. All of the fighting over this position. It does not help. We need to remove it."

Meyers's leg muscles bunched.

Durban set his cup down hard enough that the ice rattled. "There's no other choice."

Patel stood abruptly; Meyers, Paxton, and Singh jumped to their feet. "Tyler, I believe I have heard all there is to hear." Patel pulled his suit coat from the back of the chair and threw it over his left arm. "My recommendations will not change."

"I'll be along in a few minutes," Durban said. "Colonel, maybe Captain Singh would like to show General Patel around the base?"

"Of course, sir. Master Sergeant Paxton, maybe you could show Captain Singh and General Patel where we were and where we're going?"

Paxton crossed to the door and opened it, letting in Plymouth's smothering air and blinding brightness. "This way, sirs. It'll be my pleasure to give you the grand tour on such a glorious day."

When they were gone, Durban waved for Meyers to sit again. Durban got up and poured himself another cup of water. "You served with Jack for quite a while, didn't you?"

"Colonel Rimes? About seven years."

"You didn't know him in the Commandos?"

"He was already on his way out by the time I was settling in, sir."

Durban emptied the cup and refilled it. "Probably for the best. He was a bad fit for the military. Too rigid in some ways, too flexible in others."

"Like trying to salvage your son's career? Sir?"

Durban turned around, his face twisted almost in a snarl. "Colonel Rimes recommended you for a full promotion when he sent in the brevet request. Just like him. He just didn't have the leverage that day, not like he did with me. I think he was one of the few clear-headed people with the balls to do what had to be done, and that includes what he did for Timothy."

Meyers realized he'd misread Durban. "How are you and Mrs. Durban coping?"

"Mrs. Durban is back to being called Ms. Fallon, and she's living the good life off my joke of a retirement. Island hopping with her girlfriend, or whatever they're calling each other right now. I'd imagine she's drowning her sorrows with expensive drinks." Durban rubbed his gut absently. "I'm getting by okay. At least I kept my retirement after everything fell apart. Half of it."

Meyers took a drink of his water. It was cold and sweet, but it wasn't enough to deal with the heat.

"Look, Meyers, your brevet's as good as gone, but it doesn't mean you can't lose everything."

Meyers wondered what else Durban thought would matter after losing the ERF command position and rank. A year earlier, both were far outside Meyers's dreams and aspirations. After holding them and seeing how good the fit was, he wasn't sure how he'd handle settling back in as an XO or whatever position was given to him by the new commander.

"The ERF has enemies throughout the UN, people who only want to see the metacorporations extend their influence." Durban waved his cup. "This thing on Bellar? How the hell the SSC didn't see that coming…" He snorted. "Of course they did. But until this Waverley is brought to justice, the message won't be clear that the government is serious about this."

"There are a lot of people deep in the metacorporations' pockets."

"Everyone knows that. Maybe it'll be enough to root those sons of bitches out. Until then, you're just going to have to roll with it. I figure the ERF's got a year, maybe just six months. Elections will change the makeup of the SSC soon, and the economy's just gonna get worse. The kind of money they're spending on this whole thing? You need to show them results."

"You mean the new commander needs to show them results."

Durban stopped midway into pouring more water. "New commander? Didn't you hear us? Your brevet's gone. We can't satisfy anyone by putting another commander in place. They'd all just bitch and moan like the fucking world's gonna fall apart if they don't get their precious selection. We're recommending you for the position, and what we say isn't going to get challenged."

"But the Russians and—"

Durban snorted. "You got six months to prove yourself. You think putting a new commander into place is going to help that or hurt it? Let me answer that for you: It will fuck everything up. Ramawat proved that. He was the best of the candidates, and he cracked under the pressure. He wanted to show everyone that his way was the right way, but Rimes built a culture here. He built the ERF for success. The metacorporations and all their allies need to get the message: There's a price to be paid for what they did. You're the best chance this unit has to prove Jack was right." Durban considered his cup and set it down. "Don't screw this up."

He opened the door, cursed at the bright light, then closed the door behind him, leaving Meyers alone in the trailer.

He sat, unmoving, for several minutes, just rolling the information around and around in his head, then he realized he was shaking. He stood and began pacing. Six months, maybe a year. He had to begin the hunt for Waverley all over again. He had to prove Rimes had been right with his recommendation.

The odds against the ERF were long and crazy, but at least there was a chance. That was good enough for him.

THE END

ACKNOWLEDGMENTS

Thank you for reading *Turning Point*. I hope you enjoyed it. The Elite Response Force stories continue in *Valley of Death*.

This book was influenced by the events of the Battle of Mogadishu, which was covered in Mark Bowden's exceptional book, *Black Hawk Down*. If you haven't read the book or seen the movie, please make the time to do so. I worked IT support in J2 (Joint Forces Intelligence) during the mid-1990s. I was selected for a temporary duty assignment (TDY) to the Mogadishu UN forces in 1994, but I was replaced by one of my team members during my out-processing, so I remember those times very clearly.

If you enjoyed *Turning Point*, I hope you'll consider posting a review and letting friends know about the book. Reviews can be a major influencer on potential readers.

For updates on new releases and news on other series, please visit my website and sign up for my mailing list at:

http://www.p-r-adams.com

ABOUT THE AUTHOR

I was born and raised in Tampa, Florida. I joined the Air Force, and my career took me from coast to coast before depositing me in the St. Louis, Missouri area for several years. After a tour in Korea and a short return to the St. Louis area, I retired and moved to the greater Denver, Colorado metropolitan area.

I write speculative fiction, mostly science fiction and fantasy. My favorite writers over the years have been Robert E. Howard, Philip K. Dick, Roger Zelazny, and Michael Crichton.

Social Media:
www.p-r-adams.com
pradams_author@comcast.net

www.ingramcontent.com/pod-product-compliance
Lightning Source LLC
Chambersburg PA
CBHW071724190726
48292CB00003B/596